# Marked For Him

## Eden Minns

# Contents

# CHAPTER 1

X ander's POV

"Xander, your mother and I would like to see you in your office," my father murmured after peeking his head into my card room. I released a puff of air from my lips as I laid my hand of cards down.

"Oooooh, someone's in trouble with Mommy and Daddy," Donovan, my beta, teased in a baby voice. The other guys around the poker table laughed as I rolled my eyes.

"Piss off. I'll be right back," I grunted, pushing my chair back and hoisting myself up. I made my way to my office just down the hall. I figured they probably had some new information about one of the packs we would visit starting tomorrow morning.

"Pops?" I asked, entering the room and shutting the door behind me. I leaned down and pressed a chaste kiss to my mom's cheek as was customary before sitting on the couch across from them. When neither of them spoke, I raised a single eyebrow in question.

This can't be good.

"What's this about?" I pressed further.

"You know that your father and I love you very much and we just want what's best for you-" You've got to be kidding me.

"What did The Council say this time?" I growled, feeling a tinge of guilt for taking my anger out on them, but unable to control it. The Council had been in my damn business the past two years about my lack of a mate. The fact I had completely quit answering all of their calls made it so they were forced to relay their messages through my parents. I'll admit, it was childish on my part. However, so was their constant badgering.

"They've decided you're no longer fit to run the pack on your own. They've found a mate they deem suitable for you and the pack-"

"What?" I sneered. Unable to contain my instant burst of anger, I shot out of my seat. My fists clenched and unclenched, my knuckles turning white as I just barely restrained my wolf under my flesh. I was aware I was only further proving The Council's point at the moment with my inability to control my rage, but dammit!

"And if I don't go through with this mating?" I asked after a few moments, my voice more wolf than man despite my best efforts.

"If you choose to reject this mating you will be immediately removed from your position and your cousin, Justin, will take over."

"He doesn't have a mate, either!" I yelled indignantly, beginning to pace back and forth in front of them. How could The Council not see how ridiculous and unfair this whole situation was?

"He hasn't met his mate yet. He will - likely soon - and they believe he'll be more suited to handle the needs of the pack once he has," my mother explained softly. She was clearly doing everything she could to keep from provoking my already tense wolf.

"What if Mika agrees to step up to her position?" I asked, grinding my teeth. An impending headache loomed over me just at the mere thought. However, it was better than having a group of old wankers decide who I was going to spend the rest of my life with. Decide who was going to rule my pack. My people.

"That option has already been considered. Every council member was in complete agreement that Mika is wholly unfit to hold any position within the pack. Especially one of such importance as that of being Luna," my dad said. I growled, unable to stop myself from grabbing the first thing near me and launching it across the room. It was a glass container that held mints, resulting in it shattering into a hundred tiny pieces and scattering the candies all over.

"This is unfounded!" I yelled. "I'm doing a fine job running the pack! You both could have vouched for me!" I exclaimed. A feeling of betrayal washed over me. "The pack has been thriving under my rule! We're more profitable and secure than ever! These accusations are...baseless. Concocted!" I hissed before slamming my hand against the wall, causing a minor dent from the force of my anger.

"But for how long will this be the case? We've already started to see a change in you, Xander," came my mom's soft voice. "You're not taking care of yourself. Your office and house are constantly in disarray. Your wolf has a temper that's becoming increasingly difficult to manage. You don't sleep enough. And..." she trailed off, her expression turning sorrowful as she turned to my dad for comfort and silent support.

"And?" I pushed her to continue.

"The pack needs an heir," she finished the sentence, though I could see it pained her. I swallowed thickly. "As of right now, you can't provide one. And..." she trailed off yet again, looking as if she were unsure if she should continue, grating against my already inflamed nerves. "The pack is suffering in some areas. Sure, profits and security are the best they've ever been, but the orphanage is a mess. The children aren't getting what they need. The daycare doesn't have the management and leadership to keep going for the long haul. The morale amongst the women is at an all-time low. Our female warriors have begun to feel as though they aren't important with how all the attention has been focused on the men. And..." she hesitated for a breath before a steely look took over her face, "and even after everything you've been through, you continue to let Mika prance around this pack treating anyone and every one however she damn well pleases," she growled, raising her voice at me.

"She has terrorized the women of this pack to the point of near alienation. The men won't say anything because she's not their responsibility. She won't listen to me, because the last time she and I got into an argument you let her off the hook behind my back. She knows you'll continue to take her side, even if she's in the wrong. It gives her the confidence to do as she pleases day in and day out," she finished.

I didn't know what to say back to that. What could I say back to that? I just avoided her gaze, shame washing over me.

"My wolf still sees her as our mate," I husked out. I was a pathetic man, but the other half of me yearned for that....woman every day - even if he hated her as much as I did.

"Well, she's not anymore. I know you love this pack too much to just give it all up. This is your one opportunity at true happiness, Xander. Your father and I - as well as The Council - expect you to give this a real chance. Do it for yourself, honey. You deserve to have someone take care of you the way you take care of all our people every day. And if not for yourself, do it for everyone else that's counting on you. An alpha's true potential is never fully achieved until he's been mated. Think of all the amazing things you could accomplish for the pack with a mate by your side. You've already proven to be a great leader without one - minus a few hiccups. It's the only reason the council has let this situation go as far as it has," she spoke, her voice thick with emotion and eyes filled with hope.

"Did she leave her mate, or did her mate leave her?" I grunted out, finally sitting back down. I leaned over to rest my elbows on my knees. It seemed like an odd question to ask, but it was one I had to know the answer to. Maybe it was selfish of me, but I didn't want to - no, scratch that - wouldn't deal with yet another woman pining after another man while with me. Not a damn chance.

"The council has been very tight-lipped about her situation. All we know so far is that there's absolutely no way her ex-mate will ever be in the situation again. She left him. They've told us his name, but required us to sign an NDA agreement that restricts us from telling anyone else except for all high-ranking pack officials - but only after they've also signed an NDA and The Council has been faxed the paperwork evidence of it," my dad explained.

Now this piqued my attention immensely.

"Who's her ex-mate?" I asked. He didn't reply, just pushed a piece of paper across the coffee table toward me. I raised a single eyebrow before taking the pen he was holding out to me. I signed my name and waited as one of our pack lawyers came to notarize and fax the document to The Council. It was only a few minutes before he gave us the okay and left us alone once again.

"Eric Strickland."

"Beta of the Sablefur pack?" I asked, shocked. "I didn't even know he'd found his mate," I pondered aloud. We weren't allies with the Sablefur pack, but we weren't strangers either. Our pack lands were relatively close, so we often communicated with them for trading goods or hosting events to help our members have a better chance of finding their mates.

"Neither did anyone else. It was a shock to your mother and I. If the NDA wasn't a red flag, that bit of information definitely was. If his mate ran, you would think he'd be alerting every Alpha and pack in the continent to be on the lookout.""Unless he didn't want the council to find out, which could mean-"

"No. We're not going to do this. It's not our place to try and play detective to figure out what transpired between your mate and her ex. If the council is being this tight-lipped it's because she's asked them to be. I've never seen the council utilize this many precautions ever before. We will respect her wishes and allow her to tell us the story in her time," my mom snapped. My father and I immediately shut our mouths.

I wiped my hand across my face to hide the smirk I was sporting. To outside humans, our communities seemed intensely tradition-al. There have been a few times it's been stipulated that we're patriarchal cults of some sort. However, they couldn't be more wrong. When our women say jump, we ask how high.

Sure, our men were usually the only ones people usually saw outside of pack grounds, but that was because most female wolves chose jobs they could work either from home on their computers or within pack limits. Our women were the backbone of our society. Without them, we'd be lost. It made sense why I was being forced into this predicament - though I was still pissed.

I sighed deeply. "When do I meet her? And how long before we're expected to be fully mated?" I asked.

"She will be arriving tomorrow, probably after you have already left. As far as mating goes, it's up to her, but within reason. The Council originally wanted it to be said and done within a week of you being introduced, but Elder Adelia amended the terms. They're giving her a month to get comfortable here and with you," my dad said.

"With how severe the situation appears, I don't foresee a month being nearly enough time but it's not our decision, it's The Councils," my mom added with an eye roll. I nodded but kept quiet.

"We'll leave you to think about all this," my mom murmured before standing from the couch. My dad lingered for a few seconds until my mom cleared her throat and gave him an expectant look.

"Oh, right," he rushed out, getting up and following her out the door. I rubbed my face harshly with my hands. Hoisting myself off the couch, I picked up the things I'd childishly knocked over in my fit of anger and did my best to get all the glass and mints up as well. I poured myself a drink of the strongest stuff I kept hidden in my office before making my way back to the poker game I'd left behind.

"You were gone for longer than we anticipated. We ended up starting a new game," Donovan called out when he heard me re-enter the room. I just slumped back down into my seat and stared up at the ceiling, contemplating.

"What happened?" Griffin, my gamma, asked as his face turned serious and he set his hand of cards down. This captured everyone's attention. I could feel their eyes staring at me from my peripheral vision.

"That damn Council set up an arranged mating for me," I mumbled monotonously, still deep in thought. "What?" they all balked at the same time.

"There hasn't been an arranged mating in...damn near a hundred years," Donovan commented, shock lacing his tone.

"Does Mika know...?" Griffin asked. I clenched my teeth and just shrugged my shoulders. I couldn't give a shit less what she did or thought these days. Working through the bitterness has been easier said than done.

"This is gonna have more twists and turns than the trash drama T.V. shows my mate makes me watch," Andre, our head warrior, commented with an amused smile. When we all just gave him looks of confusion he continued. "You know, like Love Island? Why are you all looking at me like that?" he growled before crossing his arms. We all gave a quick chuckle at his expense.

"Maybe you should set up a planned dinner with our women. They can give you pointers on how to be a good mate," Donovan commented while cleaning up from their last game.

"You think I need pointers on how to be a good mate?" I grunted with a raised brow and a, 'I'm going to hand you your ass' expression. He held his hands up in surrender.

"All I'm saying is you've been out of the dating game since you were nineteen. Might be nice to get a woman's perspective."

"Might be a good idea..." I thought out loud. "I'll wait until we're back, though. She'll be with them for a week while we're away, so they'll be able to give me some better insight then. Why don't we call it a night, boys? Go spend time with your mates and kids before we have to leave," I said. They all nodded respectfully before slowly trickling out of the room. Donovan, however, stayed behind.

"So?" he asked, leaning back in his seat and eyeing me thought-fully.

"So?" I repeated.

"C'mon, dude. We've been best friends since we were in diapers. We all heard the commotion. Tell me what's going through your head."

"I'm so tired of being screwed over, man. This is just another thing to add to the damn list it feels like," I growled lowly before tipping my cup back and finishing my drink in one gulp. He scoffed before crossing his arms over his chest and glaring at me. "What?" I grunted somewhat defensively.

"You know I love you and think of you more like a brother, but pull your head out of your ass. What alpha do you know that gets a second chance like this? Regardless if we understand them or not, The Council has a reason for the things they do. More often than not, it's about trusting and having faith that they know what they're doing," he insisted.

I sighed. "Do you know an alpha who doesn't have a faithful mate?" I challenged back, my pride butting its ugly head.

"I get it. Mika messed around, but that's a rarity. Mika completely screwed you over, no one can deny that. But maybe this is fate's way of changing your story for the better out of this situation. For all you know, this could be The Council's way of delivering you the most amazing mate in the entire world on a silver platter as a way of saying, "sorry the first one screwed it up the first time around". You just gotta give it a chance and have an open mind. If you don't, you'll always wonder 'what if?'," he insisted. I sighed deeply before running my hand through my hair and roughing it up.

"Yeah, you're right," I mumbled with a nod. "Riley's a lucky girl," I said with a small smile that he mirrored.

"Damn right. Speaking of which, it's that perfect time of night when the boys will be in bed and she might still be awake. If I'm lucky, we can slip in a quickie if I leave now," he rushed out with a boyish grin. I rolled my eyes and waved goodbye as he lightly jogged out of the room and in the direction of his wing of the pack house.

Left alone with my thoughts, they naturally wandered to my arranged mating.

# CHAPTER 2

S carlett's POV

I was already perched over the side of my bed staring out the window when she came to speak to me. The snow pelted the ground at an alarming rate. I had a feeling we already had roughly five inches coating the ground, and the sky showed no sign of stopping anytime soon. The knock had startled me, as most things still did these days.

"Come in," I called out, just loud enough for whoever was at the door to hear.

"Scarlett?" My ears immediately perked up as a feeling of dread settled heavily in the pit of my stomach - until I remembered what today was. Elder Adelia didn't visit unless it was for something important. Today was incredibly significant for me.

It was the second anniversary of my escape from what I think Jackie said the humans call, "living hell". It was the day my physical pain ended. However, the mental pain and struggle I went through daily would persist far longer than any of my visible scars ever would.

"Good morning, Elder Adelia," I murmured with a soft smile. She came to sit next to me on my bed, peering out my slightly frosted window for a few moments before turning her attention to me. Her expression held sympathy, something that wasn't new to me. Most people here looked at me the same way. While it frustrated me to no end, I understood it.

"There are some things we need to discuss," she said with a sigh. My heart kicked up a notch in my chest. I was sure she heard it. "I'm not just coming to visit to see how you're doing. I have some news to share as well. I'm not sure how you're going to take it, my dear," she hummed, reaching for my hands - which were now shaking despite my efforts to control the tremors. I instinctively clenched them into fists to prevent the fine tremors.

"Are you kicking me out?" I husked out, fear taking hold of my vocal cords and forcing the words to be breathier than I'd intended them to be. I cleared my throat and bit the inside of my cheek.

"Not quite," she winced."What's that supposed to mean?" I growled before immediately apologizing. I was anxious and scared and had taken it out on her. She just smiled despite the disrespect.

"Don't apologize. You've come a very long way since you first met me. Do you remember how timid and afraid you were all the time?" she asked.

"I don't want to talk about this," I rushed out, pulling my hands away from her hold and turning to look at some of the generic artwork on the walls of my equally generic-decorated room.

"I do. I want to talk about the progress you've made. Despite all you've been through, you've come out the other side a strong, confident, faithful woman. You don't cower away from everyone's presence and you don't bite your tongue when speaking with others. That's something you should be incredibly proud of," she stated fiercely.

"I appreciate the kind words, but I'd like to get back to whether I still have a place to call home or not," I stated. She chuckled and patted my hand softly.

"This isn't going to be an easy conversation. I want you to know that I voted against this at every step of the process. However, the council as a whole has decided this is what's best for you and the entire Windcrest pack." The last sentence had my heart pounding in my chest as my head grew light and fuzzy. I refused to say a word until she finished explaining. Seeing my stubborn expression she shook her head and continued. "The Council has decided to arrange a mating between you and Alpha Harrington of the Windcrest pack-"

"What?!" I screeched, shooting off the bed.

"His true mate committed many acts of infidelity, thus resulting in the dissolution of their mating before it could be fully completed. He's been running the pack for four years alone and The Council will no longer let him run without an alpha female at his side-"

"That's not my freaking problem! They can't make me do this!" I screamed, my chest growing tight as I struggled to breathe.

"You're technically a ward of the council while under protective custody. They decided it's time for you to move on with your life. They believe being mated to a good alpha is the safest place you can possibly be. Thus, they've decided to move forward with the decision as it's mutually beneficial for both parties involved."

How could she speak about this so clinically? Mutually beneficial for both parties involved? This wasn't just some stupid business deal! This was my life!

"I don't want a mate! This should be my choice! This should happen on my timing, not theirs! I've been through enough in my damn life! What I want right now is to feel safe where I am! To hang out with Jackie on the weekends and to help Elder Agatha prepare meals during the week! I-I shouldn't be sold off to some...some man just because he needs a female body by his side!" I screeched. "What if I run? T-They can't stop me. I'll leave and then I'll no longer be a ward of The Council," I rushed out, my eyes filling with tears of fear. I can't do it again. I can't risk it. Elder Adelia stood and stopped my pacing with a hand to either arm, holding me firmly in place, halting the line of thinking.

"Take a deep breath, Scarlett. In and out. That's good, let's do it again. In and out," she instructed. I was shaking like a leaf in her hold, my mind racing a mile a minute.

"Look at me. Really listen to me, Scarlett," she demanded. "I know Alpha Harrington on a personal level. I've met with him under many different circumstances. He's a good man. Kind and just. He'd never lay a hand on a woman. Ever. I'm close friends with his family, his mother and I are good friends. I would've never let this happen if I didn't think you would be safe. If I didn't think you would have the opportunity to bloom and grow. I know this isn't what you want to hear, but I know what's best for you. I've been on this earth longer than I'll admit-"

"You say you know what's best for me, but you're just going to dump me in this new pack and leave!" I hissed, beginning to thrash in her arms.

"That's not true," she growled. "I made The Council agree to monthly well-being checkups. If I suspect something is wrong or you have any problems, we will terminate the mating immediately. I fought against this for long enough that I knew Alpha Harrington and all his higher-ups would be leaving the day before you arrive and traveling until at least Saturday, if not Sunday, for the renewal of their treaty contracts with other packs."

I swallowed thickly, my mind already devising a plan to get myself out of this situation as soon as possible.

"I can see the wheels turning in your head. Stop it. You've been in survival mode for too long, Scarlett. Life is meant to be lived, sweet girl. This, what you've been doing here, it isn't living. It's merely surviving. Tell me right now, honestly, that there isn't even a tiny modicum of a sliver in your being that wants to have a happily ever after with a caring mate, marriage, children of your own. Tell me right now that's not what you want and I'll help you sneak out of here without the other council members knowing," she stated, a serious look in her eyes.

I allowed myself to stop and truly think for a few moments.

Did I want the chance to have that?

Absolutely. I wasn't sure there was a female wolf in this world who didn't want a happily ever after with their mate - whether that involved kids or not. I knew she already knew the answer to her question as it was something we had discussed in one of our heart-to-hearts a while back. I just didn't know if I could handle the unknown. No matter how great she said this man was, there was still an intense feeling of anxiety inside of me. I couldn't speak, so I just shook my head no. She smiled and pulled me into a tight embrace.

"I'm so glad you've agreed. I meant what I said about sneaking you out if that's truly what you wanted, but...I couldn't be certain you'd be safe from him if I let you do that. Out there, there's no guarantee he won't find you. With the Harrington family, I'll know you're being looked after and cared for."

I swallowed thickly. "Will they know...everything?" I whispered the last word of my question.

"No. They will only be told that you were with us in protective custody and that your mate is not and never will be in the picture for you. For legal reasons, we are required to tell them your mate's name, however, whatever else they know about your situation is up to you," she said. I nodded, thankful I wouldn't have to relive that again through telling the story. Someday, I will. And someday I'll be strong enough to. That day is not today. Or tomorrow.

No one in my old pack knew what had transpired between my mate and me. No one knew the twisted, sick things that went on in Eric Strickland's mind. To the outside world, he was a picture-perfect guy with just a bit of a temper problem - something that was common amongst higher-ranking wolves. But not me. I saw him for what he really was.

A monster. A cold-blooded torturer.

I had the scars littering my back, arms, and legs to prove just how evil that man was. My skin still felt tight when I stretched, the scars still too new to relax. It took me every day of the past two years to come to terms with what I saw in the mirror when I would strip down.

At first, I would break down crying. The flashbacks were intense. So intense, it was as if I was right back in that basement, shivering on the cold floor as my body pumped out adrenaline to keep me alive. The harsh sting of an open-handed slap to the face followed by an immediate backhand the other way. Split lips and bruises were nothing to me. Bloody noses were just another day-to-day occurrence. Eric stopped taking me to the pack doctor early on. He didn't like the judging look the doctor gave him.

By the six-month mark, I was able to handle the flashbacks on my own. I'd figured out ways to stop them once they started, though my methods weren't fun. It usually meant stepping under the cold spray of a shower to shock my system.

By one year, the flashbacks were gone unless triggered. Those around me were careful not to raise their hands around me, move too quickly, or approach from behind without giving me adequate heads-up. It felt like people were constantly walking on eggshells. In hindsight, I knew they were. Nowadays, the flashbacks are mostly gone. I attributed all the progress to God's grace and my therapist. Without my therapist's amazing patience, I'd still be the shell of a woman I was when I arrived.

"You have all of today to pack the things you want to take with you and say your goodbyes. We will leave early Monday morning," Elder Adelia said.

"Next Monday?" I asked.

"As in tomorrow. Elder Thomas refused to give you more time with the news for fear you would slip out and run if you had more time to prepare," she confessed. I wanted to be annoyed, but it was a smart move on his part. I just pursed my lips and looked straight ahead out the window, though she looked like she wanted to say more, she held her tongue. Leaning towards me, she rubbed her cheek lovingly against my own. Getting up, she shut my door behind her as she left, the sound echoing throughout my mostly bare room. I blew a raspberry with my lips before looking around.

Despite calling this room home for two whole years now, I didn't have many belongings. I had five sundresses - all hand sewn by Elder Adelia except for the two most recent ones that she helped me do myself - three pairs of jean shorts, three pairs of thick winter leggings, a handful of sweatshirts, long sleeves, and t-shirts. I doubted I would be wearing anything that showed my skin; my scars weren't something I let new people see.

I had one framed photo of Jackie - my best friend I met here - and I sitting on my side table. My phone that I barely used - too afraid it would leave an electronic trail that Eric could follow right to me. A box of scrap fabric and a sewing machine to practice with. A couple of books passed down to me from other wolves that had been in protective custody and have since moved on to find homes in other packs. A hair brush and a straightener that I never used (much to Jackie's dismay), and a bag containing a few makeup products.

I tried not to think about the fact that I was able to pack up everything I owned in less than an hour. It was just stuff. Stuff didn't make you happy. I'd never had a lot my entire life, anyway. And I was okay with that. My parents dumped me on The Council grounds just moments after I was born, so I was immediately put in their version of a foster system. Funny how my life had kind of come full circle. I got bounced around a lot, so packing lightly was a necessity. I only ever kept the things that meant the most to me. That habit continued into adulthood.

There was a second knock on my door, making me wonder if someone else was here to give me any more life-changing news. Opening the door, I was met with the sight of a red-eyed Jackie whose face was glistening from tears. My throat tightened as I opened my arms for her. She immediately ran into them, knocking the wind out of me from her intensity.

"I c-can't b-believe they're making y-you leave m-me!" she sobbed. My own eyes watered as I hugged her tighter.

"I promise we'll talk all the time," I squeezed out through my tight vocal cords.

"With w-what? The phone that you d-don't even know how to u-use?" she deadpanned, trying to maintain her humor even when she was so upset she could barely speak.

"I'll learn how to use it just for you. I p-promise," I assured her as a few tears of my own leaked out and trickled down my cheeks. She didn't respond as she continued to sniffle and hiccup. "You're looking raggedy now, g-get it together," I joked, helping her wipe away her tears. She snorted before inhaling a gaspy breath.

"I'm gonna miss you so much," she whispered as her face turned sorrowful again.

"Maybe I can convince them to let me keep you. Like a package deal or something. Hey, maybe you'll meet your mate when you come to visit and the crazy stalker they're hiding you from will finally give up!" I exclaimed, trying to inject positivity into my tone.

"It's been five years since I turned eighteen, I'm not holding my breath. Melvin, however, might be. I have no idea where the hell he's at," she grunted.

"Let's hope it's long enough that he asphyxiates himself. I'm done packing and I think we need one last hurrah. I know where Adelia keeps the hard stuff, c'mon," I murmured, pulling my door closed behind me as we went.

True to my word, there was an entire bottle of brand-new brandy right where I knew it'd be. We also managed to snag a bottle of orange juice from the fridge before high-tailing it out of the main wing. We found an abandoned room on the opposite side of the house from where my room was. We didn't think to steal any glasses from the kitchen, so we went back and forth taking swigs from the brandy followed by the orange juice.

"Hey, look," I giggled, pouring a little of both into my mouth and then dramatically shaking my head back and forth. "Mini mouth cocktail," I laughed after I swallowed. Jackie giggled her head off before snatching the two bottles back from me and doing the same.

"You're gonna have to be all serious and stuff once you're a Luna. That's gonna suck," she grumbled after a long moment of silence.

"I hate to break it to you Jackie, but you're the only one I'm like this around. I usually am serious," I pointed out.

"That is so untrue. You can be a cold, callous biotch when you wanna be - just like me - but for the most part, you're sarcastic and witty. I don't think you can be sarcastic and witty when you're a Luna."

"Says who?" I challenged while raising my eyebrows.

"Worst-case scenario, they think you're not Luna material and kick you right back here. That wouldn't be so bad," she commented with a thoughtful look. I just shook my head and laughed at her.

"Adelia already guilt-tripped me into trying to make this work. You know how that is," I murmured, playing with the brandy bottle lid.

"Damn. She went for the jugular, didn't she?" she asked, sipping the orange juice.

"Unfortunately. Have you ever heard of the guy? Alpha Harrington?" I asked. Jackie immediately choked, spewing her mouthful all over the floor and me. "Hey! What the heck?" I yelled, my hands shooting out in front of me defensively to try and deflect some of the citrus spray.

"Your arranged mating is with the Alpha Harrington? The Alpha Harrington of Windcrest pack?"

"I guess so?" I squeaked out, my mind starting to run wild with various scenarios, none of them pleasant. "Is he terrible?" I asked, my palms beginning to sweat.

"Are you freaking kidding me? All that time spent hopping from pack to pack and you've never seen or heard of him? Lord have MERCY! I'm pretty sure he's the image every single unmated female in the entire world has in mind when praying for their future mate!" she yelled, getting up in my face.

"Is the fact that thousands of women picture him when planning their future supposed to be comforting? My ex isn't horrible looking either, Jackie. Look where that landed me," I grunted.

"Wrong. Your ex has crazy eyes and looks like he thinks missionary is a kinky position. You can tell there's something not quite right with him in the head. Alpha Harrington, however, is...beautiful. He's six-feet-eight inches and 300 pounds of solid-muscled deliciousness. A lot of the other alphas used to jokingly call him Gaston back in the day because that's kinda his human cartoon twin. Besides the prideful ego, of course."

"Have you ever personally met him?" I asked, hoping she had so that she could calm my nerves over the whole situation.

"Not personally, no, but I've seen him around in my old pack when he was visiting for whatever reason alphas visit other packs. Really quiet guy, but sweet from what I've heard. I guess he became pretty closed off after what his mate did to him. Word on the street says she's a real big....ya know. She's not polite," she stated with a pointed look.

"You'd have to be pretty terrible to cheat on your mate. Though, I wish all Eric had done to me was cheat on me. That was the least of his transgressions," I growled, shoving the bottles back at her just a little too hard, almost spilling one of them.

"Yeah, screw that guy. Someday, hopefully soon, he'll get what he has coming to him. But, until then, we'll toast to new beginnings," Jackie boasted, lifting the OJ bottle into the air. I smirked and lifted the brandy in response. We clinked bottles and chugged before quickly swapping them.

To new beginnings.

# CHAPTER 3

S carlett's POV

I slept the entire four-hour flight to my new home. The killer hangover I had paired with the hour of sobbing I did this morning while I was saying goodbye to everyone - especially Jackie - wiped me out. The second the personal flight attendant was done explaining the safety precautions to Adelia and me, I was out cold. I only woke up a few times when Adelia forced me to drink Gatorade to help curb my hangover - one she was both understanding of and irritated about considering she knew I'd taken from her stash.

I hadn't been feeling the nerves until the pilot announced our descent from the air. Everything felt like a blur as Adelia handed me my things from the storage compartment and guided me off the private plane. I only had a single suitcase waiting for me, which made the move pretty easy. I decided to have the one box containing my sewing machine and scrap materials shipped to my new home for convenience sake. It was incredibly clunky.

I pulled on my heavy winter coat and zipped it up as Adelia flagged down our driver. He was silent as he escorted us to an awaiting car.

"Well, isn't that a sweet gesture!" Adelia exclaimed while pointing at the bottle of champagne chilling in a bucket of ice. Her face held a smirk as I swallowed thickly but nodded. I was really regretting that brandy right about now. Taking a deep breath, I ran my hand over the leather seats of the car to distract my uneasy stomach. I didn't even want to know how much this thing had to cost.

I buckled myself in and quietly watched the scenery pass by - not that there was much to look at. Montana in January promised nothing but snow, snow, and more snow. That was something I had to look forward to for the next few months, if not more. I was okay with that, though. I loved the cold. The icy bite whipping at your face. Seeing your breath in the air with every exhale was a reminder that you were alive. Most importantly, it meant layers. Layers covering every inch of skin from the prying eyes of others whose mouths were always begging to open and ask the same, familiar question.

How'd you get those scars?

Yes, winter was my favorite time. Even if it brought back those horrid memories.

"We're not too far away. There's something I've been meaning to tell you," Adelia finally broke the silence. I looked at her, giving the go-ahead to continue.

"I was only able to bargain for a month," she explained cryptically.

"A month? A month for what?"

"Originally, all The Council members were expecting you and Alpha Harrington to be marked and fully mated within a week of you arriving. I was able to bargain and get a whole month.""A month. That's it? After everything I've been through they expect me to meet and bump uglies with some dude after only a fucking month?!" I cursed, something I hardly ever did but couldn't help in the situation. "Does that start from the moment I arrive or from the moment we meet?" I could already tell the answer by her pained expression.

"So I actually only get three weeks to come to terms with this? To be comfortable enough to let another man tear into my damn neck? You said you'd be doing monthly checkups! That you would terminate the mating if something wasn't right!" I growled, my nails digging into the nice leather beneath me. I couldn't bring myself to care that I was likely messing it up.

"I didn't lie. I will be doing monthly check-ups; the first one will be just before your required mating day. And if you still have issues afterward, well, matings can be undone by practiced healers within the council under certain circumstances," she explained. I felt tears welling up in my eyes. I felt betrayed. She'd purposely chosen not to tell me this piece of information until I was already trapped. In less than an hour, she'd drop me off and go on her merry way. I couldn't believe this.

"Scarlett-"

"I don't have anything to say to you," I interrupted her. She'd been the only consistent motherly figure I'd ever had in my life. And now here she was, deceiving me it felt like. She sighed but stayed quiet for the rest of the ride. A few moments later, we turned down what I assumed was a gravel road as the journey became bumpy. I closed my eyes, the jostling making me nauseous again. When the road turned smooth once again, I opened my eyes and just about had a heart attack. We were stopped in front of two huge, looming steel gates. Two men in towers, one on each side of the gate, stared down at the car. They gave a thumbs-up before the gate began to open. I tried to calm my breathing as we continued along a winding road, inching closer and closer to the massive house in the distance. By the time we pulled up to the front of the mansion, both my legs were bouncing from nervous energy as I gnawed at my lower lip.

My anxious buzz was swapped for confusion as we drove past the fountain in the front and continued on towards the back of the building.

"There's a separate entrance for the alpha's wing," Adelia explained.

We came to a stop at the new entrance, this one looking less intimidating. My heart rate was starting to normalize just as two huge men began making their way towards the SUV. I started trembling in my seat, doing my best to maintain my composure even though I was crapping myself internally. Who's idea was it to let me off Council grounds?!

"Relax, Scarlett. They're part of the Alpha's security team. They will not hurt you. No one here is going to hurt you. I promise. They're just going to grab your things and take them to your room," she murmured, placing a comforting hand on my shoulder. I released a shuddering breath as one of them opened the door closest to Adelia. I popped the hood on my coat, using my bun to keep it propped up and over my head so the wind wouldn't knock it back down.

"Elder Adelia, it's always a pleasure to see you," the man said, offering his large hand out for her to take.

"Thank you, Jacob. Same to you," she replied with a smile before looking back at me expectantly as I stayed rooted in my seat. I cleared my throat before scooching towards the open door. I hesitated, making brief eye contact with the man. He offered what I'm assuming he thought was a non-threatening smile. I steeled my exterior and took his hand, allowing him to help me down.

I was here. There was no turning back. I wasn't a scared little girl anymore. I'd seen and experienced too much to cower away from this. This was nothing compared to my past. I could handle this. I would handle this. And I would do it with confidence - whether it was faked or not. I said a prayer and released the breath I had been holding.

I followed behind Adelia as we approached the house and entered. She took my coat and hung it up for me. I allowed myself a brief moment to snuggle into my much-too-big-for-me sweatshirt when no one could see me before resuming a short, light jog to catch up with the two of them.

Upon entering what I could tell was the kitchen, a group of women shouted surprise! The commotion caught me off guard and I instantly pulled my hidden knife, raising it as I adopted a defensive stance. Their eyes all widened and some of them gasped with surprise. I felt my face heat with embarrassment, but there was nothing I could do about my instinctual response now. I lifted my top and tucked the knife back into its hiding place. Had we flown commercial, I wouldn't have had it on me and I wouldn't have looked like a lunatic in front of all these people. But, alas, The Council had a private jet...so here we were.

Oh well. You win some, you lose some.

They all gave me a once-over. That's when I realized I was wearing just about the worst possible outfit for a first impression ever.

"I don't always look this homeless..." I mumbled in my own defense. There was a moment of silence before two of the girls started cracking up, the rest of them soon following.

"You are going to fit in just fine!" one of them said before rushing towards me and pulling me in for a tight hug. You would think she'd be more cautious around me considering I'd just pulled a knife seconds before, but I guess not. I took a moment to analyze her as she let me go. I could tell she was at least a beta or gamma from the power she exuded, but I couldn't be certain which of the two.

"My name is Riley, I'm the beta female of the pack. That there is Peyton, she's the gamma. And last but not least is Raven. She's the head warrior's wife. She usually helps train the females of the pack, but, as you can see, she's due to pop twins out in three months so she's not allowed on her feet much. Alpha Harrington asked that we take you under our wing and help you get settled in while he's away. We thought it'd be fun to surprise you and give you the low-down on the pack before you meet your future in-laws," she said.

Okay. Okay. Blondie, Rylie. Brunette, Peyton. Raven...raven hair. I got this. Easy enough. They all gave me an expectant look, probably because I still hadn't responded.

"I'm not dumb, I promise. I'm just processing all of this," I admitted honestly.

"Oh yeah. She's gonna fit in perfectly," Raven said with a snort and a smile. "I can't freaking wait to see the look on Mika's face," she added after a short pause with a smirk.

"Who's Mika?" I asked.

"Why don't we help her get settled in and changed into something a bit nicer, girls? I know she'll want to make a good first impression with her future in-laws," Adelia commented with a terse smile. I wonder what that's all about.

"That sounds great. Follow us, we'll show you to your room," Peyton said, hopping excitedly off the stool she'd been sitting on and rushing toward me. My body went rigid out of habit. She looped her arm through mine and started practically dragging me further into the house. I gritted my teeth but let her continue - she seemed like a sweet girl and I didn't want to hurt her feelings by snatching my arm back. We walked up a flight of stairs and down an expansive hallway before stopping at a set of beautiful double doors.

"Through here is your bedroom. Jacob already brought your suitcase up. We'll just wait out here," she stated with a smile.

"You're not going to follow me in?" I asked, confused. These girls reminded me a lot of Jackie, and Jackie didn't understand the concept of personal space. They all shared an uneasy look before turning their gazes onto me.

"Um, this is you and Alpha Harrington's bedroom. He doesn't allow anyone in there, hardly ever is an exception made," she explained.

I have to start sharing a bed with him right away?! What the fuck?

"Well, you just said it's my bedroom now, too. That means I get a say in who's allowed in. Let's go," I said, not pausing to see their reactions to my words before throwing the doors open and taking a step inside. I wasn't sure what I was expecting, but it wasn't this. The kitchen had been...a bit of a mess earlier, but it was nothing compared to this. "I can see why he doesn't let people in here," I muttered sarcastically. The place was a pigsty. How in the world did this guy live in these conditions?

There were wrinkled clothes strewn all over the floor. The bed was an unmade pile of sheets and blankets halfway hanging on the floor. The small living area - yes, there was a mini freaking living room in here - had papers strewn all about. I tripped on a random shoe as I entered, almost falling. I didn't even want to know what the bathroom looked like. I couldn't even ogle at the size of the place because the mess was too overwhelming.

"Now you have to come with me. I'll get lost in...all of this," I motioned my hand around the general chaos that was the bedroom, "if you don't," I said. The girls lost it laughing again.

"Looks like some stuff already got lost. I only see one suitcase here," Peyton commented.

"I only have the one," I mentioned offhandedly. They all snap their attention to me as if I'd just confessed to some heinous crime.

"Wow, you travel light. When is the rest of your stuff being delivered?" Raven asked.

"Uh...it's not? Well, I just have one box coming, and it's just my sewing machine and some scrap fabric so..." I trailed off, my voice growing quieter and quieter as their looks morphed into that of confusion and then horror. I didn't feel the need to explain myself, so I turned away from their prying eyes and proceeded to strip all the blankets off of the bed - I would be throwing them all in the wash before I could sleep tonight anyway - and hauled my suitcase up onto the mattress. I unzipped the top and opened it. I rooted around for the only nice outfit I owned, which consisted of a chunky sweater and cute jeans that were both items from Jackie given to me this morning as parting gifts. I ignored the burning gazes of the girls as I entered the walk-in closet before shutting the door behind me so I could change.

I just shook my head in disbelief. Even the closet was a disaster. Half the clothes were hung up, and half of them were just sitting in piles on the shelves. I quickly switched out my comfy outfit and exited to find all three women with their heads close together, chatting quietly. Suddenly, I'm back in high school again. They sprang apart when they saw me and gave me sympathetic smiles. I just ignored it while repacking my sweatshirt and leggings. I'd taken my sneakers off at the front door, but I wasn't sure what I was going to wear for shoes. I couldn't put my sneakers back on, but I didn't have much else for options. I pulled out my severely worn pair of flats, but they didn't go with the baby-pink color of the sweater.

"I have the cutest pair of booties that would look amazing with that outfit. What size are you? My place is connected to yours, I can run and grab them for you to try on!" Riley offered. I glanced down at my dying shoes and back up at her. "I'm a seven," I murmured. Her eyes lit up like a kid on Christmas before she rushed off without another word.

"Do you think you could teach me how to do that?" Raven abruptly asked, pointing towards the top of her own head. I reached my hand up and ran my fingers over the three intricate French braids running down the center of my head before ending in a messy bun.

"Yeah, sure. It just takes a lot of practice," I said softly.

"Did you have sisters or something?" she asked with a look of genuine curiosity.

"Something like that...," I responded evasively. All the orphanages I grew up in had a revolving door of other girls coming in and out - me being one of them. I quickly learned how to do my hair by watching others, something that was necessary as no one ever had time to help me. Once I learned, other girls were constantly asking for me to do their hair. I didn't mind, so I got pretty good pretty quick.

"Are you hungry? Vanessa and Andrew are preparing a big brunch just for you," Peyton said. She didn't elaborate, but I assumed those were my 'future in-laws' as everyone liked to call them.

"I could eat," I nodded. Despite the nerves still present, I was starving. As soon as Riley got back, I slipped the heeled shoes on

- which did fit like a glove - and then we were off to our next destination again. Adelia watched on as a silent observer from the background. About five minutes later they dragged my body to an abrupt stop right outside a second set of double doors as a sense of deja vu from earlier washed over me.

"These doors connect the leaders' wing to the main pack dining room. There shouldn't be anyone in here right now except for our past Alpha and Luna - and maybe their daughter. Are you ready? Do you need a minute?" Riley asked, giving me another head-to-toe check. I swallowed thickly before taking a deep breath and shaking my head no. "Okay, in you go!" she exclaimed.

"Wait, you're not coming with me?" I asked, a sense of panic taking over my body, but I didn't show it.

"No, but I will be. We have things to discuss," Adelia explained, coming to stand next to me as the girls stepped back a few feet. I tried to calm my brain from the whiplash of events before Adelia pushed the doors open. I let my calm facade take over again as two sets of eyes settled on me from across the dining room. I kept my hands at my side, cautious not to fist them as I made my way to the table. When I was not but ten feet away from the table they both stood. I stopped in my tracks and staggered backward, terrified at the large, unyielding-looking man before me. His face held an impassive look as he towered over me. I wasn't a small girl - I stood about five-foot-seven the last time I'd been checked - but even in heels, he was taller than me.

The woman smacked his stomach harshly. "Smile, idiot! You're scaring her!" she hissed before turning back to me with a warm smile of her own. I couldn't help the quiet, short giggle that bubbled out of me at her words and actions.

"He often slips into alpha mode without even realizing it - a habit after being in charge for so many years. Hi! I'm Vanessa!"

the woman explained before extending a hand for me to shake. I slowly closed the distance between us and carefully accepted her hand. Her presence was warm and calming, easing my fear caused by her mate. I like her.

"It's nice to meet you," I said, my voice coming out more confident than I felt at the moment.

"The pleasure is all ours. As soon as The Council called us we were ecstatic," the man - Andrew, I was assuming - said.

"So, what was your first impression of the place?" Vanessa asked.

"Your son is very messy," I said honestly before my eyes went wide and I realized what I had allowed to slip out. "That's not what I meant to say," I rushed out. The couple both sputtered before laughing.

"Thank God. I was worried you were going to be this meek little thing. Blunt honesty is much appreciated around here," she said with a happy smile.

"Scarlett, Vanessa will be your mentor before you officially take over your pack duties as Luna," Adelia began, steering the conversation to a more serious topic right away. The next two hours were spent discussing all my upcoming responsibilities with only a short break for food - which was quite delicious. However, even the wonderful meal couldn't distract from how my head was spinning by the time we were done. I was in a daze as Adelia and Vanessa walked me back to the place I would be living from here on out.

"That was a lot to take in all at once. How are you feeling?" Adelia asked as soon as we had re-entered the kitchen. I just shrugged, almost as if on autopilot. There wasn't much I could say. It didn't matter if I was overwhelmed and wanted to scream, this was my life now. All I could do now was suck it up and move forward. It seemed to be the story of my life.

"Well, I'll be staying in a guest bedroom tonight, so if you need me that's where I'll be. I'll give you some time alone to think about everything and get to know the place," she said, giving the room a judgmental once over. I pursed my lips to keep the smirk off my face at the disgusted look on her own.

I looked around for myself and let out a grunt. Man, this place needs a lot of help.

# CHAPTER 4

Scarlett's POV

I let a small smile pull at my lips as I pushed the arms of the long-sleeved shirt I'd changed into up out of my way. I rubbed my hands together as I mentally came up with a plan of attack. After touring the entire house, I'd come to realize it was essentially a little townhouse attached to the rest of the pack house. I'm assuming it was so the alpha's family could have a sense of privacy while still being at the center of the pack just in case. I surveyed every room and realized that practically the entire place needed a good scrub down.

Everyone else saw it as work, but me? I loved it. I loved to clean, redecorate, organize and reorganize. To restore things to working order. Maybe it's because my environment - my space - was something I could control. I couldn't necessarily clean up my life, but I sure as heck could make this kitchen look like it was straight out of one of those lifestyle magazines you found lying around most convenience stores. And that's exactly what I was going to do. And - secretly - all my life I'd fantasized about having a place of my own to take care of. When you're constantly uprooted from place to place as a child with nowhere to call home, a place to call yours and make all the decisions is what you truly crave.

Normalcy.

Now, I technically did.

I decided to start in the kitchen. I gathered up all the random cups and dishes that were strewn around the house and placed them all in the sink to deal with all at once. Opening the fridge, a funky smell wafted into my nose. I scrunched my whole face upwards before pulling every item out. I threw away what was past its prime before wiping all the shelves down with a cleaning solution I'd found in a random cabinet. Afterward, I put everything back - this time with an actual purpose rather than how it had all just been thrown in before. Then I moved onto the freezer and did the same process over again. I gathered all the random items sitting on the counters and placed them on the middle kitchen counter. I turned and opened up every single cabinet so I had an idea of where things were being kept. I immediately smacked my palm against my forehead at the mostly bare sight before me.

I grabbed my phone and unlocked it just as Jackie showed me. Pulling up the notes app on the front page. I started jotting down all the things I'd need to make this a fully functioning kitchen.

How this man managed to cook for himself without any mixing bowls, measuring cups, or spoons of any sort was absolutely beyond me.

I then proceeded to move all the dishes and drinking glasses to the cabinet above the dishwasher - because that just made logical sense, less work when unloading it. I opened all the lower drawers only to come up mostly empty again - minus a single cooking sheet, one cutting board, and one large saute pan. His spice collection was also seriously lacking.

I finished adding the rest of the stuff I'd need to my list before wiping down all the countertops - one of which had a very questionable stain that took me five minutes and some serious elbow grease to get out. Lastly, I loaded the dishwasher with as many dishes as I could before adding a cleaning pod I found stored under the sink and starting it. The rest I hand-washed and put away. I giggled to myself as I remembered the time Jackie used hand soap when using the dishwasher back at the council grounds; sometimes I think she did it purposely because she was forever barred from kitchen duty after that.

Stepping back, I admired my hard work. The end result was a beautiful space that smelled fresh, clean, and distinctly like fake lemons. I smiled, the progress gave me that familiar rush to move onto the attached living room space.

I gathered up all the blankets that were carelessly tossed about and folded them. There was a beautiful wood chest hidden in the corner of the room that I decided to store them in until they needed to be used. I grabbed the few random items of clothing that were in the middle of the room, strewn about on the floor, and took them to the laundry room that was off of the side of the kitchen. Coming back, I stood in the center of the living room - if you could even call it that.

The only thing in the room was a large, plush three-seater couch, one folding dinner tray that was being used as a makeshift side table, and a massive flat-screen TV that was mounted to the wall. I rolled my eyes. Men. I added living room furniture to my list of items and moved on. The various bathrooms didn't take me too long. Eventually, I was back in what would be our bedroom. That thought still felt horribly awkward....and brought a chill up my spine to even think about considering I'd never even met the man. I'd been smart enough to bring a few baskets with me from the laundry room before coming up. I knew I'd end up needing them. I went around smelling every item of clothing, determining if it was just clean and wrinkled or if it was truly dirty. The items that looked like workout clothes I didn't even bother with - I just threw them in the basket for washing.

The clothes and dirty bedding were over half the battle. With that contained, I organized the papers in the makeshift sitting area into neat piles. In the closet, I hung up and organized both his and my clothing by color and season. His side ended up being filled while my side...well, my side looked non-existent.

Entering the bathroom for the first time took my breath away. Not because it was dirty - which it was - but because it was beautiful. There was a floor-to-ceiling glass shower that connected to a huge bathtub, one that from where I was standing appeared to have built-in jets. Oh, thank the Lord. Jackie told me about a hotel bathtub with jets she'd gotten to use one time. She said it was heavenly. It's been on my bucket list to take a bath in one ever since. I sighed dreamily while grabbing my pre-prepared bucket of cleaner and water mixture and got to work.

By the time I was done my back was aching and my stomach was growling, but the result was a bathroom I could feel clean showering and doing my business in. I carted the overflowing laundry baskets down the stairs, pausing to grumble here and there as a random sock or pair of boxers fell out.

I huffed as I dropped the baskets in front of the gorgeous double-load washer and dryer set. The Council didn't have anything nearly this nice in the communal laundry room. I wiped the sweat off my brow before throwing all the light-colored clothes in, dumping a generous amount of detergent into the respective compartment, and stabbing the start button with my finger. I turned and rested my back against the machine before slowly sliding down to the floor. My head lolled back, the sound of the clothes sloshing around almost lulling me to sleep. Despite all the hours I'd put in, I still hadn't made it to what I assumed was his poker room or his office - but those I would leave up to him.

I knew someone was here before they spoke; I'd heard their footsteps approaching the door that connected this place to the rest of the pack house. They weren't very quiet, but I don't think they were trying to be.

"What kind of magic did you use in here?!" came a semi-familiar voice from the kitchen. I knew it was one of the women from earlier, but I wasn't sure which one from voice alone. I heaved a sigh before pulling my body back up to my feet. I slumped into the kitchen, pushing the baby hairs that had escaped my braids out of my face.

"Damn, can I hire you to come and fix up my place?" Blondie - Riley - asked, running her hand along the now-spotless counter-top.

"Sorry, I'm out of commission for the day," I said, trying to muster a joking tone just as my phone started buzzing on the countertop. Picking it up, I saw Jackie's name and photo displayed on the screen and smiled wide for the first time since arriving here.

"Hello?""About time you got back to me you turd! I've been trying to get a hold of you all afternoon!" she exclaimed. I laughed lightly.

"Sorry, I've been cleaning. What's up?"

"I just wanted to make sure you made it there safely. Is he everything I said he was and more?" she asked, her tone ever so smug.

"No idea. I haven't met him yet..." I trailed off quietly, wanting to say more, but also aware I had three sets of stranger-ears listening in. "Can I text you?" I asked softly while the girls pretended to be busy, but I knew they were listening intently.

"Ugh, fine! But you better actually text me back or I'm catching the first flight to Montana - stalker potentially on my heels or not!" she said. I just smiled and said goodbye. As soon as she hung up, I typed out a quick message that some people were listening and I would call her later tonight.

"So, did you have any plans? The girls and I found babysitters for the rest of the evening. We figured we would take you out for dinner and then stop by a couple of stores. We know this place is barely even a bachelor pad, so you'll probably need more than a few things," Raven said.

"You have kids?" I asked. They appeared much too young to be mothers, but they all nodded in sync to my question.

"Why don't we talk about all this over dinner and margaritas?" Riley suggested. I hesitated for a moment. I hadn't been out in public unless accompanied by a council member ever since I'd escaped from Eric's...custody.  What if...what if he finds us?

"We won't let anything happen to you. Our mates never let us leave without at least three security men present. You'll be safe with us. Promise," Peyton said with a comforting smile. I swallowed thickly, Elder Adelia's earlier words about living echoing in my mind before I eventually nodded my head in agreement after a few minutes. However, the entire idea of leaving the house made me feel like hives had broken out along my entire body.

Apparently, they were regulars at the restaurant they'd decided to take me to. We got a table in the corner where I was able to sit with my back against the wall looking out at the entire restaurant. That was a...nice gesture. My brain was on hyperdrive the entire time we were there despite the numerous assurances from the other girls that we were "totally safe!" Any time I saw a head of blonde hair - short, long, or buzzed, you name it, my heart would beat a little faster and my palms would start to sweat.

Despite my constant alert state, I did discover that I was a fan of chips and salsa - something I'd only ever heard about before. The other girls didn't like the spicy stuff, but I loved it. Eric had always hated spicy food. I smirked while recalling the one time I'd put hot sauce all over his spaghetti. He forced me to take a bite, thinking it would affect me, but I ate it straight-faced and told him he needed to see the pack doctor. The beating that night sucked but was totally worth it.

I was slowly working away at my margarita because all I could taste was a glass of tequila with a hint of lime. The other girls, however, were sucking them down like water. They'd started to spill their life stories as soon as the liquor kicked in, and it again made me feel like I was back with Jackie. I learned that all three women met and mated their husbands right after they turned eighteen. Riley was now twenty-six with two boys, eight and five years old. Peyton was twenty-seven with three kids; two boys seven and five, and a little two-year-old girl. Raven was the youngest of the bunch at twenty-two, but even she had one boy already with another two on the way.

I asked them if they were trying to populate a sports team together. They seemed to think that was pretty funny.

"I can't remember the last time we had a girls' night like this," Raven reminisced while sipping at her virgin Shirley temple.

"I think you still needed a high chair," Peyton commented, she and Riley losing it with laughter as Raven threw a chip at them.

"They love to tease me for being the youngest in the group," she pouted playfully. "It's a running joke."

"I guess you don't have to worry about that anymore," I remarked before taking a sip of my drink, not thinking much about my comment. They were all staring at me wide-eyed when I gave them my attention again. "What?" I deadpanned, wiping at my face self-consciously thinking I must've had salsa on it.

"How old are you?" Raven inquired.

"Twenty-one, obviously," I said while pointing to the alcoholic drink I was nursing.

"I would've never guessed you were so young," Riley murmured, still staring at me like I was a circus act. I had to grow up pretty fast, I thought to myself as I fiddled in the chair self-consciously.

"I can't believe The Council decided to mate you to a man eight years older than you," Peyton added in. Now that was news to me. I was going to be mated to a twenty-nine-year-old guy? What else did Adelia choose not to tell me?! Despite my inner freakout, I kept my calm and composed exterior. I think they saw how uncomfortable the topic was making me, so they quickly changed the subject once again. By the time we were done with our dinner and drinks, I was feeling a wee-bit lightheaded and warm. Though, that didn't stop me from furiously surveying our surroundings, noting all the possible exits, and keeping an eye on the men who were with us as we left the restaurant and were driven to our next destination.

"I swear, I could live here. I mean it, I could," Peyton moaned as we pulled up to a massive yellow and blue painted building.

"What's 'IKEA'?" I asked.

"What?" all the girls gasped at the same time, causing the two security men in the front seats to chuckle softly.

"It's seriously the most amazing store ever! I get in trouble with Griffin every time I come home from here, but...well let's just say I know the best way to smooth things over," Peyton laughed with a haughty smile.

"And that's why you guys have had three pregnancy scares in the past three months," Riley commented with a smirk and a shake of her head.

"Do you not want any more kids?" I asked Peyton as the men opened the door for us and started escorting us inside.

"I'm not sure," she sighed, "I know Griffin wants at least one more so there's no middle child, but I'm content with how many we have right now. Do you want a big family?" she suddenly asked, turning the attention back on me. I didn't answer right away, thinking about my answer first. I wasn't sure how comfortable I was divulging about myself with these women just yet. Women didn't make me or my wolf uncomfortable. It was much easier for me to trust females than it was for me to trust males. Not that that was hard to understand.

"I want a really big family, lots of kids," I finally answered as we stepped inside the building. "Wow," I murmured softly as my eyes bounced around, trying to take everything in all at once.

"Told ya so," Peyton snickered before grabbing a huge blue bag made of what looked like tarp material and trying to hand one to me. It might've been the combination of the new place I wasn't familiar with, or being out in public with people I wasn't completely comfortable with, but the sight of the blue tarp triggered a memory of that cold hard basement that I haven't had in a long time.

"No," I growled roughly, glaring at the tarp bag like it had personally offended me seven times over. The anger and harshness behind my growl scared all three and even had the guards with us on alert. They took a few steps closer, one of them trying to take a position between me and the three women, but his too-close proximity to me snapped me out of the nightmare in my head. I blinked my eyes hard a few times and took a few good steps back from them. Clearing my throat as my cheeks turned pink with embarrassment as they all stared at me in confusion, questioning looks on their faces. My eyes darted to the cart to my right, my only escape from this moment. "I'll use a cart instead," I muttered while swallowing thickly and giving the blue tarp back one last disdainful glare.

"What's first on the list?" Raven asked confidently, bravely being the first one to break the silence after my mini-freak out. They all turned to look at me with friendly smiles as they caught up and fell in step with me. It was a bit unnerving, especially after the side of me they'd just seen. I wasn't used to being the center of attention...ever. Or people giving me the benefit of the doubt after getting a bit...volatile as Adelia liked to put it.

But being the center of attention was something that was going to change from now on. That was for sure. I cleared my throat, unsure how to proceed from here.

"I don't...I don't have any money," I murmured, schooling my face into a stony expression to keep my cheeks from heating with embarrassment yet again. Money was something I was never going to let myself be ashamed over ever again. Eric made sure I never had a dime to my name so I always had to rely on him. I hated it. I worked the skin off my knuckles through The Council, always putting in my fair share of work so I never felt like I was leeching off of them, but it never resulted in any monetary benefit - something that was now proving to be an issue. I had no savings to my name. No credit built up. Nothing.

"Oh, pssh, don't worry about that. We have the pack credit card. It's all going into you and Alpha Harrington's place anyway. Don't worry about it," Riley insisted with a dismissive wave of her hand. With that thought out of the way, the next worry in my mind was how he would react to me purchasing all these things without his permission. This was his home. He's been living there for...who knows how many years without a mate. It's unlikely he'll take kindly to me showing up and buying what's likely to be a thousand - at least - dollars worth of things without his permission. The thought made my hands start to sweat.

But then...the idea of doing just that had the rebellious side of me flaring up. The rebellious side that used to do things for the sole purpose of provoking Eric's demented side; the side that would lash out, beat me for hours on end, and leave me a bloody pulp. I thought that part of me was long gone. I thought she'd been buried a long time ago, during my therapy sessions. But now, a part of me needed to know if this new mate of mine was anything like my ex. Needed to test him. See if there were limits that could be and needed to be pushed. Poked. Prodded.

Yes. This was a test. For him and me. I was playing a dangerous game. Allowing old tendencies to resurface. But I needed to know. I'd done something so similar six months into living with Eric...and it ended with the scars I have on the backs of my arms.

The very corner edge of my lip edged upward a minuscule amount as I pulled my phone out of my coat pocket. I read aloud, "Mixing bowls, cutting boards, measuring cups and spoons, coffee mugs, extra cooking sheets, a set of pots and pans, cooking utensils, Tupperware, a set of knives, a new toaster that doesn't look like it's been through the wringer, a tea kettle, and various organizational things," I rattled off while scrolling down my digital list. They looked shell-shocked. "That's just for the kitchen," I continued before letting out a short, quiet laugh at their expression.

"He needed more help than we thought," Riley grunted before walking off and returning with two shopping carts.

I truly was in heaven as we wandered through the store, my pile of things growing larger and larger as we went. The warning bells in my head telling me this was a bad idea got quieter as the rebellious side grew bolder. As we moved on from kitchen to living room items we had to grab a third cart because we'd run out of space in our current ones. By the time we were finally done and in line checking out, I had everything I could possibly ever need for my dream kitchen, as well as a new coffee table and side tables, a couple of rugs, decorative pillows and throw blankets, curtains for both the living room and bedroom, dozens of various organizational bins, and a new dining room set that didn't look like it belonged inside a human frat house.

The guys insisted on loading everything up for us - all of which didn't fit and had to go in the car that'd been following us with the rest of our security detail inside. Once back at the pack house and everything was unloaded, Riley disappeared and returned a few minutes later with another bottle of tequila.

"Who wants to see how long it takes us to set all this stuff up while tipsy?" she asked. I smiled and shook my head, but had an uneasy feeling in my stomach. Minus last night with Jackie, it'd been a very long time since I allowed myself to drink. I was too afraid of losing control and not being able to defend myself.

"C'mon! Let loose with us, honey! We have to properly welcome you home! As our new Luna, it's your duty to get drunk and bond with us," Peyton insisted.

"I don't remember Vanessa mentioning that one," I joked, feeling myself start to come out of my shell at her warm smile. I felt around for my wolf, seeing how she felt about the situation. Though she was still wary of these women, she didn't feel threatened by them. That was a good sign. And, I mean, if the tarp-bag situation earlier didn't put them off, then...I might as well give them a bit of a chance? I was on pack grounds. Adelia was here too. Somewhere, at least.

"I just know there's a sarcastic sense of humor behind that smile. I'm determined to uncover it," Peyton shot back before searching the cupboards for what I was assuming was a shot glass.

"We don't have any. You'll have to use regular cups," I explained, helping her grab them from the cabinet.

"Would you like juice, Raven? Or some milk maybe?" I asked, opening the fridge before looking at her.

"Oh, that's so sweet, but I was just thinking about taking my leave for the night. My feet are killing me and I'm exhausted. Raincheck?" she asked. I nodded before accepting the glass Riley handed me.

"We'll send you updates on how furniture assembling goes so you can laugh at us in the morning," Peyton giggled as the rest of us joined in.

"Help yourself to whatever, I'm going to make a quick call," I told the rest of the girls, already inching towards the stairs with my phone in my hand.

"Oh, yes! Go ahead! We'll start taking things out of the bags for you while you're gone," Riley said while shooing me away with her hands. I took the stairs two at a time before shutting the bedroom door behind me. I dialed Jackie's number and listened as it rang.

"A woman of her word. You called," she joked. "So, spill the beans. How is it really?" she asked.

"It's not horrible. His parents seem kind - well, his mom is really sweet. I'm not sure how to feel about his dad yet. The wives of the other higher-ups ambushed me this morning on arrival-"

"Please, dear Lord, tell me you didn't pull your knife on them," she groaned, knowing me all too well. I just laughed.

"Oh, but I did. I think I scared the crap out of them, but they were cool about it. I think you would like them. They're a lot like you - no sense of personal boundaries and pretty funny. They're really working to make me feel welcome. It's a nice gesture," I said, playing with a stray fuzz on the mattress cover, making me remember my sheets and bedding were both still wet in the washing machine.

"You better not replace me!" she warned, her tone serious.

I scoffed. "No one could replace you, Jacks. Ever." She sighed deeply on the other line.

"It's already so boring without you here. Tell me what you're doing right now," she begged.

"Talking to you," I responded sarcastically.

"Scarlett, you're gonna get it handed to you. I'm gonna drive down there and body slam you or something," she cackled on the other end. I laughed along with her.

"The girls took me to some place called IKEA for all the stuff this place was missing. Talk about a total disaster, Jackie. What happened at the store is a story for in-person or whatever you call that face-to-face thing-"

"Facetime," she interjected.

"Yeah, that. But back to his house, it was a mess when I got here. I'm talking, like, the dude-who-used-to-live-in-the-room-next-to-you-last-year bad. Anyway, one of them decided it'd be fun to get tipsy and try to put away and assemble everything we bought," I explained.

"That sounds like so much fun. I can't believe I'm missing out. Send me lots of pics, okay?" she said, her tone filled with sadness.

"Will do. Love you, Jacks. So much." She said it back before hanging up. Upon re-entering the kitchen, I saw that the girls had almost everything laid out already, ready to be put away.

"You're behind, you gotta chug this to catch up," Riley giggled before shoving my glass back into my hand. I just shook my head with a small smile and tipped the cup back, swallowing a few sips before setting it back down. They took turns taking shots as they helped me put everything away in the kitchen, finding new homes in the cupboards for all the items I got. That wasn't the hard part, though.

The hard part was my head growing a bit light while the other girls were already way past the point of buzzed and one drop away from speaking in cursive as we plopped down onto the carpeted living room floor. We were trying to be quiet as I imagined Adelia was attempting to sleep, but we were highly unsuccessful.

Peyton ripped open the coffee table box and dumped everything out onto the ground unceremoniously.

"Where are the damn instructions?" Riley grumbled.

"Under your hand," I snickered. She and I looked at each other before both looking down at the crumpled packet of paper under her hand. All three of us burst into a fit of giggles, resulting in Peyton falling onto her side.

"Ouch! This just dug into my back!" she hissed before pulling the table leg out from under her. That resulted in us laughing even harder. There was a lot of bickering and laughter as we slowly but surely got the table put together. The same exact process repeated twice more with the side tables.

"Oh no! My sheets!" I yelled before trying to shoot up off the ground and make a run for the laundry room. However, I didn't see the packet of instructions that were under my foot. The moment I stepped down onto them, they slid across the carpet and caused my foot to slip right out from under me. Peyton and Riley lost it behind me as the carpet absorbed the sound of my own laughter.

"That's gonna leave a mark," I said through gasps for air while cradling my knee. I finally made it to my laundry room and somehow managed to switch the sheets over without messing it all up. The only problem now was that I had to wait an hour before I could make my bed and get to sleep. Or pretend, at least.

I exited the laundry room and was about to round the corner into the kitchen when Riley and Peyton's conversation stopped me in my tracks.

"I'm serious, Xander, she's perfect. Literally so perfect-""Couldn't be more perfect if she tried!" Peyton interrupted.

"Seriously. She's got the whole hourglass figure thing going for her. Huge hips - she's gonna give you massive kids someday. And she wants a big family-"

"No, she said she wants a really big family! Lots of kids!" Peyton interrupted - yet again - to correct Riley.

"And she's so funny, Xander. She's definitely guarded, but I think she's starting to trust us," Riley said, finally able to finish her sentence without Peyton butting in.

"How much have you guys had to drink?" came a deep, husky voice through the phone.

"Why are you asking unimportant questions right now? What's important is that-wait, shhhh, I think she's coming!" Peyton hissed. Well, that's my cue. I entered with an oblivious smile, trying to think of something to say that wouldn't give away that I'd just listened to their entire rant about how great they thought I was. I'd never heard anyone speak that way about me in my entire life. It was...nice?, but...weird? A little unnerving. I wasn't sure how to handle it.

I finally figured out something clever to say, but the look Peyton and Riley gave me once they saw me - like a deer in headlights -

made it die on my tongue as I sputtered out a laugh that slowly built up until I was laughing my head off.

"W-we've gotta go," Peyton stuttered as she attempted to hold her own giggles in.

"That wasn't one of our girls," I heard someone on the phone whisper before Peyton cut the call off.

"So, who wants to order Pizza?" Riley asked.

# CHAPTER 5

Scarlett's POV

The next morning I awoke with a bit of a hangover - the term 'awoke' being used very lightly. I didn't ever really fall asleep. The hangover, however, wasn't nearly as bad as I imagined Peyton and Riley's was considering I didn't drink nearly as much and I also chugged water and didn't fall asleep while eating the pizza we ordered, unlike the other girls.

I also didn't make it to my new bed, only the couch. Riley was snoring on the floor a couple of feet away. Her head was supported by one of the new decorative pillows and her body was covered with the throw blanket I bought yesterday evening. Peyton wasn't in sight, so I assumed she left already.

I swung my body upright on the couch, rubbing my face with my hands. The crown of my head was sore from sleeping with my hair bun in all night, but I didn't have a choice of taking it out without looking crazy. I heard a slight commotion coming from behind me in the kitchen but already knew who it was by the smell. I turned to see Adelia eating breakfast. I smiled, thankful to see a familiar face. Despite my anger at her yesterday, I still wanted a chance to say goodbye this morning.

"I wasn't sure I was in the same home when I came down this morning," she joked as I approached her. My smile widened.

"It does look pretty different, huh?" I asked, fiddling with the new produce bowl I'd bought that was sitting in the middle of the kitchen island. The only thing we hadn't gotten to last night was setting up the new dinner table, but I could do that today after she left for the airport.

"It looks wonderful in here. I figured you girls were up to something if all the racket last night was any indication," she chuckled. I winced in response.

"Yeah, sorry about that."

"Don't you apologize to me. I'm glad you're getting along with the other women. It's been a very long time since you've let your hair down like that," she pointed out, her hand coming to rest atop my own on the counter.

"I'm glad I caught you before you left," I stated as my throat grew tight.

"I wouldn't have left without a proper goodbye. Even if I had to wait all day," she murmured, her eyes becoming glassy. I bit my lip to keep it from wobbling before lunging forward and wrapping my arms around her. My body lightly shook as I cried silently.

I didn't think saying goodbye to her was going to be this hard. I think I was telling myself it would be fine to save face, but I wasn't fine. She really was the only woman I'd ever looked at as a mother figure. The only one I'd ever known. She's been the one who has cared for me since the moment I stumbled upon the council's land, bloody and on the brink of death. She nurtured me back to health until I could properly care for myself again. She's been there, holding my hand, every step of the way. Through every therapy appointment, every self-defense class, and every combat training session. Not to mention all the flashbacks, all the panic attacks. She was there.

And now, it was finally time for her to let go.

"You are going to make the best Luna. I know you're scared - I do - but you were made for this role, honey. This pack needs a strong, caring, just alpha female. They need someone who will speak for those without a voice. They need to feel loved and cared for again. They need you. I know that you can do this. I know that you're going to make me and the rest of The Council proud. Cutting you free has been the hardest decision I've ever had to make, but I know they need you more than I ever could," she wept softly, pulling back to wipe away the tears that were trailing down my face at her words.

"Don't let your past hold you back from your future," she whispered before leaning forward to press a chaste kiss to my forehead. She grabbed the bag by her feet before hooking her arm in mine. I walked her to the door and gave her one last tight squeeze. The door was opened for her as the man from before - Jacob - was there to escort her to the waiting car. She took a few steps before stopping to face me.

"One last thing, honey. If you ever see that rat bastard again - God forbid - make him hurt. That's a Council order," she smirked maliciously with a wink. She handed off her bags and slid into the back of the vehicle, waving at me just before the door was shut behind her. I waved back before doing the same with the front door, my eyes not missing the various large men who were standing around guarding the door.

"Scarlett?" Riley called out. I sucked in a deep breath and quickly wiped away any trace of tears from my face. I cleared my throat and turned to meet her gaze. She smiled, but didn't eye me sympathetically - something I was glad for.

"The sitter's probably antsy to get home by now. Are you okay if I go?" she asked.

"Oh, yeah! That's fine. Thanks for yesterday," I replied awkwardly. She smiled wide before getting up from the floor and putting the blanket and pillow back where they were.

"I'm really glad we could do that. We should definitely do it again soon. I had a ton of fun," she insisted. I just nodded and saw her out the door that connected her place to mine, not surprised that our living quarters were so close together. My ex's pack had a similar set-up.

I blew out a breath through my lips before coming to stand in the middle of the first floor. With Adelia gone, things were starting to feel real. Less temporary. Less safe. I needed something to take my mind off of the weird feelings I was experiencing. Deciding to start by making myself breakfast, I returned to the kitchen and pulled the fridge doors open. I hadn't given much thought to its emptiness yesterday after I'd cleaned it out. Now, however, it was proving to be a bit of an issue. I pulled out the eggs and various other supplies to make a simple omelet and did just that. The only sounds in the kitchen came from the quiet preparation of my food, making me wish I actually had stolen Jackie's wireless speaker like I joked I would.

Everything felt robotic as I ate my breakfast and proceeded to clean everything up from cooking it. I was again faced with the question of now what? My eyes caught the cardboard boxes sitting atop the old dinner table, making my decision for me. I moved the boxes onto the floor before scooting the old table and chairs out of my way. I pulled my knife from the discrete harness under my top and cut the boxes open before laying all the pieces out. The instructions made it a bit difficult as there weren't any words, just pictures, but I eventually figured it out. Once done with the table,

I finagled with my phone for about fifteen minutes until I figured out how to play the music Jackie had downloaded for me.

I hummed along with the lyrics as I moved onto the four chairs that matched the table. I lifted myself off the floor and proceeded to push all the chairs into the table. I grabbed the store bag with table decorations from the kitchen counter and laid out the fake plant centerpiece, napkin holder, and woven placemats on all four sides of the table. I took a step back and smiled as the whole picture started to come together - minus the table I now needed to get rid of.

I carefully took the old one apart just in case it could be reused or gifted to someone else and carried it up to the attic I'd discovered on my tour piece by piece. By the time I was done, it was lunchtime, but I wasn't hungry. I knew I needed to go grocery shopping, but that required me to leave the sanctuary of this place. As of right now, I just barely felt safe enough here. I was terrified to leave - and to leave on my own, at that.

Stop being chicken and just go get food, I scolded myself. Running up to my bathroom, I took a quick shower with the limited toiletries I had and made quick work of blow-drying my hair - it would freeze the second I stepped outside if I didn't. I pulled on a fresh sweatshirt and thermal leggings before slipping my feet into my snow boots. I found my jacket hung up in a random closet downstairs and shoved my wallet - the pack credit card still tucked inside thanks to Riley - and phone into the pockets. Despite it not being my own money, I was going to be cautious with the amount I spent. I didn't want them to think I thought money grew on trees.

I crept up to the front exit and closed my eyes, listening and feeling my surroundings. Dammit. I knew there was a slim chance the men would have left, but a girl could hope. Popping the door open, I peeked outside for a moment.

"Where are we heading, Luna?" one of the ones closest to me asked.

"I'm going to the grocery store," I replied, emphasizing it being a "me" trip, not a "we" trip. I wasn't stupid in thinking I was invincible and could prance anywhere by my lonesome safely. However, I was highly trained and skilled in combat. I could and would protect myself if I needed to. I also was good at slinking about places unnoticed and undetected. You can't do that if you have multiple massive, hulking men stomping around with you.

Like I said. It was going to be a "me", not a "we" trip. I just have to figure out how I'm getting there, I thought to myself.

"We've been specifically assigned to guard you, Luna. With all due respect, you will not be going anywhere without us," he grunted forcefully. The hair on the back of my neck immediately raised as my wolf arose, coming straight to the surface. I could feel the pressure in my eyes, telling me that their color was probably shifting between my normal light blue and the dark black irises of my wolves. Going somewhere with these men alongside numerous women who posed no obvious threat to me was one thing. There was no freaking way I was going anywhere with these men alone. I didn't trust them one damn bit. Especially when there were what looked to be at least four of them. Four-on-one aren't great numbers. Even if I could likely take them on if need be.

He gave me a confused look, but I didn't say anything in reply. I just shut and locked the door once again. Sorry, buddy, but that's not the answer I was looking for.

Alright, think Scarlett, think I thought to myself while pacing back and forth in the kitchen. It was moments later that I remembered Riley vaguely mentioning there was an attached underground garage with cars at our disposal during dinner last night.

She'd also mentioned that the keys were kept in each car's cup holders because we were the only ones with access to said garage.

Bingo.

I quickly found the staircase Riley mentioned that led to the garage - apparently, all of our units had one of these entrances to get down there. It was something I must've missed when I was doing laundry yesterday. However, I was in the cleaning zone, so I didn't blame myself.

Approaching the door, I realized there was a heavy-duty lock on the door. One that I had yet to be given the key to. I released a puff of air from my lips and pulled a bobby pin from my hair. It'd been years since I'd picked a lock - two to be specific - but I was trusting that I hadn't lost my magic touch.

Crouching down in front of it, I stuck the pin in and fiddled around with it. A few minutes had passed and I was starting to lose hope, but then the latch finally released. I pressed the handle down and the door pushed open.

"Heck yeah!" I hissed excitedly, doing a little happy dance before dashing down the stairwell quietly. I breathed a sigh of relief as I stepped inside the garage and light flooded the expansive space. I found the most modest-looking vehicle and approached it. Sure enough, just as Riley said, the door was unlocked and the keys were right there waiting for me. I started the car and giggled as I ran my hands over the leather steering wheel. I could count on one hand how many times I'd driven a car.

Come to think of it, I was lucky I was able to even get my license. The orphanage I'd been sent to after I'd turned sixteen was packed with kids and was lacking damn near any funding. The staff barely had enough time to make sure we were all still present, let alone help me practice driving to obtain my license. However, I'd been persistent enough that I got just enough practice to pass the test with a little luck.

Getting to the car and starting it was half the battle. Sitting behind the wheel with the car rumbling beneath me made me realize I had no clue where the nearest grocery store was. I pulled my phone out of my pocket and called Jackie.

"Are you missing me already?" she asked upon answering.

"Yes, but that's not why I'm calling you. I'm guaranteed to starve if I don't load up on some food here soon, but I don't know the area yet. How the heck do I use that GPS app?" I asked, swiping out of the phone call like she'd taught me to come to the home screen.

"See the little icon with the red location dot lookin thing?" she asked. I nodded dumbly before replying yes verbally. "Click on that. Now at the top it should say 'from your current location', so don't mess with that. Right under that line it should say 'to'. Click on that and just type in 'grocery store'. It should pop up with places nearby," she explained. I did as told, whooping when it came up with a place half an hour away.

"It worked! You're my hero!" I exclaimed to which she laughed. We exchanged a few more words before finally hanging up. The app started directing me before I'd even figured out how to get out of the garage, so I ignored it. I backed out and drove towards what looked to be a garage door. Sure enough, as I started approaching, it opened up automatically. Giddy with delight I eased out of the garage and backtracked to the gate at the entrance of the pack just based on what I remembered from yesterday. Thankfully, the guards on duty must have recognized the car so they let me out. Pulling onto the road, I started following the directions on my phone. I took a wrong turn at one point, so it took me a bit longer to get there than it should've, but I got there nonetheless.

I remained cautious of my surroundings at all times as I grabbed a cart and began wandering through the store. If my back wasn't covered, my eyes were constantly surveying my surroundings. I'd managed to make it through the store, gather everything I'd deemed necessary, check out, and was loading the bags into the back seat when a large, black SUV came barreling into the parking lot. They were only a few rows away from me. My heart rate kicked up as I threw the rest of my things into the back seat, not bothering to see who it was, and slammed the trunk closed. I felt bad leaving my cart where it was and not returning it to the bin, but my fight-or-flight instincts had already kicked in. I made quick work of getting in the driver's seat before peeling out of the parking lot, my heart now beating a mile a minute.

Was it irrational of me to believe that my ex had figured out I was in Montana and had already hunted me down that quickly? Yes. Was it silly that I assumed every large, black SUV was him coming to lock me up again? Probably. Was I ever going to change? Not likely. I only looked in my rearview mirror briefly enough to see that I wasn't being followed before focusing back on the road. I was excellent with directions, so I was able to make it back to the pack and up to the gates without utilizing the GPS.

I only had to wait a few moments before the guards recognized the car and allowed me in. It wasn't until I approached the garage and clicked the opener built into the car controls that my heart rate began to return to normal. I re-parked the car where it'd originally been and proceeded to load my arms up with bags, determined to get everything in one trip. I struggled to climb the stairs with all the bags weighing me down, but I somehow managed. I didn't have to pick the lock again on my way back into the house, something I was incredibly thankful for. I winced as the plastic handles dug into one of the heavily scarred areas on my left arm despite my coat providing a much-needed barrier.

The door slightly banged against the wall as I kept it open with my butt before I rounded the corner into the kitchen. Shrieking, my feet halted in place at the sight before me. The kitchen was filled with people. Along with Vanessa and Andrew, Riley, Peyton, and Raven were there as well as a girl I'd never seen before.

"Oh, thank the Lord!!" Vanessa shouted before lunging towards me. I wasn't able to block her from wrapping her arms around me as I was still loaded up with bags of food. "Are you alright?" she asked, her eyes filled with worry. I just scrunched my brows in confusion and squeezed past her to relieve my arms of the uncomfortable weight. I set all the bags down on the counter before facing her again.

"I'm finc...?" I trailed off, still incredibly confused. I looked at Riley when I heard her mutter Adelia's name followed by, 'We found her, she's alright'.

Found me? I thought to myself. A few seconds later, the front door burst open as four men came rushing in, two of them being the men from outside my door from earlier. The second their eyes found me, their expression grew angry.

"What the hell were you thinking?! Do you have any fucking idea how dangerous it is for you to leave unattended? You could've been hurt! Or worse! I specifically told you you weren't going anywhere without us!" he screamed. He continued his rant as he started stepping closer and closer to me. My chest tightened as my wolf pushed me out of the way and surfaced, ready to handle the perceived threat at hand. I turned and backed away towards the front door as he continued quickly advancing on me. I was able to get my hand in my coat and under my shirt to free my knife. The second I pulled it, his words abruptly stopped and I heard a gasp come from behind him.

"Not another fucking step," I growled out the threat, my voice barely human as my wolf had completely taken over. My hands were steady and sure, no sign of the trembling that used to come when I felt threatened. I continued backing away until my hand made contact with the door handle. I pulled the door open and dashed out as fast as I could, exploding into my wolf when I was far enough away. My shredded clothes littered the ground behind me as I dug my paws into the crunching snow and propelled myself forward as fast as I could. I didn't slow until I'd broken the nearby tree line and found a safe, concealed spot to watch the house from. I watched on silently as everyone piled out of the house, gazing at the tree line where I'd disappeared in shock, some with worry.

"She says not to go after her. If we chase her, she'll only run further," Riley called after the men approaching the trees.

"She's quick. I've never seen a female wolf run that fast ever before in my life," Andrew commented as he held Vanessa, I presumed trying to soothe her.

"Adelia wants to talk to you both," Riley murmured before passing the phone to Vanessa who proceeded to put it on speaker. I focused so I could hear what she was saying.

"Was she threatened? What happened? Why did she run?" Just hearing her voice soothed me and my wolf.

"Her guards said she mentioned leaving, they told her she wasn't allowed to do so alone. She went back inside, so they thought she was retiring for the day. They had no idea she snuck out and took one of the cars. She must've gone to the store on her own. When they realized she'd left alone, they went after her. After she got back, her head guard got aggressive and angry with her out of worry. He hadn't realized she'd react like that. None of us did," Vanessa explained. I heard Adelia sigh heavily on the phone.

"I told Elder Thomas to debrief everyone who'd be in regular contact with her about her triggers. The moron must've ignored me or forgotten to do it," she growled. My wolf snorted, she'd always hated Elder Thomas. He thought he was above everyone in intelligence and status.

"Triggers?" Vanessa echoed, the furrow of her brows deepening.

"It's not my place to tell you about her past - that I've already told you - but... it's hard to stomach for most. It's beyond anything you could possibly imagine. It's made her untrusting and wary of any male she ever encounters. Elder Thomas must've not relayed my message regarding an all-female guard team. Until she feels safe in your pack, she will never trust any man to watch after her and keep her safe. She will view them as a threat. It's not them, it's just how she's been forced to view things because of her past. I can't tell you how long it'll take for her to come out of hiding. When she does, I strongly advise she be met with a small group of females. Preferably the ones her wolf has already deemed as non-threatening if at all possible." I watched their expressions as they took in what Adelia had said. I appreciated her not telling my story for me. I didn't know when or even if I'd ever want to relive that nightmare ever again.

"It doesn't feel right leaving her out here all alone. Her wolf doesn't know these woods. There are men constantly patrolling our land. I'm afraid she'll come across one and run even further," Vanessa stressed, becoming visibly more upset. My wolf surveyed her - her tone of voice, body language, the pheromones her body was releasing. She liked Vanessa. She didn't detect any deception; that wolf was actually worried for our well-being.

"What can we do to help her? Is there anything we can do to guide her back to us and feel safe with us?" Vanessa questioned.

"I'll speak with the other elders as soon as I'm back to the council grounds in an hour or so. It's a long shot, but I might be able to send her best friend Jackie to coax her back to safety. In the meantime, just keep patrolling the border in case she spooks and tries to run. Advice your men to be on the lookout and avoid her unless nearing the border," she advised. My wolf's tail began thumping against the ground at the mention of a reunion with Jackie so soon. We loved that wolf. She was completely trustworthy in our eyes. We would protect her no matter what - even if it meant putting ourselves in harm's way.

My eyes immediately snapped to the man who'd yelled at me as he ran a stressed hand through his hair.

"I didn't mean to scare her. I had no idea she'd react like that..." he murmured, regret and guilt in his eyes. Serves him right. What man that large postures in a threatening way towards a smaller female and expects her to respond well? Idiot.

"It's fine, Maximus. None of us knew. Right now, I need you to go and help find four female warriors to take your places. I'm not risking her running again," Vanessa ordered.

"Yes, ma'am. In the meantime, Jade's agreed to monitor from here for her return," he said, looking at the female I hadn't recognized. Now that I had a chance to study her, I realized she had facial features similar to Vanessa. She had to be related in some way. Everyone besides Vanessa and Jade turned and headed back inside.

"Have you ever known anyone that was able to not only sneak away from their security detail, but to evade them after they had been found?" The girl - Jade - spoke while staring into the tree line.

"Never. She's quick and resourceful. She can assess a situation and wolf faster than any other male or female wolf I've ever met. That's a rare trait. If she can come to trust this pack, she will make an incredible Luna," Vanessa stated confidently. Her high praise of me made my wolf puff out her chest.

"I can't wait until she gets her claws on Mika," Jade said with a mischievous smirk.

"Jade, that's no way for an alpha's daughter to speak," Vanessa scolded. So Jade is their daughter...

"Oh, c'mon. You can't tell me you're not even a little excited to see her rip Mika a new one?" she challenged her mom.

"She messed with my son. Of course, a part of me wants to see her get what she has coming," Vanessa scoffed, not saying another word before she turned and headed inside. My wolf surveyed our surroundings before finding a better hiding spot and burrowing in. Despite the need for a nap, my wolf remained tuned into the female observing for us. I allowed my mind to wander to my thoughts as my wolf kept watch.

I need to find out who this 'Mika' person is.

# CHAPTER 6

Scarlett's POV

I wasn't sure how long it was until my wolf finally relented and allowed us to come out of hiding. I knew it was at least a few hours if not more. We waited until that girl, Jade, had left. It was nice to get out of my skin and spend some time in my fur. It's been a while since we've done that.

My wolf slowly trotted towards the house entrance. There was a pile of fresh clothing in a plastic bag on the steps as well as new shoes - a pair that weren't mine, which I'd ruined when I shifted. I changed back and dressed in record time. Twisting the doorknob, I was unsurprised to find it unlocked. I held my breath as I entered the house, my ears straining to catch all the noise and voices. I could hear the sound of multiple people breathing, but their speaking ceased the moment they heard the door open.

I got a sense of deja vu as I entered the full kitchen, except this time there wasn't a single male in sight. It was something I was incredibly thankful for. Riley, Raven, and Peyton were all present as well as Vanessa and Jade - she must've been watching from inside. My nose perked up as a smell that was familiar to me caught my nose. My head snapped in the direction of the first-floor bathroom as I heard a commotion coming from there. My face lit up with an ear-to-ear smile as Jackie walked out of the door. "Jacks!" I yelled, running and jumping on her. Her footing fumbled before she caught her balance once again and hugged me back.

"I heard your ass went all psycho on some dude that was just trying to protect you. They had to send in the big guns to handle this situation if you know what I mean," she bragged while dramatically tossing her hair off her shoulders after letting me down. I just laughed and punched her playfully. She was the only one who was allowed to poke fun at me for my survival instincts and she knew it.

"It's not my fault. He was yelling and getting up in my face," I murmured quietly. She gave me a knowing look that told me she understood and I didn't need to give her any further explanation.

"My mate sends his apologies. We weren't told about any...uh m, special circumstances," Jade stammered, choosing her words carefully. The word circumstances made the skin on my back, arms, and legs burn. My hand slowly moved to the area I could reach to try and soothe the phantom pain. It was a move that Jackie knew well, causing her to press her own hand against my back and gently rub it up and down. I shot her a thankful look before slowly approaching the rest of the women.

"I heard your conversation with Adelia. You don't need to explain," I said before turning my attention back to Jackie. "I can't believe they let you out!" I exclaimed as my smile returned.

"Me either. One second I'm so bored I'm trying to decide if I bug Roger by reordering all the library books out of alphabetical order again or rewatch something on Netflix and next thing I know they've got my behind on a plane to come save your behind," she said bluntly. Jade and Vanessa shared similar looks of entertainment at Jackie's extroverted attitude while the rest of the girls snorted and laughed loudly.

"I'm sure Roger's glad you're on a temporary vacation," I giggled. I noticed that all my groceries were gone from the counter, so I figured they must've put them away. That was something I hadn't thought of when I'd run.

"This place looks...incredible, Scarlett," Vanessa stated as she motioned around the room.

"Thanks. I've been pretty busy the last two days, but..." I trailed off. According to the brunch I'd had with them yesterday, my responsibilities and duties wouldn't be passed down to me until Xander and I fully mated. That was something Adelia stipulated so that all my time could be focused on becoming comfortable with my new mate. With the short amount of time we had, she didn't want me focusing on a million other things right now, too. While I was thankful for it, I wish I had something to distract me right now.

"But now she's bored," Jackie filled in for me. I just glared at her, not wanting to offend the former Luna. My wolf and I respected her. Thankfully, she just chuckled in response.

"Well, we've got a room full of women fighting to be named the best so they can guard their new Luna. Would you like to come and have a say in your team?" she asked. I nodded, rather intrigued to see the female warriors of this pack. She smiled happily before looping her arm through my own and leading me through the pack house. I felt self-conscious as every pack member we passed stared at me like I was a piece on display at a museum.

"They're just curious about you. It can be unnerving at first. It will fade once we formally introduce you and they come to know you better as their Luna," Vanessa explained. I nodded as we slowed our pace before descending the last set of stairs into what

I assumed was the basement of the pack. A set of double doors was opened for us, revealing a massive inside training area. This was like nothing I'd ever seen before. There was state-of-the-art equipment everywhere. All movement halted as we entered.

"Ladies, your Luna has voiced a desire to be an active participant in this selection," Vanessa's voice boomed throughout the space. There were a few gasps here and there as she walked us further into the room. The women parted ways as we came to stand at the front of the crowd. It was then that I noticed it was just Vanessa, Jackie, and I - none of the other girls came along. "Why don't you introduce yourself?" Vanessa whispered in my ear. I took in a slow, deep breath before releasing it. I unhooked my arm from Vanessa's and took a step forward. I squared my shoulders and straightened my back.

"Hello. My name is Scarlett. I look forward to meeting each and every one of you. This will be a learning curve for all of us, but I want you to know that I believe respect is earned, not given. You've all earned my respect as you've shown a willingness to put yourself in harm's way to protect me just by being here and competing for one of these four positions. That is more than admirable. I hope to earn your respect in return by being a leader you can trust and look up to. And eventually be a leader you can come to with anything you need, big or small. Thank you," I spoke confidently and evenly, despite the pit of nerves in my stomach at all the eyes on me. I noticed a few women smiling back at me in the crowd. That had to be a good sign. There was only a single man in the room, he was the one I assumed took Raven's position when she grew too pregnant to continue. I assumed Vanessa told Maximus - the man who'd yelled at me earlier - to make himself scarce since I would be showing up. I was thankful for that.

"Alright, ladies. Find a partner and start sparing. And remember, I want clean fights! No dirty hits! We aren't here to harm one another, we're here to show our ability to keep our leader safe!" he hollered. The noise in the room grew as they all did as instructed. While they prepared to spar, I assessed the man in charge. I identified a tick in his gate just barely noticeable to the untrained eye as he walked towards the center of the room. That's his weak spot I mentally noted before turning my attention to the women in the room.

The sparring commenced a few moments later. I broke away from Vanessa and Jackie and began leisurely walking the perimeter of the room. I examined each couple as I passed by, noting their technique as I went. I already saw three girls I knew I wanted based on instinct, skill, speed, and strength, but I still needed one more. I stopped and focused on one girl in particular in the back. She was small and her opponent didn't appear to be taking her seriously. Mistake number one. Never underestimate your opponent. Despite her total lack of correct stance and obvious lack of muscle, she was observant. Muscle and strength could be built up, but instinct was ingrained. It couldn't be learned. I watched her eyes, seeing that she'd focused her gaze on her opponent's heavy use of their right side. When she finally attacked, she went for the left, taking advantage of her opponent's weakness. If she'd been properly trained, she could've taken the girl down no doubt.

She looked embarrassed as she was taken to the floor moments later with me watching, so I gave her a reassuring smile. I sensed someone approaching me from behind and quickly turned to meet the gaze of the head instructor. He looked surprised that I anticipated his approach.

"I've picked the four I believe best suited to protect you if you'd like to come this way," he said. I nodded and followed him, but not before giving one last look to the small red-headed girl. She looked defeated.

"From left to right, it's Amanda, Greta, Tabby, and Tilly," he explained. I met each woman's eyes and gave them an acknowledging nod. Greta, Tabby, and Tilly were the three I'd already spotted. They all looked excited to be picked except for the first girl, Amanda. She looked smug and cocky. It rubbed me the wrong way. There's nothing wrong with confidence, but misplaced pride gets you hurt. And it hurts others.

"I'd like to test their abilities for myself," I said. The man nodded and motioned for the women to spread out and clear an area of mat in the middle. I called forward each girl, leaving Amanda for last. I wasn't going to compare them to my own level of skill. I had spent the past two years training practically non-stop with the best at The Council and I was naturally quick - or so Adelia said. And Eric too, or so I'd assume considering I outran him for my life two years ago while on death's door.

Right now I was just determining their ability to improve. So far, I was highly satisfied.

Calling the last girl forward, she shoved a few of the other girls out of the way as she made her way to the middle. That caused my eyes to narrow at her. There was absolutely no reason she couldn't show mutual respect for her pack sisters. With the other women, I'd gone easy. That wasn't going to be the case with Amanda.

The second the instructor blew his whistle, I was on her. She hadn't seen it coming. I had her pinned like a pretzel within a few seconds flat. I immediately released her and noticed the anger behind her eyes. She was mad that I'd bested her in front of her pack mates. She looked determined to stop it from happening again.

We resumed our starting positions once again. Unlike the first time, I laid back and waited until she attacked first. I was wildly unimpressed with the way she just blatantly attacked without giving her technique any thought first. There was no single one-size-fits-all attack; strategy had to be tailored to each opponent you encountered.

I dodged her attack immediately and had her pinned once again with little effort. There was excited mumbling from the crowd as the energy in the room grew. Amanda released a quiet growl of anger before righting herself again.

"I'd like to pull forward another opponent," I told the instructor. My comment hushed the crowd.

"What? No! Let me try again! You owe me another chance!" Amanda yelled, storming towards me and making an attempt to get in my face. I laid her out on the mat, gripping her hair and yanking her head back and to the side so her neck was shown in forced submission.

"I don't owe you anything. You have what it takes to be a great warrior with training, but I've made my decision. Do not ever get in my face like that again." I ordered before releasing her and stepping away. "Thank you for your time, but please join the rest of your pack mates," I said. She pursed her lips before turning and doing as I said. I didn't say another word as I scanned the crowd looking for the red-head from before.

"I'm looking for a small female. Red hair, lean build, a freckle the shape of a star on her upper right chest," I called out. Shocked faces encompassed the crowd as the girl in question stepped forward.

"All due respect, Luna, I don't think I'm the best choice to keep you safe," she rasped out quietly. I didn't say anything in return as we assumed a starting position. My right side was weaker due to multiple breaks to both my leg and arm on that side, so I usually stayed self-aware when sparring. However, I let that weakness show just barely to see how she would respond. I watched as her eyes immediately noted my arms lowered position and protective posturing. I smiled. I knew I was right.

I let her attack first, impressed when she went directly for the weak spot in my upper thigh. I was anticipating the attack, though, so I braced myself and kept upright. I was careful when taking her down as she was smaller than me.

"I've made my final decision," I informed the instructor as I offered a hand to help the girl up.

"Forgive me, Luna, but I don't think Minnie here is the best choice. There are stronger women to pick from," he insisted. "Amanda is at the top of her class."

"Amanda, what were my weak spots?" I asked, turning to eye the woman in question. I had no doubt the man was right and she probably was at the top of her training class - as of right now, that is.

"Um, what?" she asked, caught off guard.

"What were my weak spots?" I repeated. She floundered for a few seconds before shrugging her shoulders meekly.

"Minnie, what are my weak spots?" I asked, focusing on her.

"Right upper arm, right leg just above the knee," she stated confidently, but warily.

"Thank you for your input, but Minnie is my final choice. Anyone can be a great warrior, but only a few can be great enough to be trusted to protect the Luna of a pack. The difference between the two is instinct. I will personally see to Minnie's training. She will be a great warrior and an even better protector in due time," I stated before turning to face Vanessa, who was wearing a proud smile.

"So, about dinner. Those who live in the pack house eat in the communal dining room. Since your arrival, meals have been packed with people anxious to get even a glimpse of you. Andrew's been asked by a few members if you'll be joining us tonight. After what happened earlier today, I don't want you to feel overwhelmed, so you can absolutely choose to stay in tonight if that's what you'd like," she said as we exited the training room. The women I'd chosen to guard me followed close by.

I mulled over the decision in my head. I knew if she was asking, that meant it was almost dinner time now, so I didn't have much time to decide.

"How about tomorrow night? I'd like to have dinner with my guards and get to know them better first before greeting the pack." She nodded with a smile.

"That sounds like a wonderful idea. I'll let him know so he can pass that news along. Can I do anything for you before I join my mate?" she asked as we approached the connecting door to my living quarters.

"Bribe the council to let me keep Jackie?" I joked, though deep down I was completely serious.

"Adelia and I have already been discussing this. She's working through it on her end as we speak, but she said until they can figure out Melvin's location and keep track of him, she's safest on Council grounds," she said with a sad smile. I sighed, figuring that would be the answer. We said our goodbyes as Jackie and I meandered into my living room. She and I plopped down on the couch at the same time as Greta, Tabby, Tilly, and Minni milled around somewhat awkwardly.

"Please feel free to sit and get comfortable," I murmured, gesturing to the open spots on the furniture.

"Shouldn't we be keeping guard?" Minnie asked cautiously.

"There are six men still positioned around my living quarters. The two that just positioned themselves at the connecting door we just came through, two at the front door, one at the stairway entrance in the garage, and one at the garage exit," I answered back. "You can check if you don't believe me," I held back a smirk at their shocked faces. To my amusement, Tilly opened the door connecting us to the rest of the pack house while Tabby opened the front door. Just as I'd said, there were two men stationed at said entrances.

"How did you know that?" Greta asked in amazement.

"My wolf's senses are pretty fine-tuned and she's usually on alert," I said off-handedly.

"She's kind of a freak like that, you'll get used to it," Jackie joked with a flippant wave of her hand before immediately dodging the pillow I'd started swinging towards her head. Minnie and Greta giggled quietly under their breath while Tabby and Tilly just smirked.

Thoughts? I asked Jackie through our mind-link. She didn't ask what I meant, already knowing as this was a common conversation.

They seem trustworthy enough. My wolf didn't detect any unusual pheromones, she said back. I nodded, agreeing, but still not sold on the group just yet. I was thankful beyond belief that Jackie was here with me. I might get a little sleep tonight with her by my side.

The first few months I spent with The Council were rough, but my sleeping habits made it even worse. I didn't trust a single soul, thus making it impossible for my wolf to relax enough to fall asleep at night. I'd go days without a wink before my body would shut down and I'd finally pass out. It was a vicious cycle for about six months until I could start getting a couple of hours a night. I wasn't excited to start that entire journey all over again here.

"So, how many more days until Alpha Harrington arrives?" Jackie asked, breaking the silence. I sighed.

"Adelia said he left the day before I arrived and would be gone for a week, so he'll be back in about four days," I mumbled, my body winding up tightly at the thought of soon being confined within these four walls with a man I didn't know anything about. A man I'd never met. A man whose intentions I couldn't be sure of.

"Why don't you girls tell me more about yourselves?" I asked my guards, hoping to take my mind off of the feeling of impending doom. They nodded before finally easing themselves into the open spots near me.

"Funny enough we all just turned twenty-four, except for Minnie. She'll turn twenty-three in a couple of months," Tabby spoke first.

"Do any of you have mates yet?" I asked, taking up a relaxed posture to hopefully make them feel more comfortable around me.

"I do," Tabby and Minnie said at the same time.

"Whip out them phones and let's see photos, ladies," Jackie ordered while clapping, causing all of us to giggle. Tabby showed us first. Her and her mate were quite cute together and you could clearly see the love they had for one another. Minnie was next, but Jackie and I both jerked back when we saw the photo of them together.

"Lord have mercy, that's like trying to breed a great dane with a chihuahua!" I yelled before snorting. "His...you know must be the size of you!" I continued, unable to stop the word vomit from coming out. This caused all four of my guards to gasp before cracking up with laughter.

"I'm pleasantly satisfied, thank you very much," Minnie joked before putting her phone away once again. "I can't wait to tell him I got the position. He's going to be so excited for me," she exclaimed with a happy smile.

The rest of the night continued the same way - with all of us girls slowly growing more comfortable with one another and giving each other crap. We prepared dinner together, all pitching in to cook a dish or assist in some way. It reminded me a lot of dinners back at the council house, something that soothed both my wolf and me a bit.

When nighttime came and we all grew tired, the women had told me that two of them would stay with me overnight while the other two rested up so they could exchange places in the morning. Jackie and I chatted randomly as we got ready for bed. It felt odd falling asleep in my mate's bed with my best friend. We would've slept in one of the guest bedrooms, but we tried it and the mattresses were hard as a rock and terribly uncomfortable. Not conducive to sleeping at all.

Jackie and I stayed awake just giggling and telling jokes before she eventually fell asleep. I listened to the sounds of her soft snores, hoping they'd lull me to sleep. That was wishful thinking, though. I knew it wasn't likely.

# CHAPTER 7



Waking the next morning, I grumbled as a wave of exhaustion washed over my body. The last time I recalled looking at the clock was at three A.M. Being as it was now seven, I was thankful for the little sleep I was able to end up getting.

Jackie was still fast asleep next to me, something that didn't surprise me. She could sleep like the dead for hours on end if someone wasn't there to wake her up. It would be a while before she came to, so I rolled out of bed and wandered downstairs after changing.

"Morning, Tabby," I called out to the brunette. She stood once she saw me and nodded her head in greeting. She was the only one in sight, so I focused my nose. I sensed Minnie in the bathroom, as well as the same six male guards. "You hungry?" I asked her.

"A little. My mate and I were up late celebrating my promotion so I slept in a bit longer than I'd planned and I didn't have time to make breakfast," she explained. I eyed the hickey that was just barely peeking out from the neckline of her shirt.

"Celebrating, eh?" I teased, giggling as she cleared her throat and turned beet red. "Do you like french toast?" I asked while pulling out a carton of eggs, milk, and a loaf of bread. She nodded before holding her hand up for me to wait. She disappeared from sight and I listened as she strolled the perimeter of the room before coming back into view and doing the same with the rest of the doors and windows. I mentally patted her on the back as she finished checking things out and came to sit on a barstool across from me.

"I use cinnamon and nutmeg. Are you allergic to either of those?" I asked while pulling the spices out of the drawers. She shook her head no as Minnie finally sauntered into the room, her gait stiff and limp-y.

"Did both of you celebrate last night? Goodness. You're gonna make Jackie jealous when she finds out," I laughed.

"What?" Minnie asked as Tabby joined in on my laughter.

"You're walking crooked and she's covered in hickies. Do you want some French toast too?" She opened and closed her mouth a few times before coming to sit next to Tabby at one of the bar stools in front of the kitchen island.

"I would say no, but that smells amazing" Minnie commented before taking a deep whiff in. We exchanged light banter back and forth until I had finished cooking and plated everyone's breakfast. I covered Jackie's up so it wouldn't get too cold before she woke up.

Halfway through breakfast, the three musketeers barged into the place.

"Honey, we're home!" Riley hollered jokingly. "What smells so good?" she continued as her, Peyton, and Raven entered the room.

"Is that french toast?" Raven moaned while eyeing my food like she wanted to make love to it. I chuckled.

"Yeah. There's an extra serving for Jackie on the counter if you want it. I can make more for her when she wakes up," I said. She didn't have to be told twice before she was slumping down in the chair next to me and devouring the breakfast dish in record time.

"So, what's on the agenda for today?" Riley asked.

"I'd like to visit the orphanage," I stated matter-of-factly. Riley and Peyton looked surprised as Raven continued to be preoccupied with getting every last drop of syrup off the plate.

I made another plate of breakfast for Jackie and attached a little note letting her know where I'd be so she wouldn't worry before quickly cleaning everything up and changing. I was thankful for the new snow boots I'd been given as the orphanage was a bit of a walk from the packhouse and the sidewalk hadn't been cleared. Bringing my fist up, I knocked on the front door. The place looked decent from the outside, but it was definitely in need of some repairs. At least a new roof if nothing else.

When the door swung open, I was met with the sight of an exhausted-looking female. She couldn't have been older than twenty-five. I was shocked to see someone so young. In all my time in the system, I'd never seen anyone younger than late fifties take on the role of house mom.

"Can I help you?" she sighed as a crash echoed from behind her. When her eyes wandered to the entourage behind me, they widened.

"B-Beta Riley, Gamma Peyton. This is a surprise," she exclaimed. "Please come in," she murmured before moving out of the way so we could enter. "I apologize, I don't think we've ever met. I'm Lucy, house mother for the orphanage," she said while extending a hand to me.

"It's nice to meet you, Lucy. My name is Scarlett. I'm to be the new Luna if everything goes according to plan," I explained.

"Luna? I'm sorry, I had no idea..." she rattled off, confirming my suspicion. Everyone else in the pack knew I was coming, and had even been anticipating my arrival. It was common for packs to forget about these abandoned children - the members of the pack who needed them the most. Oftentimes the children are so ostracized they aren't able to assimilate into normal pack life when they age out of the system. They resent their fellow pack mates and act out because of it. Nearly half of all orphaned children get exiled for various crimes or go rogue before their twentieth birthday.

I was not going to let that be the case in my own pack if I had any say about it. I was going to make sure these children got what they needed from me and this pack.

"Don't apologize. I can see you've got quite the load on your shoulders," I commented with a soft smile.

"We're at max capacity right now and it's just me here. After M ika..." she trailed off, eyeing the women behind me before looking down at her feet. I could tell she was biting her tongue for fear of speaking out of turn. I wanted to know what she was holding back.

"After Mika what?" I asked, pushing her to finish her sentence.

"I'm not sure what you've heard of our ex-Luna, but she's not, um, fond of the orphanage. She's been trying to get it shut down and have the kids distributed to other packs. If it wasn't for The Council stepping in and telling her she wasn't allowed to do that, I'd be out of a job and these kids out of a home here. I used to have a few helpers, but she pulled all the funding and said they'd be better off used for something else," she explained, disdain dripping from her voice.

So this Mika woman is my new mate's ex...I thought to myself before her words registered in my mind. My wolf bristled at the new information she'd granted me. I was beginning to understand the malice behind Jade's statements she'd made to Vanessa yesterday.

"That's unacceptable," I growled, unable to internalize my anger. There was another crash in the other room, one that sounded louder than the last. I halted our conversation as I slipped past her to find out where all the commotion was coming from. Entering the room, all the children stopped what they were doing and stared at me with intense curiosity. They all looked to be around the ages of three to six. I had a feeling they could sense the power my wolf exuded. Being destined for a beta meant I gave off more dominance than a normal pack wolf. That's something that would change once I officially mated the alpha of this pack.

"Is there a reason you're standing on the tabletop?" I asked the child in question, he looked to be about five years old. I could tell he was the curator of the chaos in the room as the mess surrounded him. He had his hand raised in the air holding a toy as a little girl nearby had tears sliding down her cheeks. He shook his head no, but didn't say a word, his eyes widening as I spoke to him.

"Do you think that's a safe place for you to be?" I asked softly. Again, he shook his head no. I reached out my hand for him to take and helped him off the table.

"Mine!" The tear-stricken girl yelled while pointing toward the toy in the boy's hand.

"Is this her toy?" I asked the little boy as I crouched down to their height. He didn't respond right away, so I gave him an expectant, but soft look. That caused him to nod and look away guiltily.

"It's important that we ask permission before borrowing someone else's things. Please apologize and give the toy back and we can find something else to play with," I said sweetly but nonsensically. He reluctantly did as asked before looking up at me expectantly. I offered my hand to him once again and walked him over to an unoccupied carpet area. I sat down crisscrossed before reaching out and pulling a bin of wooden train tracks towards me.

"Should we build a track?" I asked. He smiled and nodded.

"How did you do that?" Lucy asked, her expression one of utter shock. I just shrugged my shoulders and focused on the little boy next to me. Slowly but surely the other children in the room abandoned their respective toys to come sit around me. I felt a little hand rest on my shoulder, and I turned to eye the child.

"Sit with you?" the little girl asked. She had rosy cheeks and adorable blonde pigtails that had seen better days. I nodded and scooted over enough that she could sit next to me, but she had other plans. She plopped down right in the middle of my lap and went to work with the tracks I'd been previously assembling. I just snickered in reply.

"I'm assuming these aren't the only children here?" I asked. Lucy shook her head as she and the other women watched me with curious looks in their eyes.

"The rest are in a room across the hall. They're doing school right now."

"All of them?" I asked, confused. "How many are there?"

"About thirty of them. The youngest is twelve. The oldest is seventeen. They attend school online. Sometimes they have worksheets to fill out, but most of the time they just watch videos," she explained.

"Why don't they attend school with the rest of the pack children?" I asked, growing aggravated - though not at Lucy. This wasn't her fault, of that I knew.

"Mika," she replied simply. I clenched my teeth before carefully moving the child off my lap. She looked upset, but I quickly pacified her and slipped away. Everyone followed behind me out of the room as I worked to calm my wolf.

"The schooling situation changes today. Riley, who's in charge of enrollment of the pack children?" I asked as we made our way through the building.

"Peyton has been, but it was originally Mika's job," she explained.

"I want that to be priority number one for today. All these children will be given the option to attend school with the rest of this pack," I ordered. Peyton nodded and turned to leave.

"Riley, your mate is beta so I know you have a hand in handling pack finances. I want the appropriate funding allocated to allow for three more full-time helpers for Lucy here. I also want plumbers, electricians, and carpenters out here first thing tomorrow to fix anything that needs fixing. These children don't deserve to live like second-class citizens. Lucy, how many of these children are teenagers?"

"You can come and see for yourself if you'd like," she mumbled before turning and directing me into another room. Upon entering, I could immediately sense their hostility towards me.

"What'd we do this time?" One of the older boys - I was thinking either sixteen or seventeen - grunted as he looked up from the beat-up computer he was using. He looked incredibly familiar, but I was having difficulty figuring out why.

"Come again?" I asked, coming to stand at the front of the room.

"Only time we ever get visits from hoity-toities like you is when we've supposedly done something wrong. So, what was it this time?" he repeated, leaning back in his chair and giving me a challenging look. That's when it hit me. I knew that look. I knew that thin scar running along his eyebrow.

Holy crap. I took care of this kid when I was thirteen.

"That's no way to speak to your new Luna!" Lucy exclaimed, but I waved her off.

"You've changed a lot since you were eight years old, Damien," I stated with a half-smirk. His entire demeanor did a complete one-eighty as his eyes narrowed and he sat straight up in his seat. His eyes frantically scanned my face with intensity as the rest of the room watched on intently. It was clear Damien was their leader of sorts.

"Scarlett?" he suddenly whispered, his previously narrowed eyes growing wide in shock. Seconds after his revelation, Peyton came creeping back into the room with Vanessa in tow.

"The one and only," I smiled. The room grew noisy with whispers as the other kids began talking amongst themselves in shock.

"How do you know her, dude?" the kid sitting next to him asked as he smacked his arm to try and get his attention. It grew quiet once again as they waited to hear his answer. The women behind me seemed equally as interested.

"She lived with me when I was in the Dawnfall pack. Cared for me for three years before she got bounced to the next home for beating the shit-sorry, snot, out of an older kid for picking on all of us," he murmured, still staring at me in amazement - like he couldn't believe I was really standing in front of him.

"You were one of us?" a girl in the back of the room asked in disbelief while sitting up in her seat.

"For eighteen years," I replied with a single nod. "By the time I aged out I'd been to thirteen different packs. Do any of you know if Mrs. Jameson is still alive and kicking?" I asked with an amused smile.

"Yes! That was the last place I was at before she transferred me here," the boy sitting next to Damien exclaimed with a grin.

"Ugh, she's gotta be on death's door by now. She was the worst," I giggled, half of the kids joining me as he nodded dramatically.

"Well, here's the deal," I stated, growing serious, "I know exactly what you've all been through and are still going through. That ends today. From tomorrow forward, you will all be given the opportunity to ditch this crap and attend real classes with the rest of the pack - if that's what you'd like to do. It's your choice. I also have people coming tomorrow to fix this place up. No more showers with water pressure so low you have to stand on your tip-toes to rinse your hair out, or heating units that aren't up to code for the house, so it's always cold during the winter time. I'm going to get Lucy the proper help she needs around here. And I'm sure Luna Vanessa won't have any objections to allocating the funds for a proper shopping trip for school supplies and clothing for you guys, either?" I asked, reaching forward to finger the holes in Damien's severely worn-out sweatshirt before casting a sideways glance at Vanessa.

Her eyes were glassy as she shook her head harshly. "Not a single objection. Peyton and I can coordinate transportation as well. They'll need a chaperone since they're underage, so if you'd like to go with them you can or we can certainly find a few other members to go as well. We could probably get this worked out as soon as Saturday if that's alright with you, Miss Lucy," she said.

"That would be...amazing," Lucy said on the verge of tears and nearly breathless. "I'm sorry. If you'll excuse me. I just...need to go check on the younger children," she murmured, her voice shaky as she slipped past us.

"Alright, well that's a lot to throw at you all at once. With that said, we'll leave you guys to school for now. Just make sure you get your bathrooms and bedrooms picked up so when the plumbers and other workers get here they can work without stuff getting in their way," I said. They all nodded with hopeful smiles. I smiled back at them before pushing off the desk I'd been leaning on and started to head out of the room.

"Thanks, Luna Scarlett," Damien called after me with a smug but happy grin. The statement caught me off guard. I blinked rapidly a few times before nodding and swallowing thickly. I didn't know why, but that sincere look in his eyes and the way he said my name with the title made a lump form in my throat.

# CHAPTER 8

Scarlett's POV

I stumbled out of the orphanage and meandered back to the path we'd trudged on our way here to keep from getting more snow in my boots.

"When I asked if you had sisters, and you said 'something like that'..." Raven trailed off. I stopped, turning to see all four women - Riley, Peyton, Raven, and Vanessa - staring at me with similar looks. I sighed deeply, my breath coming out in a big misty cloud that billowed into the air.

"That was easier than explaining the whole truth," I murmured, looking up into the bright sky that'd just started to release big, fat flakes of snow. I closed my eyes and let the freezing cold envelope me for a moment. My nose and cheeks started to burn with the icy chill, the sensation reminding me of the sting I'd experienced years ago. Sometimes I welcomed the pain because it was familiar. Sometimes...sometimes I wished I was back there. With him. Eric. Not because I missed him. Damn, I hated him. I despised him. There weren't enough words in the dictionary to describe the loathing I felt for that man. But...I almost think it was easier then. I didn't have to wonder as much.

The torture stopped being so psychological towards the end. The beatings were like clockwork after a while. He was predictable, in a lot of ways. I hated myself more than him for even having those kinds of thoughts. My therapist told me it was normal to think that way every once in a while. That way of life had been my normal for so long.

No, I didn't miss him. And I certainly didn't miss the woman I was when I was with him. Cowardly, timid, meek.

"Scarlett?" Riley called loudly, pulling me from my thoughts and causing my head to snap back to look at her. I blinked a few times and brushed the snow off my face. I cleared my throat, realizing by their worried faces that they'd been trying to speak to me for probably a few minutes now while I was lost in my head.

"Sorry, I got lost for a moment there," I murmured while tapping my temple, pulling the edge of my bottom lip into my mouth and nibbling at it.

"Let's get inside. It's freezing out here," Vanessa commented before starting towards the pack house again. Her hand came to rest against the back of my arm, gently propelling me forward along with her. We all stomped the snow off ourselves at the door before removing our coats and gloves. Upon entering the kitchen, we came face to face with Jackie, who was happily munching away at her plate of French toast while scrolling through her cell phone.

"Good morning!" she exclaimed as she caught sight of all of us, a thick glob of syrup dripping down off her fork and onto the front of her pajama shirt in the process. I laughed before leaning against the counter across from her.

"Your mornings are getting later and later," I teased with a snicker. She just shrugged and popped her last bite of breakfast into her mouth as the rest of the girls laughed at her expense, chewing happily as I rolled my eyes.

"So, how was the orphanage?" she asked after swallowing her bite, causing the tension in the room to rise again to awkward levels. I knew she could feel it, but chose not to comment.

"A little worse for wear, but nothing that can't be fixed up. A kid I used to live with and care for back in a pack in North Dakota is here," I said, looking her straight in the eyes.

"Holy crap, what a small world," she pondered off-handedly before side-eyeing the other women in the room. I knew they still wanted to ask their questions about my own days in the foster system if the looks they were sporting were any indication.

"You were amazing with those kids," Peyton began, a look of complete sincerity in her eyes.

"Well, I know what they're going through. I've been there before," I murmured, looking away to the window and watching the snow continue to fall outside.

"We don't want you to feel like you have to tell us the story, Scarlett. We would never pressure you to tell us anything you're not comfortable with or not ready to share," Raven stated vehemently. I sucked in a deep breath and held it for a few seconds, before finally releasing it. It wasn't that deep of a story, really. I couldn't see any harm in telling them, but I let my wolf make the final decision. When I didn't get any gut objection from her, I decided to continue.

Tucking a strand of hair behind my ear, I turned and met their eyes. "I was born on Christmas day - or so I've been told. That's what The Council healers said, anyway. My mom, or dad - they don't actually know - just...dropped me off on their doorstep in a flimsy blanket, rang the doorbell, and ran. It was the first time something like that had ever happened, so they had no idea what to do," I laughed, though my giggles died out when I realized no one else was laughing with me. Tough crowd. "Anyway. Most kids end up in the foster system 'cause their parents die in battle or childbirth and then their mates go rogue and stuff. I stayed with Elder Adelia for a couple of months until one of the orphanages had the proper resources to take care of me.

"That started my journey. I'd been in the system since I was a baby. Like you heard me say, I had been to thirteen different pack orphanages. I was transferred for various reasons. Some founded, some untrue, but that doesn't matter now. I don't know if any of you know how the system works, but most kids age out after they graduate high school and they're supposed to integrate into the pack system. Half the time that doesn't happen. Anyway, I ended up graduating high school early, and two weeks after I turned eighteen..." I trailed off, my wolf pushing to the surface to protect me from the sordid memories. I knew my eyes were flashing as Jackie's hand crossed the countertop to cover my own.

My teeth clenched together. "And I aged out of the system. The end," I ground out as my hands made fists. Two weeks after I turned eighteen, I met Eric at a mix-and-mingle event between my pack and his pack...I finished in my head.

"You said you wanted a big family, lots of kids. Does how you grew up have to do with that?" Riley asked. I nodded, thankful for the distraction, but it wasn't calming my wolf down.

"I grew up in chaos. No matter where I was, there were always at least forty to fifty, sometimes upwards of seventy kids in one house. That to me is what a home feels like, but I want stability obviously. And I want consistency. My whole life, all I wanted was a family of my own. Someone to come home to. Someone to love me..." I trailed off, falling into my head once again before snapping out of it when I realized I'd said too much. For the first time in a long time, my cheeks pinkened with a blush as looks of pity appeared on their faces. "Anyway," I rushed out, clearing my throat awkwardly. "I've always wanted lots of kids. Like six or seven. Heck, maybe even ten. I don't know," I shrugged. "I'll just keep popping 'em out until the good Lord decides enough is enough I guess," I joked, laughing along with Jackie as she cracked up across from me.

"Have fun with a prolapsed uterus," she snorted. I just picked up a piece of her uneaten french toast crust and tossed it at her with a smirk.

"Do you think you'll be able to handle that many? I can barely handle the three turds I have right now, and Griffin wants another," Peyton grunted. I chuckled.

"Yeah. I mean, the places I lived were always so underfunded I was forced to help take care and look after everyone, especially as I got older. You learn a few tricks along the way. Kids can be really funny, too. If you ever need a babysitter, let me know. I'd love to watch them," I insisted. Her eyes lit up comically.

"I could kiss you right now," she cried out. "I'll keep that in mind. However, Vanessa and I are going to head out. We've got a shopping trip to plan for a bunch of teenagers. Raven looks like she's about to fall asleep standing up, and Riley needs to go make some fixes to the budget to account for the funds being reallocated to the orphanage since Donovan isn't here to do it. We'll leave you and Jackie to enjoy the rest of your afternoon," Peyton said before waving goodbye as all the girls left through the door that adjoined our units.

"So, what shenanigans are we getting up to?" Jackie asked with a wiggle of her brows and a mischievous wink.

"Well," I stated dramatically, dragging the word out, "I bet if we looked underneath the sink upstairs in the master bathroom we'd find stuff for a bubble bath and in said very same bathroom we'd find a bathtub that has massaging jets," I exclaimed.

"SAY NO MORE!" she screamed before shooting out of her chair and bee-lining for the stairs that led to the bathroom in question. I threw my head back and laughed while chasing after her.

"Wait! Pit stop!" she yelled, coming to a complete stop in the bedroom in front of her bag, pulling out a tub of something I couldn't immediately identify.

"If we're going to have a bubble bath, then we're going to do the whole damn thing and also do face masks, too," she insisted before pushing me into the bathroom. I nodded frantically before shutting and locking the bathroom door. I started the water and set the temperature to be just past the point of burning. When it was just past half full, Jackie dumped a generous amount of bubbles in, smacked the button for the jets, stripped naked, and jumped in. I giggled my head off before following her lead.

She was one of two people - Elder Adelia being the only other person - in the entire world I felt comfortable with seeing my scars. They littered the entire back of my body starting from the lower base of my neck and moving downward. My arms were the least affected, looking like bad cat scratches while my back was the worst. My back was morphed beyond recognition of normal human skin. There were areas where the council healer had to do a graft because the damage was so deep it couldn't be saved or healed by my wolf's abilities alone.

Sinking into the water, I sucked in harshly as the temperature of the water assaulted the sensitive skin of my back for the first few minutes, but the pain eventually faded. Jackie just smiled softly at me before handing the tub of face mask over to me, having already applied it to her own face while I was dealing with my...issues. I'd discovered it was a deep sea mud mask from both the dark gray color and the earthy smell. Also, the label on the outside stated what it was.

"We're gonna be glowing when this bath is over," Jackie insisted, doing jazz hands in an arch motion over her head dramatically. I just rolled my eyes and leaned back against the back of the tub.

"You're so right. This is amazing," I sighed softly. She hummed in agreement. Neither one of us said anything for the following ten minutes until we both got back into another goofy mood. Both of our foreheads had started to bead with sweat, resulting in the mask melting away. After wiping it all off, Jackie scooped up a handful of bubbles and turned away from me for a second before turning back.

"Look, I'm Santa," she laughed. I giggled at her before shoving my hand across the water surface to splash her.

"You know they call him Daddy December in Ireland," I said. She sputtered before bursting into laughter.

"No they do not!" she screeched.

"Well, that's the translation of it. They actually call him Father Christmas, but Daddy December is way more fun," I giggled before dunking under the water and pulling all my hair in front of my face. Coming back out of the water, I carefully flipped my hair so it rested in a perfect roll on top of my head. "Look, I'm George Washington," I said in an overly-fake British accent. She lost it, cackling so hard she slipped and fell backwards into the water. Coming back up, she coughed to try and clear her lungs of the water she'd accidentally breathed in.

"That is so good," she managed to choke out. We were quiet for a few moments as a thought slipped into my mind.

"You think this Mika chick will be at the pack dinner I promised to go to tonight?" I pondered aloud.

"That's his ex-mate?" she asked for clarification. I nodded in response. "Oh, without a freaking doubt," she responded without hesitation.

"Really? You think so?" I asked.

"Are you kidding me? She's absolutely the jealous type. Nine times out of ten the people who are unfaithful are always the jealous types. She's going to want to see if you're hot. And when she sees that you're not just hot, but that you're a whole damn smoke show, she's going to be pissed. Oh, it's gonna be so good," she chuckled while rubbing her hands together.

"Will you come to dinner tonight, then? I'm sure Vanessa will let you sit by me. It'll help me feel so much more comfortable. And then you'll have a front-row seat for the drama that's apparently bound to happen," I joked.

"Wouldn't miss it for the world, babe," she murmured with a soft smile, placing a comforting hand on my arm. I abruptly pulled her in for a tight hug, pouring all my emotion into it.

"I feel like this should be really awkward considering we're both so naked right now," Jackie whispered. I started laughing before pulling away from the embrace.

"We've seen each other naked more times than I can count," I remarked before reaching down and pulling the plug on the drain. "C'mon, I gotta figure out what the heck I'm gonna wear to this stupid dinner tonight.

"You're not nervous?" Jackie asked. I just shrugged.

"Pooping bricks," I commented off-handedly.

"You don't look it at all," Minnie commented, shock lacing her tone. Again, I shrugged.

"Wearing your emotions on your sleeve is to intentionally give other people ammo to use against you. It's basically shooting yourself in the foot," I stated while continuing to make my way down the hall. I raised my shoulders and lifted my chin. Yes, I looked the picture of confidence but inside I was anything but. I was losing my ever-loving mind. I was freaking out worse than before at my guard-picking. I knew this was a very large pack and I had no idea just how many people were going to be in the dining room I was about to walk into. I knew it was going to be a lot, though.

That scared me. So much.

Showtime I told myself as we approached the huge double doors that led to the communal pack dining room. As we came to a stop in front of the doors, Vanessa and Andrew approached us just moments later. Vanessa scanned me from head to toe, a big smile pulling at her lips as she took in my new outfit - the entirety of it all thanks to Riley and her closet. She'd given me a choice of what to pick from, but there was only one thing that would cover almost everything I needed to cover. It was a beautiful long-sleeved, V-neck white dress made of the butteriest satin material. There was a pretty wrap element that circled the front and tied into a simple bow in the back just above my butt, accentuating my 'slim, hourglass figure' as Raven had said before flaring out into a short, simple A-line skirt.

I don't think it's something I would've ever bought for myself, but I loved it. It made me feel...like a woman. Delicate and soft - something I wasn't used to feeling these days. It showed off a cheeky amount of my decolletage area without being distasteful, but I had to be careful due to being gifted in the boob department. The bottom of the dress stopped mid-thigh, leaving some of my lower leg scars on display, but they were ones I could easily ex-plain away as childhood mishaps gone wrong. Bike ride accidents or something silly like that. Riley gave me a pair of simple, strappy white heels with an open toe to go along with the dress despite my claim that my feet would get cold. She assured me that with the amount of people coming tonight, the room would stay plenty warm.

I don't think she realized how unnerving that comment actually was.

"You look...stunning, Scarlett. Like an angel," Vanessa exclaimed as a single hand came up to press against her chest over her heart. The comment made my heart grow warm and fuzzy, especially considering I'd felt very self-conscious before leaving my room. I wasn't even really wearing any makeup - just a bit of mascara and some clear lip gloss.

"Thank you very much, that's incredibly kind of you," I murmured, returning her smile before turning back forward to face the double doors, my heart rate kicking back up once again.

"Okay, are you ready?" Vanessa asked me as she locked her arm through my own, giving it a gentle pat. I nodded my head once, closing my eyes and saying a quick prayer that this all went well.

There was no more time to think about what was awaiting me on the other side of the door as they were suddenly pulled open before me.

# CHAPTER 9

Scarlett's POV

A hush settled over the entire room mere seconds after my presence was noted. I swallowed the lump in my throat before releasing a shaky breath, cautious not to let my unease show.

"We're going to sit at that table right at the front there," Vanessa said, pointing all the way across the room. Of course I was going to have to walk through the entire room like I was some part of a parade. I gave her a pursed-lip smile. Nodding in understanding, I motioned with my head for us to move forward. We made our way to our seats slowly, arm in arm, down the center of the room. I made sure to smile politely at everyone I made eye contact with. Despite the nervousness, I didn't want to give off the first impression of being a cold, callous...ya know.

When my eyes caught sight of a cluster of tables containing all the children from the orphanage my smile widened enormously and I raised my hand to return the small wave some of them were giving me. The action seemed to garner the attention of quite a few pack members. Upon reaching our destined table, everyone took their seats but I remained standing.

"Would you mind if I just went to see how they're doing? With this being their first pack function they're attending and everything, it's probably really overwhelming," I murmured, my eyes seeking out the area of children once again. Vanessa smiled warmly and shook her head.

"Absolutely not. Dinner won't start for a few more minutes and I'm sure the kids would love that. Especially coming from someone who's experienced what they're going through right now," she added. I smiled before turning and walking back in their direction. Whispers followed me as I moved, bodies contorted to get a second glance as I passed, but I didn't pay it much mind. The kids looked shocked to see me approaching, but they smiled widely when I came to a stop by their table.

"Is this seat taken?" I asked, pointing to the single open spot at their table.

"Miss Lucy is sitting there, but she just left for the bathroom so you can take it for now," one of the younger-looking girls rushed out. I quickly slipped into the spot and smoothed my hands over the skirt of my dress.

"Are you guys as nervous as I am?" I whispered quietly so only they would hear me. They all laughed loudly, immediately drawing the attention of the entire room.

"Probably more so," Damien responded while trying to discreetly wipe the thin sheen of sweat away from his upper brow.

"Trust me, I highly doubt that," I joked with a light laugh. "I just wanted to come over and say that I'm glad you guys could all come tonight. Pack events can be a lot of fun, but they can also be intimidating at first. Don't let it get to your head. If you need a little word of advice, find a buddy to stick with, but make sure you don't just stick with just one another. Seek out other people and mingle. You'd be surprised how similar you are with all the other kids your age," I insisted. They looked like they were pondering over what I'd said as I heard footsteps approaching behind me. I smelled Miss Lucy before I saw her. "Well, she's back so I gotta get going," I laughed.

"How do you do that?" the oldest-looking girl at the table asked in astonishment.

"Old habits die hard I guess," I said with a click of my tongue before hoisting myself out of the chair in what I hoped was a graceful way, turning to meet Lucy with a kind smile.

"I'm so glad you're joining us for dinner tonight," Lucy gushed with a big smile. My wolf thumped her tail in my head. She liked this wolf. I did too. We sensed something very pure and warm about her.

"I was just going to say the same thing," I responded before taking her hand and giving it a gentle squeeze. "I better get going before I get in trouble for being out of my seat," I snickered. Turning, I meandered my way back to my designated table. However, upon approaching I realized that there was no longer an open seat waiting for me. The seat that was once open between Jackie and Vanessa was now filled by a woman with hair as dark as midnight and cheekbones so high and sharp, I was sure if I just merely touched them I would cut myself and bleed. Her face had a severe look to it; like she'd just sucked on a lemon and it was stuck that way.

Getting closer, she looked to be like nothing but maybe twenty pounds more than skin and bones - something that immediately made me self-conscious of my much-rounder figure. Her brows were high and thin, my guess was the product of over-plucking in her youth. I channeled my wolf forward to get a better look at the jewelry that glinted around her thin, long neck.

Mika, the cursive diamond necklace read.

So this is the woman herself, I thought with a smug smile. It had been a long time since my claws were allowed to come out and I was allowed to play. My therapist said I had self-destructive tendencies that dabbled into the side of masochism. Maybe that was so, what did I know? I wasn't the one who went to school all those years or got paid the big bucks.

So many different scenarios played out in my head of how I could approach this situation. I could play nice. Maybe even play dumb and brush it off. But I'd heard what Jade, Alpha Harrington's sister, had said about her. What the other high-ranking women said. I knew what Vanessa thought about this wolf. I knew Jackie's opinion of her. I was aware of the reputation she held and the acts she'd committed against my future mate. I was also aware that if it wasn't for her, I wouldn't be here. I might still be back in the safety of The Council's grounds without this arranged mating looming over my head.

But the final nail in Mika's coffin was that I was not a female to fuck with anymore. I was not the same woman pre-Eric. I wasn't even the same woman post-Eric. I would not let some little girl try and taunt me in front of what was going to be my pack. She could play her little games all she wanted - I would win every time. That was the harsh reality she wasn't aware of yet.

But I would make her aware of it.

I meant what I told all those women about respect being earned, not given. Unfortunately, Mika was never going to earn my re-spect. This little stunt of hers was further proof of that, but she was going to get out of my chair. I could tell by the tension that had ramped up in the room as I grew closer to the table that the pack was now distressed about the situation. I was not going to have that. If she thought I was going to beat around the bush, she had another thing coming.

"From what Elder Adelia told me a few days ago, Alpha Harrington has been running this pack alone for years. There is no reason for you to even think there is a seat at this table that belongs to you. Now, you may remove yourself from my spot and find adequate seating elsewhere. Thank you," I spoke calmly and clearly, but also loudly enough that my voice would carry to the tables around us, and farther even. Her face immediately morphed from an expression of soured smugness to one of shock.

"Excuse me?" she balked, shocked but trying to sound intimidating at the same time. Really, it just grated against my skin and provoked my wolf. I took a single threatening step forward.

"I did not stutter and I will not repeat myself. You have exactly ten seconds to remove yourself from the seat you knew was reserved for me and me alone before I personally see to your removal. And I can promise I will not be gentle," I spoke in a similar fashion as the first time. This time, the whispers that followed my statement were so loud that the volume in the dining hall was like a quiet roar. She looked around, seemingly embarrassed, before scoffing and rolling her eyes as she crossed her arms over her chest and leaned back in her chair.

"That's cute. Is this some little skit you like to do?" she challenged. I didn't say another word. Silently, I walked around the table to where she was sitting. The noise in the hall fizzled out with each step I took toward her until it was so quiet you could hear a pin drop. When I was finally behind her, my body was vibrating with tension. I hooked my foot around one of her chair legs and jerked the chair out from where she was scooted into the table.

She gasped in surprise, but she shouldn't have been shocked just yet. In a flash, I threaded the fingers of one hand into her hair. My other hand curled tightly around her neck. I jerked her body upwards while kicking the chair out from under her. Shifting my weight, I used my other leg to swipe her legs out from under her body. They were the only thing keeping her upright, so she fell to her knees. Both her hands went to the one I had wrapped around her neck, curling into her skin to restrict her flow of air just enough to induce panic. Using the hand that was curled in her hair, I jerked her head to the side, forcing her to bear her neck to me in a show of complete submission.

"It's such a pity you didn't listen. Maybe next time you'll learn to respect those around you," I murmured. Looking up, I scanned the eyes of the entire room.

"From here on out, respect and kindness to others are two key things this pack will keep in mind when interacting with one another. Give it and you shall receive it. If you have a problem with anyone, no matter their ranking - real or perceived" I gave a twist of Mika's hair, causing her to squeal, "- report it and it will be dealt with swiftly and justly," I stated vehemently.

"Now, why don't you go find the adequate seating I mentioned earlier?" I said to Mika, my tone syrupy-sweet before I dropped her like a sack of potatoes. Her face showed nothing but humiliation and embarrassment as she made the walk of shame out of the pack dining hall. "I guess she lost her appetite," I commented off-handedly before picking up the chair I'd knocked over during the entire ordeal, turning it upright once again so I could take my seat. Jackie snickered beside me at my last comment but hid it behind her hand as I scooted myself up to the table.

"I cannot believe you just did that," she managed to get out between her giggles.

"Yes you can," I smirked back at her before redirecting my attention to the rest of the people at our table who seemed to have completely lost their ability to keep their jaws off the floor. "So, what's on the menu tonight?" I asked nonchalantly. Raven snorted before forgoing her attempt at trying to hide her own laughter. Seconds later, Riley and Peyton joined her as they began laughing out loud too. Alpha Andrew smirked behind his hand.

"Do you sign autographs?" ]'[

Jade bluntly asked, causing the entire table to erupt into soft laughter, something that seemed to ease the lingering tension amongst the pack. I didn't miss the fact that her mate wasn't sitting beside her tonight - something that ate away at me. I knew it was because they felt the need to continue to hide him away from me still. I would need to make nice with him soon.

"They weren't sure what you'd like, so they prepared a simple chicken parmesan dish seeing as most people tend to like pasta and chicken," Vanessa finally spoke, answering my earlier ice-breaker. I nodded as my stomach growled quietly. We didn't have to wait but a few minutes before numerous people came flooding into the room with several plates in their hands. Just as Vanessa had said, a heaping plate of chicken parmesan with spaghetti noodles and green beans was set down in front of me. A basket of garlic bread that smelled so good my mouth watered was placed in the middle of our table and I had to clench my hand into a fist to keep from immediately snatching a piece up.

"This looks heavenly," I hummed as my mouth watered.

"Thank you so much, Luna. I'll let the cooks know. They'll be very pleased to hear that," one of the servers boasted with a big smile before leaving as quickly as she came. The atmosphere of being back with a normal pack had me mentally slipping back into the old habit of waiting for the Alpha to take the first bite before beginning to eat my own meal.

Once Andrew - default Alpha since my future mate was away - began eating, the clattering of various cutlery on plates grew in volume throughout the room. Dinner passed by pleasantly, but I still felt like a museum exhibit on display by all the eyes I could feel on me. I made sure I ate in a manner that would be deemed lady-like. I didn't want to give a bad first impression...if I hadn't already with my display of dominance over Mika. Though, I had a feeling that the girl being put in her place was a welcome change for once.

"Wow, I might kidnap your guys' cooks and bring them back with me when I leave. That was incredible," Jackie moaned while leaning back in her chair and patting her now-rounded belly. I giggled as did Vanessa.

"When are they coming to get you?" I asked, trying my best to keep the disappointment from my voice, but failing horribly. I had to look away to keep my emotions at bay. She sighed deeply.

"Later tonight," she mumbled apologetically. That caused my gaze to snap up to her own.

"What?" I hissed. "Why so soon? You've only been here one day!" I exclaimed in a whisper-yell. She sighed, looking like she liked the idea of leaving tonight about as much as I did.

"Talking them into letting me leave just for the one single day to help get you back to safety was like pulling teeth. They wouldn't even entertain the idea of letting me stay a second longer," she grunted," with a purse of her lips.

"I wish there was a way I could keep you here forever," I husked out before clearing my throat and schooling my face before any-one could catch onto my wavering emotions. Just then, the doors to the dining room opened and a tall, handsome man entered. He walked with an air of confidence that told me he was defi-nitely related to the alpha family in some way - the similarities in appearance he shared with Andrew cued me into that as well, though he was leaner in stature. If I had to guess he was probably my new mate's cousin.

"Ah, the man approaching is Justin, Xander's cousin," Vanessa leaned into me to whisper. Bingo. Damn, I'm good. I nodded to acknowledge I'd heard her. I appreciated her informing me as he was making a direct beeline for our table with determination in his gate.

"Oh my God," Jackie suddenly breathed out quickly beside me. I turned my attention from Vanessa to her, but she wasn't looking at me. Matter-of-fact, her attention was completely and totally enraptured by Justin. And that was a look I knew and recognized. It was the same look I remember sporting the moment I saw Eric when I was just a naive little eighteen-year-old.

"Oh my God," I parroted her, smacking my hand down on Vanessa's arm and giving it a gentle squeeze to pull her attention toward the pair. Justin had since taken mutual notice of Jackie, a new vigor behind his steps as they quickened towards our table.

"I'll be damned," Andrew laughed softly as he took notice of the situation at hand.

"Mate," Justin growled deeply, the words reverberating around us as he was just a few feet away. Jackie was frozen, unable to do anything but stare directly at Justin in shock as he made his way around the table to her. He pulled her up out of her seat in one swift movement, burying his face in her neck and breathing deeply. My eyes welled up with tears of happiness for her. Jackie had been waiting for this moment for five years and it was finally here. She wouldn't tell anyone because she liked to act like a tough girl, but deep down she was like every female wolf that wanted the happily ever after with her very own prince charming.

"I guess this means I get to keep her forever," I commented with a laugh, reaching up to wipe away the moisture around my eyes before the tears could fall. Jackie finally snapped out of the daze she was in and laughed happily. Her eyes sparkled in a way I'd never seen before, it made a warm fuzzy feeling encompass my chest that I hadn't felt since before I met Eric.

"Hey, Justin, is it?" I called, catching his attention immediately as he briefly pulled his face away from Jackie's neck to look at me quizzically. "Sorry, Jackie, but I'm doing it for your own good and because I love you. Hi, I'm her best friend. She's had a bat-shit crazy stalker after her for the past five years named Melvin and he's gone to some crazy lengths to get to her - to the point of her being in protective custody of The Council for the past three years. I'd suggest you bite that shit ASAP. For safety purposes," I rushed out. His expression changed from shock to anger to sheer determination - to keep Jackie safe I was sure - all within a matter of seconds.

"Way to throw me under the damn bus, asshole," Jackie grunted while throwing me a playful glare. I just smirked and blew her a dramatic kiss.

"What are you two still doing here?" I asked with a raised brow. "I'll call Elder Adelia for you and explain the situation. Have fun. Use protection. Or don't," I teased cheekily, giggling my head off when Jackie's cheeks lit up with a bright red blush. Justin wasted no time throwing Jackie over his shoulder and carting her back out the door he'd come in, whatever he originally came for had been completely forgotten.

Rightfully so.

# CHAPTER 10

S carlett's POV

I hadn't seen Jackie in the two days since the dinner where she and Justin first met. I was fully expecting to hear every single sordid detail when she finally emerged from their hibernation.

True to my word, I had called Elder Adelia the moment I got back to the confines of my own bedroom. She was ecstatic, albeit completely caught off guard by the news.

"So now you guys have to leave her with me," I stated smugly, knowing it was most likely Elder Thomas' decision to pull her back to council grounds as soon as physically possible. My words had made Adelia chuckle on the other end of the call.

"I'll be sure to deliver the news to Thomas at once. I'm sure he'll be just thrilled with all the paperwork he'll now be required to fill out in light of Jackie's new situation," she murmured back sarcastically.

"Do you think this will make Melvin finally back off?" I'd asked her after a brief moment of silence. She sighed, the sound telling me she was deep in thought.

"I'm not sure. That man is completely unhinged, that much we already knew, but it's hard to say if this will finally be what breaks the weird obsession he has with her or what makes him snap this one last time. The heads of The Council were already planning on coming down for a visit once Alpha Harrington returned from his travels, so we can use that time to discuss the best course of action in keeping both Justin and Jackie safe as well. Have they already begun the mating process?" She'd asked. I snickered.

"Most definitely if the look on Justin's face and the way he carried her out of the dining room like a caveman was anything to go by." Elder Adelia laughed at my response.

"Well, that's wonderful to hear. I'm so glad Jackie is finally getting her moment. She's got the sweetest heart, despite how she likes to keep it guarded behind that crass humor of hers. I need to go speak with Thomas and alert him to the new changes and catch up the other members before they get on the plane to collect Jackie. There's no purpose for that now. I'll see you soon, Scarlett dear," she'd murmured softly before hanging up.

Without Jackie around to keep me company, Peyton helping Vanessa plan the pack shopping trip that was to take place, Riley still working on rearranging the finances, and Raven's pregnancy taking a toll on her the last few days, I'd done nothing the last 48 hours but spend time with all four of my new guards. Most of that time was spent training them, but we did take breaks for food and rest.

It was about two in the afternoon when we'd decided to finally call it quits for the day as I could see the girls were exhausted. Their stamina was something we definitely needed to work on, but it was only day two. I needed to remind myself to pace myself and have realistic expectations. They were already doing amazing as it was and I could tell they were pushing themselves to prove their worth to me. I didn't want them getting hurt in the process.

"You guys are doing amazing," I complimented while tossing them all small hand towels to wipe away their sweat. Their faces lifted with small, tired smiles. Their bodies released pheromones of pride. Good, they should be proud of themselves.

"So...are we ever gonna talk about that little showdown between you and Mika from dinner the other night?" Minnie asked after taking a long swig from her bottle of water. I just cocked my head to the side and raised a single brow.

"What about it?" I asked nonchalantly, but inside I was anything but. I'd strategically avoided speaking about this with anyone, but secretly I was dying to know how the entire ordeal was being perceived from the outside.

"What about it?" Minnie repeated, gawking. "How about the fact that not a single female has been able to make her cower in fear like that ever before!" she exclaimed, excitement practically dripping from her words.

"It easily made it into the top five best moments of my life and I wasn't even the one who got to do it," Tabby added in, the other girls nodding in agreement with her. Well, that had to be a good sign.

"So...I take it my little display wasn't poorly perceived by the pack? I was afraid I might've given off the impression that I was an aggressive tyrant," I finally replied, letting down my emotional walls just for the moment to get the validation I'd been needing.

"No!" they all exclaimed in unison. "For the first time in...I can't even remember how long, the women of this pack have hope. You're the one who gave them it, Luna Scarlett," Greta stated soundly with a warm smile that I quickly returned. My wolf pushed her way to the surface, wanting to assess these women once again when it was just the four of us alone - no Jackie present to give us a sense of possible false reassurance. She immediately thumped her tail in approval. She liked these females. She sensed an urgency towards our safety from them that resembled the feeling we got around Elder Adelia. She wanted to meet their wolves, the true test of trust for us.

"Well, thank you. All of you," I said, meeting each of their gazes. "It's been a while since I've been able to let my wolf out to stretch and sniff around. Lord knows I don't have anything else going on. You guys wanna join me?" I asked, knowing that what I was asking them was weighed with meaning. Meeting someone's wolf was quite a big deal. It was who you were at your core. Their eyes grew wide before they all nodded without hesitation.

"Absolutely," Tabby rushed out.

"My mate is patrolling right now near one of our favorite clearings. I could let him know we're coming so we aren't bothered and no male wolves approach to see what's going on," Minnie commented. All four women knew why they'd been chosen to guard me, they knew my hesitancy around men. The fact that she was making arrangements for us with my best interest in mind without me even having to ask had my wolf purring in my head at her thoughtfulness. Yes, we liked that wolf very much.

We all changed into much warmer clothing for the trek out to the clearing Minnie had spoken about. Each one of us had a duffle bag in hand - a necessity to store our clothes in after we'd change out of them. We'd likely end up heading back to the pack house in our wolf forms. It would be much too hard to get our clothes back onto our bodies once they were wet from the snow.

We broke the treeline and entered the large clearing. It really was perfect. My heart sped up. This was a big moment for me. Not only would I be meeting four new wolves, but I would be exposing a piece of myself to four new people. Our skin side was represented in our fur side in minor ways. Like my hair - the color of milk chocolate - mirrored that of the brown-colored coat of my wolf. Or the skin of my back. Mangled and scarred, mirrored in the way my wolf was missing almost all the fur of my back.

They were bound to notice. I knew they would. The sight of it would raise questions. They could ask about it later, but I wouldn't answer. Seeing the scars on my wolf was different from seeing it on my skin side. They didn't look the same. They weren't the same; the fur side didn't endure the kiss of the whip the way my skin side had to.

We all parted ways briefly to strip down to nothing so we wouldn't ruin our clothes before shifting. The change happened quickly now, different from when you first shift. Instead of the intense pain I used to feel, it was mundane - like popping a knuckle. Emerging from the confines of the trees, I came face to face with the three other wolves. They were lying on their bellies with their snouts resting between their paws. A docile pose. My wolf casually stalked forward, stopping to lean down and sniff each female one by one.

I saw the second their eyes caught sight of my back. Their pupils blew wide, a quiet whine coming from their chests. Once I was done assessing them, they sat up from their lying position and sat back on their haunches. I mirrored their posture, giving them a single nod that told them they could come acquaint themselves with my scent. They moved slowly and carefully, taking my wolf in. I was bigger than all three of them. Tabby's wolf made the mistake of pressing her snout to my back, an action that caused my wolf to snap at her and release a deadly growl of warning.

All three females immediately jumped back, their heads going down as their necks went to the side in a show of submission. My wolf released a huff of breath before going to them and rubbing her cheek against each one of them, accepting their apologies in a way.

After we were done rubbing our scents into one another, Minnie's wolf hopped forward and nipped at my wolf playfully. When we didn't take the bait, she yelped, goading us to play. That started an all-out game of chase. Wolves loved a good game of chase.

I wasn't sure just how long we were out there, but one thing I was sure of was my wolf trusted these females. No matter how entranced we were in our game, they were always in protection mode.

I'd just rolled Minnie onto her back and pounced on her playfully when I heard someone approaching. I immediately stood guard, my ears perking up as my eyes focused on the spot where I could hear the person approaching. I didn't blame the other girls for not hearing them first - my senses were heightened and attuned from the past trauma. As soon as I was on guard, the four of them positioned themselves around me with teeth bared. At that moment, my wolf knew we could completely trust these females without question. Raising my nose to the air, I recognized the scent as one of the original four male guards that was assigned to watch me - not that I knew his name.

"Luna Vanessa sent me to tell you that dinner will be served soon," the man said, remaining at a distance. One of my guards must've linked him that we got the message because he left as soon as he came. I didn't have the ability seeing as I wasn't an official pack member yet. The girls waited to stand down until he was a decent way away before turning to me for direction. I turned and sauntered off to grab my duffle in my mouth before returning to them. They understood and quickly did the same. Minnie led the way back to the pack house, taking the route she said would avoid any pack patrolmen.

My heart pounded in my chest as we grew closer to the open area surrounding the pack house. The idea of someone besides these four girls seeing the scars made my stomach churn. When we got close enough that I knew where I was going, I broke away from the group and ran as fast as I could to the door where I'd first entered the pack house with Elder Adelia. I was thankful there weren't any men keeping guard there right now. It allowed me to shift and quickly slip inside. I grabbed a towel from the laundry room that was just off the entrance and wrapped it around my body, tucking it under my arms to keep it upright.

My hair was a wild mess of damp tangles and I had goosebumps all over my body. I exited the laundry room and entered the kitchen, checking the clock on the stove. There was no way I would have enough time to shower and make myself look presentable enough for dinner with the pack tonight with the little amount of time I had. I also didn't have anything to wear - that was becoming a real issue.

I felt horrible about practically ditching my guards. I hoped they wouldn't get in trouble for it. Although, it's not like they didn't know where I was. They could easily come find me if they needed to. I was almost positive they would be following behind me as soon as they themselves changed. I sighed deeply, my stomach rumbling as all the training from this morning and the playing from earlier hit me at once. I grabbed a glass from the cabinet and filled it with juice from the fridge before chugging the entire glass. I needed to hurry and get dressed before-

"Scarlett, dear, are you back yet?" Vanessa's sweet voice called out. Before something like that happened I thought to myself. Dammit! The upper portion of my shoulder blades as well as my entire arms were on full display due to the way the towel was positioned. I clenched my hand in the fabric and whirled around, my brain kicking into high gear to think of a way out of the situation at hand. Duffle I immediately thought before dropping the towel and sprinting to the bag I'd dropped by the front door. I ripped my heavy coat out of the bag with frantic hands - ignoring all the other garments that spilled out as well - before quickly pulling it on and zipping the front closure, not paying any attention to the fact that I'd accidentally caught my skin in the process and slightly cut myself on my lower stomach.

"Oh, Goddess, I'm sorry. You should've told me you weren't...decent," she stammered as her cheeks turned a light shade of pink, her eyes examining my current state of half-dress as well as the clothes littering the floor around me. "I didn't mean to barge in on you, I was just stopping by to see if you would be joining us for dinner again and was going to walk down with you if you were," she explained. We both gave my current state a once over at the same time.

"I don't think I'm presentable enough for dinner with the pack tonight, so I think I'll just eat here. Enjoy a quiet night in before..." I trailed off, not wanting to outwardly say before your son shows up and ruins what little peace I have with his male presence and the horrible awkwardness that it's bound to bring, but I think she caught onto what I was feeling anyway as she smiled sympathetically.

"That sounds like a good idea. Sometimes it's nice just to have a bit of time to ourselves every once in a while. I wasn't sure if anyone's told you, but I think all the men are due to arrive back sometime around mid-morning tomorrow, so you'll have a chance to sleep in a bit," she said with a smile. I gave her my own smile back, but it felt tight and forced. The thought of me 'sleeping in' was laughable. I was going on day four of basically no sleep at all - I'd had a collective four hours if I was lucky at this point. It was starting to wear on me. If this were a normal situation my crash would be coming soon, but with the impending idea of sharing a bed with a man I knew nothing about, I had no idea when the next time I would be getting a night's worth of sleep would be.

She stuck around for a few more minutes as we discussed how our days went - after I had changed of course. We eventually said our goodbyes and she left for dinner. As I predicted, when she was exiting my guards were just entering.

"You scared us when you took off." Minnie was the first to speak.

"One second you were there, and then the next we felt a gust of air and you were just gone," Greta added with astonishment. The corner of my mouth pulled up. Speed and stamina were the first two things I worked on when my body regained enough strength when I was first taken into protective custody. I figured if Eric couldn't catch me, he couldn't ever torture me again.

"Sorry, my wolf and I are very selective of who we're around..." I answered, my response slightly cryptic, but I could tell they knew exactly what I was talking about by the looks on their faces as they glanced at one another.

"You can ask, but I can't promise you you'll get an answer," I husked out, staring at my hands where they were spread out on the kitchen countertop.

"Our wolves are reflections of ourselves," Minnie began, "as I grew older and my hair got darker, so did my wolf's fur," she stated. I nodded but didn't say anything. "Your back and arms..." she trailed off, her voice quivering before she cleared it. I swallowed thickly before crossing my arms over my chest.

"How...?" she continued before trailing off, seeming at a complete loss for words. I just shook my head.

"Some things are better left in the past. I'd like to keep it that way," I murmured, my tone flat - completely devoid of any emotion. Inside, I felt anything but. I wondered if I would ever be free of his reign over me, or if he'd always have this invisible hold. "I'm gonna skip the pack dinner tonight. You ladies can go shadow the men who are patrolling the perimeter entrances and exits if you want to pick their brains and get some experience. I'm just gonna lay low the rest of the night," I mumbled. They shared similar looks of worry that I chose to ignore before nodding and leaving me alone in the kitchen.

I slipped onto one of the barstools and propped my head up on my arm. I was so tired, but my mind was still wired and on high alert. I didn't have the energy to cook, but I needed to eat. Hoisting myself out of the chair I pulled the fridge open once again and surveyed the contents. All of it required far too much effort.

Suddenly, there was a knock at the front door - which was actually the back entrance. My brows furrowed and I immediately pulled my hidden knife. I skulked along the wall silently, slowing my breath so that even with heightened hearing, no one would hear me approaching the door. I closed my eyes and carefully pressed my ear to the wood to listen.

"What the hell is up with knocking?! I told you, just yell in and tell damn woman I'm here to visit! Knocking will just freak her out! I bet you she's already at the door with her ear pressed up against it listening to everything we're saying with a knife in one hand ready to strike!" Jackie hissed at whoever she was talking to. Despite my desire to throw the door open and pull her into a hug, I waited a moment and sniffed out the pheromones of everyone standing around. Male. But...oddly enough...I didn't detect any danger, I unlocked the door and whipped it open.

"See! What did I say!" Jackie yelled, pointing at me and my knife that - in hindsight - I should've put away. It was then that I saw her mate was the one she was talking to, something that made me bite the inside of my cheek to stifle my laughter. I tucked the knife back into it's holster before moving out of the way so Jackie could come in. I was surprised at my wolf's reaction to her mate. Despite being a male and a stranger, she wasn't immediately distrusting of him. I knew it had to be due to his mating with Jackie and my wolf's immense love for Jackie.

"So, any chaffing?" I asked cheekily as we all sauntered into my kitchen. Justin laughed loudly as Jackie just pushed me playfully while threatening to maim me. Once she settled in beside me, I turned to look at her and ask if she'd eaten dinner yet, but she immediately cut me off with a loud gasp.

"Scarlett Lane Rockwell," she scolded using my full name. "When was the last time you slept, for God's sake?" she demanded angrily, sounding every bit like an angry mother. I sighed and rolled my eyes, trying to playfully brush off her concern but I knew how bad the circles under my eyes were getting despite my efforts to contain them. Jackie always saw right through my act.

"Well, let's see. You were there. We had brandy," I joked, referring to the night before I'd left on a plane to come here. She gave me a look filled with sadness.

"You're taking a pill tonight. Justin can sleep outside the room and keep watch at the door and I'll sleep with you. And don't you dare try and argue with me!" she growled as I opened my mouth to do just that. I released a frustrated puff of air through my nose before leveling her with an irritated glare. She was a very newly mated female and she was going to make her mate sleep outside the bedroom while she slept with me. This was stupid.

"It's fine, Jackie. I'll crash eventually-"

"Like your fucking wolf is going to let you fall asleep once Alpha Harrington shows up. As if. I know you both better than that," she hissed just barely above a whisper. Her eyes held so much concern for me that it made me feel guilty.

"Only if it's okay with Justin," I murmured only so she could hear. If her mate wasn't okay with it, then I simply wasn't going to sleep until I literally dropped to the floor and my body shut down. It'd happened once before. If that's what it took, then that's what it took.

"You're sleeping outside her bedroom tonight and keeping watch while I sleep with her in the bed," Jackie stated matter-of-factly while looking directly at her mate. My entire body froze up and my breath caught in my throat as I waited for his response. He didn't look at all happy about the arrangement, but he just nodded in acceptance. I blinked a few times, shocked.

That's it?

"You look like you're trying to solve all of life's problems," Jackie commented with a laugh. I wasn't sure how to respond. Of course, I knew that other mates interacted much differently than how Eric interacted with me. I wasn't stupid, but part of me had been programmed to always expect the worst out of every male, every mate, I ever encountered. My therapist said it was one of my many survival tactics. If I automatically expected the worst, I could plan accordingly to protect myself ahead of time.

If I were to have ever spoken to Eric in such a manner...a slight shiver ran up my spine before I immediately pushed the thought away as my skin began that odd phantom burn.

"Are you hungry?" Jackie asked, pulling me out of my head and back into reality. I immediately nodded as my stomach growled in response.

"Starved."

"Well, let's order something in. I've been craving pizza for the past couple of days ever since we got drunk and you mentioned it without following through," she taunted.

# CHAPTER 11

X ander's POV

I rolled my neck trying to work out the kinks that had settled there from the hours I'd spent in the car over the past several days. I wanted nothing more than to be able to come home, plop down on my couch, kick my feet up, and mindlessly watch the sports coverage that'd be on before the hockey game tonight. Maybe get a bit of pack paperwork done. Just relax. However, I knew none of that was in the cards. It wasn't even nine-thirty yet and I already knew today was going to be a damn chore if the text my mom sent me about this Council meeting I had to attend was anything to go by.

"So...you getting nervous?" Beta Donovan asked as we pulled up to the pack gates, stopping briefly before they let us in.

"And what is it I have to be nervous about?" I asked monotonously while watching the land pass by out the window. The guys teased me relentlessly the entire way back, making me wish I didn't choose to share a car with all of them for these trips every year. He didn't reply as we came to a stop at the front entrance to the pack. His mate made an appearance, waving frantically at our car despite the fact there was no way in hell she could see in with how blacked-out the windows were. I sighed deeply before swinging my door open and getting out. Gamma Griffin and Head Warrior Andre followed my lead. Donovan was already out of the driver's seat and picking his wife up to greet her. Peyton popped out and jumped on Griffin, smothering him in kisses as well.

I was thankful that I wasn't the only one who wasn't getting a proper greeting home as it seemed Raven wasn't a part of the greeting committee this time around.

"And where would my mate be on this fine morning?" Andre asked no one in particular.

"She's not feeling too well. The baby's really been taking it out of her lately. She told us to tell you sorry, but to give you this," Peyton said before blowing a kiss. Andre just smiled and shook his head.

"I apologize if I'm interrupting, but we need to meet. Now. Please follow me," came the stern voice of someone I had only spoken with a handful of times; Elder Adelia. She was a serious-looking woman with light gray hair, crow's feet, and a no-nonsense scowl that could scare even the toughest of men. Everyone immediately straightened before nodding and quietly following behind her. We all exchanged similar looks of confusion. While I knew there was a meeting with The Council due to my mother's heads up, I hadn't been given a single detail ahead of time about what would be discussed.

Upon entering my dad's office, I saw that my parents, the three highest-ranking council members - Elder Thomas, Agatha, and Isaiah - and four of the best pack warriors we had were already waiting for us. Raven was also sitting next to my mother - something that confused Andre. My interest was immediately piqued by the odd group of people.

"Does anyone care to explain what's going on?" I asked as we all settled into our seats.

"Not before these are signed by those who haven't already signed them," Elder Adelia said before handing out papers to everyone except my parents and me.

"Is this a non-disclosure agreement?" Riley asked aloud as her eyes scanned the document.

"Yes. Every single one of you will be required to sign that regarding everything that is going to be told to you in this room. Alpha Harrington, Vanessa, and Andrew have already signed theirs. There are pens on the table just there. Please don't waste any time, we're on a strict schedule," she stated while glancing at the watch on her wrist. Unsure looks were exchanged all around as everyone signed the papers and handed them forward. After everyone's pages had been collected, Elder Adelia looked to the ceiling and took a deep breath.

"The NDA form is because the people in this room right now are the only people who have the privilege of knowing the name of Scarlett's ex-mate. You are not to speak his name to anyone for any reason. Is that understood?" Elder Adelia spoke, her tone calm and even but there was an edge to it that had the hair on the back of my neck rising - despite the fact that I already knew who my future mate's ex was. "If the subject of doing business with their pack is to ever come up around those who are not privy to this information, you are to find an excuse as to why you cannot do business with said pack and move on. Are we clear?"

"What's with all the secrecy?" Maximus, my sister's mate, and one of my good friends, asked. Elder Adelia looked like she was at war with herself before running a stressed hand down her face.

"It's not my story to tell. What Scarlett chooses to tell you, if she ever chooses to tell you, is up to her and her alone. However..."

she trailed off, clearing her throat while sharing a look with Elder Thomas before focusing her attention back on all of us. The look on her face told me that we weren't prepared for whatever she was about to say.

"What I can tell you is that there is a Contract of Retribution with her mate's name on it signed by all four council members as well as Scarlett filed away at The Council headquarters," Elder Adelia rasped out. I felt my jaw slacken as all the air left my lungs. What the fuck. The noise in the office grew as people voiced their shock.

"What is a contract of retribution?" Raven asked, looking embarrassed that she didn't know. I didn't blame her. Had I not been required to take a course in the history of our kind due to my alpha status, I probably wouldn't have known either.

"It means that whatever that asshole did to her, it was so bad the council signed an agreement that states she can deal with him however she damn well pleases without any legal consequences - and anyone who gets in her way can be dealt with as well. And if she happens to get caught by the human authorities in the process, the council will help clear her name," I ground out through clenched teeth unable to believe what she was telling me.

"There have only ever been two instances where a Contract of Retribution has been utilized in the history of The Council's existence...that's how severe someone's act of injustice has to be against another of our kind," my mother murmured, her voice breaking towards the end as her eyes shone with tears.

"Now you can understand why when you came at her the way you did - voice raised and posturing the way you did - she reacted accordingly," Adelia spoke to Maximus, who was sporting a look of both understanding and guilt.

"Her ex-mate is Eric Strickland, the beta of the Sablefur pack-" Adelia continued without hesitation.

"Oh my- that pack is within the state," Riley gasped.

"Now you understand the severity of the situation and why his name must stay in this room. If someone were to find out for any reason and it was to get back to him...we have no way of knowing what he would do. But I didn't ask Vanessa to call this meeting just to tell you the name, and we don't have much time left before we need to leave. I need you all to listen very closely. Especially you, Xander," she stated, fixing me with a serious look.

"She's untrusting of anyone, but especially men. The one who was supposed to care for her and love her more than anything. ..well, I think you can fill in the blanks. She's worked hard to get where she is, but change is difficult for her. You're all going to have to try your very hardest to accommodate her needs if this is going to be a smooth transition - or as smooth as it can be. She has no idea I'm here saying this and she would probably kill me if she knew I was, but I'm doing it for her. To the men - you cannot just blindly enter rooms if you sense her there anymore. You need to knock and announce your presence. It won't be a forever thing, but it will help her come to trust you. Don't get too close or invade her personal space, her wolf will sense it as an unspoken threat. Don't raise your voice, yelling triggers her fight or flight response. Don't put your hands on her - even if it's in a friendly manner - unless you give her a heads-up that you're going to do it first. And the biggest thing - I cannot stress this enough - do not ever touch her back for any reason under any circumstance whatsoever. That last one goes for you too, ladies. Do I make myself clear?" Adelia asked with finality, pushing herself up to a standing position with her hands clasped in front of her.

We all shared similar looks of interest at the last demand but nodded.

"She didn't seem to have any major issues being around Riley, Peyton, and Raven," my mom commented off-handedly, seeming confused by all the rules that had just been outlined.

"They're women," Adelia murmured with a sad smile. "Now, I'd like to speak with Xander alone for the last few minutes of my time. The rest of you can gather in the pack kitchen and I will come and address you when I'm done," she instructed, giving everyone a 'get out now' look. Once we were alone, I gave her all my attention. I was shocked speechless when she let down her hardened expression and just looked like a concerned mother.

"I need you to really listen to me, Xander. Scarlett is the strongest woman I've ever met in my entire life. What she's been through...it should have killed her. But it didn't. She wouldn't let it. She fought tooth and nail to be here. To survive. She's kind, loving, and fiercely loyal to those that she loves. But she won't show it. Not at first. I have no idea how she's going to react to being around you, but I beg of you to be patient and mindful. I know you've been burned before, too, but...to be honest, you're going to have to set your own insecurities and reservations aside for right now and focus on just Scarlett. If you can make her feel safe and get her to come out of her shell, you'll be the happiest man in the entire world with her as a mate and a Luna," she insisted. I blew a breath of air out of my lips.

"How the heck am I supposed to establish a connection with her if she's too scared to even be around me? Never mind the idea of intimacy. If she's not comfortable just being in the same room as me, how in the world is she going to be comfortable enough to let me mate her?" I grunted, running a frustrated hand through my hair.

"You can't give up before even giving it a chance," Adelia scolded with a glare.

"I'm not giving up, I just don't see how this is going to work. She's been through a lot, that much is obvious, and I don't want to freak her out, but we only have three weeks left. The council didn't give us much time to work with and the clock is ticking," I stressed. By the look on her face, this was something she'd been stressing over too.

"Xander, you're a smart man. I'm sure you'll figure something out once you meet her," she said before turning to exit the room. "Come, let's go meet the others so I can properly introduce you to your new mate."

"Now?" I deadpanned, my palms beginning to sweat. I couldn't remember the last time I was this nervous. I was an alpha for crying out loud! I didn't get nervous. Well...not about stuff like this.

"No time like the present, dear. Let's go," she ordered, opening the door and gliding out. I chewed on my lip as I followed behind her. The mood in the kitchen was bleak as we entered, everyone's heads were pressed together as they were all whispering furiously.

"Enough!" Adelia snapped quietly but effectively. "I've linked for Jackie to bring her down and she will immediately know what's happening and has been discussed if you all don't lighten up. Her intuition is sharp, so put on a smile and make sure it's real." I ran a hand through my hair again to try and dispel some of my pent-up energy, but it didn't help. I decided to try and take care of my hunger instead by rummaging through the pack fridge while we waited. I was pushing aside a head of lettuce when I heard the voice.

"Jackie, seriously! I'm not putting on the damn blindfold!" A feminine voice growled playfully. It was followed by that same harmonious laugh I'd heard days earlier over the phone echoing off the walls. "What's the surpri- I'd know that smell anywhere!" the voice rushed out before the patter of footsteps quickened dramatically. A burst of brown rushed past me and clobbered Elder Adelia. All of us watched in shock as the harsh old woman smiled wide and laughed - actually laughed - before wrapping her arms around the woman's small frame. Well, small compared to me, I guess.

"You should watch that potty mouth of yours now that you're going to be a Luna," Elder Adelia commented with a scolding tone.

"Well what damn fun would that be?" the girl shot back sarcastically. Her comment and tone pulled a genuine laugh out of me. It must've caught her off guard because her gaze immediately snapped to mine. Her wide, happy smile dropped off her face within seconds as her eyes cooly assessed me. I noticed the way she tried to take a subtle step backward.

"Well, I guess we should make some proper introductions then, hmm? Scarlett, this is Alpha Harrington - but his first name is Xander. Xander, this is to be your Luna and mate, Scarlett." If I wasn't so enthralled by how incredibly beautiful she was, I wouldn't have been such a damn moron. I would've actually remembered everything Elder Adelia had just told me mere minutes earlier about all of her triggers. But no, I didn't. What did my dumbass do instead? I took four quick steps forward and reached my massive hand toward her to try and shake hers, effectively invading her personal space. That's like, what, 90 rules I just broke? Way to go, Xander. That's just perfect, pal.

I wasn't sure what I was expecting her to do. Run? Maybe. Cower? Maybe. Pull a knife on me from where it was hidden up her sleeve and press it against my pants zipper before I could even take my next breath? Fuck no. My eyes widened comically to the size of saucers and I swallowed thickly. A thin sheen of sweat formed on my upper brow - she was pointing a very sharp object at a very vital organ of mine. I moved my hands so they were up at my sides in a surrendering position.

"Scarlett, he didn't mean to scare you," Elder Adelia murmured softly into her ear while gently stroking the outside of her arm. That seemed to snap her out of the daze she was in. Her eyes went wide with a deer in the headlights look before they dropped down to where her knife-wielding hand was positioned. She quickly sheathed the weapon while rapidly shaking her head back and forth.

"I didn't mean..." she whispered so softly I almost didn't hear it. Her body started shaking with fine tremors, a terrified expression washing over her face. She clasped her hands in front of her and dug her nails into her skin, the action confusing me as it appeared to be causing her pain. I didn't have time to dwell on it as she ducked her head and tilted it to the side in a show of submission, the tremors in her body getting worse.

"Oh dear, this isn't good," Elder Adelia rushed out with a look of worry before trying to get Scarlett's attention. Standing there, watching the scene unfold before me, I felt helpless. I knew they told me not to touch her, but something in my gut was telling me otherwise. I needed to do something.

"Scarlett," I spoke softly. Nothing.

"Scarlett," I tried again a bit louder. Again, nothing.

"Scarlett," I grunted out a third time, but this time I used a bit of my alpha command. Her head snapped up to look directly into my eyes. I slowly reached out and gently rested my hands on the sides of her arms, rubbing my thumbs back and forth across her skin in what I was hoping was a soothing manner. "It's okay. I didn't mean to scare you. It's my fault and I'm sorry. It's okay." I spoke confidently and evenly, hoping to stop whatever the hell this reaction was. Her breathing, which had started to hasten, began to slowly return to normal as the course tremors in her body eventually eased until they were completely gone. She blinked a few times until the fog in her eyes cleared, her cheeks tinted a light shade of pink in embarrassment before she roughly shook my hands off her arms and took a large step away from me. She peeked at everyone else out of the corner of her eye - I'm assuming to see if they were watching - but they were all pretending to be deep in conversation with one another. I shouldn't have found the relieved breath she tried concealing as cute as I did.

"How'd you sleep last night?" my mom asked her, breaking the tension in the room and drawing Scarlett's attention away from both me and what had just transpired.

"Alright. I did end up sleeping in a bit, actually. Jackie and I didn't get up until about half an hour ago," she replied, hardening her expression. I was amazed at her ability to so quickly bounce back from the panic attack she'd just had seconds ago. "I think you should ask Justin how he slept, though," she said with some amusement in her tone - though I could tell it was forced - shooting Justin an apologetic look. The girl she'd come in with - Jackie - laughed before leaning up to press a kiss to the mark on Justin's neck - woah, wait a minute? What? That's new. Definitely going to grill him about that later.

I watched Scarlett intently as she made her way through the room. The way she eyed Donovan, Griffin, and Andre up and down. She was taking in every single detail about them, her body poised in a way that every single muscle looked like it was ready to strike at any moment. I watched as her eyes lingered over the scar where Donovan broke his right arm, beyond impressed she'd even caught it but wondering if that's why her eyes lingered there.

Maybe I was giving her too much credit. When she was done assessing each of them I watched as her eyes surveyed the room, darting to every door that led out of the room - lingering extra long on the one that led outside to the back patio before strategically positioning herself in the room so she was closest to that door.

I then let myself just take in her appearance. Damn, if we could make this work I was going to be one lucky bastard. Griffin had gotten in my head right after the news was broken to me - saying some nonsense about me possibly getting a carbon copy of Mika.

With long chocolate brown hair, a full voluptuous figure, and thick pouty lips, Scarlett couldn't be more different from Mika if she tried. And that was just as far as looks went. I wasn't stupid enough to assume they were anything alike on the inside, either. Mika was a woman in a league of her own as far as attitude went and I wasn't interested in what she had to offer at all. That was for sure.

"Well, us Council members really must get going. I hope you do settle into your role here perfectly, Scarlett. Don't forget, Monday marks three weeks until you're to have completed your mating. It was good to see you once again. You too, Jackie. We'll be in touch," Elder Thomas suddenly muttered before grabbing his briefcase and ushering the rest of The Council members to follow behind him with a wave of his hand. Adelia gave Scarlett a sympathetic look before hugging her one last time. A whispered promise of seeing her again before the month was up before saying goodbye.

# CHAPTER 12

X ander's POV

"Well, if my favorite brother isn't back from his press tour," Jade announced dramatically as she entered the kitchen, pressing up on her tip-toes to press a chaste kiss to Maximus's lips.

"Scarlett, I keep meaning to come and find you to tell you - I think you're going to need to just create one autograph and then make a ton of copies to save yourself time. Pretty much every woman in the pack wants one at this point. It's all anyone is talking about," Jade laughed with a big smile.

"An autograph for what?" Griffin asked, raising an eyebrow before looking Scarlett's way. She smoothed her hands down the front of her dress, her face not giving away a single emotion.

"Mika was out of line. So I put her back in it," she stated simply. Her words and expression caused all the women in the room to burst into laughter, but Scarlett just shrugged as her demeanor remained the same. "I left a loaf of banana bread in the oven when Jackie dragged me away. I need to go check on it," she spoke softly before quickly leaving the room.

"I better go check on her," Jackie rushed out before kissing Justin quickly and rushing off in the direction Scarlett had left.

"What the hell happened with Mika?" I demanded the second I knew she was out of earshot.

"Oh, just hold on. Someone apparently caught the entire thing on video. They started recording the second they saw Scarlett walking back to the table after Mika sat down in her seat. They knew something was going to happen, but no one knew it was going to be this legendary," Jade shrieked, giddy with excitement as she turned on the massive TV that hung on the wall opposite us before connecting to its screen sharing system. After a few clicks, the video was broadcast and playing.

"From what Elder Adelia told me a few days ago, Alpha Harrington has been running this pack alone for years. There is no reason for you to even think there is a seat at this table that belongs to you. Now, you may remove yourself from my spot and find adequate seating elsewhere. Thank you," Scarlett's voice spoke calmly and clearly. I couldn't see Mika's face from how far away the person was, but I would've paid anything at that moment.

"Excuse me?" Mika replied. Her voice always grated against my nerves. Scarlett took a threatening step forward. You're kidding me. Was this actually happening?

"I did not stutter and I will not repeat myself. You have exactly ten seconds to remove yourself from the seat you knew was reserved for me and me alone before I personally see to your removal. And I can promise I will not be gentle," came Scarlett's voice again. I don't know what it was about hearing her command Mika in such a confident way, but I felt the front of my pants tightening. The pack erupted into whispers in the background of the video. I saw Mika looking around - I knew her well enough to know she was embarrassed that Scarlett was making her look bad - weak - in front of the entire pack. Mika scoffed and crossed her arms over her chest before leaning back in her chair.

"That's cute. Is this some little skit you like to do?" Mika challenged. Scarlett didn't say another word and I watched on with bated breath as she started walking around the table to where Mika was sitting. The noise in the background of the video quieted down to nothing until Scarlett was behind Mika. I watched in absolute awe as Mika gasped in surprise. Griffin, Donovan, Andre, and I released similar sounds of shock. I was glad I didn't blink because if I had I would've missed what happened next. Scarlett smoothly removed her from her seat, taking her down to her knees in seconds as she grasped her neck.

"Are you playing with me right now?" Donovan laughed in amazement. My eyes were glued to the screen, I couldn't look away. Scarlett jerked Mika's head to the side, forcing her to bear her neck in a show of complete submission - in front of the entire fucking pack.

"It's such a pity you didn't listen. Maybe next time you'll learn to respect those around you?" Scarlett murmured before looking up and scanning the entire room. "From here on out, respect and kindness to others are two key things this pack will keep in mind when interacting with one another. Give it and you shall receive it. If you have a problem with anyone, no matter their ranking - real or perceived - report it and it will be dealt with swiftly and justly," she stated, doing something to Mika that caused her to cry out at the exact moment she mentioned someone's perceived ranking. Holy shit.

The video ended with Scarlett saying, "Now, why don't you go find the adequate seating I mentioned earlier?" to Mika in such a sweet tone I had to laugh.

"Yeah, I want one of those autographs whenever she gets them made," Griffin stated. "Dammit. I'm so pissed I didn't get to see that in person," he grumbled.

"You're being awfully quiet," my mom commented, eyeing me pointedly.

"No one is upset with Scarlett, are they?" I asked. I didn't want that drama on my hands. Not when I already had a hoard of things I needed to deal with. Especially not for Scarlett's sake.

"No one besides Mika's little group of minions. And some moms were a little peeved that she was so aggressive in front of their kids, but they liked her takeaway message. And they dislike Mika enough that the pros outweighed the cons," Jade said. I nodded.

"I'm gonna go unpack my stuff and take a shower. You guys want to meet in about an hour and a half to go over some of the paperwork from this past week?" I asked the guys.

"Actually, son, I'm going to do that. Why don't you spend the day with Scarlett?" my dad suggested with a look that said it was less of a suggestion and more of an order. I raised both my eyebrows and took a deep breath in before nodding and releasing it.

"O-kay. I'll see you guys later then. Let me know if you need anything," I grunted before walking off. Coming to the door that connected my living quarters to the pack house, I noticed there was a door sign and a welcome mat on the floor. Those are new. So was the woman positioned outside the door clearly keeping guard.

"Alpha Harrington," she nodded respectfully before moving aside so I could enter. I just nodded back with a confused look before going to twist the knob to enter. "Uh, Alpha. I know it's your house, but...um, maybe...maybe knock....first?" the woman suggested awkwardly with an apologetic expression. Dammit! How did I forget that one too? I nodded before wrapping my knuckles against the wood three times and pushing the door open.

I stopped and turned around, checking to make sure I was actually at the correct wing of the house before entering the place again. Yeah, this is definitely the right wing, but this looks absolutely nothing like my house...I gazed around the place in confusion. Jackie, who I'd gathered was probably Scarlett's best friend, saw me enter and whispered that she would be upstairs in the guest bedroom watching TV if she needed her before quickly disappearing.

"I decorated a bit," Scarlett remarked from the kitchen where she was dumping another bowl of batter into a freshly greased loaf pan. Her eyes watched me closely as I edged my way towards her. I took a deep inhale, the smell around us making my mouth profusely water. Was this what it was like to actually have a good mate? Your place was clean, nicely decorated, and smelled like freshly baked banana bread?

Man, I really have been missing out.

By the look in her eyes, she was waiting for my reaction to the new look. Her entire body was coiled tightly, the tension in her shoulders obvious. "A bit?" I chuckled, coming to stand across from her at the kitchen counter, staring down at the loaf of banana bread that looked like it'd just come out of the oven. My tongue came out to wet my lips as the smell wafted up into my nose. Pure heaven. My reaction seemed to catch her off guard for the briefest of seconds before she masked her surprise.

"Would you like a piece?" she asked after putting the other pan in the oven and setting a timer.

"Yes, please," I replied, probably a little too quickly based on the slight upward curving of the edge of her lips. She pulled out a knife before carefully cutting a thick slice and setting it on a small plate. I expected her to hand it over, but she ventured over to the fridge to pull out a tub of butter. Smearing a thick layer that instantly melted over the bread, I greedily took the plate from her as she handed it over and dug in. I consumed about half the slice in one single bite.

"Holy shit," I groaned before finishing the rest of the piece in record time.

"Would you like more?" she asked. I looked up and scanned her face, trying to get a reading on what the hell she was thinking but there wasn't a single emotion there for me to go off of.

"Depends. Am I allowed to eat the entire thing without you getting mad at me?" I asked, giving her a cheeky smile - one I knew had my dimples popping. I figured it wouldn't hurt to try and flirt a little. I hadn't been laid in....I didn't even know how long - at least four years? - so I was severely out of practice. It was unbecoming of an Alpha to sleep around and I just didn't have the time these days to try and pursue Mika. Nor was I willing to stoop to that level of self-deprecation. Sex wasn't worth that to me.

However, if Scarlette and I only had until the end of the next three weeks to make this thing official, I needed to work on my charm a bit. Her eyes darted down to check the dimples out before shrugging. I'd be lying if I said my ego wasn't bruised.

"I sorta baked it for you. If you want to eat it all right now, then you're more than welcome to," she responded evenly. "But if you're hungry, I could make you a proper breakfast. I went grocery shopping earlier this week," she continued, breaking our eye contact to finish cleaning the bowl from the bread she'd made. I couldn't remember the last time someone besides myself cooked me breakfast.

"That would be nice. I can help if you want," I offered. She dropped the bowl she'd been washing, the sound of it banging startling her a second time before she looked up at me in shock. It was the first real emotion I'd seen her show since we'd been alone. That seemed like a win in my book.

"What?" she finally asked, slightly breathless.

"I said I can help cook breakfast if you'd like," I repeated, pushing off of the chair I was on to stand. She craned her neck to look up at me, making me aware of our severe height difference. She had to be at least a foot shorter than me. And besides all her curves, she was much smaller than I was. Feminine in a way that had my wolf licking his lips appreciatively in my head. If I wanted to, I could pull her into my chest and completely wrap her in my embrace. The thought alone had my mind wandering to how nice all those soft, thick curves would feel pressed up against me. Nicer than Mika's unfaithful bony body that's for damn sure. Some men are into that kind of thing, and that's cool. But I know what I like and it was staring right at me.

She cleared her throat, her eyes holding a glare when I finally came back to reality. I scratched the back of my neck awkwardly when I realized my wolf had flooded the room with mating pheromones - the fucking jerk. I might as well have just been sporting a full-on boner and said, "hey, I'm thinking about banging you right now!" because that would've been just as discreet.

"I got a few things out while you were...thinking," she commented with a pointed look. I chuckled and rounded the counter, mindful to leave a few feet of space between us. Looking at everything she got out, I noticed she'd apparently planned on making pancakes, eggs, bacon, and...potatoes? I'm not sure what she had in mind for those.

"What can I do?" I asked before resting my hands on my hips. She hesitated for a second before sliding the potatoes over to me and handing me a peeler.

"Could you peel these for me, please?" she asked. I nodded and immediately got to work. We worked in comfortable silence, me peeling and her creating the batter for the pancakes.

"What next?" I asked. She didn't say anything as she grabbed a big bowl and filled it with water, before handing both it and what looked like a cheese grater to me. The corner of her mouth curled upwards for half of a second as it did earlier, but this time in reaction to my utterly confused face.

"I always grate the hashbrowns into water so that the potatoes don't oxidize while I'm grating them," she explained. Picking up a potato, she proceeded to show me exactly what she meant before stepping out of the way so I could continue.

"What happens if the potato oxidizes?" I asked while grating away. She furrowed her brows at me like I was crazy for asking. Maybe that was a stupid question, what did I know? I don't cook meals like this often. I did just the bare minimum.

"Nothing, really. It just doesn't look as appetizing," she mumbled softly before getting a big griddle out - one that I knew for a fact I didn't own before she moved in here - and turning it on. Once I had all the potatoes shredded I looked to her for my next direction.

"I know you said it makes them look more appetizing, but this looks gross," I commented as my nose scrunched up while peering into the bowl of foamy and milky water with shredded potatoes. This time the corner of her mouth did pull up in a smile before disappearing. Score.

She pulled out a strainer and handed it to me before pointing to the sink.

"Now you use cold water to rinse the potatoes until the water runs completely clear and there's no more starch clinging to the potatoes," she explained.

"How come you don't want the starch?" I asked absentmindedly as I began rinsing them.

"Because that's what causes issues when you're cooking them. It can stick to the pan and cause them to burn," she explained. Once I was done rinsing the potatoes, she walked me through the process of thoroughly drying the potatoes to make sure they weren't too wet - she assured me if they had too much moisture in them that, too, would prevent them from cooking properly.

I watched her in awe as she poured a copious amount of vegetable oil and slapped two large slices of butter into a skillet pan before dumping a huge mound of the potato shreds into it and covering it to cook. "Not good for the heart, but it's good for the soul," she murmured so softly to herself with a laugh that I don't think she meant for me to hear it.

"Something someone used to say to you?" I asked. Her eyes snapped up to me before she pushed a lock of hair behind her ear in a bashful manner.

"I lived with a pack in Georgia for three months when I was fourteen..." she stopped, looking conflicted about how much she wanted to say. She flipped the pancakes and bacon that were cooking on the griddle. I assumed to give her something to occupy her time while she contemplated what to say to me.

"The orphanage was way overcrowded. Since I was one of the oldest girls I was expected to help care for the littles-"

"You were an orphan?" I interrupted, immediately regretting the move when she eyed me pointedly and continued her story.

"The house mother's name was Jacinda, but she had us all call her Momma J. She was..." she trailed off, a genuine smile pulling at her lips that had my mouth going dry and my heart beating just a little faster. "So funny. And the sweetest woman. She cared so much about all of us kids. She taught me all I know about how to cook, especially soul food. That's what she always used to say to me, though. 'It's not good for the heart, but it sure is good for the soul'," she said with another laugh before her expression turned somber.

"How come you were only there for three months?" I asked while reaching forward to lift the lid to check on the hashbrowns. She abruptly smacked my hand away with a harsh, don't! before her entire body seized up with tension. Every muscle looked coiled and ready to spring into action at the drop of a dime.

"Sorry," I muttered weakly, taking a step back to hopefully appear like less of a threat. "Is there a reason you have to leave the lid on?" I asked, carefully pointing towards the pan that she'd just smacked my hand away from. I knew she was expecting me to lash out, but I wasn't sure how long I was going to have to stand here like a dumbass before she realized I wasn't going to behave like some kind of barbarian. There was a slight tremor in her arms before she took a slow step back and quickly took the pancakes and bacon off the griddle, never once turning her back to me or taking her eyes off of me for more than a couple of seconds.

My earlier question remained unanswered as she took the lid off the potatoes to flip the hashbrowns. They cooked for a few more minutes as we remained in tense silence while she finished up the scrambled eggs.

The tension in her body remained as she piled the food onto a plate, surprising the hell out of me as she handed it over to me with her eyes downcast and her head slightly tilted in submission.

"Thank you," I said before making my way to the new dining table. I resisted the intense urge to dive in and stuff my face as I waited for her to join me with a plate of her own. Thankfully, I didn't have to wait too long. I was surprised when she chose to sit in the seat to my immediate left instead of directly across from me like I figured she would to put some distance between us.

"This smells amazing," I commented, hoping to try and bring back the light mood from earlier. She nodded her thanks as she moved her hands to rest them in her lap. I didn't realize what she was doing until after I'd taken my first bite. Only then did she reach up to grab her fork and cut a piece off of her pancake.

"You don't need to do that here," I stated after I swallowed my food - my tone probably harsher than it should've been due to the way she slightly jumped, but I'd already showcased what an idiot I was around this woman.

"Do what?" she asked with narrowed eyes. The statement seemed like a challenge. Whatever I said and did from here was a test it felt like. If only I'd studied.

"Wait for me to take the first bite. I get it's some...respect thing in front of the pack, but not when we're in our own home. Or at any informal gathering, for that matter. We're equals," I insisted while looking directly at her, making sure I kept eye contact the entire time I spoke. She looked like I'd just spoken a foreign language, but I chose to leave it and continued eating. We didn't say another word to one another until I was almost done with my food. It was almost easy to forget the uncomfortable silence because of how good the food truly was. I need to thank this Jacinda woman personally.

"I got transferred," she abruptly spoke, catching me off guard. I furrowed my brows in confusion. "I was only with Mama J for three months because they transferred me. It wasn't by choice - it rarely was - but that was the one time I actually wanted to stay. It wasn't because I had caused trouble. I liked it there, but they didn't have room for me. And since I was the oldest, I was costing the most money to feed. Therefore, I got the boot," she explained. I wasn't sure why she was suddenly opening up, but I wasn't going to question it.

"Have you ever tried to reach out to her again? Mama J?" I asked.

"Last I heard she was still running that same orphanage. I always wanted to try and travel back to that pack when I turned eighteen to see her, but...I never got the opportunity," she husked out, a haunted look in her eyes before she looked down at her plate to avoid my gaze.

"Maybe we can look into that after the mating. The busiest time for pack business is just about over, so we should be free to travel here soon for small periods at a time," I offered before scooping up my last bite of food.

"You'd take me all the way across the country just to visit an old orphanage house mother?" she rasped out quizzically, looking so unsure I thought I might've said something wrong.

"Yes...? Unless that's not what you wanted," I spoke quickly, afraid I might have misinterpreted her words. Trying to understand her was like trying to put together a 1000-piece puzzle that had no picture and was just a solid color.

"Can you excuse me, please?" she asked, looking like she was ready to bolt. I furrowed my brows but just nodded my head. I threw my hands up, completely lost when she did make a run for it the second I conceded.

What in the world had I done wrong?

# CHAPTER 13

S carlett's POV

My legs carried me away from him as fast as they possibly could. Approaching the bedroom I would share with him in less than twenty-four hours, I threw the double doors open. I was so lost in my thoughts I didn't even realize Jackie had followed me into the room and was right behind me. It was something that hadn't happened to me in a very long time. I released a startled yelp before wrapping my arms protectively around myself.

"Girl! What the hell are you doing up here? I've been eaves-dropping the entire conversation - he's amazing!" she hissed out. I wasn't sure what came over me, but I gave into the emotions of vulnerability I was feeling and broke down into tears. I covered my face with my hands, embarrassed and wishing the ground would just swallow me up whole.

"Talk to me, Scarlett. Tell me what's going on," Jackie coaxed, gently leading me over to the sitting area in the room. She eased us down onto one of the loveseats as I furiously wiped the stupid droplets away. My chest heaved up and down as I hiccuped, trying to catch my breath. I looked into Jackie's eyes, allowing myself to take the comfort she was offering as I processed whatever the heck it was I was feeling.

"You're confused and scared," Jackie whispered, voicing my emotions for me. She leaned forward and pulled a tissue from the box on the coffee table in front of us, handing it to me before wrapping her arm around my shoulders. I nodded, the revelation of my feelings making me cry harder.

"My wolf doesn't trust him and neither do I. She doesn't even want to give him a chance or the benefit of the doubt. Or at least didn't...but then he's saying things that Eric would've never have said-"

"Like you being equals," Jackie interrupted with a knowing look. I nodded. "Or offering to help you make breakfast. And then actually following through," she continued. I remained quiet for a moment.

"It seems too good to be true, Jackie," I whispered, a scared tremor in my voice. "Eric was never a romantic, but things were at least cordial at first. What if this is like that? I-I can't do that again," I rushed out, my breathing beginning to pick up as I felt myself start to sweat and flush all over.

"Scarlett, look at me," Jackie demanded. I did as she said, staring into her serious gaze. "That is never going to happen again. The council would never allow it. I would never allow it. This is my home now, too, remember? When you and I made that promise a year ago that we would always watch out for each other, that wasn't something I took lightly. Forever and always, okay?" she said, raising her pinky between us. I released a shaky breath before hooking my pinky around hers and repeating her words.

"Something about him makes me careless," I confessed, my pinky still interlocked with her own. Her brows furrowed as she waited for me to explain. "It scares the shit out of me. I've never felt so out of control in my entire life. Even when I was with Eric. I was always one step ahead, I never lost my head around him," I said. The moment when I slapped Xander's hand away from the skillet lid flashed in my mind before I continued speaking. "When Adelia introduced us, this tiny, small, completely insignificant part of me was immediately intrigued because..." I trailed off, not wanting to say the words out loud.

"Because you're attracted to him," Jackie finished for me, clearly holding back a smug smile for my sake. "Scarlett, do not beat yourself up over the fact that you find the man you have an arranged mating with hot," she demanded.

"I'm not beating myself up over it," I grumbled, side-eyeing her. "I just...it was the first time since I met Eric that I realized me and my wolf were both checking a male out because we were into them, not because we were assessing the threat they posed," I revealed.

"Scarlett that's...huge," Jackie balked, looking at a loss for words.

"I have no idea how to process any of this, Jackie. Most of me wants to deal with this the way I've been dealing with everything the past two years to keep myself safe, but that small insignificant sliver of me..." I stopped, unable to even speak the words aloud.

"I think you should go at whatever pace feels right to you, but bear in mind that you have three weeks until you gotta do the naked tango with that beautiful, beautiful man downstairs," she giggled. The thought had a swarm of nervous butterflies arising in my stomach.

"I need to tell him I'm still a virgin," I rushed out bashfully. "Best to just rip the bandaid off now instead of waiting."

"Oh boy. I forgot about that. Most people would assume you and Eric did the deed with how long you were together," she nodded thoughtfully. "Oh please let me eavesdrop on that conversation too. I just bet his reaction is gonna be priceless," she begged. My cheeks flamed in response as I grabbed a decorative pillow from next to me and whacked her with it.

"No!" I hissed with finality before quickly standing and straightening the skirt of my dress. "How do I look? Like I've been crying my eyes out?" I asked pathetically.

She laughed, "yeah. C'mon. Let's fix you up before you go back down there." I allowed her to pull me into the attached bathroom and pick and prod at my face for a few minutes. I did look better coming out than when I went in, so I was thankful for her help. I was mindful not to fidget too much as I steadily made my way back to the kitchen-slash-living room where I was hoping to find Xander. Thankfully for me, he was relaxed on the couch watching TV so I didn't have to go searching. He gave me his full attention the second he saw me, something that was a bit unnerving, but I didn't show it.

"There's something we need to talk about," I stated, keeping my tone diplomatic as I folded my hands in front of me. He raised his eyebrows in question before reaching forward for the remote. Turning off the TV, he repositioned himself so he was sitting up rather than casually slouching back. I took a deep breath before sitting on the opposite end of the couch, leaving an entire seat cushion of space between us. I fiddled with my fingers in my lap for few a brief seconds before giving myself a mental shove to get on with it.

"I'm not sure how much they told you about my past mating-" I started, but he cut me off.

"Just his name," he informed me. I nodded. I knew he would already know that much as Adelia had disclosed this to me. This was good. The less he knew, the less I had to disclose and explain.

For now, I guess. I could just come right out with what I wanted to tell him and that would be that.

"As far as our mating in almost three weeks goes," I said, stopping to clear my throat as I shifted uncomfortably in my seat, "I think it's important for you to know that I'm...I'm still a virgin," I rushed out while staring straight ahead at the blank TV in front of us. He'd been taking a sip of water at that exact moment, resulting in him choking on it profusely. I turned and eyed him, noting his wide eyes of surprise.

"Sorry...what?" he gasped, a few remnant coughs following his words. I squared my shoulders and met his gaze head-on.

"I'm still a virgin," I repeated with more confidence in my tone than before. A long period of silence followed.

"Scarlett, can I ask you about your past mating?" he questioned, looking like there were a million of them burning on his tongue. I sighed deeply before rubbing at my temple, feeling an impending headache already starting to arise there.

"I'd rather you didn't, but that would be a bit unfair of me considering what I just told you," I answered honestly.

"How long were you together?" was his first question. Wow, starting with a hard hitter. I met his gaze briefly before staring down at my fingers in my lap.

"Just briefly over a year," I stated matter-of-factly, hoping he didn't hear the waver in my voice as my mind recalled why I'd run in the first place.

"A year?" he sputtered.

"Infidelity on our partner's behalf is something our pasts have in common," I revealed cryptically.

"But even with infidelity considered, the marking is a very powerful force to ignore. And to be left incomplete for such a long amount of time...?" I huffed before turning to meet his gaze once again.

"He never fully marked me. He refused to do it at first and after a while I stopped asking him to," I stated before giving him a look that said I wasn't saying another word on the subject. Just speaking about it made the memories want to creep back up and overwhelm me. I tried to push them away, but they were a force to be reckoned with.

I could smell her on him the minute he stepped foot into our bedroom. It made my stomach churn with self-hatred and the need to vomit. I bit the inside of my lip so hard it bled, my need to say something so strong but the bruises from this morning's breakfast slip-up were only starting to develop. He said the Alpha had a last-minute question about the end of the quarter finances. It was the same excuse he used two nights ago when he came back smelling like that woman who cleaned the pack offices.

It used to be a sick game of his he'd play with me. One of his favorite mind games. I used to beg and plead for him to finally mark me and take me to bed. But he would always say he 'wasn't in the mood'. Afterward, he'd disappear for a few hours and come back reeking of a different pack female. He'd show back up later and grab me by my hair - which was always in a pony because that was the easiest for him to jerk me around with - and he'd twist it around his hand real tight. Sometimes he'd pull me up off my feet and dangle me in the air, sometimes he'd just throw me across the room. Then he'd spend hours telling me how inadequate I was. How disappointed he was to have a mate like me. Fate had been unfair when pairing him with me. No male deserved someone so lowly. Someday, he was going to do me a favor and put me out of my misery. He'd rough me up just enough that the aggression he'd built up during the day wouldn't bother him and keep him from falling asleep before dragging me to bed with him; keeping me tucking tightly against his body so my nose was assaulted with smell of the sex he'd just had with another female less than an hour before all night long.

"Scarlett?" Xander's soft voice finally pulled me from the blackness clouding my vision. When I blinked it away, I realized I was clutching my hands together in front of my chest with my nails digging into my skin as my body gently rocked back and forth - a position I'd been forced into by Eric so many times I couldn't even count. Uncurling my hands I swallowed the thick lump in my throat before smoothing my thumb over the half-moon shapes my nails had accidentally dug into the skin on the backs of my hands.

"Would you like to go for a walk around the pack house?" he asked, entirely abandoning his previous line of questioning. His offer stunned me into momentary silence. It was times like these where I couldn't help but compare how different he was from Eric. Earlier in the kitchen helping me cook. Asking me questions and actually listening to me when I spoke. And now asking me to be seen with him in front of the pack.

Eric only permitted me to leave our wing of the pack house twice the entire time we were together. And both times were within the first few weeks we'd met. Every other time was when I'd snuck out. Not that I made it very far. I was always beaten severely for it. It looked like he was about to revoke his offer since I was taking forever to reply, so I quickly blurted the first thing I could think of.

"I just need to get my shoes." He nodded and stood to wait by the door that linked our place to the rest of the pack house. I grabbed my simple, worn-down flats as they were the only thing that would go with the hand-sewn long-sleeve dress I was wearing. I quickly slipped them on my feet. I stood slightly behind Xander as he opened the door and waited for him to leave first. I gave Tabby a soft smile and wave as we passed her on our way out. Upon hearing Xander awkwardly clear his throat I looked up to see him holding his hand out for me to take. My body coiled with tension, unsure of what to do as I stared at the offered hand.

"You can say no, Scarlett. I won't be angry," he said. "I just thought we could start with something small so you could get used to my touch," he murmured gently before lowering his hand back down to his side, not missing a step as he continued walking down the hall. His comment started an all-out war in my body. Then I started to think about what Jackie said about only having three weeks. Who knew how I would react once I actually touched him? Who knew how my wolf would react? How long would it take for me to get used to his touch? What if it took me three weeks to get used to it and I waited three weeks to finally find that out?

My head grew dizzy with the idea, but then the sound of his soft laughter snapped me out of my daze. "What are you laughing at?" I demanded, my steps coming to a halt as I stared at him. He had an easy-going smile on his face that only furthered my anger. I felt that familiar feeling of rebellious energy rise in my body as his smile grew to the point of one irritatingly sexy dimple popping out.

"I can practically hear your thoughts racing a mile a minute," he chuckled. I ground my teeth as my wolf rose to the surface. She wanted to challenge him. To push him. She wanted confirmation that he was going to snap like Eric always did. I knew she was only getting like this because I was under high levels of stress, but I couldn't help it; couldn't stop it.

"I'm glad one of us finds this humorous," I growled, malice lacing my tone as I glared at him. The amusement dropped from his face within seconds. Here it comes I thought, but all he did was sigh with resignation.

"I didn't mean to upset you. I'm sorry if I did. I was trying to lighten the mood," he explained, his tone apologetic with an irritated edge. My wolf paced in my head. This wasn't what she was expecting. We were prepared for violence. It's all we'd known. Now...now I had the oddest feeling of guilt. I felt like a total jerk. I just stood there feeling like an idiot. He turned and continued walking, towards where I wasn't sure, but I followed anyway.

After a few minutes of mental ping-pong with myself, I decided to just say, well...screw it. Biting the inside of my cheek, I reached forward and slid my hand into his that was closest to me, my hand sporting a minor tremor as I did so. His steps faltered for a millisecond before he caught himself. He adjusted the hold so that our fingers were interlaced before giving my hand a gentle squeeze. I didn't want to admit how much I liked the way my hand felt in his much larger one.

We settled into a comfortable pace beside one another despite his much longer legs. I expected the silence between us to feel uncomfortable, but it didn't. I wasn't desperately searching for something to talk about. It was...nice as much as it was strange. Though my wolf was still on high alert.

"What would you like to see first, the pack library or the movie room?" he asked while peering down at me. I didn't even have to give the question a single thought.

"Library," I answered confidently.

"The library is one of the largest rooms in the entire packhouse. Members are constantly donating to it from their personal collections. It started out as one wall of bookshelves when the packhouse was first built back in the 1900s. Obviously, that structure has long since been torn down and replaced by this new one, but those original bookshelves are still in this packhouse to this day," he said, coming to a stop at a pair of huge double doors. He let go of my hand - something I was surprised to say disappointed me - and opened the doors for me.

The sight of the massive room before me took my breath away. When you first stepped inside there were five old, worn-down wooden bookshelves. They had clearly seen better days, though they were still holding books.

"Those are the original bookshelves?" I assumed, walking up to them and running my hand along the fading wood.

"They are. A group of our elder pack women come together every year to do a bit of upkeep on them to ensure they continue to remain in the best shape they can for as many years as possible. All of these books are actually picture albums. They contain memories that date back as far as the late 1800s," he murmured, running his hand down one of the spines with a thoughtful look on his face before pulling it out of its spot.

"That's amazing," I breathed out. He flipped the book open before a wide smile encompassed his face, those dimples making another reappearance.

"This was my favorite one to look through as a kid," he said absentmindedly while flipping through the pictures before turning the book so I could see the photo he was looking at. It was a much younger Vanessa and Andrew smiling with so much love at one another. Vanessa was in a wedding dress while Andrew was dressed in a formal tux.

"Their wedding day," I stated knowingly, a smile of my own pulling at my lips. My eyes moved to the next picture, one of Vanessa and a toddler who couldn't have been older than two years old. The picture was in black and white, but I had a sneaking suspicion that the boy in the photo was Xander.

"Human weddings on top of regular mating ceremonies were just becoming popular within werewolf society when my parents found each other," he started to explain when he saw the look of curiosity in my eyes. "Being Alpha and Luna, they didn't realize that a big extravagant wedding would be expected of them, but every pack loves a good reason to party. They were already pregnant with me from the night of their mating, so they decided to put the wedding off until I was old enough to be a part of it. I was their ring bearer."

"I'm assuming that's what's expected of us as well? A big extravagant wedding after the mating ceremony?" I inquired, looking away from the picture to meet his eyes. He looked surprised that I was even bringing up our mating.

He breathed deeply. "Most likely, yes. However, nowadays they're typically intertwined together. Most people do both at the same time these days, but the wedding can wait. I don't want...to overwhelm you. I saw what my sister went through to plan her wedding and that was a nightmare. We can take our wedding at whatever pace we decide," he insisted vehemently.

# CHapTer 14

Scarlett's POV

I'd come to realize that I really didn't like it when people surprised me. Well, what I truly mean is that I didn't like it when people didn't live up to the preconceived expectations I had made up in my mind about them.

I had been living with Xander for three days now. Living was a very loose term. Despite my intense fear of sharing a bed with him from the get-go, he had insisted on sleeping in the guest bedroom. The conversation started with me awkwardly hovering by the bed after I'd changed into my pajamas - which consisted of a long-sleeve shirt and pajama pants with my hair hanging down my back, freshly brushed. He emerged from the closet in nothing but a pair of boxers. He smirked after catching me ogling his body plain as day before I realized I wasn't even trying to be discreet about it.

The man obviously trained rigorously, that much was clear to see. My eyes didn't miss the multiple large scars slashed across his chest and arms, something I wanted to ask about but refrained from doing. I turned my gaze to my feet and shifted my weight from foot to foot as I tried to quell the heat in my burning cheeks.

It was then that I realized my wolf had released just the tiniest scent of desire from my body. Cue mortification in three, two, one.

I knew Xander had smelled it. His eyes briefly shifted before he gave his head a firm shake and grabbed a pillow. The one I hadn't been sleeping on the past few nights. He tucked it under his arm as I gave him a questioning look due to the gesture.

"You can sleep in here to get more comfortable with your surroundings, but I don't think it's wise for us to sleep in the same bed right away. There's no need to overwhelm you on night one. I'll be in the guest room just down the hall if you need me for any reason," he told me before walking out. I never thought I'd get my jaw back into place after that conversation. Ever.

I expected him to kick me out of his bed. Tell me to get lost and sleep in the guest bedroom. I mean, this was his bed. He was a large - scratch that, huge - man. This bed looked custom-made. There was no way he would fully fit on the bed in the guest bedroom comfortably. But, despite all that, the guest bedroom was where he'd resided every night since he'd arrived back. I felt awful considering all I did in his massive, comfortable bed was toss and turn until the sun came up and I finally surrendered to the fact I wasn't getting any sleep again.

Despite the fact my Luna duties were being put off until after our mating, Xander still spent the majority of his days tending to his Alpha duties. Except for the day they had originally returned. I didn't mind, though. I was still incredibly torn on where the heck my brain, body, and wolf stood where he was concerned. One minute I was open to the idea of mating with him, and the next I was on the verge of having a panic attack.

I was thankful to at least have the company of my four guards that I trusted when Jackie was off screwing Justin's brains out. I couldn't blame her. Their bond was still new. Or so I figured was the case. What did I know? I'd never had that kind of connection with anyone, so I had nothing to compare it to besides stories people told me about their experiences.

With it being day three without any sleep, I didn't foresee myself being able to spend the entire day training with my guards like I had the previous two. I wouldn't be able to sustain myself much longer if my days kept on like this. Throwing the covers back with a grunt, I pulled myself out of bed and proceeded to shower and brush my teeth. I slipped into one of the few outfits I had before making my way down to the kitchen. With how tired my body was starting to become, my stomach wasn't feeling particularly hungry. That meant breakfast was out of the question. I plopped down onto the sofa, rubbing my hands down my face to wipe away the remnant sleepiness before I was left with a feeling of what now?

My eyes caught sight of my sewing machine and the box of fabric that had just been delivered yesterday. Finally. It has apparently got lost in the mail for a short time. Well, I guess I could try sewing another dress I thought to myself. I was lacking in the wardrobe department and there wasn't anything else for me to do except sit around and twiddle my thumbs while I waited for Xander, or somebody else, to show up. I lugged the sewing machine to the dining table and plugged it in before picking out the fabric I wanted to use. I chose a new roll of incredibly soft, baby-pink jersey material that Elder Adelia bought me for Christmas last year. I'd been eyeing it online for some time, but I could never justify the outrageous price for an entire roll of it.

After picking my fabric, I also pulled out a few pieces of scratch paper and a pencil from the box that housed the sewing machine. I drew up a rough-looking stencil with my measurements in mind, hoping the final product would turn out even half as good as the last dress Adelia and I made together. With my stencils complete, I cut the fabric accordingly before beginning to slowly sew the pieces right-sides together. As a beginner, it usually took me forever and a day to sew because I was terrified of going too fast and messing up a stitch.

I lost track of time as I worked on the dress, having to rip a few messed-up seams here and there. I had the top half completely done and was attaching the skirt, feeding the material through the needle when a knock at the door caught me off guard and pulled me out of the zone. I forgot to take my foot off the lever when I looked up as Xander walked through the door - no surprise considering he was the only person I wasn't comfortable with who was ever able to catch me off guard. It resulted in the needle accidentally stabbing my finger. I cried out before ripping my finger away so I could hopefully avoid getting any blood on the light-colored fabric of the dress. I cradled the finger in question to my chest while my eyes scanned the fabric for any spots of blood that might've landed on it.

"Are you alright?" Xander's deep voice right next to my ear caught me off guard for a second time, making me jump yet again. I sighed deeply, trying to mentally calm my racing heart.

"I'm fine. I wasn't paying attention and stuck myself," I muttered as my finger started to sting more intensely.

"Let me see," he said, reaching forward for my hand that I was holding to my chest. I furrowed my brows before slowly extending my hand for him to inspect the injured finger. This request interested my wolf immensely. It was a minor bleed so it would be healed in a few minutes, but I eyed him closely.

"You got yourself pretty good," he commented off-handedly before wiping my blood away with the hem of his shirt - something that shocked me speechless and made my wolf thump her tail once. She was....unsure. He continued to inspect the wound for a few seconds before releasing my hand. "What're you making?" he asked, his hand picking up the pink fabric that was dangling off the table and fingering it. He let the fabric drop from his hand as he took a seat next to me at the table.

"A dress. I'm not so sure how it's going to turn out," I confessed. That made him smile.

"I took the day off early so we could go into town for a bit of shopping. I couldn't help but notice that your side of the closet is rather...bare," he stated with a wince. "There's a nice shopping mall about an hour from here. It's pretty popular with all the pack women. Or so I've been told."

The thought immediately made me sweat. Leaving to get groceries thirty minutes away was one thing. Going an hour away was an entirely different thing. Montana was a big state, but I had no idea who I could potentially run into at a shopping mall an hour away. Who's to say I wouldn't run into one of Eric's men who would recognize my smell? They probably wouldn't remember my face because they hardly ever saw me, and when they did my face was usually mangled with busted lips and bruises, but they would know my smell. And then they'd run back to Eric and tell him where I was. He'd be angry. So angry. He'd know exactly where to find me. He'd come after me.

No. Too risky. Not worth it. I shook my head back and forth rapidly. "No. No, thank you," I rushed out before swallowing the thick lump that had formed in my throat.

"You don't want to go shopping?" he marveled. It wasn't that I didn't want to go shopping per se. I knew I needed new clothes. However, shopping had always been more of a chore rather than something I actually enjoyed. I didn't want to voice my fears out loud. I knew they were probably irrational, but that didn't matter to me. I'd fought so hard to get out of that vile man's grip. I didn't want to jeopardize my freedom for something as meaningless as clothes. I just shook my head no at his question before placing my hands back on the fabric and starting to sew again.

"Can I ask why?" he questioned, his tone telling me he didn't believe me. I stirred over the question for a second, my hand instinctively going to the worst of the scars on my back. Looking at him, I saw that his gaze had followed the movement of my hand. "You'll be safe with me, Scarlett. No matter where we go," he stated confidently.

I had to choose my next words very carefully. "I'm...not saying I won't be safe. I'd just much rather prefer to do any shopping online." He narrowed his eyes quizzically before leaning back in his chair.

"Is that how you did things when you lived with the council?" he asked. I could feel my wolf growing closer to the surface. She was quickly becoming agitated with his questions. They made us both feel stripped. Bare. If I told the truth and said yes, he would ask why I didn't have more clothes than I did. That would lead to me avoiding a conversation about Eric controlling me with finances. If I lied and said no, then he would continue to push the subject of why I didn't want to go out to do my shopping. He'd started talking again, but my wolf had tuned him completely out. She wanted to test him again. Push him. Push his buttons. Make him snap.

Interrupt him while he's talking. That was one of Eric's biggest pet peeves and one of the surest of ways to secure a beating.

"Scarlett, if this is an issue of money-"

"I'm not foolish enough to not know where your pack is located," I abruptly cut him off, my tone abrasive as I squared my shoulders and shot him a look over my eyelashes from where I'd been focusing on my hands. He stopped talking and waited for me to continue with an annoyed look. My wolf waited. "And you're not foolish enough to not know that the Sablefur pack is located within the same state - how many hours away I'm not exactly privy to, but I'm sure you are. I'd rather live the rest of my life with nothing in that closet than go to this mall you're speaking of and chance..." I finally stopped, biting my tongue when I realized that in my anger and rebellion, I'd said far too much. I swallowed thickly before clearing my throat, going back to the final few stitches with shaking hands that I knew he could see.

He didn't say a single word, just sat there studying me with a watchful gaze. I forced my body to relax so as to seem like his presence wasn't affecting me, finally getting my hands to cooperate and stop shaking. I could freaking do this. He still hadn't moved when I pulled the finished dress out from the machine and cut the attached string loose. I held the garment out in front of me and examined my handy work, impressed with myself and my ability to whip something decent together all on my own.

"Scarlett," he grunted, his tone harsher than anything he'd used with me ever before. My heart began to pound in my chest as my entire body readied itself for a fight. My wolf immediately raced to the forefront - the pressure just beneath my eyes a familiar feeling - ready to leap into action if needed. I just quirked a single eyebrow up in response, untrusting of my voice to portray the confidence I needed it to at the moment.

"I told you I could protect you. I meant that. I would put myself in harm's way to keep you safe. We won't go today, but you need new clothes. I'll take tomorrow off early again and we're going to that mall. There's very little chance anyone from your old pack will be there. Plan accordingly for the trip," he ordered while standing from his chair, preparing to leave to go back to work I was assuming. I felt the pressure behind my eyes as they shifted colors, my wolf coming completely forward. I just told him I wasn't going, but maybe he needed his fucking ears cleaned. I was not going to sit here and be told what I was and wasn't going to do, I'd had enough of that with Eric.

Push him. Make him break. Snap the resolve.

"I don't know who you think you are to give me orders and expect me to just nod my head and blindly follow them, but that's not how this is going to go. I very clearly just said I was not going to that mall. I'm not going to repeat myself," I growled, pushing out of my seat and looking him square in the eyes. "And I can fucking protect myself. I've done it before. I did it for a year. And then again for two more after that. I can do it again," I hissed.

"Who do I think I am?" he rumbled, taking a single step towards me, his own eyes flashing. I steeled my spine to keep from stepping away in fear, but my legs were secretly shaking. "Who do I think I am? I'm to be your mate. That's who I know I am. I'm the man who simply has your best interest in mind and wants to take care of you if you'd stop fighting me every step of the way!" he continued, his voice beginning to raise in volume and anger. I carefully eased back a few steps, hoping he wouldn't notice so I could bolt - but, of course, he did. He released a resigned growl before turning and quickly making for the exit before I could, but he paused on his way out.

"Oh, and I think it's high time we started sharing a bed. I'll see you tonight," he stated before shutting the door behind him with a slam. I sucked in a harsh breath as my entire body started to sweat. He's punishing me. He has to be. This is how it all started with Eric - the mental games. I knew it. I fucking knew it. They're all the same. This was too good to be true. I knew it.

I wouldn't let myself tuck tail and run, though. I refused. He wanted to play games? Fine. I could play with the best of them.

He had no idea what I could endure. I'd play his little games until the day Elder Adelia showed up right before our required mating. The second she did, I was forcing her to see this man for what he truly was before getting me the hell out of here. Things wouldn't go back to normal like I'd wished they could with Jackie being stuck here with her mate and all, but hopefully, she could come visit every once in a while.

Later that night when dinner was done cooking, I slipped into the new dress I'd sewn. The color made me look like the embodiment of innocence and femininity. I'd decided to cook something hearty but simple tonight; thick potato soup and a homemade French baguette with butter spread to dip in the soup. I'd yet to make anything home-cooked for dinner. Matter-of-fact, I hadn't cooked a meal for Xander since breakfast the first morning we'd met. He usually was gone until dinner, and then Vanessa would send someone to deliver a portion of whatever the pack was having to our place every night for us.

I already told her we wouldn't be needing food tonight as I was cooking. I could hear the smile in her voice when we'd spoken about it. If only she'd known I'd had an ulterior motive behind my actions. I felt bad - like I was deceiving her - but I pushed it away.

I glanced at myself in the microwave's reflection. I smoothed down the soft curls I'd done to my hair as nervous butterflies flitted around in my stomach. He wants to play house so bad and act like a mated couple despite my bare neck? Fine. I'll bite. I'll play dutiful little mate. I've done it before. I can do it again. Forcefully pushing away a few dark memories that wanted to surface, I picked up a serving spoon and stirred the soup just as three quick knocks came to the door.

Show time. I didn't turn as I heard him enter, but I bit my bottom lip when the smell of his beta and gamma met my nose. So we have company...I picked up the hand towel I'd been using and wiped my hands, but it was only an excuse to keep my hands busy as I turned to meet all three of their eyes. I met Xander's...apprecia tive gaze first. His eyes wandered up and down my body before finally landing on my face. His irises flickered for a few seconds before settling down. I averted my gaze to meet Donovan and Griffin's briefly, nodding in acknowledgment. They returned the sentiment with looks of equal unease. Why, I was unsure.

"Will you both be staying for dinner?" I asked. I highly doubted they would. They both had families of their own to return to, but I figured it was the polite thing to ask. And I hoped it would irritate Xander. It would've pissed off Eric, that much I knew.

"No," Xander grunted out before either of them could respond, though Donovan had opened his mouth to reply. He closed his mouth briefly, shooting Xander an amused smirk before turning his attention back to me.

"Thank you for the offer. It smells wonderful, but both of our mates are waiting for us with dinner of their own," he responded. I nodded, my eyes tracking Xander's every move as he crossed the living room and entered the kitchen.

"What's for dinner?" he asked followed by a slight lick of his lips, his eyes wandering to the pot behind me with curiosity.

"Potato soup," I answered simply, wondering why the men were with him if they weren't coming to eat with him.

"We'll go grab those documents from the office and then we'll be out of your hair," Griffin stated looking back and forth between Xander and I before grabbing the back of Donovan's shirt and pulling him with as he approached the stairs.

The tension grew ten-fold after the men had left as promised. I served him a big portion of soup and bread. Tonight, I didn't wait for him to start eating before I took my first bite. Not a single word was exchanged between the two of us as we ate.

Or as we cleaned up from dinner.

Or as we got ready for bed.

Setting my toothbrush back in its normal spot, I squeezed my hand into a tight fist to quell the tremor before releasing it. I ran my hands over the front of my long-sleeve top to rid them of the sweat they'd accumulated. Xander had already changed and done his entire night routine. Turning, I stared at the bathroom door. I told myself I would give myself ten more seconds in the safety of the bathroom before I opened the door to discover if he was serious about us finally sharing a bed.

10...9...8...

# CHAPTER 15

Scarlett's POV

3...2...1...I slowly reached out and grasped the doorknob, holding my breath as I turned the cool metal and pushed the door open. It felt like my stomach dropped to my ass as I saw him lying on the opposite side of the bed from where I usually laid. My mouth instantly went dry and I struggled to swallow the lump in my throat. My tongue felt too big and my head felt fuzzy.

You can do this. Don't let him win. You made it through Eric. This is a walk in the park compared to what you've been through. I released a silent, shaky breath before strengthening my resolve and walking out of the bathroom. I kept my face stone-like and impassive as I approached the bed, avoiding eye contact as he glanced up from his phone to look at me. I methodically pulled the covers back from my side of the bed and got in. My entire body felt like there were pins and needles all over my skin as I climbed under the covers and rolled onto my side so my back was facing him. Every single instinct in my body was screaming at me for turning my back on the enemy, but it was strategic. I had to let him feel like he didn't scare me. Didn't threaten me. He wasn't someone I gave consideration to; not one worth a second thought in my mind.

Every single muscle in my body was tense as I reached up and turned off my lamp, leaving the only other light in the room coming from his. I could feel his eyes on me, coasting over my body, before he sighed deeply and turned off his own light. The tension in my body rose as we were cloaked in darkness. My wolf instantly rose to the surface, on high alert and constantly scanning the sounds and smells around us for any detection of an attack.

I didn't know what to expect when Xander said we would be sharing a bed from now on. With Eric, I was so used to him holding me hostage against his body while awake - his only intention being for me to smell the other women and what they'd done together on his body - but then the second he'd fallen asleep, he would naturally release me and turn completely away. Even in his sleep, when he was no longer in control of his conscious brain, he hadn't wanted me; hadn't yearned for me the way a mate was supposed to. The memory made a single tear slip down my cheek, catching me by surprise. I quickly wiped it away, hoping like hell Xander wouldn't be able to smell its saltiness and start asking questions.

I released a silent sigh of relief when I simultaneously felt the bed shift and heard Xander roll onto his side. Glancing over my shoulder, I saw his own back facing me. Good, he didn't plan on touching me. The bed was so big that even with how large Xander was, there was at least a two-person gap between our bodies - something that brought me some mental comfort. Though, it didn't ease my body.

Day five of no sleep, here we come.

I wasn't sure exactly how many hours I'd been lying there wide awake when it happened. The 'it' in question was Xander rolling over, his huge hand sliding over my upright hip and curving around to my stomach, his palm flattening over my belly as his fingers splayed wide. Then, as if that wasn't enough of a massive shock to my freaking system, he roughly jerked my body back against his own and laced his legs through mine. His hand moved away as his beefy arm took its place locked against my stomach at the exact same time his nose dove down into the crook of my neck.

I gasped quietly as my entire body completely froze in utter shock before a raspy groan of contentment rumbled out of Xander's chest. I didn't dare move - not that I could have even if I wanted to. He was quite literally wrapped around me like a boa constrictor. I tried my best to process what the HELL had just happened. Even my wolf was stunned - and that never happened.

I angled my face just the tiniest bit to get a whiff of his skin, picking up his pheromones, and was stupefied. He was....asleep. Fast asleep. Completely passed out. Not a single trace of consciousness to be found. Lying here, wrapped around me with his nose pressed against the most intimate area of my body breathing in my scent...that's where- I cut the thought process off as my throat grew thick with emotion and my wolf started thumping her tail against the confines of my head.

She wanted to hate this man. And his wolf. How were we supposed to hate this man and his wolf after this? How was I supposed to hate him when the most primal side of him wanted ...this? There was no mark urging this on. There was no mating pull to encourage this behavior. There was nothing that could be influencing him to want me other than just...him wanting me. Something about that revelation had the smallest bit of tension in my body releasing as I carefully turned in his arms to face him. As I turned and moved out of our position, he released a quiet, slightly annoyed growl in his sleep before moving us so we were pressed against one another and his nose was once again in the crook of my neck.

My heart sped up. What if this was a fluke? It was possible. Highly likely, even. I didn't know anything about him or his sexual tendencies. What if he had a woman in his bed every night? What if he was one of those Alphas that screwed a new woman every week just because he could? He was certainly handsome enough to get away with it. What if this cuddling was just a result of always having a woman in his bed? The thought made me angry, but I couldn't be sure. I knew Jackie would know - she always knew the hot gossip like this. Plus, she would now have the inside scoop since she was screwing his cousin.

However, I also wanted to test this theory beyond just tonight. What if he only pulls me close tonight and my heart is racing for nothing? I'd feel really, really dumb, now wouldn't I?

But, it wasn't just that night that he pulled me close after falling asleep and held me there the rest of the night. It was the next night, and the night after that, and the night after that...each morning was the exact same as the very first. I would close my eyes and steady my heart rate and breathing. He'd awkwardly untangle his body from my own before slipping out of bed, quickly change into his suit for his day of work, and exit the room quietly as if nothing had happened. The only good that came from that first night of awkwardness was he dropped the shopping trip talk the next day altogether.

I had called Jackie the morning after the first night to ask her about Xander's past with women before me. I had to know if I was the hundredth woman warming his bed. If I was getting another Eric - but I guess without the cheating aspect as they'd have come before me.

I didn't want to admit that the jealousy that'd reared its ugly, fat head when the original thoughts took root that first night instantly went away when Jackie cackled right after I asked her about it.

"You're kidding right?" she had giggled.

"No, this is serious! No one's told me about his recent activity. Just that his mate isn't in the picture because he was cheated on. A lot of guys that get cheated on go out and screw everything with a pulse. I need to know if I should've bleached those sheets we slept on before we slept on them. Or if I should've thrown out the whole mattress," I growled.

"Relax, babe," she shot back defensively. "Justin told me he hasn't even looked at another woman since they had their marks dissolved and their souls unbound. Justin said they've tried multiple times to get him to hook up with random humans to release all that frustrated energy, but he never went for it. Always said it was never right for an Alpha to sleep around," she had explained. I also didn't want to admit how much I liked that answer.

"Ugh, I can't even imagine how good your guys' sex life is going to be once you finally mate. He's going to be releasing years of pent-up sexual frustration and you're going to be finally experiencing everything for the first time with a dude that is rumored to be gifted with a dick the size of-- baby, c'mon you know your dick is the only one I care about. Justin, come back. I was just teasing Scarlett. Baby, please? I'll do that thing with my tongue you really like?" And then the line went dead and that was the last I heard from her the rest of the day.

In hindsight, I was sorta glad she was so wrapped up in her mate right now. If she wasn't, she'd be here to see the atrocious bags under my eyes. She'd see how sunken in my eyes were from eight days without nearly any sleep at all. It was a miracle I was able to cake enough concealer over my face to keep Xander from asking questions, but I could feel the inevitable coming - the black dots that would surround my vision for just a few seconds before they eventually surrounded everything and pulled me under without warning - holding me captive for hours, maybe days. I'd started to hallucinate a few days ago, but it was nothing compared to what it used to be, so I just ignored it. The things I used to see and hear...yeah, I wasn't scared by these ones. I just had to keep reminding myself that it wasn't real and continue moving along.

I was too tired to eat anything except for dinner - which was the only meal Xander and I shared as he was usually caught up in work. So much for us spending the majority of our time together before our mating? I was too exhausted to question it, though. Everything took too much effort the past couple of days. Even training.

I wasn't sure how long it had been since Xander slipped out of bed this morning, but I finally pushed myself up and off the mattress. My legs buckled, but I was able to get a hold of the bedframe in time to keep myself from going down. I peeled my eyes open, the burn in them so intense it was almost unbearable. When the blurriness in them finally went away and my eyes focused, I realized I was staring at the bathtub in the bathroom.

Yes, a bath sounds so nice my sluggish brain conjured as I pulled my wolf forward and used every last ounce of energy she had to put one leg in front of the other before I was eventually standing in front of the jet-laden monstrosity. Filling it with scorching water I couldn't be bothered to close and lock the door before stripping and slipping into the water. I cried out quietly as I plopped down into the water, too weak to slowly ease my way in and give my skin the necessary time to adjust to the heated water. A few tears slipped out of my eyes at the searing pain, but it slowly subsided as I gently stroked my back and arms carefully.

My arm shook with exertion as I grabbed the bottle of bubble bath and squirted a generous amount in. The smell was nice as the bubbles began accumulating until there was a decent film over the top of the water. I let my head lull back against the porcelain back of the tub wishing my mind would just finally shut off and let me sleep. I just want to sleep.

"Hey!" the voice jostled me upright, some of the bubbly water, spilling over the side of the tub. I sucked my bottom lip into my mouth and dug my teeth into the soft, pliable flesh, scratching my nails against the sides of the tub roughly.

I sucked in a harsh breath as tears welled up in my eyes. If you don't speak, you can't anger him. He won't be provoked. I told myself. The water suddenly felt like it was boiling and the scars on my back were searing. I mistakenly released a choked sob of pain as a tear rolled down my cheek. Eric laughed wickedly, a glimmer of delight in his eyes.

"The nerve pain pills didn't help, did they Scar-lett. Such a fitting name for you, my mangled girl. I always said I'd make your body match that name of yours," he smiled wide before lathering his tongue over his bottom lip to wet the chapped thing - a habit I always hated. My chest heaved with the effort I was using to hold back my wails.

"Scarlett?" came the sound of a distant voice, but I was so delusional I didn't even register that it hadn't come out of Eric's mouth as his image loomed over me. I picked up the closest thing to me  - a candle I'd placed on the ledge of the tub - and chucked it as hard as I could at Eric's face. A mangled, distressed scream hurled from my mouth as it left my hand.

"Scarlett Lane," I immediately snapped back to reality. Only one person used my middle name. Turning my head to the side, I came face to face with Jackie. Immediately, I knew two things: firstly, I was busted for my insomnia streak based on the horrified look on her face. Secondly, Eric had been a hallucination. I sighed with relief, laying my arms on the edge of the tub and resting my cheek against them as I watched her eyes gloss over with tears. A huge wave of guilt slammed into me at the sight.

"I'm fine, Jacks. Please don't cry," I slurred, my tongue feeling thick. I watched as her chin quivered slightly before her cheek puckered in - meaning she was biting it to try and keep from crying harder. Dammit.

"I'm going to grab your pills and then you're sleeping," she stated before turning and leaving before I could even get a word in edgewise. I brought my hand up, rubbing the headache that was starting to form at my temple before releasing the breath I didn't know I'd been holding.

Xander's POV

"I see there've been some major changes in the budget over the past few days? Can we go over that?" I asked, turning my attention to Donovan as I slightly turned myself in my chair. I fucking hated these mid-month meetings. They happened every month like clockwork and despite their importance, they grated against my nerves. They typically consisted of about 20 people from different major areas of the pack. Because of the new year and the renewed pack treaties we'd signed this month, this one had been particularly grueling.

"So, the orphanage needed a lot of things that we weren't aware of-" Donovan had started to speak, but was interrupted as the doors to the large conference room we were in were abruptly, and aggressively, thrown open. I was surprised to see Justin's mate, Jackie, standing there with both a terrified and angered look on her face. It was an odd mixture of emotion. Uh oh, what did Justin do this time?

"Honey, you can't just barge into my meetings. I'll come find you when I'm done," Justin rushed out in a whisper before shooting everyone in the room an apologetic smile.

"Like hell I can't!" she growled before doing something I wasn't expecting - she turned her angered look from Justin to me. "Do you even pay any attention to Scarlett at all?" she hissed, a look of fury on her face. I threw an expectant look at Justin - it was his mate who was completely out of line after all - before meeting her gaze once again and squaring my shoulders.

"Excuse me?" I questioned. "It took me one look at her to know she's probably been I'd guess seven, maybe even eight, days without a single hour of sleep. By looks alone, and knowing her as well as I do, I can confidently say her body is going to shut down on her sometime within the next two hours - if not sooner. Any good mate would've noticed that something wasn't right by now. What the hell have you been doing? Because being even a half-decent mate isn't the answer!" she sneered before quickly turning on her heel and darting off. I felt my father's disappointed stare boring holes in the side of my face as my heart pounded in my chest.

Scarlett didn't seem like she was sick or hurt...

I cleared my throat before pushing out of my chair. "If you'll excuse me. This meeting is now concluded. We'll reschedule and pick back up at a later date," I rushed out before my legs quickly carried me in the direction Jackie had gone. I hastened my pace as I grew closer to our place. What if something is seriously wrong and I'm too late? Fuck.

The thought had me practically sprinting the rest of the way. I didn't bother knocking when I got there. Dashing up the stairs, I followed the scent to the bathroom where I found Jackie kneeling next to the tub.

"Please, Scarlett, just take the pill. I'm begging you. Last time you were gone for a week. Please," Jackie begged, her voice taking on a hysteric edge as she pushed a pill against Scarlett's chewed up lips. I saw her nostrils flare a few moments after I'd entered the bathroom, her body jerking up slowly and sloppily as if she were drunk. When her eyes centered on me, they were unfocused and hazy. All the air knocked out of my lungs at the sight of her. She looked...bordering death. What had happened? How could I have possibly missed this? I just had dinner with her last night. I sat across from her. I would've noticed if it was this bad. I would've noticed this. Wouldn't I?

"We need to get her out of the tub. If something happens while she's in it, she could drown," I insisted softly while unbuttoning my suit coat. I slipped it off and tossed it onto the bathroom counter. Undoing my cufflinks, I also tossed them away before rolling the sleeves of my dress shirt up my arms so as to not get them wet.

"When she's like this, she's dead weight. I can't lift her, but she won't let you near her when she's naked," Jackie responded knowingly, peering back at me with that same worried look in her eyes. I nodded before turning and coming face to face with a shattered mess of glass and... candle wax? I ignored it but made a mental note to ask about it later before quickly making my way to the closet. I pulled a t-shirt of mine off of the hanger and grabbed the first pair of her underwear I could find. I quickly came back to Jackie's side and handed the items over.

"Get these on her. Even if they get soaked, it's better than nothing. We need to get her out of there," I insisted before turning my back to give some privacy. The way Jackie spoke to Scarlett while she maneuvered her limbs into the articles of clothing was as if she were a mere child.

"Okay. You're just going to have to go for it. She...she's going to fight you. You need to reassure her. Tell her what you're doing. Tell her you're not going to hurt her or even trying to hurt her. She needs to hear that. Even if she keeps fighting," Jackie stressed. I nodded, releasing a deep breath before approaching the tub. I crouched down, swallowing thickly as I reached my arms in and wound them around her form. The second my arm made contact with her back, her eyes shot open and narrowed at me. Her body started bucking in my arms, but I had a firm grip on her.

"Scarlett, I'm not going to hurt you. I want to make sure you're safe," I stated evenly and confidently. Her arms came up to bat at my chest, push me away, reach around and try to shove my arm away from her back. "Scarlett, I need to make sure you're safe," I grunted as I made my way towards the bed. She would soak the sheets, but there was a spare pair in the linen closet. As soon as we were close enough, I released her onto the bed. Her arms immediately wrapped around her front in a protective manner. And that's when I saw them.

The scars.

They were littered all along the backs of her arms. Some were little, but most of them were huge gashes. Thick, pink, puffy scars that told the tale of a whip held by someone who clearly had no fucking mercy. My eyes widened as I took in the sight of them. This is why I've never seen her in anything but long sleeves. She finally noticed that I wasn't looking at her and followed my line of sight. She dropped her arms quick as lightning and reached under her pillow, producing the same knife she'd pulled on me the first day we'd met. She slept with it under her pillow?!

I raised my arms in surrender as I heard Jackie come up behind me, a quiet oh no releasing from her lips.

"Scarlett, I'm not going to hurt you. I want you to sleep. You need to sleep. Jackie is going to stay with you while you sleep. I'm going to send all four of your guards up to stand watch. You and your wolf will be safe here. I'll be downstairs. No one is going to get to you. I promise," I said before slowly and carefully backing away while maintaining eye contact.

Once out of the room, I found it hard to walk away. I didn't want to leave. I wanted to stay behind and be the one to lie with her and make sure she was alright. I couldn't believe that I'd been so fucking careless with my own mate. I mind-linked for my mother to find her guards and send them immediately, letting them know it was an emergency. I could feel my mother's worry through our bond, but I didn't have time to explain and I wasn't going to air Scarlett's dirty laundry.

Not when I knew I was part of the reason she wasn't sleeping. That much I knew to be true. I'd been the absolute dickhead that pushed her three days ago during our argument and demanded we start sleeping together. I was angry and wanted to have the last word. It was childish and I didn't expect her to go through with it. But then she did. After that first night when I woke up practically wrapped around her like a damn blanket...and after the best night of sleep I'd had in years...well, I was a selfish prick. I didn't say what I'd planned to say.

I'm sorry for pushing you. I'll move back to the guest bedroom. While I've been refreshed and feeling amazing the past three mornings, she's been torturing herself. And I didn't even...didn't even notice because I'm a dick. And a terrible mate. Maybe that's why Mika cheated, not because she's also a horrible mate. I ran a stressed hand through my hair just as a frantic knock came to the door. I swung it open and met the worried gazes of Scarlett's four female guard's - faces I'd come to be quickly accustomed to in the last few days. I didn't even notice that they hadn't been around today. She must've told them to take today off so they wouldn't suspect what was going on with her.

She's smart, but not to the benefit of her well-being.

"Thank you for getting here so quickly. There isn't time to explain, but I know Scarlett and her wolf trust you four. I need you to go upstairs, assure her that you're all here for the next however many days, 24/7, and that she's safe. Go, now," I ordered. They nodded before rushing up the stairs. I then linked the six male guards who were originally hired to be her detail to come as well to take up their usual places.

I stealthily wandered up the stairs and peeked inside the bedroom doors. Jackie worked quickly as I was greeted with the sight of her and Scarlett - now wearing her usual long sleeve - lying on the freshly made bed with her four guards closely surrounding her, all touching her in some way.

I wanted so badly to go in, but I knew better.

# CHAPTER 16

Xander's POV

I spent around an hour pacing back and forth in the living room until I wasn't able to wait any longer. My wolf and I were both anxious to see how Scarlett was doing. Was she finally asleep? Had her body shut down on her like Jackie said it would? Or did she finally take the pill Jackie was trying to give her so she could fall asleep on her own?

I quietly eased the bedroom door open, mindful not to make a single sound, and entered the room. Jackie's eyes moved from where she was cradling Scarlett's head against her chest towards me before focusing her attention back on her friend. The four female guards were still positioned close by but weren't directly touching Scarlett like they had been earlier.

"Did she...?" I asked, my voice barely above a whisper so as to not wake Scarlett from her much-needed slumber.

"She took the pill, but I had to crush it up and rub it into her gums so it would work right away - get directly into her blood-stream. I was afraid waiting for it to travel to her stomach would take too long and by then her body would give out," she explained off-handedly while brushing a lock of damp hair that had fallen across Scarlett's face behind her cheek.

"How long will she be out for?" I questioned, unable to help myself as I took a few more steps towards the bed, my eyes focusing on Scarlett's form. I'd never seen her like this. So relaxed and at ease. She looked so innocent. It was completely different from how I was used to seeing her since I'd met her nearly six days ago. If I thought she was beautiful before, she was stunning when she let her guard down.

"It's hard to say," Jackie spoke before releasing a deep sigh, "at least twelve hours. Could be an entire day. Could be as long as a few days. There's no way of knowing. It all depends on how deprived her body was and how long her wolf feels safe enough to stay under," she murmured, stroking Scarlett's cheek affection-ately. Like a mother would her child.

"This is my fault," I finally ground out. I forced myself to look away from her angelic face out of shame as I stared out the bedroom window, watching the new flakes of snow fall and accu-mulate on top of the mounds that were already there. I swallowed before slowly approaching the window to shut the blinds as I let my comment sink in. The room was instantly bathed in darkness. I didn't want Scarlett to have to sleep in a room flooded with light reflecting off the bright snow.

"What do you mean?" Jackie finally asked.

"I was a dickhead and let my anger and the need to have the last word get the best of me. We had an argument about shopping. She didn't want to leave and go to the mall for fear of running into..." I stopped, knowing her female guards hadn't been told the name of her ex-mate. The thoughtful look we shared told me she knew exactly who I was talking about. "Superficially, it bruised my ego. More than that, it angered me that she didn't trust that I could keep her safe. Or doesn't trust my intentions when I say I will keep her safe. So I retaliated. I insisted that it was time we started sharing a bed as a way of growing closer. If I hadn't been so...damn stupid, she would've been sleeping at night. This wouldn't have happened," I hissed while gesturing toward her motionless body in the bed.

I ran my hands through my hair roughly as I started to pace the length of the room again, my anger at myself and my stupidity mounting again.

"While that definitely contributed, it's not the only reason for her inability to sleep. You've only been sharing a bed for how many nights now?" Jackie asked, not sparing my feelings one bit. I was glad she didn't.

"Three," I responded without thinking as I continued to pace, clenching and unclenching my fists. "Exactly. As I said before, she's probably been without enough sleep for about seven days now. Even considering the night I slept with her before you returned, it wasn't enough. Do the math, Alpha Harrington. There's a reason I said I could tell she was going to shut down just by a single look. This isn't the first time this has happened," she murmured, sadness lacing her tone. The weight of her words pulled me to a stop. I turned to look at her with a questioning gaze. She pursed her lips as her eyes grew misty. She cupped Scarlett's cheek softly before turning back to meet my eyes once again.

"When she finished...physically healing after first arriving at the council grounds and was cognitively with it, this was a regular occurrence. For months on end. She was so scared she was going to end up back...there for so long. It was like a never-ending cycle of insomnia then crash, insomnia then crash. Elder Adelia was the first wolf she finally came to trust. She was able to get her some sleeping pills. They're stronger than anything you'll see on the non-wolf market. They essentially force her body into a mini coma so she can recuperate. Elder Adelia would lie with Scarlett for however long she was out until her wolf fought the drugs off and came to," she finished.

"I didn't think it was physically possible to go so long without sleeping," I commented, a hint of horrified awe in my voice.

"Her record is eleven days straight without a single nap," she whispered as a somber, faraway look encompassed her face. Her lips pursed for a few seconds before she shook her head. I assumed shaking the memory away. She quietly cleared her throat before meeting my gaze again.

"She almost always starts hallucinating around day three or four. They're nothing major - not at first. And they're usually harmless. They were a bit different every time, but usually people. Kids she looked after and grew fond of at the various orphanages she was placed in."

"Not at first...?" I trailed off apprehensively. She released a tired sigh before surveying the women standing around the room, listening in.

"Ladies, can you do a survey of the house again, please?" Jackie asked quietly, but I knew it wasn't for safety purposes. They all sported unconvinced expressions but didn't say anything before quietly and swiftly leaving the room.

"Around day five, she'll start to hear his voice. Or used to at least. I'm not sure if it's changed - she doesn't have any patches of missing hair by her temples and ears, so that means she hasn't been pulling it out. That leads me to think therapy has altered some things permanently for the better. The worst hallucination I've ever personally seen her experience has only happened once. It was on day eleven of that one-time stretch just before she lost consciousness. There are some things she's never told even me about concerning what she's been through, but..." her voice caught in her throat as a few rouge tears slipped down her cheeks. "That day she was so out of it, she really believed she was right back there. Nothing could convince her otherwise. I can still hear her screams of agony in my nightmares, sometimes," she hiccuped out before meeting my gaze with such sad eyes. Her words made me look towards the bathroom where the shattered candle remained littering the floor.

"You nor I could ever possibly comprehend what she's been through, or what she did to get out of that situation. You have to understand and extend her grace for the self-preserving habits she has. The life she lives now - even if it doesn't look like much living to you and me - is practically paradise for her. She deserves someone who's going to do whatever possible and by any means possible to give her the sense of security she's never had." She leveled me with a harsh look.

"I'm still here aren't I?" I answered after a few moments of silence, thinking that answered her statement adequately. Wrong.

"You were still here the past three days, too," she countered, immediately making me wince. I reached up to rub the back of my neck as her words stung with truth.

"You're right. I need to step up. Have to. I came back and just kind of thought my life was going to go right back to normal. I don't know what I'm doing with her or how to take care of her, so instead of manning up I've been running away to work." I rasped out, averting my gaze to my feet in shame.

"Well, they always say admitting you have a problem is the first step in getting help," she said. I smirked.

"What do I need to do to make sure this doesn't happen again?" I asked with a determined expression.

"You're going to have to watch her after she wakes up from this. Closely. Make a good mental note of how she acts and looks when she's well-rested. She's very good about compensating for the exhaustion - both physical and mental - and covering up the physical signs as well. You need to be able to pick out the minute differences in her behavior when she starts to decline so you can recognize the need for her to take a pill. Close your eyes and take a good, deep scent of her right now," she ordered. It felt incredibly awkward, but I did it anyway. Noting exactly how she smelled - her and her wolf.

"That is what you should smell at night when she's supposed to be sleeping. Calm and relaxed. Both she and her wolf are at ease right now. When she's awake, you'll need to scent her again. She always has a tiny hint of cortisol and adrenaline mixed in when she's awake. It's very distinct. Know the difference in how she smells asleep versus awake so that you can call her out at night if she's gone more than 2 nights without sleeping. She will try and talk her way around it. Proof is the only way to cut through that.

"Set alarms at various times at night to get up and check on her. But always change them on a nightly basis to be at completely random times. She's smart and learned to school her body to fool Elder Adelia a few times into thinking she was asleep when she actually wasn't. She knows she needs to sleep, and if you can prove that you know she hasn't been sleeping, she'll take the pills. But you must be diligent," she insisted. I nodded, taking in everything she'd just told me.

"What if I had one of the guest bedrooms redecorated to look exactly like the room she slept in at the council grounds? Do you think that a sense of familiarity would help?" I asked, pondering the idea out loud.

"You would do that?" Jackie questioned, a look of astonishment on her face. I nodded without thinking.

"If it would help her, then absolutely. I could probably have it done before she wakes up if you think it would help." I replied. She looked at me with an unfamiliar expression for a few long seconds before finally nodding multiple times.

"I think that would definitely help. And Xander?" I raised an eyebrow in response. "You can't keep working all day like you have been. She's a master at flying under the radar and going unnoticed to survive. If you give her the opportunity, she'll do it. Then before you know it, your three weeks will be up, and you'll be mateless again. Because she will find a way to run. You have to hand the reins over to someone else right now. Even if it's just part-time." I nodded. Determination seeped into every pore as the word mateless rang through my mind as the image before me of Scarlett's peacefully sleeping frame burned a hole into my memory. That was not an option, and I wasn't going to allow it to happen.

I didn't say another word as I turned to head out the door. I mind-linked Donovan to let him know I was coming to meet him in his office.

"What's going on? Is Scarlett alright?" Donovan immediately asked the second I stepped into the office of his wing. I released a frustrated huff of air - at myself, not the situation - before easing into the chair across from his desk.

"She will be. I need to take a couple of measures to make sure this doesn't happen again. Which is why I'm here. I'm going to be doing a bit of renovating to my living quarters, so expect to see some invoices coming to you. They'll be handled through my personal account. And about that state-of-the-art security system we were testing out in the communal living quarters? Do we have results back yet from...what's the kid's name?" I muttered, trying to think of the young pack member that mated in about six months ago. He was insanely gifted with computers and technology.

"Alistair? Our head of technical security?" Donovan filled in for me a bit sarcastically. I nodded with a snap of my fingers in his direction.

"Yes, that one."

"We did. It's the best money can buy as far as he's concerned. Nothing else has come to the market like it or that can compete with it. He's installed a system to protect it from even the best hackers with it being digital. It's about as secure as we could possibly get. Why?"

"Perfect. I want it installed everywhere. Every single external pack door. Triggers on every pack window. I want cameras installed to watch cameras. I want to be able to see absolutely every inch of the exterior of the pack house and I want it in high resolution. Get as many men as it takes for it to be done by the end of tomorrow. I don't care about the expense. Contact Alistair and inform him about the change in the system so he can get in and secure...whatever needs securing once it's installed. And tell him that I want to be debriefed on how to use the system and be able to check the footage at any and all times," I stated nonsensically. His eyes had gone wide and his mouth was slightly agape by the time I was done speaking.

"Are we good? Do I need to cover anything again?" I asked, having someone else I needed to talk to.

"Uh, no. I got everything," he mumbled. I hummed in reply and pushed out of the chair, quickly making my way back to my own office. It was one of the two rooms Scarlett had left untouched - along with my poker room - and it was blatantly obvious. It was a complete disaster compared to the rest of the house and was at odds with the decoration. It felt cold and sterile in here as opposed to the rest of the place that now had a warm, soft appeal to it. The way my childhood home felt growing up.

Starting up my computer, I pulled up my video chat and typed in the number elder Adelia had given me in case of emergency or necessity and called it. It rang for what felt like forever until she finally answered.

"Xander, I've only just settled back home," Elder Adelia said in greeting with a worried furrow of her brow. I couldn't help the amused grin it pulled out of me.

"Don't ask," I said while running my hand through my hair and down the back of my head. "I need to ask a favor of you Elder Adelia. For Scarlett's sake."

"Anything," she insisted without hesitation. I could tell she loved Scarlett. It was clear to see.

"She's not sleeping," I began, my words causing her face to morph into the exact same expression of worry Jackie had been sporting earlier. Before she could stipulate about the situation, I continued talking. "I'd like to transform one of my guest bedrooms to look exactly like her room back at the council. If I could get some pictures of her old room to give to the decorator, that would be great. And if at all possible - if someone hasn't moved into her space yet - have you ship her actual furniture including the bed frame, mattress, bed sheets, all of it, here so that the room is filled with familiar scents as well. That would be great, too," I finished.

"I knew I made the right choice when I overruled Elder Thomas and chose you," she whispered, her voice thick with emotion. I smiled before her words registered in my mind.

"Wait, overruled and chose me?" I asked, a million questions flooding my mind at that moment.

"I'll have the furniture packed up and overnight shipped by the end of the day. I'll send a swatch of the paint we use. It's the same generic color throughout all the bedrooms in the living quarters. It was wonderful speaking with you, Alpha Harrington," she mused before ending the chat abruptly. I slumped back against my office hair and crossed my arms over my chest. What could she possibly mean by 'chose' me? Choose me from what? Who else was in the line-up?

I didn't let myself mull over the odd statement for long. I left my office, eager to get back and check on Scarlett again. I eased the door open quietly, wanting to rip it off its hinges when it creaked even the slightest. I mind-linked for one of the pack maintenance men to come oil it now. Then I corrected myself to just have them drop the oil off at the front door - I didn't want to risk their presence alarming Scarlett's wolf and waking her.

"She hasn't been very restless or moved much at all, which is good. It could also mean this is going to be a longer slumber," Jackie explained as I slowly inched closer to the edge of the bed. The four female guards had positioned themselves in various places around the room, but didn't pay me much mind past a respectful nod and 'Alpha Harrington' when I entered. My eyes darted to one of the sofa chairs in the sitting area of my room. Before I could think better of it, I was making my way over to it, quietly picking the chair up and moving it to sit right next to the side of the bed.

Jackie watched me carefully as I sat down in the now-relocated chair. She quirked an eyebrow at me in silent question.

"I'm having a state-of-the-art security system installed throughout and around the entire pack house. No inch of this place will be untouched. It's the best that money can buy. I'm going to set up a device so Scarlett can have access to view the entire perimeter of the house in real-time at whatever time she wants. We have stringent border security, but I figured this would hopefully help her feel safe here. Also, all her original furniture from her council room is being shipped here to go into the room to be redecorated. Elder Adelia is going to overnight express it as well as the paint swatch of the walls," I informed her.

I wasn't sure if my plans were well perceived as I was focused on Scarlett. An intense urge to reach out and grasp her hand - like the way we had when we went for a walk around the pack house - grabbed hold of me. I placed my hand flat on the mattress and slowly inched it towards where her own was, fingers splayed against the soft sheets - I think she must use that stuff my mom always talked about...clothes softener I think it was called?

"Alpha Harrington," Jackie whispered softly in warning. I was monitoring her face, and even as I inched closer she didn't stir. She didn't grow restless. I paused for a brief second as I was a hair's breadth away. I picked my hand up gently and with a delicacy I didn't know I possessed, I placed it atop of her own. Maybe two seconds passed before her inner eyebrows furrowed inward and down. She took a deeper breath than the one before. Her fingers twitched a few times. I took it as a positive sign and slightly curled my fingers around her palm.

Big mistake.

Still dead asleep, her hand snapped to snatch mine in a vice grip. It took every ounce of self-restraint I had inside not to shout in pain. I knew for a fact at least my pinky finger was broken, if not more. I bit my lip to keep from yelling. Doing the only thing I could think to do in the moment, I started to rub my thumb back and forth across the knuckles of her hand that was currently squeezing the life out of mine. After a minute of my gentle stroking, her brows unfurrowed and the pressure around my hand slowly began to release. I let out the breath of air I'd been holding. Turning my head, I leaned down to wipe the few beads of sweat that had accumulated on my forehead onto my shirt sleeve.

Scarlett lowered our still-joined hands back to the bed. I didn't dare stop caressing her hand for fear she might take mine hostage again. And hers were so soft. And small. Dainty. I wondered what they would feel like pressed against my cheek. Or the back of my forehead when I didn't feel good and she was checking if I felt hot. I liked those scenarios a lot.

I widened the area of my touch to the back of her hand and not just her knuckles. Eventually, the rhythmic motion of my caressing tired even me. I couldn't help but lean forward to rest my head against the mattress. I wasn't sure what time it was, but the comforting smell of her soothing pheromones and the soft touch of her skin against my hand lulled me into a deep sleep.

# CHAPTER 17

X ander's POV

My eyes shot open as my wolf awoke me. He sensed someone approaching. It was an entirely new habit he had developed over the past three days. I wasn't sure how, and it wasn't intentional, but it came in handy. The hand Scarlett had pressed against my upper chest twitched as the person grew closer to our bedroom doors. I scented the air, identifying the person as Alistair just as a light knock sounded from our bedroom door. Scarlett's fingers fisted the material of my shirt. Her breathing grew lighter and a touch quicker.

'Leave. I'll meet you in my office,' I mind-linked him. I listened as his footsteps fell away, but kept my gaze focused on Scarlett. The further his footsteps sounded, the more Scarlett relaxed. I lifted my hand from where it was stroking the side of her hip and cupped her cheek. The pad of my thumb swiped along her cheekbone, just a bit more defined now than it was prior to her slumber. I mind-linked for Jackie to come and lay with her in my absence.

"I'll be back soon," I murmured - so softly it was barely more than a rumble from my chest - just as I heard the door open and Jackie enter. I carefully extracted myself from her grasp and allowed Jackie to take my place. I peeked at the alarm clock on the nightstand before I went, reorienting myself a bit. Six-thirty? Damn, that was a killer four-hour nap.

The past three days have been...so odd. However, if I had a choice after today then all of my rigorous training days would be immediately followed by a mid-afternoon nap with my mate. My body wasn't sore. I wasn't tired. I felt refreshed mentally and physically - like I could go an entire training session with the pack warriors all over again with no issues.

The journey in getting to where Scarlett and I now were was a long and careful one. She and her wolf - but mainly her wolf - were comfortable and would allow me to lie next to her in bed. And not only allowing me to lie next to her but even going so far as to take the initiative in her sleep to reach out and touch me.

It started with that first night. I fell asleep right there with only my head on the mattress and her hand held in my own. That's how things stayed for a few hours until my upper back was completely cramped, locking up on me in the middle of the night. I gently eased inch after inch of my upper body onto the bed under Jackie's watchful guidance. It took a couple of hours, but the awkward hunched-over-slash-lying position was better than the hovering position I had been in previously.

Then, things progressed from only stroking her knuckles and hand to stroking her lower forearm. It was something I'd done in my sleep and she hadn't objected to. Or at least that's how I took it because she and her wolf had still been contentedly asleep, not threatened by me or my touch. So I continued it while I was awake.

I felt a bit dumb for how giddy the small progress - having my upper body on the bed and touching her forearm - made me feel. Somehow, I couldn't quell the notion that I'd just won an Olympic gold medal from how Jackie watched on with a look of wonder. However, truly nothing could compare to how it felt when Scarlett started slowly gravitating towards my body. It typically happened when I would return throughout the afternoon after being frequently pulled away.

I would slowly resume my awkwardly hunched-over position. Before I could even reach for her hand, her chest would press into the mattress ever so slightly as she rolled a bit my way. Her hand would inch towards my direction. When I would take her hand into my own, engulfing the tiny thing in the warmth of my giant ones, she'd release this damn adorable sigh that sounded just like contentment. Or at least, I wanted that to be what it was. Hoped it was.

That evening was when Jackie brought up the idea of me fully lying in bed with Scarlett. I'd been vehemently against the idea at first. Under no circumstance did I want to cause her any more problems than I already had. What if that's what caused her to forcefully wake up and the first thing she saw was me lying there like an idiot? She'd freak out! She'd never trust me again.

Despite voicing all these concerns to Jackie, she reassured me. She had already thought about those scenarios as well. However, with how Scarlett and her wolf had been reacting to me so far, she didn't foresee any of them occurring. She told me when I was here, touching her, Scarlett actually slept more soundly.

I wasn't so sure about that. I think she said it to make me feel better. I'll admit, I did like the idea a lot.

So, despite my nerves about the situation, I slower than ever before eased into a sitting position on the edge of the bed under Jackie's encouraging and watchful eyes. Once seated, I just did my normal hand-holding and stroking. After a few minutes, I eased down onto my back. My head resting on a normal pillow felt foreign after how I'd been sleeping. I waited on my back for a long time, afraid the closeness - despite the large gap between us - would put her wolf on high alert. But it never did. Once I was sure the coast was clear, I turned onto my side so I was facing her. I took a leap of faith and didn't wait before reaching out to stroke her forearm.

I was tense for a while, not wanting to make a wrong move. Once I relaxed and was nearing sleep, though, was when it happened. I felt the shift in her pheromones for the first time as she leaned towards me once again. It was the most relaxed she had ever seemed. I would be a liar if I said it didn't make me excited. Since then, this has been our default position.

"What can I help you with, Alistair?" I asked, getting out of my head as I entered my office where I promised to meet him. He and I have been spending quite a few hours together over the last day and a half. Ever since he finished working on the security system, he's been teaching me how to use and navigate it in easy-to-manage increments of time.

"Mika approached me about half an hour after you and I finished our session today," he revealed. That stopped me in my tracks. Absolutely nothing good could come out of Mika approaching the head of the technical security department. Especially when almost everyone in the pack has seen the recent security changes that have taken place.

"And?" I prompted him to continue.

"She tried to convince me that she was to have clearance within the new system. When I didn't entertain her lies, she tried to bribe me with sexual favors. Apparently, no one has told her that it's not common practice to hump whoever you want after you've been mated and married. She seemed rather shocked and upset that I turned her down," he stated with a matter-of-fact tone. I wanted to laugh at the situation, but I couldn't with how serious it was. Why did Mika want clearance? What the hell is she up to?

I grated my hand over the getting-longer 5 o'clock stubble that had been growing for a bit too long. It was something I'd been neglecting ever since Scarlett went to sleep. I paced back and forth in front of my desk.

"Did she give any indication as to why she was supposedly supposed to have clearance?" I asked.

"I didn't think to ask. I did, however, add in a few more iden-tification authorization factors and tracking measures to ensure recognition if someone who shouldn't be trying to get in makes an attempt right after she left my office."

"Good. That's very smart. How's the search for a team to mon-itor the live footage going?" I asked. He shrugged.

"It's going. Some really good candidates so far, but the interview process has been slow. I should have more results by the end of the week." I nodded, exchanged a few pleasantries, and thanked him for his time before parting ways. As I made my way down the hall, I intended to head back to the bedroom, but then my stomach released a loud howl of hunger. To the kitchen it is.

Scarlett's POV

I could hear the vague sound of Jackie's voice somewhere in the distance. I couldn't make out any words - quite frankly, it sounded a lot like the adults in the charlie brown special I got to watch once at Christmas time at the orphanage in the Dusk pack. I wasn't sure how long I'd been out for, but it had to be a while. It was weird, this time around.

When I took the pills, I always got knocked out cold for an extended period of time. Then, after my body got enough sleep to recover just enough, I would get periods of cognitive aware-ness. Similar to this. It felt like swimming in black nothingness, but I could hear a bit of nonsense around me. Only enough to distinguish whose voice it was. If my wolf wasn't threatened, and my body really needed it, I would slip back into the realm of unconsciousness. On the other hand, if she was, she fought damn hard against the sedative and I'd wake up. There were never periods of lucidity beyond the unrecognizable words.

This time, though...I had a long period of unconscious-consciousness. I couldn't be certain what exactly caused it, but I had a guess. When the odd moment occurred, I woke up in a way...but my wolf didn't. I'm unable to fight off the drug without my wolf's assistance. While I knew my skin side was refreshed and ready to get up...my wolf, for the first time in three years, felt safe enough to relax and let her guard down to restore herself. I had no idea why. I didn't care, though. I just knew it made me want to cry big fat tears.

While I was lucid in my mind, but still under, I could hear actual conversations going on around me, despite being physically passed out.

The first conversation freaked me out. I thought I was dreaming - something I've never done before when using one of the pills. It was Jackie speaking in a hushed voice to who I knew to be Justin. Or was an educated guess based upon the content of the conversation. It also had to be a phone call, because it was a one-sided conversation.

The next conversation made me so much more confused. Because it was between Xander and Jackie. They were discussing the renovations Jackie had essentially forced Justin into doing in their now-shared house. They talked like old friends. I didn't understand. I had no idea how much time had passed between the first conversation and the second one.

Or the third and present conversation that rocked me to my core.

Jackie's phone rang. I only knew that it was her cell because I recognized the ringtone immediately. It was the Imperial March from Star Wars. She set it for all The Council Elders as a joke. She'd been staying with them long enough to know she could get away with it on the off chance any of them heard it.

"Elder Adelia, how was your day?" Jackie asked. So it's either evening or nighttime. Good to know. "She's okay. Still sleeping. I've been waiting for your call all day because I wanted to tell you this on the phone instead of in my text this morning. It was just too big for that. Last night we decided to take a leap of faith and have him lay with her. And - would you stop yelling!" she hissed quietly. I couldn't imagine what Edler Adelia was saying on the other line because I was freaking out too. He did what??

"I said shc was still asleep, didn't I? Actually, if you'd stop interrupting, I was going to say that she didn't become restless. Not even once! Instead, her sleep patterns actually grew more stable because of his presence. When he laid with her, her pheromones changed to match his after he'd fallen asleep. That's never happened before, Elder Adelia. She's never even done that with me. Or you!" Jackie exclaimed matter-of-factly. Her pointed statement shocked me. If I had a conscious jaw to drop, I would.

Your sleeping wolf altering their pheromones to match the person they were sleeping alongside was something you usually only ever saw among the closest of wolves - mothers and their pups, identical twins, or long-time mates. Couplings of that sort. It made absolutely no sense that my wolf - who trusted no one that deeply - did such a thing with a man she didn't even know...

"I don't know what this means. Or was it's going to mean for her or her wolf when she finally wakes up. I just know I've never seen her look this good this quickly with how horrible of shape she was in before. His presence is making a difference. I have a good feeling she could wake up soon," Jackie finished.

Apparently, that was all the cue my wolf needed to decide now was the time she felt fully refreshed and ready to go. On Jackie's cue of the word 'soon', she started pushing against the weight of the drug in my system. I felt pins and needles all over my body. I fought to pull my eyelids apart. Finally, painstakingly, I got a single eyelid cracked just ever so slightly. What felt like the brightest of lights assaulted my retina. I slammed the eye back shut and released a small, discontented groan.

"Oh my goodness, she's awake!" Jackie gasped. "Scarlett, honey!" Jackie immediately reached for me. She rubbed my arms, helping me slowly sit upright as I tried to ease my eyes back open. Jackie already knew my needed routine after one of these long stints of sleep. I needed to sit up and stretch because I was always sore from lying for too long without proper movement. Then, I needed to get up and move around - usually on the way to the kitchen for a massive meal to restore all the calories I wasn't taking in while I was out.

Once I was able to successfully pry my eyes all the way open without feeling like I was staring directly into the sun, I gave Jackie a small smile.

"So, how long was I out for?" I rasped out, my voice hoarse and groggy. She chuckled softly.

"Three full days. Not your best record I must admit," she teased. I was amazed it was that brief considering how good I felt and how long I'd gone without sleep. But then, I remembered the conversation I'd overheard. She must've seen the confusion on my face because she patted my arm and stood to help me up. "C'mon. Let's go make you something to eat," she insisted.

"I hope it's multiple somethings," I murmured seconds before my stomach released a massive rumble for emphasis. She laughed with a shake of her head. After standing and steadying myself, I realized I didn't immediately reach for my knife to arm myself.

That's...odd. I scrunched my eyebrows together, unsure of what I was feeling. I didn't feel threatened in this room anymore, which was ironic considering this room was the reason I just came out of the situation I was in in the first place. I felt safe in here. I didn't feel like I needed to arm myself while I was in here. But then when I think about taking even one step out of this room, my instincts come rushing back and my hand itches for my knife. I didn't get it one bit.

I shook my head, dismissing the weird thoughts, before grabbing the knife and stuffing it into its usual spot. Jackie gave me ample time to meander down to the kitchen. I was surprised to scc it looking in a similar state of dismay as when I first showed up.

"I'm only asleep for three days and it looks like a bomb went off in here," I muttered with a huff. A mere second after I spoke, I heard a loud crash coming from the laundry room before a haggard-looking Xander quickly appeared in front of us. Shirtless. There was a shadow of stubble growing on his face and his hair was unruly; it looked like it'd been a couple of days since its last wash. If I had to guess, he'd just been running his hands through it out of frustration, too. My eyes wandered a bit further down and...

And he had chest hair. Chest hair. He always wore shirts to bed prior to...the situation, and I hadn't noticed it the first night I checked him out. But damn was I noticing it now.

I cleared my throat quietly and looked down to my feet, trying to distract myself from the sight in front of me. And the newfound feelings of...comfort? From my wolf? That was incredibly unnerving.

"You're allowed to ogle your mate, Scarlett. It's not a crime," Jackie teased me with a snort before walking further into the kitchen. "What did you do?" she asked, pointing towards the shirt I just now noticed was hanging from Xander's hand. He seemed to have forgotten about it too as he continued staring at me intently.

"What? Oh. I spilled sauce on it and can't get it out," he growled, lifting the shirt back up to glare at the offending spot. I laughed. Well, I attempted to. What came out was an unusual, foreign garbled noise that made me cough as a result of my voice being rested for so long.

"So, what do you want to eat?" Jackie asked me.

I sucked in a deep breath before saying it all in one go. "French toast, pizza, loaded nachos, a salad with all the best toppings, and a fat t-bone steak medium rare." Jackie just rolled her eyes at me. "I'll eat whatever you put in front of me, Jacks," I giggled as my stomach rumbled a second time right on cue. She pulled out a loaf of bread and began making me a big helping of French toast - the easiest thing on my list. I had practically tuned the world out as I scarfed my food down faster than was probably safe or healthy when the sound of footsteps approaching our front door stopped me mid-chew. I lifted and turned my head towards the door before the three knocks came. I swallowed the bite I had in my mouth and reached up to touch my hidden knife for reassurance as I tracked Xander with my eyes. I didn't miss the way he expanded himself to his full height and power when approaching the door. I don't recall him doing that when I first met him. It had to be for my benefit...

Opening the door, Xander accepted two big plastic bags in one hand and a distinct-looking box in the other. What is he up to...?

I set my fork down on my plate as I continued to scrutinize him from where I was seated. Xander shut the door with his foot before turning back towards us.

"What is all that?" Jackie asked. He made his way back to where I was sitting and started pulling out styrofoam to-go boxes.

"Loaded nachos, a salad with all the best toppings, a fat T-bone steak medium rare, and a pizza. You didn't mention toppings, so I just got you cheese," he stated while popping the tops off the containers and sliding them over towards me. My mouth watered as I eyed all the food I'd jokingly - but not so-jokingly - requested. Minus the French toast I had already been eating courtesy of Jackie. "I put in an emergency special order with the pack kitchen. They were more than happy to oblige. Here, you'll need this by the way," he said while getting a steak knife out of the counter drawer. However, instead of just reaching over to hand it to me, he set it down on the countertop and slid it across to me. I don't know what it was about the intentional action, but it made my heart skip a beat and butterflies form in my stomach.

"I also have some things to show you when you're done eating. I've been working on them while you were resting." I nodded before immediately digging into all the food. I wasn't ashamed of the fact that I finished two-thirds of everything I was given. By the time I was done, I was stuffed but completely satisfied.

"I don't know where you put all of that," Xander commented in complete astonishment, but there was a hint of pride in his voice. I just shrugged and patted my belly.

"So, what's the first thing to show me?" I asked, my curiosity getting the better of me. He smiled before grabbing a tablet off of the counter behind him. It was a bit bigger than my hand and required a long complicated passcode to unlock it.

"This is your personal device. It will show you a live, 24/7 view of the security camera system we just installed all around the pack house. You can keep this device with you at all times so you can check the perimeter of the house whenever you please. No matter the time of day. They also record and store up to a month's worth of video. Anything beyond that is sent to a backup storage device which can be accessed on an external computer if you have a specific time and day you want to check." I hesitated in taking the tablet from him. I almost couldn't believe that he'd gone to this length to...to make me feel safe? He extended his hand toward me, encouraging me to take it.

I clicked through some of the cameras before pushing a lock of hair behind my ear and biting the inside of my cheek. I said it before, and I'll say it again, I really don't like it when people don't fit the preconceived notions I have of them.

"The other one is my favorite of the two, personally," Jackie butted in, piquing my curiosity even further. The corner of Xander's lips edged upwards. A bashful look took over his face.

"Well, don't keep me waiting. What is it?" I asked, my fingers gripping the tablet in my hands harshly as my stomach upended itself. I wasn't sure if I was even ready to see the next surprise. The security system was already so much to try and wrap my head around as it was.

"Follow me," Xander instructed before heading towards the stairs. The feeling I got in my chest, a pull of...want to follow after him from my wolf, made me want to run back to the bedroom I'd come from. To transport back to the day I fell asleep. I didn't understand it. The last time I felt this pull it led me straight to disaster and anguish.

"This is it," Xander spoke as we came to a stop in front of one of the many guest rooms. The smell of fresh paint caught my nose. I immediately wanted to see what was behind the door. He twisted the knob and pushed the door open. I felt all the air rush out of my lungs at once. I had to suck my bottom lip into my mouth and bite to stop it from quivering. I moved past Xander's large frame and wandered into the middle of the room. While it was bigger than the one I had back at the council, it looked otherwise identical. The dreary eggshell white walls and painfully standardized furniture would've been an eyesore to anyone else. However, to me they brought a sense of peace; a calm I had been aching for ever since my arrival here. I reached my hand out and ran my fingers along the thick bed quilt, snagging them on a tear. A tear that I would know from anywhere. Because I made it.

"I meant what I said when I told you that I can and will do anything to keep you safe. And I want to make sure you're happy. Sleeping is important, Scarlett. I'm so sorry I was an awful mate and didn't see the signs before it was too late. I won't let it happen again. I promise. I hope sleeping in a room that brings a feeling of familiarity can ease your mind and allow you to settle in more comfortably from here on out," he stated. I had a hard time swallowing the lump that formed in my throat as I listened to his words and continued to examine the room.

"You did this? On your own?" I asked for clarification. For whatever reason, my wolf trusted and felt safe with this man. I didn't understand it. I couldn't fathom why so soon after all that we had been through...but, just maybe, I was starting to.

"Well-"

"Yes. He did. We were discussing ways to prevent what happened from happening again and he suggested this entire idea all on his own. He orchestrated the entire thing. He coordinated with Elder Adelia to have your actual things sent here. It was all him. Don't let him tell you otherwise," Jackie butted in from the doorway. She gave me a meaningful look before disappearing once again.

I couldn't explain the feeling that blossomed in my chest. I felt just like that cartoon character in the Christmas movie Jackie had forced me to watch. The one whose heart grew three sizes in just a single moment. Except my heart wasn't growing, it felt like it was coming alive for the first time in three years. As I turned to face Xander and meet his gaze, a feeling of warmth spread all over my body. My eyes welled up and my nose stung with the unshed tears. Ones I was desperately trying to hold back. A single, traitorous tear slipped down my cheek as I stared at the only man who'd ever made me feel cared for in my entire life.

And then I did something I never thought I would ever do. Not in a million years. I took the three small steps forward to close the gap between us. I gently lifted my hand to press against his chest.

And then I kissed him.

# CHAPTER 18

Scarlett's POV

I knew the kiss caught him completely off guard by his abrupt intake of breath and rigid body posture he was sporting. Add the fact that I knew he was expecting to initiate everything between us because of the situation at hand. However, his surprise only lasted a mere second before he quickly responded. And damn, did he respond.

I'd only ever been kissed four times in my entire life. Twice by boys I'd met growing up in the orphanage during my young, teenage years. And twice by...anyway. I was not going to ruin lucky number five - no, perfect number five - by thinking about my past. I allowed myself to become lost in the way Xander tasted, how soft his lips were, and the way they moved effortlessly against my own.

The longer we kissed, the more control he slowly took. He shifted his body closer to mine before thoughtfully wrapping an arm around my butt, careful to avoid my back, as his other hand rested on my hip. The action, in all its carefulness and sensuality, drove me absolutely wild. My hands had a mind of their own. They traveled up from where they rested against his chest to his head, fingers diving into the already messy locks.

I think we would've been standing there making out like hormone-crazed teenagers for the rest of the day had we not been interrupted.

"Jackie said you were awa-oh!" Vanessa's high-pitched exclaim of surprise snapped us out of the bubble of bliss we'd created. I ripped myself away from him, mortified beyond belief that she'd caught us going at it unashamedly. I felt like my red-hot cheeks would never cool down. Especially not when she was looking between the two of us with the happiest smile I'd ever seen her sport. I wanted to find a quiet hiding place and just crawl into it for the rest of the foreseeable future.

"Mom," Xander grunted. I could feel the annoyance rolling off of him in waves. I had to bite the inside of my cheek to keep a smile from breaking out in amusement. So he must've enjoyed that as much as I did, then.

"Right, um, sorry! I'm gonna go find your father!" she rushed out quickly before darting off. The smile never once left her face. Xander released another annoyed grunt followed by a low, short groan.

"You can say no, however, she's going to go share this finding with anyone that will listen. h

How about we get out of here before she does so? The library has a secret spot that most people don't know about. It's pretty secluded-"

"Yes," I rushed out. I furrowed my brows, shocked at the words that had come out of my own mouth. And at how quickly they had. He smiled widely, both his dimples popping. My wolf and I both took a long, appreciative look. Wow...the Lord really did amazing work on this one.

"Scarlett, are you listening?" he asked.

"No," I dumbly responded, still staring at him. He sputtered briefly before bursting into deep belly laughter that I could practically feel the vibrations of. I felt my face heat with embarrassment all over again.

"Too busy checking me out, huh?" he teasingly shot back with a smug smile.

"Yes. I love your dimples," I answered honestly. I felt that familiar rebellious energy I was used to...but it was different this time. It felt...good, not destructive. He looked taken aback by my honesty. A light shade of pink dusted the tops of his cheeks as a bashful look overtook his face. I liked his reaction far more than I wanted to admit.

"Well, it's a good thing I can't get rid of them then, yeah?" he cheekily replied. I giggled under my breath, the action feeling foreign with anyone other than Jackie, but it felt nice. Not even a second later, the room was flooded with the same mating scent he'd exuded the morning we cooked breakfast together. I wasn't sure how to react. I'd turned him on, on a primal level, by just... being me. Not by how I looked, but by my laugh. Something that was just part of who I was. The thought made my throat tighten with emotion.

I spent a year never being enough for the man I was supposedly destined to be with, but it's been less than a week with a man who barely knows me and I feel...seen. Wanted.

"So, should we go?" he asked, clearing his throat as his eyes shifted a few times before settling back down. I nodded and turned towards the door. Out of the corner of my eye, I saw his hand instinctively move toward my back before he immediately pulled it away and ran it through his hair in an awkward save. It felt...wrong? I wanted the intimacy that came from his touch.

However, no matter the amount of progress we had made, I didn't feel ready for that step yet. I wasn't sure if I ever would be.

Walking down the hall, I stopped a few steps after I didn't feel his presence following. Turning, I gave him a questioning look. He quirked an amused eyebrow at me before a similar smile followed.

"As much as I love the look you're sporting, I think you'd probably prefer to change before wandering around outside of our wing," he commented, motioning his hand up and down my body. My eyes widened as I glanced down. I realized I was still in the outfit Jackie had thrown on me before I conked out. I shook my head at my idiocy and quickly turned the trajectory of my steps back to our bedroom. I changed into a pair of leggings and a sweatshirt before rejoining Xander in the hallway.

We made our way down and out to the hallway. I knew Tabby and Minnie would be standing watch - I could smell them. They both smiled widely when they saw me. Similar looks of relief showed on their faces.

They nodded their heads respectfully and murmured, "Good evening, Scarlett". I nodded back while returning their smile. However, the smile dropped off of my face as the feel of Xander's hand confidently taking hold of my own stole all of my attention. I had the knee-jerk reaction to snatch my hand away out of surprise, but I didn't. After a second or two, the instinct wore off. I let the warmth of his hand overtake my own. It was soothing. I liked it.

"You ladies can stay here and hang out. We're just going to take a stroll together for some privacy," Xander told them. Nodding in acknowledgment, he turned to lead us down the hall. I wasn't sure what it was about the statement, but I didn't like it. It made me feel uneasy. My wolf may have put her trust in him - and as weird as that was for me - a teeny sliver of me still wasn't sure what to think. The wolf side didn't have to endure Eric's torture; I did. So what if all of this was a ruse to gain my trust? And then what? What happens when we're all alone? Why did we need privacy?

I vaguely recognized that it was ridiculous for me to be having these thoughts, but I couldn't stop them. I hadn't realized how lost I'd gotten in them, either, until Xander brought us to a halt inside the library at the end of a secluded row of bookcases. The space was cramped. Too cramped. I threw his hand away from mine and took a few quick steps back. He looked over his shoulder questioningly. Clearly seeing the guarded gaze in my eyes from our surroundings, he huffed with a quick shake of his head.

"Well, this is where I was telling you about. I'm going up there. You can come up with me if you want," he whispered. I creased my forehead at the word up. Seconds after, he reached between the small space created by the wall and the last bookshelf to reveal a slim, tall ladder. I took a couple more steps back as he braced the ladder on the bookshelf before ascending to the top. I continued watching as he went before he finally disappeared at the top. He peeked his head over the ledge before whispering, "Your choice," only loud enough for me to hear with a bit of straining. Then, his face disappeared again.

I looked around, scanning the surrounding rows of bookshelves. I looked back up to where he'd disappeared. My curiosity was dying to know exactly what was up at the top of these shelves. It was a fantastic hiding spot. I don't think you'd ever know the space was there unless someone explicitly told you. However, I didn't like this one bit. Being alone with him in the bedroom was one thing. Small, enclosed spaces where I couldn't be found unless someone was told was another entirely.

And brought back too many memories.

I gave the hiding spot one last glance before turning to explore the rows of books nearby me. I had just discovered a large section of romance novels when a familiar scent hit my nose. The faintness of it told me the person was just entering the library. I slowed my breathing and honed my hearing to try and catch whatever was said.

"So, anything?" came Mika's familiar voice.

"Nothing more than what I already told you last time. People are being annoyingly quiet about her," came another familiar voice, but one I hadn't expected to hear. Amanda. I hadn't intended to make an enemy out of her when I overlooked her for Minnie the day I picked my guards. Despite my reasoning, that's exactly what I'd unintentionally done.

"Ugh, you've got to be kidding me. There's no way that freak hasn't woken up by now! I mean, seriously! It's been, like, six days!" she screeched quietly, annoyance heavy in her tone. I rolled my eyes. Someone needs to get her a calendar. Then, my mind immediately skipped over the irrelevant fact that she got the timeline wrong, instead focusing on the revelation that she even knew about my...very long nap.

How did she even find out? Who told her? Was there a mole in my security team? Who all knew in the first place? I focused back on their conversation, putting the important questions on the back burner for now.

"I don't know. All I know is she has to wake up on her own. I guess she went a really long time without sleeping 'cause of some past situation. I don't fully know. I wasn't able to catch all the details," Amanda murmured, sounding deep in thought. Almost like she was trying to recall what she'd heard from her memory.

"Whatever. Boo-hoo. I mean, seriously, what a drama queen. Right? I heard all this 'pity me' bullshit has to do with her ex-mate or something because he didn't want her and now she's got some complex about it. My money is on her making the whole thing up, whatever it is. I told Caroline that too," Mika said with a snort of laughter followed by Amanda joining in.

Hearing these people talk about that private part of my life - the torture I'd endure for nearly 365 days - as if it was something I'd made up made my skin itch with disgust. My stomach churned. I felt like I was going to vomit the entire contents of my oversized meal from earlier all over the love stories in front of me.

My money is on her making the whole thing up...those words just kept echoing in my mind on repeat. I heard and smelled Xander approaching from behind, snapping me out of my head. The laughing stopped as he grew close.

"Ugh, and have you seen what she wears? And I'm not talking about the clothes she borrows from the other leaders' mates either. It looks like something you'd see at the freaking thrift shop," Mika sneered.

"I guess that suits her well. I heard she was an orphan from the day she was born. Dropped off at the council grounds like trash. Second-hand clothes for a second-hand kid. Her parents didn't want her, so I guess it makes sense that her mate didn't, either," Amanda added in with a snicker. The scent of another wolf entering the library cut their laughter short. Mika and Amanda must've taken their arrival as their cue to leave based on the sound of their giggles fading in volume.

"Scarlett-" Xander began, but I motioned with my hand for him to stop. I didn't care what he had to say. It didn't matter to me. He wasn't the one who'd said those horrible things. They did. What I needed to know was how they had become privy to the knowledge they had, and if they'd tainted other pack members with this absolute garbage through word of mouth.

I blinked back the few tears that had surfaced before swallowing hard. I turned and exited the library. I carefully slipped past Xander as I went, mindful to stare straight forward as to not lock eyes with him as I exited. I could feel his presence lingering behind me as I made a determined bee line for one of his most frequently used conference rooms. The only reason I knew this was because it was the biggest one. Entering the room, I searched high and low. I covered every inch but came up with nothing. That's when I remembered Xander said he'd been working closely with Alistair recently.

I turned and exited, Xander still following close by. I smelled my way to the correct office by the distinct scent of electrical equipment. I knocked a few times before entering without waiting. The man behind the desk scrunched his eyebrows in confusion before standing.

"Can I...help you?" he asked. I didn't answer before beginning to search his office just as I had the conference room. I refused to believe there was a mole amongst my security detail. After searching for a few minutes, I finally placed my hands along the underside of his desk opposite where he had been sitting. I slid until they hit something small and round - about the size of a dime - and relatively flat. My eyebrow quirked upward before I plucked the item off the underside of the desk and revealed it.

"Is this supposed to be there?" I asked, looking at the man whose suddenly completely pale face told me all I needed to know.

"I have no idea how that got there," he sputtered. Taking the offending item from me, he pulled it close to his face to examine closer.

"What is it?" Xander asked from behind me.

"A recording device," the man and I said at the same time.

"Son of a-" Xander began angrily but was cut off.

"It has to have been Mika. She's the only one who's been in this office besides you and me. It was when she came to try and convince me to give her security clearance. I had no idea she stuck this there. I didn't know Mika was even smart enough to think of that," the man admitted. I took the small device and dropped it to the ground before stomping on it a couple of times - just for good measure.

"You can go train with the warriors or something. I'm going to go hang out with Jackie," I said to Xander without any further explanation. I quickly slipped past him before he could put up a fight. I sped to where I knew Jackie's new quarters were. She was the only one who could do true investigative work with me. And she was absolutely getting roped into this one.

I knocked quietly on her door, only having to wait a few moments for her to answer. "Gotta go dig, you busy?" I asked using our signature saying. She released a large huff of air, clearly knowing this wasn't going to lead anywhere good before slumping against the door frame.

"Alright. Fine. I'll bite, but if we get into any legal trouble you're taking the fall this time," she grunted. Her resignation caused me to giggle. I wasn't sure where Mika usually hung out. I hadn't even had time to tour the entire pack grounds, so I had no idea what I was even dealing with yet. With that in mind, Jackie and I changed into hoodies and just prowled. We put our hoods up and masked our scents. It meant we could lurk about practically undetected - that's how we liked it.

We stopped at the pack dining room first, but that was a bust. Then we lingered around the library - since I had seen Mika there earlier. That, too, was a bust. We finally stopped at what looked like a communal pack TV area. There were quite a few younger females and males lurking around. They looked to be anywhere from 18 to 23 if I had to guess. Jackie and I stood at the door as I strained my ears to listen. She hadn't asked what we were looking for - she knew that she usually found out along the way.

The group talked about random, unmated wolf things for about fifteen minutes. Stuff like who was having a party that weekend, who was going to be turning 18 soon, and something about rumored new pack transfers that were coming. It was nothing of real importance. We were just about to leave and call this dig a loss when one of the males suddenly piped up, stopping me in my tracks.

"So, Mika told me something interesting the other day."

"Oh, yeah? Was that before or after you guys hooked up?" one of the older-looking guys in the group asked before snickering cheekily. My top lip curled up in disgust.

"After, obviously," the first guy laughed. "Supposedly, our new luna is in a coma or something. Self-induced I guess. She's, like, majorly screwy in the head. Mika said she made up this whole elaborate story about her ex-mate abusing her or something and pretends like it keeps her from sleeping." The entire group laughed loudly as he finished telling them his juicy gossip. My stomach twisted into knots. I don't know who she paid - or more likely screwed - to find out what she knew, but I was praying she didn't have an exact name.

"That's messed up! Is she just, like, laying there? Like she's sleeping beauty refusing to get out of bed?" one of the girls asked before laughing her head off - as if the idea was the funniest thing in the world to her.

"I don't know, but I feel bad for Alpha Harrington, man. Mika's an...okay screw I guess. If you're desperate. But can you imagine getting two duds for a mate?" he asked.

"I don't know about dud, Duke. Did you see the new chick at that dinner? She's, like, a 12/10. Can you imagine getting to hit that from behind? Damn. Plus, Mika's always spouting off from the mouth. I bet she's blowing smoke up your ass. Especially after that chick put Mika in her place that night," the guy from before interjected. At least someone was using some common sense.

"Yeah, but think about it. Have you seen her since that one night?" The 'sleeping beauty comment' girl said. The entire group seemed to consider what she said as if the story actually had merit. I just scoffed quietly and rolled my eyes. I'd heard all I needed to hear. I didn't need Mika's poison spreading any farther than it already had. I didn't even have a clue how far it had truly spread.

I needed to do something. And I needed to do it quickly.

# CHAPTER 19



S I spent the rest of the evening hanging out at the orphanage. I just wanted to go somewhere that I didn't feel as if everyone around me was judging me. I wanted to go somewhere I felt like I temporarily belonged.

The kids had shown me all the new things they got while out on their shopping trip. I was bummed I didn't get to go with them since I was out cold, but it didn't seem to dull their spirit one bit. They were all so excited just to simply own something that was theirs and didn't come three generations passed down. It made my eyes water more than a little. The older kids also showed me the laptops the pack budgeted for since many of them expressed interest in going to college as well. I was more than impressed by all that Riley had done in such a short period of time. But, then, the sun gave way to the moon and it was soon bedtime for all the kids. And that meant it was time for me to go home.

I somberly reminisced over the loud breakfasts I shared growing up as I cooked a very silent one the next morning. I wasn't sure where Xander was. He was up really late doing who knows what. I was already asleep by the time he came to bed and he awoke before me. My only indication that he'd been in the bed was that his side was warm and smelled like him this morning. I was too preoccupied with the fact that I actually slept last night to focus too much on his absence.

I had just taken my last bite of omelet when I sensed Riley, Raven, and Peyton approaching. They knocked for approximately two seconds before swinging the door open with a loud, "Helloooo? Anyone awake??" I just shook my head with a small smile and swiveled on the barstool I was perched on to meet their gaze.

"Oh, good! You're up! We have fun news!" Peyton exclaimed. "We're going shopping!" she chirped with an excited clap. I groaned before rubbing my eyes with my thumb and index finger. Shopping is was got me into the prior situation I had been in - if you wanted to get technical.

"I'm not in a shopping mood today, but thanks for the invite," I spoke, hoping the lame excuse would work. I should've known I wouldn't be so lucky.

"Pssh, whatever. You're going with us and that's final. Your wardrobe is so sad it makes me cry when I walk in there. It needs some serious TLC and we're going to restock it today. Get some shoes and your coat on and let's go. Alpha Harrington already gave us his credit card for you," Riley said, pulling out said card and doing a little dance with it in between her hands.

"Uh, just...give me a second," I murmured before hopping off the stool and quickly moving past them towards the front door. I bolted out and sensed my way to where Xander was hiding out - likely because he didn't want to face my wrath he knew was now waiting for him. Jerk.

I pinpointed his location down to his office and threw the door open. I ignored the other men's questioning gazes thrown back and forth between Xander and me.

"If I didn't want to go shopping with you, I sure and hell don't want to go shopping with the girls," I growled out, unable to keep the irritation I felt from seeping into my voice.

"Scarlett," he started, but my wolf and I released a quiet mixture between a growl and a huff as I crossed my arms over my chest and glared at him. He chuckled at the response before pushing himself out of his hulking desk chair and making his way to me.

"The women have been to this particular mall hundreds of times. They've never seen anyone from the Sablefur pack there. Ever. I promise you, it's going to be-"

"If you say fine, I'm going to..." I trailed off, only loud enough for him to hear. He smiled. Those damn dimples that made my knees quiver made an appearance.

"Fine," he finished with a husky laugh. "There're a few representatives from a neighboring pack that we're allies with coming to fix some treaty documents that were improperly filed on their end. They alerted our pack registrar that they would be traveling here out of courtesy since it was their mistake. However, with our current situation, I tried to call and let them know we would just send someone to them. They didn't see our email in time and were already on their way. They're going to be here in a couple of hours. Therefore, you're going shopping with the girls today," he explained calmly. My stomach did that little flutter thing I'd heard Jackie talk about before. It wasn't as intense as when he showed me the Council-like bedroom, but it was a close second.

He'd made accommodations for me without me even asking; without even having been told to. I wasn't sure what to say back to him. I still didn't like the idea, but I understood it now. I sighed - partially out of resignation, but partially....well, as I stared at his beautiful face, I didn't want to admit that it was also partially in admiration.

"Scarlett, sweetheart, you're going to be safe. I promise. And I don't take that lightly. If I could go with you, I would. I wouldn't even let you go if I thought there was an inkling of a chance something could happen to you," he insisted. I wasn't sure if I even caught the rest of what he had said after he called me sweetheart.

Sweetheart. The word just kept replaying over and over in my head. I'd never been called a term of endearment ever before. With Eric, it was always 'mistake' or 'unwanted'. Most often he called me 'mateless' and that one stung the most. Xander called me sweetheart.

Whereas Eric's nicknames made the skin on my back sear with phantom pain, Xander's made my tummy flutter with butterflies. I swallowed thickly before finally nodding, realizing I probably looked like a weirdo just standing there staring at him, one hand on my tummy and the other on my back.

"Okay," I whispered so softly I wasn't sure he even heard it. My gaze momentarily flitted down to his lips as my tongue dashed out to wet my own before I met his eyes again. The corner of his mouth quirked up just a tick. He brazenly stepped forward, his hand coming up to rest against my cheek as he simultaneously leaned down and pressed his lips against my own. The kiss only lasted a few seconds, but it felt so much longer. Xander pulled away first but stayed close enough that his lips were grazing my own as he spoke again.

"Use my card. Get whatever you want. No exceptions. I mean it," he mumbled before pecking my bottom lip a final time and sending me on my way with a charming smile. I was so entranced by the smile, I'd forgotten to put up even a little bit of a fight before just nodding and sauntering back to our place. The girls were waiting around patiently, all three of their faces pulling into knowing smiles as I got closer and their noses raised into the air. Thankfully, they kept their comments to themselves. Kissing Xander was already overwhelming enough as is, I didn't need anyone questioning me about it or - heaven forbid - teasing me about it, too.

I quickly dressed and we got going. We met up with the rest of the entire entourage of people that were accompanying us - which included my four female guards, the four male guards originally assigned to me, plus Jade, and Jackie - as we exited the main front doors of the pack house. I watched the scenery zoom by for what felt like ever, but was really only a couple of hours before we finally slowed our speed and pulled into the parking area of a massive shopping center. It was a cluster of big malls in one area. Supposedly, this was the place to shop.

Entering the mall, I was slammed with what felt like a brick wall of adrenaline. There were too many smells, too many noises, too many people. They were moving around me too quickly. My neck felt like it was going to break as my face snapped in every single direction. I couldn't find a way to get my back against a wall. I felt too exposed. The last time I had gone shopping without an entire escort of Elder Council members was before Eric. I was fourteen years old and my boobs had grown too big to contain within the built-in bras of the worn-down tank tops I was given as hand-me-downs.

Right now, with the way my heart was racing, my face flushing, and my chest tightening as the panic gripped me, I'd be okay if I didn't do this again for another seven years. That much I knew.

"Scarlett," Jackie's calm voice murmured right next to me, but I barely heard it through the white noise that was growing louder and louder.

"Scarlett," she husked out, harsher this time, effectively cutting through the fog in my brain. I glanced to the side to take in her soft and concerned gaze. "It's okay. Remember what Xander said? You're safe," she reassured me.

Sweetheart. The word rang through my head again as my wolf thumped her tail in my mind. I swallowed my thickened saliva before breathing deeply and nodding a few times. I cleared my throat and continued forward on shaky legs. Our ascent towards the first store was painfully slow as I found it hard to let even a single passing stranger by without a brief glance. Eventually, though, we made it there. Jackie knew me well. I'd been dreaming about this place since I was sixteen and caught a glimpse of the alpha's daughter of the pack I was housed at sporting the cutest workout outfit through the orphanage's dingey window. Any time I had internet access - which wasn't often - I would look up their clothing. When Jackie and I got close, it was something we started doing together.

"I don't know what lemons have to do with working out," Jackie started.

"But damn if I care," I finished our favorite saying as we sauntered into the store's entrance. I released a sigh of contentment as I gazed around, just taking it all in - and for a positive reason. Everyone else fanned out - well, except for my four girls who stayed close by me, alert the whole time. I walked along the outer perimeter of the store, feeling the material of the butter-soft leggings between my fingers. I heard the human sales associate approaching from behind and turned to meet her stare.

"Would you like to try a pair on?" she asked with a friendly smile. I hesitated for a second. The price tag winked at me under the bright studio lighting of the store and my eyes widened for a moment.

"Uh," my breath caught in my throat, "I don't think so-"

"Yes, she will. I'm around a size six. I think with her hips and booty she's either a six or an eight. Why don't we grab both just in case?" Peyton suggested from a few feet away, walking fast towards me. I sighed, seeing the look of determination on her face and knowing she wasn't going to give up this battle.

"Perfect! Here are both those sizes, let's get you that dressing room! Anything else you want to snag before we head back there?" the girl asked.

"I grabbed some stuff I thought would look cute on her," Raven said as she waddled up from behind us, her arms full of hangers causing my eyes to widen comically. All of the women practically forced me into the dressing room with all the clothing items in tow. I went with the bigger pair of leggings first and they fit like a glove. My jaw dropped until my mouth was slightly agape as I ran my hands down the fronts of my thighs and around to my backside in a sweeping circular motion. The material felt incredible against my marred skin. So comfortable.

I slipped off everything I had on top and grabbed one of the neutral-colored bras and full-length hoodies. I skipped the cropped ones completely for obvious reasons. I slipped it all on before zipping the black jacket up. The bra, even though just a measly sports bra, was more supportive than any meager thing I had ever owned. It took the weight of my boobs off of my shoulders for once and made me feel like I could actually go for a decent training session. The material of the jacket felt identical to that of the pants and caressed the particularly painful patches of skin on my back. I wanted this in every color.

I was never one who particularly liked shopping. No matter the age. Growing up, there was never any money for even the essentials, which meant you got whatever you got when it came to things like clothing. Even when I was old enough to get a job within the pack at 16, that money almost always went to buying more groceries for the home I was staying in or helping with the bills to keep our utilities on. Most packs didn't care if we had hot water during the middle of winter or not. And then, when Eric came into the picture, I had less than nothing. He controlled every single cent. I wasn't allowed to have a bank account. Nothing was ever in my name. He ensured that he exerted complete control over every aspect of my life.

"Well? What's taking so long? Let us see!" came Jackie's inpatient demand. I sniffled quietly before wiping away the brief tear that had trailed down my cheek. I steeled my exterior, making sure I looked put together. Opening the door, there was a collective gasp followed by a couple of squeals.

"Damn I have got to start training with you," Riley exclaimed with a big smile.

"You're buying all of this. No questions asked," Peyton stated with finality before turning on her heels and disappearing. I furrowed my brows before turning back into the stall to try on the rest of the clothing. I ended up liking everything I tried on, but left the more revealing items untouched.

Leaving the dressing area, I came face to face with a bag-riddled Peyton looking like she was waiting on us.

"What...?" I asked.

"Oh, this is all yours. Various items in your sizes in different styles and colors. By the look you gave, I could tell there was going to be a major fight at the cash register so I just went ahead and got them for you. We can move on to the next store," she finished with a cheeky smile. I pursed my lips at her cleverness before huffing in annoyance. Damn her and her intuition.

The rest of the stores pretty much went the same way. Apparently, no one was here to shop for anything. They were solely interested in assisting me in expanding my wardrobe. It had been about two hours and I'd accumulated a variety of clothing items besides just the athletic wear from the first store. I now had dresses, blouses, jeans, shoes, and heels despite my abundant protests against them.

"Okay, Raven is ready to call it a day so this can be our final stop. I think it's the best closer for the trip," Riley giggled mischievously. I quirked my eyebrow upwards in question as I stared up at the sign that read La Perla.

"Do we have to do this? Seriously?" One of the male guards groaned as two of them joined in his sentiments. Though Maximus didn't seem to share their feelings as his hand slid around Jade's waist and a smug smile made its way to his lips.

"You want a future heir for this pack? Shut up," Riley shot back. Future heir? Her words didn't make sense to me until I'd truly taken a look around and realized we were in a lingerie store. My cheeks instantly felt like they were on fire and I wished the ground would just swallow me whole.

"C'mon honey-buns, we've got 15 days to seal the deal. It starts with getting comfortable with the idea of it. Start picking stuff you like out, I'm going to start over there," Riley said before wandering to the left side of the store. I blew a raspberry with my cheeks before surveying the various scantily clad mannequins on display. One in the far corner caught my eye. It had on a pretty, all-white silk material nightgown. The straps were thin and the V in the front was way too low cut to be considered comfortable - I mean seriously. If you wore this thing to bed, you were going to wake up with at least one boob outside the gown, if not both. There was a cheeky slit up the left thigh, too. It was pretty - if it wouldn't have exposed....everything I was insecure about.

But, then again, being naked while we mated was going to do that too, so...

I glanced around again at some of the racier pieces on display and wondered if I would ever be able to feel sexy in my own skin. Whether I was stark naked or prancing around in one of these barely-there pieces of lace scrap fabric. Feeling that rebellious nature rise up inside of me, I suddenly whisked through the rack of white silk nightgowns in front of me. Finding what I believed would be my size, I snatched it into my hand. I quickly walked towards a racy red bra and panty set that were completely see-through mesh except where the most intimate areas needed to be covered in which there were patches of opaque lace. I picked both pieces up along with the matching garter belt as well.

I continued on, grabbing anything and everything that caught my eye and suited my fancy. My arms were full and I needed a basket after just a mere twenty minutes. Riley glanced at me over her shoulder and giggled before giving me an approving thumbs up. I bit the inside of my cheek, about to suggest we check out, when I smelled it.

Or rather him.

# CHAPTER 20

Scarlett's POV

It was a bit of an ironic situation, really. Part of me wanted to laugh about the whole thing. When there was no perceived threat, I did what most would consider 'overreacting' and my body went into panic mode. However, when there was a very real, very threatening situation at hand, I didn't hesitate for a second. My heart didn't skip a periodic beat nor did I have to catch my breath in fear. The adrenaline kicked in, my wolf took over, and I just reacted.

I moved systematically and methodically. Within a matter of seconds, I was out of sight of every single guard and woman I was with. I didn't know how much time I had, but I needed to move quickly. The scent had already drifted closer than when I first smelled it. I moved as fast as I possibly could without making noise. Slipping from the entrance of the mall, I maneuvered through the crowd while keeping my head down.

Before I knew it, I was outside - but not safe. Nowhere was safe. I took off towards the parking lot and subsequent forest that lined the interstate at a dead sprint. Once I'd broken the treeline, I didn't think twice before shifting into my wolf and forcing my legs as fast as they'd go.

I would remember that smell from anywhere. It was the one I remember lingering in Eric and I's wing the most before I escaped. It was the Gamma of the Sablefur pack. He'd been one of the two people who'd known about my tie to Eric; knew what Eric was doing to me. Worse yet, he'd helped Eric with...the thoughts had my heart racing once again just thinking about being in the same building with someone in that circle again. A menacing growl escaped from my throat as I dug my paws into the earth and drove my body forward even faster.

I didn't think I'd been running that long. I must have gotten lost deep in my thoughts because I could already see the front gates of the pack house coming into sight. I slowed my pace, contemplating my next move. I didn't want to alert anyone to my arrival. I changed my course a couple of hundred feet before leaping over the huge wall. I strained my ears as I approached the front door, shifting fast when I didn't hear anyone. I rushed in and quickly hid behind the first door I saw since I was stark naked. It turned out to be some sort of storage closet of sorts.

I quieted my breathing and listened once again, trying to hear and figure out who all was in the pack house right now.

It was quiet for a few seconds before I heard Vanessa's deeply concerned voice call out. It was slightly muffled before becoming a tad more clear. I think she was somewhere upstairs.

"Xander! It's an emergency. It's Scarlett. She...something must've spooked her. She didn't even say anything to Jackie. She just disappeared from the mall. They've been looking everywhere for thirty minutes and no one can find her."

Wow. A 2-hour drive ran in just thirty minutes? That's nearly a personal record for me. I didn't have much time to be impressed by my wolf's speed and stamina because a feral, angered roar rang throughout the packhouse. The intensity of it caused the hair on the back of my neck to stand.

"Why wasn't I informed sooner?!" Came the sound of Xander's pissed-off growl. "She could be anywhere by now if someone grabbed her!" His words were followed by a loud clattering commotion. It was dark inside the closet I'd abruptly shut myself in, but I reached up and felt around the shelf above me. My hand came into contact with something that felt akin to a blanket. Score. I pulled it down, expertly draping and wrapping it around my body so that all the necessary areas were fully covered. I listened for a few moments before slowly twisting the doorknob and pushing the door open. Peeking my head out, I didn't see anyone around. I slowly inched my way out and dashed up the stairs and down the hall. I could just see the door that connected the alpha's wing to the pack house. I was almost there when-

"Scarlett?" I wasn't dumb enough to stop and see who was calling my name - I was only wrapped in...whatever this was after all. "Scarlett!" came my name a second time, but much closer and much more confident. I slowed my steps before releasing a raspberry through my lips. I hugged the material around my body tighter as I carefully turned around. I was faced with an entourage of people. Xander being the one who called my name. Vanessa stood nearby him as well as all of the high-ranking pack members. I assume they were in a meeting before Vanessa came to tell Xander about me running off. A few men were standing behind them; men I didn't recognize. All of them were staring at me as if I had suddenly sprouted a second head right in front of them.

"Yeah, that's my name," I mumbled dumbly, having no idea what else to say in the current situation.

"Is that the spare rug for the front entrance?" Vanessa asked, confusion evident in her tone while eying the material wrapped around my body. Maybe that explained why it was particularly stiff.

"Get Maximus on the phone now. I want to know why I was lied to. She did not go missing thirty minutes ago," Xander sneered, speaking to no one in particular. However, it was clearly a command for someone. I had been taking small steps backward - carefully so I didn't alert the group. Some of the gazes were making me feel uneasy. My wolf was already right under the surface from what had just happened. She was surveying the wolves with an intimidating glare forced through to my exterior.

Glancing up, Xander took notice of what I was doing. He tracked my gaze back to the men I didn't recognize before abruptly standing to his full, threatening height. He was posturing, that much was obvious. "Get back in the room. And if you stare at my mate for a second longer, I'll make sure it's the last thing you ever see," he growled. Their eyes widened for a single second before they dashed back into the room from which they came.

"Xander this is a picture that was taken forty minutes ago, look at the time stamp," Donovan said, stepping up from behind Xander. He extended his hand in front of Xander's face to show him something on his cellphone - the picture I assumed. Xander's eyes narrowed at the screen. He scrutinized the photo for a few seconds before his gaze moved to me. He met my eyes for a split second before they traveled down my body, taking in my current state of dress.

"You ran all the way here in your wolf form? In forty minutes or less?" He asked, his brows furrowing. His face took on a worried and impressed expression simultaneously, an odd look combination to see.

"I guess so," I murmured, desperate to retreat to our bedroom where my wolf and I both felt a pull to right now. It was the only place we truly felt safe. Especially right now.

"Tell the men that I apologize, but our meeting is being postponed. An emergency has come up. We will accommodate any needs they have, but we'll have to have this meeting tomorrow morning at the earliest," Xander spoke over his shoulder to Donovan.

"But they just got here," Donovan husked out looking slightly stressed. I shifted back and forth on my feet awkwardly, wanting to slink away if I could get the chance. Unfortunately, there were still too many unmoving eyes on me.

"I don't care. This meeting is only happening because of an initial mistake on their behalf. We're being very accommodating in the first place. I have something more important to take care of right now," Xander growled out. Turning, he gave me his attention once again. His glare softened considerably when we made eye contact. "Come on, sweetheart," he hummed while approaching me.

Whatever it was about that word - and the way it made me feel when he said it - instantly had the minute splash of adrenaline still pumping through my body come crashing down. His arm slowly raised to wrap around my rug-covered shoulders. He guided me towards the door I'd been previously making a mad dash for. I hadn't even realized I had practically melted into his side until I'd already done so. I even went so far as to press my face into his chest as we walked, breathing in the smell of him. It was almost as if the behavior was second nature. I pulled myself away a bit and cleared my throat to compose my muddled brain as we entered our place. I turned to face him, pulling the rug tightly around my body like a safety blanket.

"Why don't you go change while I do a sweep of the place since the girls aren't here?" he asked. I wasn't sure why his suggestion hit me so hard. Probably because of what just happened. My emotions were running high. I was still terrified no matter how much I didn't want to admit it. Something about him just knowing there was something off in the first place, and assuming the task my guards always did as soon as we got home because they weren't here, had emotions I didn't want to name for fear of doing so swirling in my chest.

I swallowed thickly. "Okay," I husked out, my voice hoarse and tight with emotion. I quickly slipped on a pair of leggings and a long-sleeve shirt. Mika's harsh words from yesterday rang in my ears, but I quickly brushed them away. Her opinion didn't matter to me. It never would.

Xander was just finishing up when I re-entered the kitchen. The look of serious concern on his face had my stomach doing funny things. I didn't know what to think.

"What happened, Scarlett?" he asked, looking like the answer was pivotal to his well-being. Thinking back to exactly what had happened made all the feelings hit me once again. My knees went weak as my lower lip threatened to tremble before I pulled it into my mouth. I looked away, unable to maintain eye contact any longer. I heard rather than saw him move around the kitchen island, coming to stand right next to me.

"Scarlett," he whispered just before his hand came up to softly rest on the top of my shoulder. Normally, with anyone else, my wolf wouldn't have allowed the touch. Not in an area so close to such a vital part of my body. But Xander? He...he was different. And oh how that scared me. I squeezed my eyes closed tightly to try and keep the tears at bay that I could feel forming. His calloused hand traveled slowly from my shoulder, across my collarbone, ever so gently up the delicate skin of my neck, and finally cupping my cheek. I let my eyes flutter open and saw the upset look in his eyes.

"I'm sorry," he started before having to stop himself. He clenched his jaw in what I could tell was contained anger. "I should've been there. For whatever it was," he stated with so much conviction and sincerity that my resolve finally snapped. The first sob bubbled out of my chest so unexpectedly that it even caught me off guard. Once it made its getaway, there was no stopping the torrent that followed. The crying came fast and hard. So hard I could barely breathe.

Xander looked dumbfounded. Clueless as to what to do. He looked like he wanted to hold me, but didn't know how. That just made me even more upset. Among the many things Eric had taken from me, he'd even taken the simple ability of the man in front of me to give me basic comfort.

Take it back. Don't let him have the power anymore. Overpower the memories.

I'd come to decide that sometimes the rebellious thoughts in my head weren't always all that bad. Sometimes I liked to think they could be useful. I decided this was one of those times. I followed my own mind's advice and pushed past every doubt and fear, taking the one thing I wanted at that moment; true comfort from the one person I was craving it.

I pushed his hand away from my face, ignoring the flash of disappointment in his eyes, and immediately lunged at him. Wrapping my arms around him, I buried my face in his neck as he often did to me at night during his sleep. I knew he was completely unprepared for my reaction. His body remained stark still for a few seconds following my hold. Finally, he responded. His tense muscles relaxed and his frame curled around mine. His face turned to press his cheek against the side of mine. He rubbed his scent into my skin in a manner I'd only ever seen mates do when they were soothing their partner. Seconds later his hand threaded through my hair. The other arm wrapped around my waist at a painfully slow rate. My breathing quickened for a couple of seconds at the feeling, but....that was it.

"It's okay, Scarlett. I'm here. He's not going to get to you. He can't get to you. I won't let him. I promise. I've got you, I'm here," Xander's words gently landed against the side of my face. Though his voice was soft, his tone was confident. His hand moved vertically to span the entire length of my back as his palm pressed against my shoulder blade, holding me tighter against his body.

His words, paired with the physical feeling of him having my back, had my wolf and me letting our guard down as I completely relaxed into him. I allowed him to be the one to solely protect and watch out for me - while fully conscious - for the first time since before Eric. It was...euphoric. My wolf and I were practically drunk on the overtly male pheromones he was releasing in waves. It was essentially his way of overwhelmingly staking his presence in our home. It guaranteed anyone would think twice before entering. He was ensuring I felt safe with him, even after I'd shown him that I trusted him.

I wanted to bask in all of it. I couldn't help myself as I released my locked hold around his neck, allowing myself to slowly slide down his body before my feet gently touched the floor. I didn't move, though. I remained pressed firmly against him, my palms flat against his pec muscles as I hummed under my breath. My wolf took over and instinctively burrowed my face back and forth across his chest, pressing his scent further into my skin.

"Are you...smiling?" Xander asked softly, sounding unsure - like he almost didn't even want to ask the question, but was too curious not to. My eyes, which I hadn't realized I'd closed again, fluttered back open. I reached my hand up to my face and realized that I was, indeed, smiling. The dumbfounded look on Xander's face made my smile widen even more seconds before releasing a quiet giggle.

His reaction was instantaneous. The smell of his mating pheromones flooding the room was so strong it almost made me choke. I didn't have but a few seconds to react as his face quickly descended, his lips capturing mine in a searing kiss.

We'd made out before, but it had been nothing like this. This kiss made me hot all over; made my clothes feel suffocating. I wanted his hands anywhere and everywhere all at the same time. It was maddening.

He must've felt how I did. He scooped me up into his arms with a big hand positioned under each of my thighs. Turning, he started for the stairs. However, he stumbled his way over to the couch instead after losing his balance from closing his eyes to kiss me. I giggled at the action before pulling him back down for another heated kiss. I must've been unknowingly pulling at his shirt. The next thing I knew, he leaned back and tossed it off somewhere behind him uncaringly. I didn't even get to appreciate the beautiful sight before. Seconds later his mouth attached to the delicate, intimate area of my neck. He began placing hot, open-mouthed kisses everywhere. He suddenly hit a spot that made stars and black spots dance around the periphery of my vision. My mouth dropped open as a loud, long moan fell from my lips. Hearing my response, Xander doubled his efforts on the area.

I brought my legs up to wrap around his hips. I was unable to contain myself when they jerked up to grind against him on their own accord. One of Xander's hands found my right hip before he pulled me down hard while simultaneously grinding his hips upward. It all felt so good, my mind went totally blank.

"Xander," I husked out, his name nothing more than a needy moan of desire on my lips. Unfortunately, that was the exact moment someone entered our house and interrupted all of it. We have got to get a lock. Or a sock for the doorknob. Something. Anything.

"I, uh...think I've interrupted something," came Donovon's mirth-filled voice. My eyes shot open at the voice. Xander stilled momentarily before pushing himself up over my body so that his weight wasn't crushing me. That might feel kind of nice, come to think of it...His gaze wasn't focused on me as he glared over the back of the couch at who I knew was his beta.

"29 years old and I can't get any fuckin' privacy in my own home," Xander growled

"You're the alpha and you think you get privacy? Psh. Maybe for your honeymoon. But whatever you got going on down south, I'd suggest you take care of it. And quickly. I'm doing you a favor right now whether you think so or not. The whole crew just showed up from the mall worried as hell about Scarlett. Therefore, all of them plus your mom will be here in about two, maybe three, minutes. So, again, you're welcome. Now retuck it and put your shirt on before they show up," he laughed. Xander grumbled under his breath before leaning down to press a few last kisses to my lips.

"This is gonna be painful for more reasons than one," he grimaced, climbing off the couch and helping me do the same. I made the mistake of glancing down at his zipper region, my jaw nearly hitting the floor. I composed myself and quickly looked away before he caught my reaction - the one he missed while putting his shirt back on. My nether regions ached just thinking about our future mating. Then, the utter shock of simply thinking about that event purposely - and not with disdain either - completely derailed my line of thinking. However, I wasn't able to get caught up for too long. Mere seconds later the front door opened once again and a hoard of people - the ones I'd been with earlier - came swarming into our living room.

"Please, make yourself at home," Xander muttered grumpily. I liked the childish reaction to us being interrupted far more than I would admit. I covered the humorous smile his reaction brought to my face just before elbowing him in the stomach.

"Scarlett I'm so glad you're okay!" Riley exclaimed, rushing over to me to roughly pull me into a tight hug. I did my best to return the hug, but my arms were crushed against my sides from how she had been grasping me. "I took my eye off of you for literally one second and then you were just gone! I don't think we'll ever be able to show our faces at that mall ever again. We made such a commotion looking for you," she laughed off-handedly. The comment, however, made me freeze all over again.

"Did you say my name?" I asked, unable to stop the racing of my heart as the scenarios already started up in my head. What if he heard them while they were searching? Smelled my scent on them? Put two and two together? Just as my thoughts started to spiral out of control, I felt Xander's strong arm wrap around me from behind. His palm flattened against my lower belly, which was now twisting into knots all over again. He pulled me back against his big frame. He didn't say anything, just rubbed his thumb gently back and forth across my skin while cocooning me in his hold. It was enough to have my heart gradually coming back down to its normal pace. I carefully, slowly leaned back into his hold.

I let out a deep breath before making eye contact with Riley once again - who was sporting a mischievous grin on her face. Her gaze pinged-ponged back and forth between Xander and me.

"Well, once we found out that you were fine and had just come back here, Jackie figured there wasn't any harm in finishing up our shopping before heading back. So we went ahead and grabbed the stuff you had in your basket," she said as her smile grew wider. She stretched her hand out to offer me two large white bags with gold La Perla lettering on them. My cheeks tinted pink as all the women in the room snickered. Vanessa cleared her throat while avoiding eye contact.

"Well, we just wanted to make sure you were alright and to see to it with our own eyes. So, we'll just give you two some privacy for the rest of the day, then," Jackie spoke dramatically. Raising both of her eyebrows suggestively, she finished the ridiculous gesture with a wink. I couldn't help the snort I released at her antics.

"Oh dear," Vanessa whispered when she caught on to what Jackie was hinting at. I heard Xander groan under his breath, but it was so quiet I was sure I was the only one who heard it.

"C'mon, Luna V, you wanna be a grandma, don't you? Just don't think about the logistics. Let's go people, move out," Jackie instructed while motioning towards the door with both her hands. Once they were all gone and the door was locked behind them, Xander turned to face me with an amused smile.

"Have I told you I like your best friend?"

# CHAPTER 21

S carlett's POV

    I giggled at his statement, "No, but that's nice to hear."

"So..." he began. He ignored every shopping bag the girls had left for me - and there were a lot of them - and went straight for the fancy-looking bags that I knew were filled with lingerie. The corner of my mouth curved upward as I pulled one of the bags towards me. I was feeling emboldened. I was sure if it was because of the encounter on the couch earlier, or the look in his eyes that he was giving me right this very second. Whichever it was, something about it made me want to give him a little show. I wanted to prance around in the lingerie that simply seeing on the mannequin made me feel sexy. I also needed something to get my mind off what Riley said earlier about making a scene at the mall.

The thought of Xander getting a look at...everything. Well, to be totally honest, it downright terrified me - but that made it a great distraction. I didn't know what he would think or if it would change his opinion of me. However, he had to see them eventually. I didn't want to be forced to show that side of myself on the day we mated. Anticipating his reaction during such a big moment would make it impossible for me to relax. I cleared my throat, choosing to ignore the small tremor of my hands as I spoke.

"I bought some...things. For you. Well, they're technically for me, but I got them for you," I spoke, beginning to ramble as doubt crept into my mind. However, I could see that I'd piqued his curiosity and...something else. Something darker. He brought his hand up to rub over the lower half of his face before slowly releasing a deep breath through his nose.

"Yeah?" he asked, a huskiness to his voice that hadn't been there just seconds prior. I nodded, swallowing the lump in my throat. Ignoring the raging nerves in my stomach, I took the final leap of faith - feeling like I might faint as I did so.

"I thought I could try some of them on for you. Give you a little-"

"Yes," he growled out, not even letting me finish my sentence before agreeing to the offer. I smiled. My confidence had been boosted a smidge by his eagerness. I grabbed one of the bags and started moving toward the stairs. Neither one of us spoke as we made our way to our bedroom - the one we'd been sharing every night since I'd come out of my deep slumber. Part of me felt bad that he went through all that work to remodel his guest bedroom just for me. However, I had a strong feeling he didn't mind one bit seeing as I was in our bed every night.

Once we'd entered the room, he took a seat at the sitting area. He rested against the seat, spreading his legs wide as he leaned back and placed his arms behind his head. He looked relaxed, but completely imposing at the same time. The sight of him - so big and so male - made me give a sigh of want. The smug smile that pulled at the edges of his lips told me he had most definitely heard it. I narrowed my eyes before strutting toward him and plopping the bag I'd had in my hands down onto his lap.

"You pick what you want to see first," I stated, resting my hands on my hips. He raised a single eyebrow before a boyish grin took over his face. He reached into the bag and pulled the first item out. It was the simple white silk nighty I'd developed a love-hate relationship with at the store.

"My pajamas are too hot at night with how you wrap around me. I had to get something lighter to sleep in," I explained. I don't know why, but I liked how he still gave the piece thought and attention despite its chasteness. Well, chaste compared to everything else in the bag. It wasn't at all what I had actually had in mind for pajamas. However, after feeling his skin pressed against my own earlier, I didn't want to go back to long sleeves at night; not when it was just the two of us. I mean, after tonight he'd be seeing what I had originally intended the sleeves to cover.

"It's soft, I like it," he commented before setting it down with care. Reaching back inside the bag, he pulled out the next item. I immediately wanted to hide seeing what it was. It was probably the sexiest piece in the entire bag. One I knew for a fact I hadn't picked out myself. I wasn't gullible enough to think it had accidentally ended up in my cart when I dropped it to the ground as I plotted my escape from the store. This had Jackie written all over it. The dark, almost blood-red set hardly covered anything at all. Most of the covering was done by the sporadic lace and accompanying garter belt. I might as well just walk out naked for what this set was going to accomplish.

"This one," Xander stated confidently, holding the mere scraps of fabric out for me to take. I hesitated.

"Are you sure? You haven't seen anything else in the bag yet," I pointed out, hoping he might reconsider and continue looking through the rest of the items. I secretly hoped he would forget about this piece and pick something else entirely.

"Never been more sure about something before. I want to see this one," he insisted. I swallowed thickly. Taking it from him, I headed for the bathroom. Just before I shut the door, with the wood cracked ever so slightly, I paused.

"Xander, um...I just want to warn you. I don't...I don't look like other girls do," I rasped out, my voice breaking halfway through my statement. I squeezed my eyes shut, hoping he wouldn't question it. My words were vague, but there was no way I could go out there like nothing was wrong. Not without some kind of heads-up or forewarning. I mean, my entire backside was absolutely mutilated.

"Is that supposed to change my opinion?" he asked. His tone held genuine confusion. I didn't reply. I started the nerve-wracking task of stripping down bare and pulling the skimpy outfit on. I worked slowly. Eventually, I completed the last task of clipping the garter belt to the red-tinted stockings Riley had apparently purchased to go with the set. I finally garnered the courage to take a final look in the mirror. I mean, I did look really good. Then I turned and my stomach plummeted.

I'm gonna make your body match your name.

Eric followed through with that promise, that was for sure. I didn't wait a second longer. I had no desire to torture my brain overthinking Xander's potential reactions a second longer. Taking a deep breath, I twisted the doorknob and carefully pushed it open.

If I wasn't so nervous, I might have giggled at how cute the immediate jump to attention he did was. He sat up a bit straighter in his seat, his eyes solely focused on me. I watched the way his brain processed the sight of me as his gaze shifted from my face to my body. His tongue peeked out to wet his lower lip before pulling it between his teeth. His eyes darkened seconds before they began shifting from the hazel shade I'd come to love to that of his wolf's. *That's a good sign at least.* He leaned forward in his seat, positioning his elbows on his knees as he rested his face on a single clenched fist. He continued silently looking me up and down, his gaze covering every inch of me.

"Do a spin for me," he grunted, though it almost sounded more like an aroused growl than words. I bit the inside of my cheek before closing my eyes and slowly turning, one step at a time. I could tell the second he saw the worst of the scars on my lower back, upper thighs, and backs of my upper arms. A vicious, murderous growl - so loud it was nearly deafening - resonated throughout the room. I'd be shocked if the whole pack didn't hear it, too.

"Move your hair," he demanded, his voice barely human. I'd been smart enough to leave it down so the length covered most of my back. Xander wasn't dumb, though. A single tear slipped down my cheek as I reached up and swooped my hair over a single shoulder.

"I'm going to skin him alive," he seethed, the sheer rage in his voice sent a chill down my spine. Overtop the numerous other bone-deep scars Eric had given me, was one final one. A large X was carved over the entirety of my back from each shoulder down to the opposite hip.

"So every male will know you're a reject. Damaged goods. Unwanted. Marked forever, but not how you wish to be. Isn't that right Scar?" Eric had said. I was so lost in my thoughts. I didn't realize Xander had gotten up from his chair and approached me until his hands landed on my shoulders. I jumped and released a startled cry.

"I'm so sorry," he husked out, sounding physically pained. "I wish I could take away all the hurt he put you through. But I can't," his words landed softly against the side of my face. He gently turned me to face him. "What I can tell you without a shadow of a doubt, Scarlett, is that someday soon - when you're comfortable and you're ready for it - I'm going to put my mark on you. And then I'm going to spend every single day for the rest of our lives doing whatever I can to help you forget the ones he put on you," he stated. The conviction in his voice was so strong it made my knees weak.

"Why not now?" I asked. The warm fuzzy sensation in my entire body felt way too similar to the thing Jackie described as love. I emphasized my question by tilting my head ever so slightly, further exposing the bare skin of my neck. My heart pounded in my chest and I held my breath. I'd put myself in this position countless times. I'd begged the wrong man for this same thing on so many occasions, only to be flat out rejected over and over again.

The hesitation I saw in his eyes was an immediate gut punch. It felt like someone had knocked the wind out of me. I swallowed thickly, harshly biting the inside of my lip to prevent it from wobbling with emotion. I was about to shove myself away from him until he spoke.

"I don't know that I'll be able to stop at just the mark," he rumbled out, the shifting of his eyes starting back up again. Then the hesitation made sense, and my emotions did a complete 180. I don't know that I'll be able to stop at just the mark...I don't know that I'll be able to stop at just the mark...able to stop at just the mark...at just the mark...

I gripped the fabric of his shirt in my hands and held it tight. All I could do was simply shrug my shoulders in reply. My knees wanted to give out as his words continued to run through my mind on replay. Apparently, that was all the convincing he needed. He tangled his fingers in my hair and pulled my neck into a further submission-bearing position. He began lathering my skin with a slew of open-mouthed kisses. I released a soft sigh of his name as he hit that same spot from when we were on the couch. I was only able to enjoy the feeling for a few seconds before the harsh sting of his teeth piercing my skin followed. It felt like all the air was forced out of my lungs. Thankfully, the harsh pain only lasted a split second. Then, the mind-numbing, all-consuming pleasure took over. It was so intense it took my ability to stand as my legs gave away. I leaned all my weight against Xander to stay standing.

Sealing his mark, Xander's hands were everywhere. His touch felt like magic. I wanted to be wrapped up in his embrace completely and never leave it.

"How fond of this are you?" Xander husked out when he was finally able to tear his lips away from sucking on both sides of my neck. It took me a second to realize he was referring to the brand-new lingerie set I was wearing. He pinched the garter between two fingers. I hadn't realized his other arm snaked its way around my body and was cupping as much of my ass as he could possibly fit in one hand.

I gave a harsh shake of my head. "Don't care," I rushed out.

"Good," he growled. Fisting the material in his hand, it appeared as if he was going to rip it away. However, he hesitated for a moment. "Is me ripping this off of you until you're completely naked for me going to trigger any memories I need to avoid?" he asked. Yes. I'm in love. I hooked my hand around the back of his neck and harshly jerked his face down to my own. The kiss was borderline violent in intensity. I proceeded to cover his hand with my own and helped him rip the garter and panties off in one go. I begrudgingly pulled away from our kiss for just long enough that he was able to slip his shirt off. Next to go was my bra. Xander tore it in two at the middle of the cups before pushing it off my shoulders. I made quick work of his belt and pants zipper before he took over and shoved them down his legs.

Stepping out of his pants, he reached for me. He hoisted me into his arms by the backs of my thighs. I released a quiet squeal of surprise. I was fascinated by how easily he multitasked in carrying us to the bed and kissing my neck. It was much more coordinated than our previous attempt downstairs. I expected him to drop me on the bed. Instead, he lifted me a bit higher on his hips and crawled onto it with me. When my back finally hit the mattress, I took a few seconds to ogle - really appreciating his body. He was sculpted like a fine piece of art. Damn, I got so lucky.

"Do you want to keep going?" Xander asked, breaking through my haze of mating pheromone-induced lust. I had to blink a few times to understand his question.

"Yes. So badly," I practically whined. I quickly realized how borderline pathetic it had sounded. Did he want to stop? Is that why he asked? What if he was having second thoughts?

"Scarlett," the rough utterance of my name pulled me from my thoughts. The dark look in Xander's eyes captivated me. "I'm so hard it hurts right now. I have about two seconds of self-control left. I'm lucky I have any at all. I need to know if you still seriously want this or if I need to leave. I want this bad, sweetheart, but if you want to wait I need to know right now," he groaned. I started shaking my head vigorously.

"I want this!" I rushed out breathlessly, emphasizing my point by reaching down and gently grasping at Xander's 'so hard it hurts' manhood. I was probably better off not doing that. Getting a handful of just how well-endowed he was... It made my entire nether region cramp in anticipatory pain. Xander moaned loudly before burying his face in my neck. I could see the prominent vein on the side of his neck bulge angrily at the restraint he was showing. I gave his member a squeeze before beginning to move my hand up and down his length.

He pulled his face away from my neck. Adjusting his body, his hands were resting on the mattress on either side of my face. "Scarlett, baby, that feels incredible, but you have to stop or you're going to make me blow my load before I've even gotten inside of you," he grunted. I scraped my bottom lip with my teeth as I stilled my hand. The term of endearment had my nether regions flooding and throbbing more intensely.

Baby. I like that one too.

"Hurry up, I want you inside me," I rasped out, unsure where the confidence to actually say that comment had even come from.

"Fuck," Xander hissed before kissing me hard. I was confused when he slowly worked his way down my body leaving a trail of wet kisses right to where I was throbbing for him. I thought he wanted to mate?

"I want to make sure this feels good for you. It'll help if you've already come and are relaxed," Xander said when he looked up at me. He must have seen my slightly confused face.

I wasn't sure what to expect from any of this, but the second Xander put his mouth on me I felt like I was going to explode. I could barely catch my breath. It was so good and so much all at once. First he used his tongue. Then he added a single finger. I arched my back before hissing at the slight sting when he added a second finger. I didn't have time to focus on the slight burn because moments later his lips latched onto my clit and sucked. I couldn't even formulate a coherent thought. The only thing I could do was moan his name over and over. His fingers curled inside of me as he increased the pressure on my clit. That's when I came. Hard. He continued to suck and stroke me until I'd ridden out the last wave of my orgasm. My body felt like putty as he pulled away, wiping his face with the back of his hand. That's so sexy. I want him right now.

"Condom or no condom?" Xander asked with a smirk as he readjusted our position, once again settling between the V of my thighs. The image of having a pup of my own immediately flooded my brain at the question. it had my wolf whining with deep want in my head so loud I almost winced outwardly. Was I ready for a baby yet? Absolutely not. But if this was something my wolf - who was the reason I was still alive today - was more than ready for and clearly wanted this deeply...

"No condom," I answered soundly. He had already been leaning over to open the nightstand next to us, likely anticipating a different response. His eyebrows shot up before a wide smile graced his face. Yes, I love this man. And those dimples. His smile grew even wider.

"Just so we're clear - the condoms aren't leftovers or ones I've had from anything recent. They were kind of a gag gift from my beta and gamma after they found out about our arrangement," he informed me. His words were followed by him sliding his hands up my thighs in a slow caress. His eyes followed the trail his hands made in an appreciative manner. I didn't know how he knew the thought was going to cross my mind. Knowing the condoms were new and intended for us made me breathe a sigh of relief.

I brought my hand up to gently rub one of the arms that was positioned next to my head, the touch catching his attention. "I'll be as gentle as possible," he reassured me. Leaning down, he captured my lips in another searing kiss. My eyes had closed, but they flew open with a gasp a few seconds later. The feel of Xander rubbing his tip up and down my sex sent the most delicious sensation throughout my entire body. With one last teasing nip at my bottom lip, he lined himself up and slowly eased inside of me. I was expecting pain. At least a throbbing. However, there was only a pinch of discomfort followed by mind-numbing pleasure. Xander released a few garbled curse words under his breath as he finished easing his entire length inside of me.

I brought my legs up to wrap around his hips as his pelvis met my own. When his body brushed up against my throbbing clit, I grabbed onto his shoulders and dug my nails into his skin. The sensation was too much. Too good.

"You fit perfectly," Xander growled against the shell of my ear just before he finally started to move his hips. The rhythm wasn't slow or fast, it was just right. I nodded my head in agreement with his previous words, but my pleasure-high brain couldn't even come up with the most basic response in reply. All I could do was moan. I clenched my legs around his hips as he picked up his speed. He reached down, sliding one hand along my hip before lifting it slightly. The new angle had me crying out. I let my hands drag down his back. Grasping his firm butt, I pulled him into me harder. The action must've been the cue he needed. Moments later his pace switched from slow and steady to something much more satisfying.

Xander shortened his thrusts, his length just barely leaving me before he buried himself to the hilt once more. The sound of the headboard banging against the wall with every thrust was nearly drowned out by our collective moans.

"I'm gonna-" I finally managed to husk out as I felt my body winding so tightly with pleasure that it was nearly unbearable.

"C'mon, Scarlett. Take us there, baby," Xander growled against my ear before nipping at the skin on my neck just below it. It didn't take more than three more thrusts before I threw my head back into the pillow. I damn near screamed as my orgasm slammed into me like a freight train. Xander's fingers that were holding my hip dug into my skin before he followed me into the abyss of pleasure. The force of his orgasm had me yelping as I continued contracting around him rhythmically. The entrails of my own release were not dying down in intensity.

The sound of our mutual panting was the only sound in the room as we both slowly came down from our intense highs. When my brain could finally form a thought, I removed my grip from his body. I realized, regretfully, that I'd dug my nails dug into his skin.

"I'm sorry," I winced as his eyes traveled to where I was examining the scratches and grooves I'd made in his back and sides with my claws.

"Never apologize for that. That tells me I'm doing my job right," he smirked cockily. I giggled softly while trailing my hands up his chest and around his neck, playing with the short hair at the nape of his neck. He started to pull out a few seconds later, but I halted the movement by pressing my foot against the back of his thigh. He gave me a questioning look.

"Don't pull out just yet. I like feeling filled by you," I said. My eyes went wide as my cheeks heated with a blush. I once again shocked myself with my own bold confidence to say what I was thinking and wanted. His eyes darkened immensely as he licked his lower lip.

"Say it again," he growled as he sank back in all the way and circled his hips.

# CHAPTER 22



Scarlett's POV

I wasn't sure what time it was the next morning when I woke up, but it was the greatest night of sleep I've had in my entire life. It was likely a combination of my body being so blissfully exhausted when Xander and I finally called it a night, as well as the luxury of having my mate by my side as I slept. I wasn't entirely sure what to do with being so well-rested.

I released a very necessary stretch, arching my back upwards as I did so. The movement caused the blankets and sheets to fall away from my chest and down to my midriff.

"Mmm," Xander released a deep hum of appreciation. "Good morning indeed," his sleepy rasp followed the sound from next to me. I turned to see his eyes trained directly on my bare chest. I giggled in response. In a flash, Xander grasped me and adjusted our positions so I was straddling his waist as he lounged underneath me. Sex last night only consisted of missionary and a very lazy - but still satisfying - final round in the middle of the night. I had only been asleep an hour when Xander woke me to do it from a spooning position. Remembering how he'd slipped inside me as we cuddled had my lower region lubing up appreciatively.

"How sore are you?" Xander asked as a look of need took over his face. I shrugged one shoulder before leaning slightly forward to brace my hands on his chest. I closed the remaining gap between us and softly, teasingly, kissed him. "Are you gonna line yourself up or do I need to do it for you?" I mumbled against his lips. He cursed under his breath before rushing to do as I asked. He helped me sink back down on him, releasing a hiss as I finally enveloped all of him. I didn't have a clue what I was doing in this position, but I had a good idea of what I was supposed to do. Going off of instinct, and what felt good, I found a pace that had both Xander and myself moaning loudly within seconds. His hands found my butt, occasionally moving me to hit a specific angle that pulled a series of deep, appreciative groans from his chest.

I was so close to my orgasm that I could taste it when Xander's previously closed eyes shot open as he jerked up in bed. I choked on a gasp. The shift in position forced him so deep I felt like all the air in my lungs was squeezed out of me. I looked at him with utter confusion as he grasped the bed sheet and hoisted it up,  covering my back just seconds before our bedroom doors came flying open. I clung to his shoulders as my mouth dropped open, this time with a gasp of surprise. Well...and maybe a little something else. He was massaging my cervix at this angle.

"Get the fuck out!" Xander roared, his arms moving to wrap protectively around my back. I glanced over my shoulder to see the silhouette of a man's body retreating fast as anything. Xander definitely scared him. Xander was still seething a minute later. My body was too keyed up from not realizing someone was coming to just resume our prior activity and finish what we'd started. I groaned unhappily before dropping my forehead down onto his shoulder.

"I was so close to coming," I complained, my tone whiny more than anything. Xander huffed out a laugh.

"I'll make up for it later," he rasped out before pressing a kiss to the side of my head, smoothly maneuvering me back onto my back before pulling out. I grimaced, the discomfort of all the rounds we'd gone last night and now the one this morning finally starting to make an appearance.

Xander had a really hard time leaving me this morning once we'd gotten out of bed to go find out whatever he was apparently so desperately needed for. I giggled as I surveyed the fridge thinking about how he'd left and come back three different times for 'just one more kiss, then I'll actually go'. My stomach growled loudly, bringing me back to the task at hand - feeding myself. I was famished. Jackie wasn't wrong when she said sex was a fantastic workout. I couldn't decide what I was in the mood for, so I pulled out all the items to make a little of everything that I was craving. Thinking about Xander having to abruptly leave without breakfast had me tripling everything I was cooking to accommodate his hefty appetite.

Xander's POV

"Someone better be dying!" I growled as I entered my office, my tone harsher than it probably should've been. Dammit, could you blame me? I was right in the middle of being ridden by my mate. I wish I could say it was a boner killer but I'm still hard as a rock. It was damn uncomfortable.

I was greeted with both silence and smug, knowing looks from all of my men. "Well?" I prompted, getting even more pissed off at not being answered.

"The men from the Dawn pack are threatening to leave within the hour if the business they came here for isn't finished. They also said they will sever our ally agreement. As much as I hated...i nterrupting you, it was necessary," Donovan rushed out, the smirk still not leaving his face.

"Threaten to leave? Over a single day delay?" I grunted in annoyance before walking farther into the room and rounding my desk to sit.

"Xander, it's almost four-thirty in the afternoon," Griffin snickered, trying to hide his amusement and failing.

"What?" I deadpanned, my eyes immediately finding the clock on the wall and realizing they weren't lying. It actually was four-thirty. Scarlett and I slept the entire day. "Shit. Call them in," I ordered before running my hands down my face. Three irritated-looking men sauntered into the room a couple of minutes later.

"Gentlemen, I apologize for the severe delay," I noticed how their nostrils flared - obviously taking in my changed scent that was distinct to mated males. I raised a single eyebrow in question. Shit, I'm just going to have to address this. "Obviously, you can tell that my mate and I completed the mating process last night. It was an unforeseen turn of events and I want to apologize again for the inconvenience it's posed for you all," I spoke calmly and clearly. There was a second of silence before a huge smile broke out on one of their faces. He appeared to be the leader of their little group.

"I was damn irritated having to wait, but no one can be upset about an Alpha finally claiming his Luna. Congratulations, Alpha Herrington. We're all very happy for you," he finished before reaching his hand out to shake mine. I grasped it and accepted the handshake, grateful the truth seemed to subdue them. It took me longer than necessary to re-read through the agreement. I wanted to be sure nothing had changed before signing it and my mind refused to quit wandering to Scarlett. Once our business was said and done and we'd escorted the men to their vehicles, the barrage of questions ensued.

"So..." Donovan spoke before letting his implied question float between us but continued when I just smirked and stayed quiet. "It turns out it wasn't Patty-cake you guys were playing behind that door. I already knew that though because your entire upper level smells like sex and pheromones," he ribbed. "Just for the record, I would've rather been skinned alive than interrupt you this morning, but, well, you know." I chuckled in response.

"You're lucky I knew it was you. I think anyone else would've gotten skinned alive in response," I murmured. They all stopped at the door to our main conference room, but I kept walking.

"Where are you going?" Griffin hollered after me.

"Where do you think?" I asked him in a 'duh' tone. "To finish what Donovan interrupted this morning," I finished with a lop-sided grin. They all hooted and hollered after me as I finished the rest of the walk to Scarlett and I's door. The thick scent of breakfast food slowly wafted into the hallway and I knew I was in for a treat. The idea of breakfast followed by bending her over the table had my footsteps quickening.

"That was fast," Scarlett commented from behind the griddle as she saw me make my entrance. My eyes immediately went to the shirt she was wearing - it was one of mine. Breakfast is definitely going to have to come after table sex I immediately thought to myself.

"Do you think you can multitask?" I gruffly asked. My barely-dissipated erection from earlier came back so quickly I was surprised I didn't get light-headed from the rapid shift in blood flow from one head to the other.

"Multitask?" she asked, her tone filled with confusion.

"Yes. Can you flip pancakes while being fucked from behind?" I asked while coming to stand next to her at the kitchen island. I smelled the shift in her scent immediately as her eyes glossed over with need.

"I'm always willing to try something once," she murmured breathily. Safe to say, the pancakes were completely black on one side before Scarlett finally remembered to flip them. I just couldn't help myself; I was addicted to her and my impulse control was apparently non-existent when it came to her. I think if she just merely breathed my way, I'd get hard. She could ask me to give her the world and I'd go research how to accomplish that.

"How's your omelet?" she asked after we'd both scarfed almost half of our plates down.

"Fantastic. The best omelet I've ever had I'm pretty sure," I immediately responded with a smile. I could hear her sweet, feminine voice in my head - the sound was just slightly fuzzy.

"I bet he's just saying that." I knew it was her own thought as she looked away bashfully.

"Really, I'm not just saying it. You're the best cook I've ever met. Better than my mom - but don't tell her I said that," I said followed by a soft laugh. She giggled, but there was a perplexed look on her face. "What is it, sweetheart?" I asked, a dreamy look overtaking her face as the pet name left my lips. I've known exactly the effect it had on her since the first time I'd used it. I was just glad I affected her as much as she did me.

"It's the craziest thing, but you always seem to know exactly what to say in response to what I'm thinking," she said. I sat back in my chair to study her face, wondering if she was messing with me despite the lack of sarcasm in her voice. After a few seconds, I realized she wasn't teasing at all - it was a genuine statement. It took me a whole two seconds to realize that no one has ever taught her about the connection mates have after completing their bond - one of which included being able to hear each other's thoughts when tapped in or not blocking them.

"It's because I can hear what you're thinking, sweetheart. Has no one ever told you that?" She sat up much straighter in her chair at my statement.

"What?" she demanded. I could hear her heartbeat kick up ever so slightly as I nodded.

"It's something that comes with the mark and bond thereafter. If you're not blocking my thoughts and I'm not blocking yours, I will hear them inside my head almost as if they're my own. However, it's not my voice, it's yours. That's how I know they're from you," I explained. Her mouth opened and closed a couple of times before she slumped back in her chair.

"How come I can't hear yours?" she asked, appearing a bit put off by not having access to mine. There was no malicious intent behind blocking her from getting my own, I just didn't want my wolf and I's...intense thoughts about her to freak her out when we had just mated.

"I've had mine blocked so that you didn't get overwhelmed by my wolf," I answered honestly with a rakish grin. "I can teach you how to tap into mine or how to block me from getting in to hear yours or from having them passively come to me," I continued.

She nodded enthusiastically. I explained the various processes. Some were difficult to explain, but she caught on quickly - a fact that didn't surprise me as I'd realized she was incredibly smart. I had her test out blocking me by thinking about anything and seeing if it came through. She got the most adorable smile of pride on her face when she knew she had done it successfully.

"Okay, now how do I hear yours?" she asked with excitement. I couldn't help the smile that came to my face. I released a deep breath before cueing my wolf and removing my own block. A few seconds later the image my wolf had been showing me all morning popped back into my head. I knew the second she got it as her cheeks turned bright red and her jaw dropped slightly. My wolf was, admittedly, completely out of control. I don't think he'd ever be fully satisfied unless I found a way to keep Scarlett on her back 24/7.

"That was my wolf," I explained with a snicker and a slight shake of my head.

"I can see why you kept me blocked now," she giggled back. "However, I'm not opposed to the idea..." she trailed off, clearly referring to my wolf's desire. I groaned, pushing my chair away from the table and quickly reaching for her. I swiftly swooped her off of her chair and plopped her down on my lap. She immediately moved to straddle me as her hands dove into my hair. Our faces moved toward each other at the same time, our lips meeting in a searing kiss. She still wasn't wearing any panties from our pre-breakfast workout. I'd used them to wipe off the cum that was dripping down the inside of her thigh. The memory had me growling into her mouth as my hand found the thick flesh over her hip and pulled her to grind against me.

Unfortunately, we didn't get far - yet again - as I could hear and smell Jackie approaching quickly. I couldn't find it in me to pull away as Scarlett grew more into the kiss, sucking my tongue and effectively pulling a moan from me.

"Well, well, well, if it isn't the newest mated couple screwing like bunnies anywhere and everywhere they possibly can," Jackie called out, her tone filled with mirth as she entered our place. She leisurely made her way toward us.

"I lied earlier about liking your friend," I grumbled against Scarlett's lips when I finally pulled away. She giggled at my statement before peering over her shoulder at her best friend.

"Well apparently not because we keep getting interrupted," Scarlett shot back with faux irritation.

"Mm, yes. Sorry about this. Justin spilled the beans to me as soon as he got back this morning that you'd finally done the naked tango. No one's happier for you than I am," she said while reaching the table and pulling out a chair to sit. Scarlett squirmed uncomfortably, clearly thinking about her state of undress and our current position. It wasn't doing anything to help with the raging erection I now had. I held the shirt she was wearing, which was long enough to be a dress, down to keep her covered. I gently turned her on my lap so she was no longer straddling me and leaned her back against my chest to face Jackie.

"Did you just come to see if Justin was lying to you?" Scarlett asked with a smirk.

"No..." Jackie trailed off as a regretful look overtook her face. This can't be good. I felt Scarlett tense immediately. I placed my hand on her thigh and began rubbing soothing circles over her soft skin.

"Look, I hate to be the one to have to tell you this, Scarlett, but there's no way I can keep it from you and I know you'd kill me if I did. Mika's stirring up trouble again, except this time she's really crossed the line. She successfully spread a new rumor around the pack halls that Xander and you aren't mated yet because Xander still loves her. She said, and I quote, to 'give it just one more week and he'll be crawling back to me'. I've also heard whisperings about Xander wanting 'nothing to do with that lying, conniving bitch and her annoying fake sob story'. I know we talked about you addressing this with both her and the pack, but I think it has to be sooner rather than later. I hate that she's forcing your hand in any of this, but I refuse to let her stand around and disrespect you," Jackie finished, a harsh edge to her tone from the anger of the situation.

"I've had enough of her. I'm contacting the council and requesting an immediate eviction and relocation. She's poison to this pack and always has been. I will not allow her to try and turn even a single pack member against you," I spoke, my anger seeping into my tone. Scarlett's hand came up to cover the one on her thigh.

"That will help, but it's not going to solve the issue of her already spreading the rumors through the pack. There will undoubtedly be people who believe her, even if they don't say so," I murmured before sharing a thoughtful look with Jackie. "Call your mom and tell her that we will both be attending dinner with the pack. Everyone will only have half an hour to scramble together but I'm sure they'll want to see how we interact," I stated before pushing myself off of his lap to get ready for dinner.

I sauntered into our closet and rooted around the rack looking for the specific dress I knew Jackie had purchased for me. She'd jokingly said that it was going to be my 'coming out' dress. Slipping it on, I took a deep and shaky breath before smoothing my hands down the front of the semi-fitted pearl-white silk dress. It had an ultra-thin strap that hooked around my neck to hold the dress up. The entire back was fully exposed from my shoulders all the way to the dimples on my lower back.

"This is it," I whispered to myself.

# CHAPTER 23



S carlett's POV

    I picked up my phone, texting Jackie to take Xander with her and I would meet them in the dining room. I just needed a few more minutes to collect my thoughts. I used the time to finish throwing on some mascara and sweeping my hair into a simple updo. I also didn't want Xander's massive, hulking frame to be the focus of the room when I walked in. I needed to make sure all eyes were only on me as I dispelled the fabricated lies Mika had spread. Checking the clock on my phone, I was going to be a couple of minutes late. I hurriedly grabbed my phone and threw my shoes on before making my way to the pack dining hall.

I could hear the endless chatter going on inside the room. The only separation were the double doors. I let out a shaky breath before grasping both doors and throwing them wide open. The second I did so, every set of eyes in the room tracked to me. I swallowed and scanned the room. I quickly set my sights on the table where Xander and the rest of the high-ranking pack members were sitting. I kept my eyes straight, not making eye contact with a single pack member as I slowly made my way into the room and toward Xander. The previously silent room began erupting in gasps of horror and hushed words spoken amongst one another.

I could feel the tension in the room instantly transform to sorrow. There were even a few mournful whines released into the air. As I grew closer to the center of the room, I caught sight of Mika in the corner of my eye. I switched the focus of my gaze from Xander to her, unblinking as my glare hardened. She hadn't seen my back yet, though she swallowed thickly as her eyes broke my stare and trailed over my arms.

I finally spoke when I was just a couple of feet from her. "Spread another lie about what I went through - something you can't even begin to understand or even imagine - and I will make sure it's the last thing you do. You can trash talk me about anything and everything else. Keep my past out of your mouth," I growled before continuing the rest of the distance to our table. Xander immediately stood to embrace me when I was finally within arms reach of him. His arms wrapped around my body and he rested them gently against the bare skin of my lower back.

"You're the bravest woman I know. I'm so sorry she pushed you into feeling this was your only option," he murmured against my temple. I sighed before pulling back and looking up into his eyes. He quickly swooped down and captured my lips in a sweet kiss. I knew it was both because he wanted to and as a display to the rest of the pack. I was his, he had chosen me. Pulling back I turned to face the room of shocked faces.

"I understand there are many false allegations going around about me. Rumors concerning my past and subsequently my in-volvement with Alpha Herrington. I think it's plain to see that these allegations are completely baseless. I may be your Luna, but that doesn't mean I have had a perfect life. I'm not a stranger to pain and I know many of you aren't either. If anyone has any questions about my intentions, or wishes to question my integrity, you can come to me directly. I have no issue answering any questions as best as I can without reliving painful moments of my past," I spoke. I scanned the crowd and met the eyes of multiple pack members as I did so.

I turned and sat in the seat that Xander had pulled out for me. There was an incredibly awkward silence plaguing our table. Vanessa was trying to shield her face from everyone. Her quiet sniffles and gentle shaking of her shoulders gave away the fact that she was crying. Xander's father had a tortured look on his face as his jaw clenched and unclenched. The hand that wasn't stroking his mate's back to comfort her was balled into a tight fist, his knuckles white.

"You're all acting like you're the ones with a mosaic of scars on your body. Lighten up," I finally spoke, breaking the thick tension at the table. Xander released an amused snort before using the hand of the arm that was draped across the back of my chair to gently stroke the skin of my shoulder.

"Good sex must've loosened you up and restored your sense of humor," Jackie commented, causing Vanessa to release a sound between a gasp and a choking noise. She proceeded to turn a bright shade of red. Riley, Raven, and Peyton let out quiet giggles at both Jackie's words and Vanessa's response. Feeling light and playful - more so than I ever had before - I decided to give Jackie an equally cheeky response.

"Must have," I murmured with a smirk that I quickly hid behind my glass of water. I was fully aware that many pack members at the tables immediately around us were intently listening to every word we were exchanging.

"So, what finally did it?" Jackie pressed further, a mischievous look on her face.

"Jackie, I don't think-" Vanessa began, looking like she'd rather be anywhere than at that table listening to a discussion concerning her son's sex life. I couldn't say I blamed her.

"He makes me feel safe," I commented with complete honesty. I was shocked that I'd even answered her, let alone told her the truth. The answer made me get a warm, tingly feeling in my chest that I knew wasn't heartburn. It also...didn't feel like it was my own? My brows furrowed slightly as I glanced at Xander next to me with a questioning gaze. He leaned down to press a soft kiss on my forehead. This time the butterflies that erupted in my stomach were definitely all mine.

"Amongst many other things," I added, trying to dispel the new wave of awkwardness my answer had brought on. It clearly made everyone think about my very public display tonight and the indications behind what I'd said.

"Other things?" Xander was the one to ask, looking both smug and curious.

"Are you fishing for a compliment, Alpha Herrington?" Donovan teased from a few seats down. Xander just laughed softly in response, but immediately went silent when I'd sent him the images my wolf was playing through my mind; very naughty ones that conveyed exactly what we liked about him that fit into the category of 'other things'. Xander's eyes went black as he licked his bottom lip.

"Giving your mate blue balls at a public dinner isn't considered polite, Luna Scarlett. Just in case no one has ever told you," Raven commented with a laugh. Everyone else joined in with her, clearly detecting the change in Xander's demeanor.

"I'll make it up to him later," I commented off-handedly, not-so-subtly maneuvering my hand to his thigh and giving it a light stroke. My remark caused all the men at the table to roar with laughter before releasing a few teasing hoots and hollers. The rest of the dinner went smoothly. My scars were still a very interesting subject to the pack as it didn't sound like much conversation was happening around us.

"Luna Scarlett," came a soft baritone voice behind me. Immediately recognizing it, I turned to give Damien a smile. I nodded for him to continue. He shifted nervously on his feet as everyone at the table's eyes set on him. "I just came to tell you congratulations on your mating from all of us. Um, from the orphanage? Yeah. And thanks again," he said softly, a hue of pink splattering his cheeks. My smile grew immensely.

"Thank you, Damien. I appreciate it more than you'll ever know," I said, sincerity in my tone. He was the first member - outside of high-ranking officials - to formally acknowledge my officialized status among the pack. Something I didn't take lightly. He didn't hang around long - only enough time for me to ask how school was going now that he was attending with the rest of the pack children.

Things continued going smoothly with conversation starting to pick up more around us. That is, until dessert was being served and Xander's father decided to speak up.

"So, when can I expect you two to make me a grandpa?" There was a playful look on his face, telling me that he had no real expectations and that he was just jumping onto the teasing wagon - as everyone else had along the course of the evening. The corner of Xander's mouth turned upward into a lazy half-smile that made one of his perfect dimples pop.

"Who knows? Could be in just nine short months, I suppose," he commented off-handedly, taking a bite of cheesecake to hide his cheeky smile. I giggled behind my hand, anticipating his parents' reactions. However, a huge crashing noise sounded behind us.

"DON'T TOUCH ME!" Mika's distinct voice screamed at the top of her lungs at one of her minions. She quickly stormed out after. By the looks of things, the crash appeared to be all the plates from the table Mika had been sitting at swiped to the floor in her rage.

"Well, apparently someone's not happy Xander's been shooting his baby juice inside you," Jackie muttered under her breath. It was only loud enough that I could hear. I sputtered out a laugh before giving her an incredulous look. "What? Clearly it's the truth," she snorted. Everyone looked at us, curious as to what we were talking about.

"On that note, I think we'll take the rest of our dessert to go," Xander said as he stood from his chair. Everyone at the table eyed his already empty plate.

"You have such pressing matters that you can't stay a little longer?" Vanessa asked, looking only slightly serious.

"If you want to be a grandma, yes," he shot back with a mischievous smirk.

"Xander Joseph!"

Xander's weight fell completely against me, pushing me further into the mattress as I panted in an attempt to catch my breath.

"Doggy's definitely my favorite so far," I commented as my breathing continued to slow and even out once again.

"Fuck, I love you so much," Xander groaned out against the shell of my ear. "Oh, shit, am I crushing you?" he rushed out before swiftly pushing himself up, removing his weight from my body.

"Mmm, I kinda liked it," I murmured softly, "however, my knees are starting to ache from being on them in this position for so long," I said. He chuckled, moving onto his back. Once settled, he shifted my body so I was tucked against his side. I pressed my face into his chest. A few minutes passed before I decided to bring up the thought I'd been mulling over since we'd retired to our bedroom for the night.

"So-"

"I can already tell I'm not going to like whatever is about to come out of your mouth solely based on that opening," he huffed out. I laughed softly in response.

"I'd like to start training again. And with someone who's appropriately matched for me as far as skill set. I don't want to lose my edge just because I left The Council. I don't think there's anyone among your female warriors suited to spar with me-"

"Then you will train with me," he immediately growled, though it was soft and more gruff than anything. I fought to keep the smile that wanted to break out on my face at bay. I lifted myself up so I could get a proper look at his face.

"You don't think that would be too much of a distraction?" I asked, purposely batting my lashes and beginning to trace barely-there, teasing lines across his chest with my pointer finger. He swallowed thickly. Taking a deep breath, he shook his head harshly.

"No. I don't. It may be hard to believe, but sex isn't even close to the most important thing to my wolf where you're concerned. It's your safety. I can't promise when we're done training that he will just let you shower and go right to sleep, though," he said. A grin that couldn't be described as anything other than wolfish pull at his lips. It was at that moment I knew Xander was purposely allowing his thoughts to roll over to me.

An image of him and me in the shower slowly appeared in my mind. I was kneeling in front of him. His hand harshly gripped my hair, pulling it back and out of my face. He was simultaneously using the grip to yank my head back and expose my neck. His other hand gripped my breast, tweaking the nipple to a hardened peak.

My hands were wrapped around his painfully erect member, the throbbing tip just about to enter my mouth.

My breath caught in my throat at the image. Remembering his words - that the most important thing to him was my safety - made warm fuzzies envelope my chest. An increased surge of moisture added to the already growing wetness that was accumulating between my legs. This man made me feel so wanted in the best ways.

"I've been having real trouble reaching that spot in the middle of my back when I shower. Think you can lend me a hand?" I leaned in to whisper against his lips. I trailed my hand down and wrapped it around his dick as I said the word hand. He released a long hiss as his hips jerked upwards into my palm.

Safe to say Xander got me dirtier before finally helping me clean up during that shower. Not that I was complaining one bit.

# CHaPTer 24



Scarlett's POV

It was so, so irrational. I knew it. I knew it was. I couldn't help it.

Ever since Xander had started training me a month ago I literally couldn't keep my hands to myself. It was like a light switch went off in my brain or something. I simply couldn't get enough of him. I mean, don't get me wrong, Xander wasn't complaining. No one, really, was complaining in a sense. I think it was actually Beta Donovan who joked and said over text, "Xander is so well laid I could probably start a war with every single pack right now and he wouldn't even bat an eye." Xander even laughed when he read it if I remember right. I'm not entirely sure - I was sucking him off in his office when he read it to me, so my memory is a bit hazy on that one.

Xander's ease could even be felt by the pack from what his father had said in off-handed comments during a couple of shared dinners at their house. The pack knew their Alpha was better rested. Less anxious. That feeling of ease then passed onto the pack. Victoria - despite her utter despair at knowing exactly why - couldn't be happier for us. Every time she saw me, she gave me a tight hug that eventually turned tearful and told me how glad she was that I was there. I wasn't an overly emotional person, but I relished those hugs despite feeling mostly awkward during them.

Elder Adelia's visit had come and gone before I'd even realized I'd been here a full month. Xander and I hosted. We'd invited his parents to join as well given the circumstances of it. It was still considered a visit from a member of The Council afterall. Afterward, Elder Adelia and I shared a heart-to-heart over a mug of warm cocoa. There was more than a little splash of brandy in it.

Sitting on the couch next to her felt like old times. She told me all about how relieved Roger was that his library wouldn't ever again be rearranged out of Jackie's pure boredom. However, she also said there was now a kind of quiet the house hadn't had since Jackie and I became friends. She said everyone had noticed. I smiled sadly at her, realizing it was her way of telling me she missed me without outwardly saying the words and making me feel guilty. We promised to call each other at least once a week to stay in touch.

Xander and my's "provisionary period" we were given at the beginning of our mating had been up for exactly three weeks. We were still adjusting to spending much less time together every day. It was difficult since his parents completely stepped back and Xander and I were expected to resume all our normal day-to-day functions as Alpha and Luna.

It really wasn't that big of a deal...except it meant that I had to learn to be okay with only having sex once in the morning. And then I had to wait all day until I got him to myself at night. Or I had to get creative and find ways to sneak in quickies. I'd discovered very quickly that only one orgasm was simply not enough to get me through. I wasn't sure how anyone functioned with just one to start the day. Or even none? Preposterous.

Luckily for Xander and me, I'm a very creative wolf.

This morning was a perfect example. Xander told me he had an early meeting he couldn't miss and the ten-minute shower quickie was all we had time for. I had smartly worn a flowy dress today and doubled up on all my morning tasks, delegating as I went. When lunchtime came, I snuck my panties off. Easy access and comfy for straddling, or doing it on the desk; I wasn't going to discriminate. I popped the cotton material into my desk drawer before making the quick trip down the hall to Xander's office. I gave three quick knocks on his door before peeking my head in. I smiled widely when I saw he was alone. I quickly locked his office door behind me, my body thrumming with excitement.

"Scarlett, baby, I told you I had back-to-back meetings all day. Is something wrong?" The stress line on his forehead made me feel bad for interrupting his work. I folded my hands against the small of my back and leaned against the wooden door. I bit the corner of my bottom lip before silently admitting defeat. I would have to sulk back to my office and mourn our afternoon orgasms alone. I really missed getting to spend uninterrupted time with just him and me.

"No," I sighed before clearing my throat. Xander, though, knew me too well. Or I forgot to put my block up and he quite literally read my mind.

"Come here," he said, motioning me forward as he pushed himself a short distance away from his desk. I moved from where I was positioned at the door to stand between his spread legs. This wasn't helping my situation at all. There was something so sexy about how powerful he looked sitting in his big desk chair looking so manly and in charge.

"Scarlett, I asked you if something was wrong," he pressed again, reaching out to rest his large hand against my hip before allowing it to slide down to the side of my butt. Just as I went to open my mouth, the phone on his desk rang. He sighed heavily before pressing the speaker button and voicing an answer all the while not taking his eyes off me.

"Alpha Herrington, your 1:30 is on the line to speak with you," the voice echoed. I threw my head back and quietly groaned, practically falling into his chest. I pouted like a petulant child. When did I get so pathetic? This man's ability to screw me docile is uncanny.

"Can you just tell them I'm going to be a little bit? I had a minor unforeseen event come up that I need to take care of quickly, thank you," he mumbled before ending the call and turning back to me. I felt the subtle vibration of laughter from his chest against mine, telling me he likely had an idea why I was so irritated.

"Sweetheart, tell me what's wrong," he husked out softly against the shell of my ear. I pushed back against his chest so we were face to face again.

"What's wrong is we only had sex once this morning and you always give me at least two orgasms and if you don't do me right now I will....I don't know. Spontaneously combust probably!" I cried out as I fisted the expensive dress shirt he was wearing in my palms. "And don't you dare laugh at me!" I growled out, seeing the look of amusement on his face.

"I would never, baby. I take this very seriously," he said with an amused expression. "Are you wearing panties?" He asked, the tone of his voice getting me hot all over. I shook my head fervently. He made a tsking sound at me with his tongue a couple of times before murmuring, "My naughty girl. Walking around without anything on under this pretty dress." I preened at the compliment. It was one of my more recent sewing projects.

His phone had already started to ring again as he gently pushed me back so he could stand, but his eyes didn't wander from my face. He leaned down and captured my lips in a sweet kiss. It didn't last very long before they wandered down my jaw and to my neck. His hands on my hips slowly walked me back until my butt hit the edge of his desk. His teeth raked up the side of my neck to my ear. Goosebumps covered my entire body as he blew out his hot breath there before speaking.

"You want me to fuck you on it or bent over it, sweetheart?" he husked out, his hands leaving my hips to begin lazily undoing his belt. The sight made my mouth water for his cock, which I could already see straining against the fabric of his expensive slacks.

"Scarlett," came his domineering voice - the one he had to use often in the middle of sex. I just couldn't stay focused long enough when it came to him. I sucked my bottom lip into my mouth, scraping it with my teeth harshly as I forced myself to make a decision. I wanted both, but we didn't have time for that. He popped the buttons on his pants and raised a single brow, a warning that I had about two seconds left before he made the decision for me.

"Over it," I rushed out. He grabbed me by the waist and spun me just as his phone started ringing for the third time. I couldn't even find it in me to feel sorry because I was soaking wet, dripping down the insides of my thighs. He threw the skirt of my dress up to uncover me. He released an appreciative whistle before pressing me forward, my hips touching the cold flesh of his oak desk. Seconds later I heard his zipper slide down, almost crying in relief. I knew I wouldn't have to wait much longer for what I'd been desperately needing all afternoon. The fourth phone call started just as his thick length slipped through my lower lips to coat himself in my running juices. He abruptly pulled back and sunk all the way in me with one firm stroke.

I gasped at the intrusion. My walls clenched and released rhythmically as I fought to keep from coming right then and there. Something I'd discovered - much to Jackie's displeasure and annoyance - was I happened to be one of those rare women that could come by just penetration alone. That didn't mean Xander's fingers weren't insanely magical, though. I went to swat them away as he attempted to play with my clit, much to Xander's confusion.

"If you do that I'm going to come right now and I want this to last longer than 15 seconds" I whined. Xander chuckled darkly. Shoving my own hand away, he made quick work on my sensitive nub. He simultaneously circled his hips, his cock still balls deep. I couldn't keep my long moan quiet as I suddenly came.

"I intend to get at least two orgasms out of you, baby," Xander insiste. He never let up as he started working me over through my orgasm. His fingers were relentless on my clit and his thrusts worked in time with his fingers. By the time our 'quickie' - which actually ended up being 35 minutes - was over, I'd had three orgasms and my legs were practically jello.

My upper body was laying against Xander's desk - which was currently supporting all of my weight - as he pressed chaste kisses to the back of my neck. He cleaned our collective come from between my legs and down my thighs - where it'd run after he pulled out.

Unfortunately, the sweet moment was ruined when the door handle jiggled. It was followed by someone banging on the door. "What the fuck, Xander! Why is your door locked? I've tried calling you four or five times now! What the hell is holding you up?!" Beta Donovan's voice yelled through the door.

"I'm sorry. We should've waited until later at home," I murmured softly, practically half asleep. Xander laughed softly at the lack of remorse in my words.

"Nonsense. I needed something to help relieve a little stress. This was exactly what I needed." He helped me slowly stand from where I'd been half-laying, half-leaning. He held my weight as I wobbled over to the couch. I sat with a slight grimace - at which Xander smirked before he proceeded to his office door to unlock it. Beta Donovan and Gamma Griffin came barging into the room.

"Oh, fuck. Could you have at least sprayed some Febreeze or something? Maybe think about it next time so it doesn't smell like your dick," Beta Donovan muttered with a grimace. He waved his hands in front of his face. I couldn't help the laugh that bubbled out of my chest at his reaction. Xander's scowl curled up into a smile before he smirked and winked at me.

"It's my office. If I want to have sex in it, I will. That's one of the perks of being Alpha," he joked.

"Well I hate to burst the post-coital bubble, but he wants an answer. Now. Well, actually, he wanted an answer an hour ago." Donovan grunted, a stressed look coming over his face. I watched as Xander's face morphed into one of anger, but I could see the underlying tenseness and anxiety. There was something he wasn't telling me.

"Who's the 'he'?" I asked. All eyes in the room snapped to me, almost as if forgetting I had been sitting right there.

"No one," Xander grunted out immediately. I cocked my head and raised an eyebrow at him and his reaction.

"No one?" I repeated.

"No one," he growled back, crossing his arms over his chest and adopting a defensive stance. "I have other things I need to get done before I'm finished for the night, so I'll see you when I get home," he stated, so much finality in his tone that it sparked a fire in my gut. I pursed my lips and nodded my head up and down slowly.

"I see. What would those things be?" I asked, watching as the vein in his neck began to bulge.

"Alpha duties."

"Mm. Mhmm." I felt bad for Beta Donovan and Gamma Griffin because I could tell by the incredibly uncomfortable stance that they did not want to be in the room with us anymore.

"Beta Donovan, who were you discussing?" I asked, moving my gaze from Xander to make direct eye contact with him.

"Beta, Gamma, you're dismissed," Xander quickly growled. I had to clench my teeth to keep from yelling at him in anger. Neither of them could ignore the Alpha command. They both cleared their throats awkwardly, giving a respectful bow to Xander and me before leaving quickly.

We stared at each other for a few seconds. When it was clear he had zero intention of telling me anything, I sucked back the tears my eyes wanted to release. "I'll make your bed in the guest room."

"I have a bed," he shot back with heat.

"Yes. You do. And tonight, it will be in the guest room," I snapped with equal anger.

# CHAPTER 25

Xander's POV

I paced back and forth in Donovan's kitchen. He stayed quiet and just watched me.

"You know she'll be safe with us if you decide to take her," he finally spoke. I attempted to massage out the crick in my neck with no luck as an involuntary growl left my lips.

"I don't like the thought of her leaving our pack grounds. She's most comfortable here," I husked out, forcing my wolf, who'd crept up during the encounter, down.

"But she's safest with you," he reasoned. I gripped the edge of his kitchen countertop and allowed my head to drop down. The mere idea of leaving Scarlett behind instead of taking her with me on this trip was upsetting enough that it had caused a forced shift earlier today right in the middle of my office. It's not like we were a brand new mated pair - it had been a little over a month now. However, it might as well have been with how needy I still felt for her and whenever I was around her.

There was just an ease when I was with her. We had a routine down. She always awoke early to make breakfast while I got ready for the day. Breakfast was usually silent as neither of us were huge morning people. We typically spent lunch apart as we both worked away at this list of things required of us by the pack. My favorite time of day was when our work days were over. We would cook dinner side-by-side while talking about our days. There was always a dessert of some sort - I'd quickly learned my mate had a terrible sweet tooth. Over dessert, she'd tell me stories from growing up in the orphanage. In return, I'd share my own childhood stories. Once we cleaned dinner up, we'd take a long relaxing shower together. Sometimes it would turn heated. Most of the time, we'd only exchange soft kisses and gentle touches. Scarlett had come to love when I would carefully wash her back. I spent a lot of our post-shower time gently massaging her back with the tonic we got from the pack doctor to help with the nerve pain she suffered with. We always ended our nights wrapped in each others' arms. Being away from her for even a day seemed like torture.

"I think you should talk to her-" Donovan's words were cut off by my harsh growl.

"Not a single person will speak a word of this to her until I've made a decision and subsequent plan. She's been through enough. She shouldn't have to shoulder this choice," I grunted.

"I can understand where you're coming from, and your concern, but I don't think you're giving her enough credit. I think she'd want to have a say. She'd at least want to be involved rather than kept in the dark."

"Yeah, well, speaking of. My little stunt of throwing you and Griffin out to keep her in the dark supposedly bought me a one night stay in the guest room," I grumbled, annoyed beyond belief. Donovan's light-hearted chuckle met my ears. I threw daggers at him with my eyes.

"Your mate is being generous. Whenever I piss Riley off she'll strip all the guest beds of their linens and put me on the couch." I shook my head at his admission before releasing a deep sigh.

"I'm gonna go talk to her," I mumbled before turning and leaving his place. The pit that had been in my stomach most of the day only worsened with each step I took closer to home.

"Alpha Harrington," one of Scarlett's guards nodded to me before moving out of the way of the door. I acknowledged her before entering. Our place was quiet, which wasn't necessarily unusual. However, there was something different. I couldn't place my finger on it until I sauntered further into the first floor. Usually when I came home, the first thing I saw was Scarlett moving around in the kitchen grabbing out the ingredients for whatever we were going to cook. Tonight, however, she wasn't anywhere in sight. I'll be fixing my own supper. And eating it alone it seems. Fuck. I tried to roll out the tension in my shoulders, immediately turning to the stairs to go in search of her.

I came to a stop right in front of our bedroom door. I noticed the offensive pile of things neatly stacked at the foot of the door. It consisted of my pillow, a pair of the boxer shorts I usually lounged in until I discarded them to sleep, and my toothbrush. I felt a surge of anger rush through my belly. When she'd made the comment about kicking me out of our bed, I didn't think she was actually serious. My hand grabbed and attempted to turn the door knob only to find it locked. I balked. She locked me out?

"Scarlett?" I called out. I heard some shuffling behind the door, my anger flared. "Scarlett! Open the fucking door!" I yelled. My demand was followed by the muffled sound of a door - my guess was our bathroom - slamming shut. Moments later I heard our bathtub turn on. My anger shifted from the situation to myself. Now not only was I kicked out of our bed, I had to miss out on our shower time. Her skin was always considerably more stiff at the end of the day. How was she possibly going to reach to use her cream? She was now unknowingly punishing herself too. I growled in frustration before snatching the offending pile off the floor. I trekked into the guest rooms closest to our bedroom. It just so happened to be the one I'd redone for Scarlett. Despite the bed not having the greatest mattress, the sheets and blankets were all hers. It meant the room was still saturated in her scent. That was at least a bandaid over the wound.

Regardless of having the comfort of her scent, I tossed and turned on the bed. It was impossible to find a comfortable position. I was so used to Scarlett's soft body pressing up against mine. I would tangle a leg between her own while I buried my face in her neck and breathed in her scent as I fell asleep. Without her to hold onto, and effectively cuddle into, I couldn't find the right angle. This sucked.

I glanced over at the clock and sighed in defeat at the bright red letters glaring back at me. Damn near three in the morning and I hadn't even been able to relax. I sat up in the bed and harshly rubbed a hand down my face, wiping away the exhaustion.

"Fuck this," I grunted. Snatching my pillow off the bed, I made a determined beeline for our bedroom. She didn't know this, but there was a key of sorts for the bedroom door. Only I knew where it was stored. Rummaging around in the hall closet where I kept it hidden, I pulled it from its spot. I made quick work popping the lock and throwing our door open. Not much to my surprise, Scarlett was awake and pacing in front of our windows. Her gaze met mine, quickly turning from worry to irritation when she saw me.

"You can be pissed off at me all you want. You can give me the silent treatment. You can yell. I don't care. But I'm not sleeping without you," I stated in a tone that left no room for argument. I sauntered towards our bed, throwing my pillow back in the spot where it goes. "Quit being stubborn and get in here, baby," I demanded after she hesitated a few seconds. She released a soft sigh before following me to the bed. Despite her upset demeanor, the second she climbed in, she curled up into my body like she did every night. The action immediately put my wolf, who'd been pacing in my head all night, at ease. My arms wrapped tightly around her waist and cinched her body as close to mine as she could possibly get.

"I don't like you hiding things from me," she whispered in such a soft voice I almost didn't hear it. My eyes shut as I clenched my jaw. The tone of her voice made my heart squeeze. Dammit, I'm a bastard.

"Everything I do is to keep you safe and happy. I never want you to be stressed or to worry about anything," I murmured against her temple before pressing a soft kiss where my words had landed.

"But in doing so, you did the exact thing you were trying to avoid," she said while turning in my arms so we were face-to-face. I brought a hand up and stroked her cheek. I was momentarily side-tracked by how beautiful she was as she nuzzled into my hand. A thick knot formed in my throat so tight I almost choked around it as a feeling formed in the pit of my stomach. A feeling I'd never felt before. It made me realize that I hadn't even noticed what was happening until it had punched me right in the gut. It was so slow over the past few weeks; like a thief in the night, this woman had so easily crept in and stolen my heart.

"I love you, Scarlett. If anything happened to you..." I trailed off. The constriction in my throat from simply the thought of having to go a day without her in my life was too much to bear. I had to swallow hard to get it to ease enough to try speaking again.

"You won't let that happen," she murmured, her wet eyes glistening with unshed tears I could see in the moonlight streaming in from the open curtains. "Say that again. Please," she begged softly, her tone almost desperate.

"I love you. More than I did yesterday and less than I will tomorrow. Everything you do is perfect to me. If anyone ever tried to take you from me, I would search the ends of this earth and kill anyone who got in my way to find you. I would do anything for you," I stated vehemently. A single tear slipped down the side of her face as her soft, delicate hand reached up to caress my cheek.

"I love you too," she rasped out, "so much". A warmth spread throughout my whole body. It was another sensation I was experiencing for the first time. My mind was made. This woman isn't leaving my side. Not for a minute.

We moved towards one another at the same time, our lips connecting as I moved over her while sliding between her legs with practiced ease. Her arms wound up to lock around my neck. We parted only long enough to shred the rest of our minimal clothing before our bodies found one another again. There was no sense of urgency like there usually was from us both before our first orgasm - so needy for the other we couldn't help but rush things the first round. I took my time with every caress, every kiss.

When I finally sank into her, it was like our first time all over again. Every sensation was magnified. The hand at the base of my neck lightly scraped my scalp as it ventured into my hair before grasping at the strands and giving a light tug, Scarlett's tell tale sign that she really liked whatever I was doing. Our bodies were just a hair's breadth apart, every inch of skin practically molded together. I trailed my kisses from her lips down to her jaw, my thrusts becoming a touch rougher as she gave the skin near my ear a soft nibble. The change in pace had her moaning my name appreciatively before biting my ear lobe.

"I-" she gasped when I leaned to add more pressure to her clit with my pubic bone, "-love you," she panted out against the shell of my ear. I couldn't, and didn't want to, stop the moan that barreled from my chest at the profession. My balls started to tighten and pull against my body. I quickened my pace just a touch, but increased the strength of my thrusts. Scarlett was always asking for it harder rather than faster. I'd grown to learn when I was close to coming and needed her to get there faster, this was the answer.

It only took a couple thrusts before Scarlett was digging her nails into my shoulder hard enough to draw blood as she threw her head back against her pillow.

"Look at me, baby. Look at me, Scarlett," I ground out, never easing up on her. Her eyes immediately snapped open to stare into mine. "Mine. You're mine. Say it," I growled out.

"I'm yours," she husked out, just barely holding on to the edge of sanity before her orgasm hit. I slammed into her a final time and sealed our mouths again. Taking every last cry of pleasure she had for myself because I was one greedy bastard when it came to this woman. Her orgasm triggered my own, and I waited for the high to slowly subside as the aftershocks left her body.

"Are you asleep on me already?" I murmured in amusement, staring down at Scarlett's completely relaxed and limp form. The small, amused quirk of her lips gave me my answer.

"You're still inside me and half-hard. I don't think I could possibly fall asleep like that," she snickered breathily. I was immediately fond of the idea.

"Might be kinda nice for Xander Jr. to have a snuggle buddy all night long," I commented. Her reaction was instantaneous. Her eyes shot open and she leveled me with a serious look.

"Don't you go getting any ideas just because I let you hang out for a while after sex," she insisted. I chuckled before leaning down and lathering her neck and chest with kisses, some I purposely placed in her ticklish spots. The action caused her to release that adorable giggle that was music to my ears.

She laid silently in my arms for a few minutes before she started squirming. I released her so after sex clean up could ensue. Most of the time it meant me changing the sheets from all the come and sweat we'd worked up while Scarlett peed and fixed her hair - typically that time was littered with complaints about how 'ratty' I'd made her hair from all the pulling, grabbing, and running my hands through it. That wouldn't change anytime soon, though. I loved her hair.

"Did you get your cream put on?" I asked her as she exited the bathroom wearing a new night slip. She gave me a sheepish expression.

"Kind of," she murmured with a shrug of her shoulder.

"C'mere," I beckoned, reaching for the tub of thick cream on her nightstand. She pulled the nightgown off silently as she came to rest between my legs. Turning, she exposed her back to me so I could properly lather the medicine on her back.

"Can you take the day off?" she asked softly as I continued massaging. I sighed deeply, eyeing the clock that now read 4:15. If I didn't, I would have to be up in an hour. But I really shouldn't.

"There's so much I need to get done..." I trailed off, finishing with her back and gently turning her to face me. I helped her slip back into her pajamas as every single one of the things on my to-do list flitted through my mind.

"Are you going to tell me what made you so upset earlier?" she asked, shifting so she was pressed against my chest. Her hands wound up and around my shoulders where they began running rhythmic circles into my skin. I sighed deeply, knowing we needed to discuss the topic sooner rather than later.

"It's the Dawnfall pack in Wyoming," I started, waiting for any sort of reaction.

"I was in an orphanage there once when I was younger. I can't remember exactly how old I was, but it was sometime between nine and eleven," she revealed. I was less than shocked by this admission. My mate had lived in more states and packs than I could keep track of at this point.

"I don't know what it was like when you lived there, or if you even remember much, but to date the pack doesn't have a great reputation. It's not a bad pack to live in, per se, but the Alpha is fierce. He's not one you want to cross or even think about getting on his bad side. He's nearly impossible to get into communication with and he has almost no treaty alliances with any other packs. But he would make a great ally if I can get him to agree to a treaty. I've just barely gotten my foot in the door. However, he wants to have the meeting on his pack grounds. This is the first and only formal meeting he's agreed to thus far after months of negotiation and communication..." I trailed off, already feeling a new tension headache coming on.

"I see," she murmured softly, looking deep in thought.

"I wasn't sure what I wanted to do. Leaving you here seemed like the most logical answer because this is where you and your wolf feel the safest. However the thought of not taking you with makes me physically ill. I can't do it Scarlett," I stated with finality, my forehead wrinkled together with the stress I was feeling.

"Then I'll go with you," she reasoned as if I hadn't been stressed over this practically every second for the past 48 hours.

"What?" I balked.

"The place I feel safest isn't here because it's our pack. It's because you're here, Xander. I am safest and feel safest wherever you are. If you're going to this pack for the meeting, then I'll go too." I scanned her face closely for a few minutes, looking for any hint of possible deception for my benefit. Making sure she wasn't just saying it to soothe me.

"You're sure?" I asked. She just nodded. I released a heavy sigh.

"Okay then. I'll let him know that you'll be attending and all the names of our security team who will be coming as a result of that," I stated. She just smiled sleepily and nodded. "I figured you could talk with his Luna while you were there, too. Maybe try and discuss some of the changes you've made to our orphanage and how they've been successful for our pack," I added as we climbed back into bed. I felt the familiar sensation of her happiness blossom in my chest after I'd spoken.

"Mmm, you're gonna get such a special wake up call tomorrow when you go into work late," she hummed lazily. I couldn't help but laugh and shake my head. Couldn't say no to that, now could I?

# CHAPTER 26



I kept the snicker that so desperately wanted to bubble out of my chest to myself as I watched Xander move around our home. There was an intense look on his face. He was barking orders at everyone who even stepped foot inside our door. He'd been tense since two nights ago. After he finalized his plans with this Alpha we were going to visit, the change happened nearly immediately. I'd already forgotten the alpha's name - something I would need to ask Xander as soon as we were settled in the car and his feathers weren't so ruffled. His wolf was so on edge he wanted to make someone guard our bedroom door this morning while we had sex. It was the fastest no he'd ever gotten from me. We compromised by doing it doggy so he could face the door 'just in case'. As much as his over-protectiveness made me almost want to roll my eyes, my wolf and I loved it too much to do so.

I quickly realized we had everything we needed; the cars were packed, everyone was ready to go, and we were only waiting on Xander's go-ahead. I called his name and got his attention.

"Should we head to the airport now?" I asked. He huffed before nodding. When everyone saw Xander meandering towards the car, they followed suit. Maximus was driving and Jarrod - one of the four male warriors Xander had originally picked to guard me - sat in the passenger seat. Xander sat next to me in the back. His hand quickly found my thigh with a strong grip seconds after he finished buckling himself in. It didn't leave its spot the entire car ride. Or during the flight.

I could feel his uncertainty through our connection as our car approached the main gates to the Dawnfall pack. However, you would've never guessed he was feeling anything based on his exterior. I was certain I was finally seeing the true Alpha side of Xander; the side of him that only needed to come out in situations such as this. I would be terrified of him if it weren't for him being my mate.

"Don't get out of the car until I get you," Xander's calm, collected voice commanded. I wouldn't have known he was speaking to me if it weren't for the slight squeeze he'd given my thigh just before he spoke. I covered his hand with mine and wrapped our fingers together. Leaning over, I forced his face to turn just enough so I could give him a proper kiss on his lips. His rigid exterior softened just a smidge as he responded to my touch. I was caught off guard when he abruptly deepened the kiss, taking it from short and sweet to a heated makeout with overt groping above our clothes.

"Xander," I finally chastised under my breath. I was certain my cheeks had turned numerous shades of red as his men kept their backs ramrod straight and their faces forward, not sparing a single glance back at the two of us. He just cracked a boyish smile in response. I gave an exasperated eye roll before gently stroking his cheek with my hand.

"Alpha, we're here," Maximus softly spoke, bringing the car to a stop. In a moment, Xander's playful exterior vanished. Back was the overly serious and intimidating Alpha I'd seen a few minutes prior. Xander pressed a soft kiss to my temple before exiting his side of the vehicle. I folded my hands in my lap and waited. I didn't know what exactly Xander was waiting for, but I was relieved when the stuffiness of the car evaporated the second he opened my door for me. He gave me a single wink while reaching out his hand for mine.

I wasn't sure what I expected of the Dawnfall pack alpha. He was much younger than the previous one I'd caught glimpses of occasionally during my time here. I figured it meant this must be the previous Alpha's son. I knew they only had the one and he was a good few years older than me. However, I couldn't for the life of me remember his name. Damn me for forgetting to ask Xander.

"Scarlett, this is Alpha Damien Huxley," Xander introduced me as we approached the equally intimidating man. Although, Xander was definitely more physically imposing. However, I could tell this man had secrets just from the look in his eyes.

"Wonderful to meet you, Alpha Huxley," I spoke while politely extending my hand for him to shake, praising my voice for not quivering or breaking on any of my words. He grasped my hand in a firm shake as he briefly met my eyes.

"You as well, Luna Harrington. Imagine my surprise when Alpha Harrington brought up bringing a mate with him during our final conversation regarding this meeting," he responded. Though his words were kind, I sensed the hint of annoyance surrounding them. I just gave him a small smile.

"I do apologize if my presence has put a damper on this meeting. It's quite hard for me to be away from my mate this early when the bond is still so fresh," I shot back, taking all the responsibility despite the need being mutual. I didn't want him to get the idea that I was a weak area of Xander's - especially if this meeting didn't go well. The Alpha just hummed in response before motioning us inside. We only got a short distance into the foyer when he stopped. One of his men approached him to speak in a hushed voice. For the first time in over a month, my wolf's guard was completely up again. I'd forgotten how exhausting it was shortly after entering the foreign packhouse.

I clung to Xander tightly as Alpha Huxley escorted us through the halls and toward a room similar in style to Xander's own office. Not a word was spoken amongst the large crowd of Xander's men as well as the few men Alpha Huxley had with him as we settled into the room.

"Incredibly lively bunch," I muttered. My eyes widened after I realized I had allowed the sarcastic comment to slip. All of Xander's men fought back snickers of laughter and smiles of amusement. Alpha Huxley's men were better at hiding their reactions. "Do Felicity and Jasmine still run the orphanage here?" I asked, trying to distract from my inappropriate comment. Alpha Huxley's penetrating gaze snapped to me, his eyes narrowing for a second as they darted all over my face - assessing me.

"I'm not sure," he finally responded. My brows furrowed together at his answer, though I wasn't shocked. Most packs, especially the higher-ranking wolves, had little to nothing to do with their orphanages. It was even so in my own pack before I came along.

"Alpha Harrington, I'm assuming you've had plenty of time to look over the revised agreement I sent back to you," Alpha Huxley commented, turning his unnerving stare towards my mate.

"I did. In regards to section 36b and disclosing all previous pack contracts...there are some new circumstances we need to discuss that followed my mating." Xander's response made my back go ramrod straight in my chair. I refused to look anywhere but at the blank, white wall directly ahead of me. The curious, fleeting glances from all of Alpha Huxley's men seared my skin.

"And what would these new circumstances be?" Alpha Huxley asked, his tone conveying his distrust immediately.

"There is a prior contract that exists, though it's not one specifically signed by my pack or regarding my pack. However, it does still affect my pack, in a way. And, due to its nature, will affect our decision to sign a treaty or not based upon your...response to it." Xander explained cryptically.

"You're speaking in riddles. If I knew this prior to your coming, I would have canceled this-"

"I have a contract of retribution. With The Council," I abruptly interrupted Alpha Huxley. The room went silent. Alpha Huxley gave me the impression he wasn't a man who was ever interrupted without consequence. However, my words threw him for such a loop he just stared at me. "It's in regards to my original mate. I won't say true mate because that man is the farthest thing from a mate to me - and as far as I'm concerned, Xander is my true mate - but he is a wolf in a position of power. For obvious reasons, our pack will not conduct any kind of pack business with his pack - including alliances."

"Someone has to go through more than one can imagine for The Council to offer a contract of retribution..." Alpha Huxley trailed off, his eyes never leaving the side of my face. I nodded once. Xander's warm arm wrapped around my shoulders as his hand rubbed soothing circles into the arm he was holding.

From the spot where I was tucked into Xander's side, I saw a flash of movement as the door to the office we were in was opened. Peeking around Xander's wide frame, I focused on the person standing in the doorway. My jaw couldn't have dropped faster when I realized who I was seeing.

"Roni?" I rasped out, my tone quiet and unsure. The woman's name coming from my lips seized the attention of every single one of the men from the Dawnfall pack. The woman in question snapped her gaze toward where she'd heard me call her name. She took a few more steps into the room. The closer she got, the more sure I was about who this woman was.

"Scarlett?" came her inquisitive voice in return.

"Oh my gosh, Veronica!" I squealed, softly pushing away from Xander and darting towards the familiar woman. I was incredibly grateful for the distraction from our current conversation. There were lots of excited yells as our bodies crashed together in a warm embrace. She gave a few tiny jumps of excitement while still holding my body in a death grip - something that apparently still hadn't changed since we were younger.

"What the hell are you doing here?!" Veronica demanded curiously. "More importantly, what the hell happened to you? You never kept in touch like we promised! I swear, I sat by the phone for weeks after you left. A rumor started going around the system that you'd disappeared. No one had seen a trace of you in...months!" she exclaimed. I felt my skin prickle with awareness. All eyes in the room dawned with a hint of understanding, but the most intense stare I could feel boring into my back was my mate's.

"It's, uh, a long story...as for what I'm doing here, however, I tagged along with my mate. He and the Alpha are meeting about a possible treaty," I explained. She gasped before abruptly turning her gaze onto Alpha Huxley - much to everyone's surprise.

"Eeek! Damien, what the hell are you waiting for? Let's sign the treaty and have an early dinner to celebrate!" Veronica exclaimed, her happiness contagious like it had always been.

"It doesn't work like that, honey," Alpha Huxley said to her, his glass exterior melting for just a moment as he addressed her. His response had her pouting. Her lower lip puckered out comically.

"Doodle bear," she whined, giving him what I could only characterize as puppy dog eyes. Alpha Huxley sighed heavily.

"Why don't we break for dinner first. Alpha Harrington, you and your Luna can join me and mine. We can discuss the treaty while our wives catch up," he reasoned. That wiped the frown off Veronica's face, but it seemed to have transferred to mine at Alpha Huxley's words. Wives.

I knew Xander could tell something was bothering me during dinner. It was the bond; I'm sure he could sense my soured mood through it. Despite that, I tried my best to be upbeat and cheery with Veronica through all our catching up we had to get through. I'd wholly avoided her line of questioning about where I'd disappeared to - Veronica always did have a short attention span. It allowed me to easily maneuver to a different subject. Thankfully.

I'd learned that her and Damien had only been mated for five months. They met when he was traveling back home after a meeting in another state. He saw her broken down on the side of the road and stopped to offer a helping hand. The rest was history according to her.

"I wish I had our wedding album to flip through with you right now! I remember how obsessed we were with all things weddings when we were younger. We'd find every wedding catalog at the thrift store and cut out the things we liked then glue it into a journal. I still have mine! Do you still have yours?" My stomach churned uneasily at the question, nausea bubbling in my stomach. The answer was no. I didn't. I didn't have anything that belonged to me before the age of 18. I had no idea if any of that stuff still existed or if Eric destroyed it all during the time he was torturing me. Or if he did it after I'd gotten away.

"I think it got lost in my last move," I finally answered with a tight smile. I blinked back the moisture in my eyes as the bright room lights glinted off the surface of her beautiful wedding ring.

"Alpha Huxley, thank you for dinner but I think it's about time my mate and I turn in for the night. We can pick this conversation back up first thing tomorrow morning," Xander's strong voice spoke, effectively signaling our leave.

Back in our room we'd been assigned for the duration of our stay here, I could tell Xander was tense. He seemed unsure of how to navigate the conversation he wanted to have.

"Scarlett?" He called after me as I changed and did my nightly routine.

"Hm?" I murmured in response.

"Don't 'hm' me. You're upset. I can't do anything about it if I don't know why you're feeling this way," he gritted out. I sighed heavily as I finished braiding my hair and tying it off with a hair tie. Grabbing my toothbrush, I wrestled with my brain on how I was even supposed to approach the subject. I didn't want to. It felt...well, it made me feel like I did when I was with Eric in a way. Like this pathetic girl who was about to ask a man for something he didn't want to offer, only to be shot down.

"Scarlett," Xander grunted, his stance taking on a more serious posture.

"When Alpha Huxley referred to me as your wife, you should've corrected him. We're not married," I finally commented, looking away. I focused on pasting my toothbrush as if removing the plaque from my teeth was the most important thing ever at that very moment.

"What?" Xander deadpanned, genuinely confused. "The fact that I didn't correct another alpha in regards to our marital status is what you're upset about?" he continued. I felt the tears welling up in my eyes again at how ridiculous he made it sound. And at how stupid I felt for how deeply the situation was upsetting me.

I spit the foamed toothpaste from my mouth. "Well?! We aren't married!" I yelled, wiping my mouth with the back of my hand before throwing my toothbrush across the counter and storming past him into the attached bedroom. He caught me by the arm before I could get too far, whirling me around to face him.

"And that's why you're upset? Because we aren't married yet?" he inquired. I shoved against his chest, wanting to have my pity cry under the covers where he couldn't see my tears.

"You mentioned us getting married and having a wedding weeks ago. You've never brought it up since. I take it that you changed your mind. It's fine," I hissed, attempting to yank my arm from his embrace.

"Scarlett, I didn't bring the wedding up again because I didn't think it was a good time. You were still acclimating to the pack, and then when you were more comfortable I was slammed with pack business after being away for so long. I apologize that it hasn't been the first priority on my list," he stated, a hint of agitation in his tone. It was a tone he'd never used with me before. This was all my fault. I knew that now. I was being insecure and completely overreacting to a minor situation, but I couldn't help the absolute pit in my stomach that formed from the tone he'd just used with me.

"Oh," I rasped out, swallowing hard. I forced my mental block up, not wanting him to see the emotional chaos that was going on inside my head. It wasn't his fault and I didn't blame him for it.

"Scarlett," he grunted out, his tone even harsher, "don't do that. Don't block me out when you're upset. He turned me so I was fully facing him before sighing heavily. He pressed a kiss to my forehead before pulling us towards the bed in the middle of the room. He took a seat on the edge and pulled me to stand between his spread legs.

"An engagement comes before a wedding. That involves a proposal. Going off of what I know about you, I'm guessing you don't want some elaborate, extravagant proposal where there are hundreds of sets of eyes on you when I ask you to marry me." His words made me snicker. The mere thought alone made me almost break out in hives.

"Absolutely not," I answered almost immediately. He smirked and nodded.

"Something intimate and personal then?" I nodded again. "Do you want to pick out your ring with me, or do you want it to be a surprise?" he asked. I didn't even need to ponder the question.

"Surprise me." We stayed in the same position as he slowly massaged circles into my hips. I could tell he was wrestling with something else but refused to invade his thoughts to find out what it was.

"Scarlett, what Veronica said earlier..." The knot in the pit of my stomach that had seemed to completely dissipate came back ten-fold now at his words, "It has to do with what happened to you with him, doesn't it?" Xander tentatively asked. I didn't respond right away. "About you not keeping in touch? People thinking you'd disappeared?" he prodded. I ran my hands over his shoulders and down his arms, the physical contact calming me a minor amount. I nodded, unable to get any squeaks of sound past my constricted vocal cords.

"Did he kidnap you?" he asked. I shook my head no. I bit the inside of my cheek hard enough that it drew blood. A few more minutes passed between us in silence before I was able to attempt to speak.

"I had just turned 18 two weeks prior. My pack and the adjacent pack were hosting a mix and mingle for single wolves with a handful of different packs. Me and a group of newly 18-year-old girls from the last orphanage I'd been in in Utah decided to go for fun. We just wanted to get ourselves out there since we didn't have much experience at pack events. Veronica came with us, but she was twenty at the time. She was a rare case of someone who'd aged out but was allowed to stay because she helped the orphanage mom's run the place.

"I met Eric an hour into the event. He was only there because he was with his Alpha renewing business contracts at my pack at the time. Otherwise, he never would've traveled that far for a mix-and-mingle event. Those were his exact words to me one time. I knew instantly what he was to me. He did too. I didn't even get to say goodbye to anyone I'd come with. I didn't get to grab any of my things; he must've sent someone for them later in the middle of the night.

"I should've known by how he went about everything that ni ght...it was all foreshadowing for how he would end up treating me. But I was just a young, naive girl. All I wanted was love and a family. I never expected he could ever treat me the way he did." I didn't realize I'd started crying. It wasn't until Xander's soft fingers brushed the tears away that I noticed. He didn't say a word, just let my word vomit continue.

"At first it just seemed innocent - sweet, even - how he gatekept me from the rest of his pack. He didn't want me to leave his quarters alone, so I didn't. That only lasted a week. Then I wasn't to leave his quarters at all. Then I wasn't to leave his bedroom. Eventually, after three weeks, I grew sick and tired of the same four walls and only seeing him every single day for maybe two hours when I was awake - if I was lucky. I lashed out. That's...that's when it all changed. He used it as his opening to really let his monster out.

'That first beating was the worst of them all; I wasn't prepared for it. I had no idea he was capable of hitting me. Capable of causing me that kind of pain. There was no gradual lead-up. I couldn't breathe after he was done. It turns out he'd fractured a few of my ribs from how hard he had been kicking me." I paused as Xander's hands fisted on my waist and his jaw clenched so hard I could hear his molars grinding. I grasped the side of his face with my hand and stroked it before continuing. "He only took me to the pack doctor for the first six months. Then he stopped. I don't think he wanted anyone to know about me or even have cause to ask questions about me. About that time is when he started cheating - though I don't even know if you could call it cheating. We certainly weren't sleeping together and what we had didn't resemble any kind of relationship. However, I would take that over the sleep deprivation, starvation, and subsequent whippings. He got the alpha involved later on. They would test out new tools for the rogues that trespassed on me first to find the ones that left maximum damage with the most pain inflicted-""Scarlett," Xander choked out, his voice breaking halfway through. Our eyes met and that's when I saw the gathered tears in his own hurting gaze. "I don't...I can't hear anymore, sweetheart. Not right now." I nodded in understanding. The Council had to conduct my testimony for their records over a week's time for the same reason.

The rest of the night, we were both quiet. We didn't need to swap words. His tight hold on my body said all he needed to say as we drifted off to sleep in each other's arms.

# CHAPTER 27

S carlett's POV

The next morning, Xander and I joined Veronica and her mate for breakfast - per Veronica's insistence. The atmosphere seemed a bit more tense than the meal we'd shared together the night prior. I couldn't put my finger on why. Eventually, Xander and Alpha Huxley's conversation veered to one about business as it had the night before. Veronica gave me a look I knew well.

"Hm?" I asked under my breath.

"Hm what?" she whispered so only I could hear.

"You haven't changed one bit, Roni. I know that look. Something's not right. What's up?" I asked. She sighed softly, taking a small sip of her juice before sitting back in her chair with a thoughtful look on her face.

"Damien and I had a long conversation last night that started with how I knew you," she began. I raised a single eyebrow, nodding for her to go on. She hesitated, tucking a strand of hair that had fallen out of her neat bun behind her ear. "It was a rather tense conversation. He accused me of hiding things from him intentionally-" she cut herself off as her voice grew gravely with emotion. My gaze quickly shifted to the men beside us to see if they'd caught on to the sudden change in the air around us. They thankfully hadn't - yet anyway.

"And? Why would he think that?" I asked softly.

"Because I never told him about any of my past in the system. Not a single bit of it." She gave me a hard look when my face contorted into one of confusion. "Those weren't happy times for me, Scarlett. Not most of the time, anyway. I want to disassociate myself from that life as much as possible. I figured when I met my mate, it was a chance to reinvent who I was," she explained.

"Oh..." I trailed off. "I guess I can understand," I replied, though I wasn't sure I meant what I said.

"Did you tell Alpha Herrington about your childhood right away?" she asked, her tone slightly accusatory.

"Well...yes," I stated with an unsure shrug of my shoulders. "You and I never spoke about our reasons for being in the system back in the day, but I was there from birth. The system is the only thing I ever knew. It might have been different for you, and I'm sorry if that's the case. However, the times I had, until now with Xander, were the only good times I had in my life. Our experiences were very different," I explained. Though my words only caused a deep fissure of confusion to furrow on her forehead. I knew why; she didn't know about my past with Eric. I wouldn't be enlightening her.

"The house I was in with you was the first and last one I was placed in," she began as a look of anguish crossed over her face. "My parents were killed by a human that was driving drunk on their way back from a vacation." Her confession saddened me. I think I would rather never know my parents than lose them after knowing their love my whole life. I reached across the table and grasped her hand within my own, giving it a firm squeeze.

"I'm so sorry, Veronica. I can't imagine the pain of losing both your parents like that." She swallowed hard and gave my hand a squeeze back before pulling away.

"What about you? Have you ever thought about looking for you birth parents? Seeing if they're still out there?"

"What?" I asked softly, but not because I hadn't heard her. I had. I was just having a hard time processing what she had asked. I was caught completely off guard.

"You know, you have the resources to find them now - being a luna and all. I'm sure it wouldn't be all that difficult, really. You have half of their DNA after all. Alpha Herrington has access to most of the shifter population via database. It would just be a quick search. Unless they weren't registered or they were never part of a pack, they'll show up."

I sat in the dining chair, just blinking rapidly at her. Everything she said was logical, but I felt like my brain wasn't firing on all cylinders. Thankfully, I was saved from having to answer when Xander called my name. Looking up to meet his gaze, I realized he'd said something after my name that I hadn't caught.

"What?" I asked unintelligently. Xander's familiar, warm smile graced his face - I hadn't seen it much since we showed up here; he'd been all business so far. The smile eased some of the anxiety that had built within my chest.

"I asked if you and Veronica had a chance to discuss the changes you've made to the orphanage." It seemed like I just couldn't get away from this damn topic today. I quietly shook my head. "If you wanted to talk with her about it, now's the time. Alpha Huxley and I have finalized our agreement. All that's left is to sign the papers and make it official." I nodded again in response, blowing out a big breath of air before turning back to Veronica.

She smiled at me before shaking her head. "I know that look as well as you know mine. Clearly what I just suggested has your brain completely scrambled. How about you come back and visit, maybe in a couple weeks, and we can chat about it?" she asked, a knowing look on her face. I agreed, thankful for the break she was giving me. I couldn't help the fact that my brain was swirling with the thoughts that my own parents could still be out there.

Later that evening, Xander and I rode back to the air strip in silence. I appreciated him leaving me alone with my thoughts- of which were still completely tangled in knots. It wasn't until our flight was making its descent from the air back onto our own territory that he finally spoke up.

"What did Luna Huxley say that's got you all flustered?" I braced myself for our landing before answering him.

"She made a comment about...about my parents," I paused when he gave me a questioning frown. He waited to ask me his follow-up question until we were seated in the car.

"What about them?" he prodded.

"That they're probably still out there somewhere. She said with your resources, it would be easy to find them," I murmured, still mulling over the idea.

"She's correct, but..." at his hesitation, I studied him closely.

"But what?" I asked, my temper flaring for some reason. He sighed.

"Do you think that's a good idea?" I furrowed my brows at his response, annoyance flooding my body.

"So you think it's not?" I grumbled back, diverting my gaze from his. I instead peered out the window of the SUV that was driving us home.

"Scarlett, that's not what I said-"

"But it's what you're thinking," I growled back, interrupting him. I took a deep breath, trying to calm my fizzing irritation.

"I don't want to see you get hurt, sweetheart. For any reason," he murmured. I could feel my defenses crumbling as the pet name left his lips, his tone so genuine. I relented, turning to meet his eyes again.

"I didn't say I was going to find them and meet them. I just wanted to know who they were," I mumbled like a petulant child.

"What if you don't like what we find?" he asked, always the voice of logic and reason.

"What if I don't look at all? Then I'll always have that 'what if' lingering in the back of my mind," I insisted. He sighed heavily at my statement.

"Okay, but tomorrow," he replied as we pulled up to the pack house - a welcomed and familiar sight to me, "tonight I just want to enjoy some alone time," he stated, a fire sparking in his eyes.

"Xander!" I hissed, smacking his arm lightly as my cheeks heated. The men in the front hightailed it out of the car, clearly having heard and understood exactly what Xander meant.

"It worked didn't it? I guarantee we won't be interrupted while we watch that movie you put on our list last week," he insisted.

"Oooh I just bought a new box of that popcorn you really like," I said as he grasped my hand to help me from the vehicle.

He perked up, his eyes shining with excitement. "Butter lovers?" I giggled and nodded.

"Best mate ever," he whispered before pecking my lips softing and escorting us inside.

# Chapter 28



Scarlett's POV

True to his word, Xander called me to his office the next day. It was only a couple hours after I'd had lunch. I gave him a harsh glare when his eyes had lit up with mirth seeing how I hobbled into the room and up to his desk.

"You look sore, baby," he commented. I growled softly before smacking his hand away from my waist. My actions only pulled a lighthearted chuckle from him.

"I am sore - all over - and it's your fault!" I accused. He just smirked back.

"You certainly weren't complaining this morning," he pointed out while ignoring my annoyance and pulling me onto his lap. I just huffed and rolled my eyes, allowing him to caress the skin of my thigh under my dress he'd already pushed up. I leaned forward and took the computer mouse into my hands, minimizing everything he'd been working on.

"Where's the database?" I asked as he pressed soft kisses to my jawline and neck.

"Did you wash with something different this morning?" he asked, his nose pressing against the top of my head as he took another thoughtful whiff of my hair. I laughed softly at how easily distracted he was.

"I got new shampoo and conditioner. You love the way that lotion I've been using smells and I found their hair care line the other day. It was in one of the packages when we got back," I answered off-handedly.

"You smell incredible," he groaned. I snapped my fingers a few times, getting his full attention again.

"Right the database," he said, pausing just long enough to point to an icon on the home screen. Pulling it up, it seemed simple enough to use. I started by searching for myself. I was amazed at all the information that came up, my jaw dropping slightly. There was a mostly up-to-date photo of me, next to which were all the known statistics about me; my birthday and age, hair and eye color, color of my wolf, height and weight, and current pack I belonged to. Under the section containing all the basic information was the date I was dropped off at The Council, the entire list of orphanages I'd ever been placed in, and the exact dates I'd stayed in each one.

"This is a little freaky," I commented with a slight shiver up my spine. I brushed it off and attributed it to Xander's earlier kisses. The next section was devoted to "matings". I hated that even though The Council worked to remove all ties linking him to me, I knew exactly whose name was listed first. The blacked-out section with REDACTED written in bold red letters stared back at me. The date we met spanning to the date I showed up on Council grounds was across from where Eric's name had been blacked out.

"It's scary how precise all of this information is," I murmured as my eyes stopped at the exact date Xander and I had sex for the first time. It was listed with the word CURRENT written inside parenthesis next to his name in bold letters. "How could they possibly know the exact day we consummated our mating?" I asked, not really seeking an actual answer.

"I, uh, had to tell them. For documentation purposes - not solely related to this database," he revealed sounding somewhat sheepish. My cheeks reddened at the thought.

Choosing to ignore his statement, I scrolled to the next section, which was titled "familial relations". There weren't any names listed. The void section made me swallow the sudden surge of odd emotions that had lodged itself in the base of my throat.

"This is what you're looking for," Xander stated, his hold on me tightening. He'd probably felt the onslaught of emotion I'd just been bombarded by through our bond. I rubbed a hand over the forearm anchored across my waist. I stared at the link he'd pointed to. It was the only thing listed a few spaces down from the top of where I presumed my family would've been listed. It read "suggested familial members".

"Why does it say 'suggested'?" I asked.

"It populates files of other individuals whose DNA is in the database and matches your own. This feature was developed in the 60s when there was a boom of kidnappings happening due to abnormally low birth rates amongst our community. The feature was necessary in reuniting families. It was never removed from the database, even after it was no longer regularly used."

I nodded, my cursor slowly inching toward the link. I hesitated for a moment before straightening my spin and clicking. The first profile that came up was an older woman with graying brown hair. She looked like a much older version of me. It took my breath away. Her hair was the exact same shade as my own. She had a soft smile on her face in the picture.

"Margaret Anne Turner," I read aloud with a shaky voice, "72 years old. Member of the Nightwalker pack. Mated and married to Jeffrey Keith Turner. One sister and a brother. Three kids of her own. How am I supposed to know who she is to me?" I asked Xander, though based on our numerous similarities, I already had an idea. He took the mouse from my hand and started clicking around the page. Finally a pop-up that had both our faces with a slew of random colors and lines came up. "Is this supposed to mean something to me?" I asked. Xander chuckled.

"No. Only Alphas are given training on how to read the results for security purposes. Based on the percent of genetic matching, she would be your grandmother," he revealed. My eyes continued to frantically scan her face. I must've gotten my cornflower blue eyes from her.

"How come she popped up first?" I husked out, growing emotional from the knowledge that I had a grandmother out there.

"She's the highest percentage match to you in all the results," Xander explained, sounding somewhat saddened. I swallowed thickly. So my mom and dad weren't in here? I didn't want to outright ask, but I had to know.

"Why wouldn't my parents come up first? I have half of their DNA." Xander seemed hesitant to answer.

"There are some instances where wolves didn't make it into the database due to one reason or another. Sometimes it meant their birth was kept a secret, or they went rogue before The Council knew about them and could get their DNA." I nodded before taking control once again and scrolling past her file. The next face was another woman who looked to be in her mid-30s and was the spitting image of my supposed grandma. My heart started to beat faster.

"Elizabeth Joanne Friedman. 47 years old. Member of the Nightwalker pack. Married to Dennis John Friedman. Two siblings, a brother and sister. Who is she to me?" I asked, unable to stop the anxious quiver in my voice. Xander did more clicking before the same pop-up appeared.

"She's your aunt. Likely on your mother's side based on the results." I didn't speak. I couldn't stomach to scroll anymore. I don't know what I'd been wanting or expecting with this excursion, but I had a sick feeling in the pit of my stomach. I had an entire family out there. Did they know about me? If they did, did they ever try to find me? Why weren't my parents in the system?

My head grew dizzy with all the questions that were racing through it. Not long after, a headache began to throb in my temple.

"I don't want to look anymore," I croaked. Xander hugged my small form tightly to his own, not saying a word for a few moments as he held me.

"Do you want to go meet them? I have a treaty with the Nightwalker pack. It's in the same state as Momma J's orphanage. We can visit both in the same trip," he offered. I mulled over the idea for a few minutes. No matter how upsetting the information had been, it didn't stop every base instinct inside me that wanted a family. Not that Xander wasn't my family - because he was - but I'd grown up not belonging to anybody. I'd believed it was just me against the world.

This little database had changed everything about that belief.

"I think I do..." I trailed off, my tone still slightly unsure despite my words.

"Why don't I give you the number for the pack's Luna? You can speak to her about our pending arrival and plan the trip whenever you're ready. I just need at least a week to prepare to leave so I can handle business on my end before our departure." I agreed, my chest growing tight with how much I loved and appreciated him. He wasn't a very talkative man; only when he needed to be for me. The speed at which he had learned to care for me - better than

I could myself - had frightened me at first. He was so observant and acted without me needing to say or do anything. I don't know how I did life before I knew him.

Not very well, that's for sure.

I didn't say anything, too emotional to speak as I leaned down to press a passionate kiss to his lips. Slipping from my spot on his lap onto the floor, I kneeled in between his spread legs. Xander's face morphed into a smug, knowing grin.

"I'm sure we have time for a little afternoon snack?" I asked while reaching for his belt. Xander just leaned back into his office chair in response, welcoming my touch. I'd only gotten the belt and top pants button undone when his office door flew open. My hand paused on his zipper as my face snapped towards the direction of the intruder.

"Seriously?" Both his Beta and Gamma grunted in unison as they stayed put just a few steps inside the room.

"We're gonna be busy for twenty minutes. Go grab some coffee or something," I stated boldly. Their faces revealed their shock at my words before Beta Donovan snapped out of it and pulled Gamma Griffin behind him. As soon as the door was shut I turned back to an amused Xander. "Where were we?" I asked while continuing to lower his zipper.

Since leaving his office, the decision of choosing whether to visit my family or not weighed heavily on my shoulders. I invited Jackie and Jade on a girls' spa outing. However, even the relaxing atmosphere couldn't take my mind off of it.

There was really no doubt in my mind that I wanted to meet them - even if they weren't my parents. I was just...afraid. What if I wasn't good enough? What if that's why no one ever came for me? What if I showed up and was shunned like a fool? That would hurt worse than not having family at all.

I jumped at the feel of Xander's large hands resting on my shoulders as I continued to stir the pot of soup I'd started cooking for dinner. He gave them a gentle squeeze before pulling me back into his embrace by my hips.

"I could see your mind working a million miles a minute from the front door," he whispered against my ear before giving my temple a soft peck.

"What if I'm not good enough for them?" I suddenly asked him, shocked the words even came out of my mouth. His face turned perplexed.

"I don't think that's even possible, sweetheart. Everyone loves you. You're perfect," he stated with so much conviction I felt my heart skip a beat or two.

"You have to think that, I'm your mate," I sighed. My response had him laughing much to my confusion.

"That's horribly false. Just look at me and Mika; I didn't think anything good about her for a long time before you came into my life. I kicked her out of the pack without a second thought. A mate bond only goes so far," he stated adamantly. Dammit, he has a point.

"Whatever subconscious idea you've mustered to make you ask me that, squash it. Your past is not a predictor of the future." I mulled over his words for a few minutes, the ding of my preset bread timer pulling me back to reality.

"Would next week work for you?" I asked after we'd started eating in peaceful silence. The corner of Xander's mouth lifted slightly.

"I can make it work as long as their Alpha and Luna agree to the visit." From that moment, it felt like the phone number Xander wrote down for me was burning a hole in my pocket.

# CHAPTER 29

Scarlett's POV

My stomach turned with anxiety and my head throbbed from the tension of over-thinking as the pilot announced our descent. I'd had plenty of time during the five hour flight to think - and rethink - my decision to meet my family. Xander originally said he needed a week to prepare, but it only took the weekend. I think he knew if I was given any more time to ponder the idea, I'd back out. He wasn't wrong.

Once we landed, Xander gave my hand an encouraging squeeze. "Are you ready?" he asked. Suddenly, a massive wave of nausea - from the combination of my nerves and the change in altitude - hit me like a ton of bricks. I quickly snatched the vomit bag to my left and hurled the entire contents of my stomach, which wasn't a lot to begin with. Xander just rubbed my back in soft, reassuring strokes as I wretched a few more times. When I finally felt a bit more stable. I dropped the bag into the trashcan across from my seat and wiped my mouth on the napkin Xander offered me.

"Okay. I think I'm ready." Xander just gave me an amused smile. He extended a breath mint to me before pulling himself out of his seat. Upon exiting the jet, we were quickly ushered into a large black SUV that would take us to the pack house. According to Xander, it was always customary to greet and converse with the Alpha and Luna regardless if your business in their pack involved them. Stupid formalities.

Pulling up to the pack house, I could see two figures standing outside waiting for us. They were older - likely in their 50s if I had to guess - and seemed nice if their smiles were anything to go by.

"Alpha and Luna Harrington! It's a pleasure to have you," their Alpha called out as we exited their vehicle. Xander confidently strode towards them, shaking the leaders' hands before pulling me into his side.

"The pleasure is all ours. Thank you so much for allowing us to visit on such short notice," Xander replied politely.

"Well, it's not every day the new Luna of a favorite alpha of ours finds some long-lost family members in our pack! We're incredibly excited for you both. Please don't let us stop you from getting on with your reason for being here!" the luna exclaimed, excitement obvious in her voice.

"Thank you so much. It was wonderful to meet you both," I said softly, shaking both of their hands. Xander ushered us back to the vehicle we were being escorted around in. He mumbled to the driver - telling him the family we were off to visit - before he settled back in beside me. My knees bounced as our drive continued. I gnawed at my lower lip so hard I tasted the familiar tang of metallic blood in my mouth.

"It's going to be fine," Xander murmured against my ear while simultaneously rolling the tortured lip from between my teeth. I released a shaky breath and nodded just as we pulled up to a large country-style home. It was nestled in a thick clump of trees. Per my request, the Luna hadn't informed the family of our visit, nor the nature of it. I felt slightly guilty ambushing them like this, but it made this whole ordeal easier for me.

Xander got out first, rounding the SUV to open my door and help me out. My entire being felt shaky and unsteady as we slowly trudged our way up to the front door. Xander knocked loudly and we waited. Suddenly, I wondered what if they're not home? I felt stupid now for not having the Luna notify them ahead of time.

Just as I was about to turn and give up, the front door was pulled open, leaving just enough room for a head to pop out. Despite the screen door still separating us, I could see it was the face of a younger gentleman. His brows scrunched together in confusion before he cleared his throat.

"Can I help you folks?" he asked, his voice wavering - obviously having felt the power from Xander's wolf and recognizing his status.

"Hello. I'm Alpha Harrington and this is my mate. We've come to speak with Margaret Turner. Is she around by chance?" Xander asked smoothly. I was thankful Xander could tell I was already overwhelmed and spoke for me.

The man's gaze turned further confused before he stiffly nodded.

"Dennis? Who's at the door?" A soft, feminine voice called from inside the house. Suddenly her face appeared in the doorway. I instantly recognized her as the woman Xander said was my aunt. Her eyes scanned Xander's large frame before they settled on me. She drew in a sharp breath before her hand slapped against her mouth. "Oh my God," she murmured between her fingers, gripping the man's forearm with white knuckles.

"Momma!" The woman - Elizabeth wasn't it? - shouted behind her, the sheer volume of which made me want to wince. "Please, come inside," the woman insisted, her tone shaky and giving away the tears in her eyes that had yet to fall.

We followed the couple inside to a quaint living room. Pictures were littering almost every surface as well as a collage on the wall. It felt like a true home filled with memories.

"What's going on, Lizzy?" the man whispered.

"Are you blind?" she hissed, her hand gesturing towards me. "How can you not see it?" Before the man could respond, there was a creak in the floorboards before the older woman I recognized as my grandmother joined us in the living room.

"Elizabeth, what could possibly be so important that you're shouting loud enough for the next pack over to hear every syllable?" I smirked at the response, unable to help the quiet snort I released. That seemed to catch the older woman's attention and her eyes snapped to me. Her tears were nearly instantaneous. I had no idea what to say or do. I stood there awkwardly as the older woman cried, soon comforted by Elizabeth's embrace.

"It's like looking at my sweet Josephine," the older woman wept.

I began the conversation the only way I knew how. "My name is Scarlett," I offered weakly. However, my words only seemed to further upset the woman. "I-I'm sorry. We'll go," I rasped out, grabbing Xander's arm and turning to leave.

"No! Please!" I stopped, turning to face her. "My name is Margaret. You...you look just like your mother when she was younger. I'm sorry for the tears. I just...where is she? Your mother?" the woman asked, but there was a desperation in her voice. My heart fell.

"I was hoping you could tell me," I responded, hating the way her expression turned from one of hope to one of anguish.

"I don't understand?" Margaret said. Sensing the shift in conversation, Xander stepped in.

"How about we all have a seat? This might be a long conversation," he offered. Margaret motioned us towards a loveseat as the rest of them took a seat on the nearby couch.

"When I was born, my...my mother dropped me off at The Council and fled. The blanket I was wrapped in was a bright scarlet red, so that's what Elder Adelia named me." I opened my mouth to say more, but realized I was just rambling what I knew to fill the silence, so I snapped it back shut. Snuggling into Xander's side, I hoped to hide away from their sad, inquisitive stares.

"She abandoned you?" Margaret asked, her voice so soft I almost didn't catch it.

"Um, I guess so? I stayed with The Council for a couple of months until an orphanage opened up within the state," I explained. I hated the pain my revelation was clearly causing the woman. It was plain to see in her eyes.

"Your mother was...free-spirited, to put it nicely. She'd always been a bit more troublesome than her siblings as a child, but I just figured she was headstrong and rambunctious because she was the youngest. When she turned 13, she ran from home for the first time; left the pack completely to go to heaven knows where. She never would say. I was sick with worry for weeks. Finally, after she'd been gone for nearly three months, the Alpha declared her a rogue. It broke my heart. Then, one day, about three weeks after the declaration, she just...showed back up. By law, I was supposed to report the reappearance to the Alpha, but I couldn't. She was my daughter. I was just glad she was back. She only stayed with us for four months after returning, then she was gone in the wind again.

"It was like that for the next five years - off and on running. Her father and I never did tell the Alpha when she would come back every once in a while. She always stayed with us for a couple months here and there. Just after she turned eighteen and we celebrated her birthday, she was gone the next morning. None of us have seen her since. Had I known that would be the last time I'd ever speak to her or see her beautiful face..." Margaret's words were cut off by soft sobs. "W-we didn't know that she'd found her mate, let alone had a child." I swallowed the thick lump in my throat as it constricted with emotion. "I always held out hope that she would return, if only for a brief visit, but she never did. I can't help but wonder if she's even still alive," Margaret cried.

"Don't say that momma," Elizabeth scolded, unshed tears filling her own eyes.

"She turns 40 soon," Margaret hiccuped out, pushing off the couch to approach the wall of pictures. She grabbed one of the bigger frames and pulled it down. Slowly making her way over to me, she gently placed the picture in my hands. An unexpected tear slipped down the side of my cheek as I stared at it. It was practically a mirror image of myself, if only a bit younger-looking. I brought my hand to the woman's face, running my fingers over the image as if I would be able to tell anything about the woman if I just touched her.

"We called her Josie for short," Elizabeth supplied, watching me take in every single detail of the photo.

"Josie," I whispered softly to myself.

"She'd be so proud to know her daughter was a Luna," Elizabeth continued as a sad smile took over her features. "She always told me she'd grow up and do bigger and better things than anyone could ever imagine." I suddenly became too overwhelmed by it all. My chest felt too tight, my breaths too shallow.

"Excuse me, please," I rushed out before setting the picture down and running out of the house. I stumbled down the front steps before tripping towards the SUV. I slammed into the front, splaying my hands out wide on the hood as I gasped for air.

"Breathe, Scarlett," Xander's strong voice commanded behind me. I felt his body cocoon my own from behind, his repeated commands helping me to draw bigger lungfuls of air in and out. The fog in my head slowly cleared as the tears came hot and fast.

"She had everything I've ever wanted! A family! People who loved her! People who looked out for her! And she just threw it all away! Threw me away!" I screamed. "I hate her! I hate her, I hate her, I hate her!" I cried hysterically, thrashing against Xander's embrace until his strength overpowered my own and he held me down against his chest, releasing soothing words like I'm here and I love you and I'm never leaving your side. I wept into his chest for what seemed like forever. I didn't have it in me to quit the pathetic show of weakness.

"Scarlett?" Came Margaret's soft, unsure voice from the front door. I peeked one eye over my shoulder at her.

"We can't change what's happened in the past, but we can decide how we want the future to go. I'd like it very much if you'd come in and stay for dinner." I pondered the invitation in my head. I was already here, might as well see it through.

"Okay," I spoke hoarsely. Xander placed one final kiss to my forehead before intertwining our fingers and leading me back into the house.

Despite my dramatic meltdown, dinner was...nice. Different. There was a slightly awkward atmosphere surrounding us, but that didn't stop the conversation from flowing. They told me all about themselves and what they did for a living. Apparently, my grandpa was off collaborating on some construction project with another pack. Margaret kept saying how upset he was going to be when he found out he missed meeting me. She made me promise to return again when he was back.

As nice as meeting them all was, I was more than ready to move on with our trip. I liked my family a lot, but I didn't know them well enough to be having any slumber parties just yet. Besides, after the emotional toll the day had taken on me, I was more than excited to see Jacinda tomorrow after seven long years.

I could smell the house before I even saw it, a huge smile overtaking my face. Xander chuckled softly at my reaction as we rounded the corner. We made our way up the drive to the small orphanage I used to call home once upon a time. The place had definitely become more run-down since I'd lived here, but it still exuded the same charm I'd fallen in love with soon after settling in. I couldn't help myself as I dashed from the car and to the front door, pounding my fist against the crooked frame.

"Who in the hell is banging at my damn door!" Momma J's southern lilt floated towards me, making me smile even wider. The door swung wide open with gusto and I came face to face with the one woman - besides Elder Adelia - that ever felt like a mother to me.

"Momma J," I sighed happily.

"Oh my goodness! Scarlett, is that you baby?" she said while pushing the door wide open and snatching me into a bone-crushing hug. I eagerly welcomed the embrace and squeezed her back. "Okay hold on, lemme see you," she spoke, pushing me to an arms distance away. "Look at you! You so tall now! And beautiful! I always knew you was gonna be a pretty girl!" she laughed, tears clouding her eyes. "My my, how you've matured. And who's this young man, hmm?" she hollered loud enough for Xander to hear from his spot leaning against the car.

"That's my mate!" I beamed happily.

"Scarlett, a Luna now? Hooked herself a fine young Alpha? You sure did well for yourself now didn'tcha?" she teased with a wink. "Come on inside now. Ya'll made it just in time for lunch and it's even ya favorite." I gasped.

"Fried chicken and okra?" I asked excitedly. She laughed heartily before nodding.

"I even made some grits too. Don't think ya'll comin' in here for free, though. Ya'll can help me with the peach cobbler," she insisted. I nodded, almost forgetting about Xander as he rested a hand on the small of my back and ushered me inside.

# CHAPTER 30

Xander's POV

I watched with a permanent smile on my face as Jacinda and Scarlett bantered back and forth, catching up on Scarlett's childhood after she left Jacinda's care and then talking about our relationship. She'd left out the entire part about Eric - rather spinning a story about aging out and going to live with Elder Adelia again. It was believable enough.

"Alpha Harrington, you want another serving?" Jacinda offered. All the kids that dined with us had left the room to do whatever kids these days did with free afternoons.

"No, Ma'am. And please, call me Xander," I insisted yet again, not seeing the purpose of formalities in this place.

"I ain't eva called an Alpha by his first name," she retorted back.

"I've heard you call Alpha Presley by his first name multiple times when you were on the phone," Scarlett sassed.

"Only when he make me real mad," Jacinda shot back with a smirk. "He too scared of me to do nothin about it." I couldn't help but smile. I could see an Alpha catering to this force of a woman.

"You sure you don't want no more? You look like you could use a little meat on them bones," she insisted. I had to laugh considering I was already close to 300 pounds.

"I have to save some room for your cobbler. It smells amazing."

"You should've seen him when we first met. All muscle and no husk," Scarlett joked, winking at me from across the table.

"Fatten him up good, didja?" Jacinda laughed. "I taught this little girl everything she knows," she stated proudly.

"She's said so many times. She feeds me well thanks to you," I insisted.

"Baby, get the thing from the car!" Scarlett insisted excitedly.

"What thing?" Jacinda asked skeptically, narrowing her eyes at a beaming Scarlett. I left and returned with the heavy package I had to help Scarlett wrap the night before in our hotel room.

"Uh-uh! You did not bring me nothin'!" Jacinda stated, stubbornly crossing her arms over her chest.

"C'mon! Open it!" Scarlett prompted. Jacinda just gave her an annoyed side eye before huffing and beginning to tear back the wrapping paper. When the image on the box came into sight Jacinda gasped before whooping loudly with excitement.

"A full set of cast iron pots and skillets! You didn't. Oh, sweet girl, you didn't!" She hollered, pulling Scarlett into a massive embrace.

"You always talked about how badly you wanted them but the pack never splurged for them and never would. Now you don't have to worry about it."

"Oooohwee! I'm about to make gumbo in this tonight!" She insisted, pointing at the large dutch oven on the box.

"This calls for a celebration. Let's dig into that cobbler," Jacinda insisted, pulling a couple smaller plates from a cabinet.

"That smells heavenly," Scarlett moaned.

"Girl, since when do you like peach cobbler?" she laughed. Scarlett's eyebrows furrowed.

"I usually don't, but that smells amazing," she replied, her tongue peeking out to lick her lower lip.

"Pregnancy does crazy things to the body," Jacinda chuckled while serving a huge spoonful onto a plate and sliding it across to me first.

"Sorry?" Scarlett stated, just as confused by the statement as I was.

"Ya'll know pregnancy be changing everything about a woman's palate. Things you don't like you start to like, and things you used to love you can't stand. That sort of thing," she elaborated absent-mindedly. At Scarlett and my's confused silence, she paused with her spoon mid air and flitted her gaze back and forth between the two of us.

"Don't tell me ya'll didn't know you was pregnant," she dead-panned, still gazing back and forth between me and Scarlett. My heart began to race as my palms started to sweat.

"N-no. I had no idea," Scarlett husked out, blinking rapidly. "How do you know?"

"I've been around so many pregnant women my whole life. It's a smell you don't neva forget. You smell just a bit sweeter than you should - fertile," she explained. Scarlett was at a loss for words and I couldn't stop the tears that pricked my eyes if I tried.

"You're pregnant," I whispered, running my hand through my hair roughly as I stood and whisked Scarlett into my arms. I nuzzled my face into her neck as I held her tighter than I ever had before.

She's pregnant.

She's growing our child.

I'm gonna be a father.

Holy shit...I'm gonna be a father.

The thoughts all bombarded me one right after another. I felt like I couldn't catch my breath. I pulled back, pressing my forehead against Scarlett's as a soft laugh of disbelief poured out of me. Scarlett palmed my cheeks before swiping away my fallen tears with her thumbs.

"We're having a baby," she stated with a hiccup, the emotion clear in her voice.

"If that ain't the sweetest thing. Whew, Lord, who cuttin' onions in here?" Jacinda exclaimed before releasing a loud sniffle and patting at the corner of her eyes.

I couldn't help my following reaction. It wasn't something I could control or stop if I wanted to.

"Jacinda, this has been fantastic but I think it's time we get back home." I stated soundly.

"What? We just got here! We can't leave yet!" Scarlett exclaimed, eyeing me like I was crazy. Jacinda just chuckled softly.

"He just protecting what's his, baby. S'okay. You can come back and visit me anytime. The door always open," she insisted. Scarlett glared at me as we made our way back to the airport, arms crossed over her chest.

"Don't give me that look, sweetheart," I grunted, my skin itching like I had hives. The second my wolf registered that Scarlett was pregnant, my skin had felt too tight and I was on high alert. Nothing was going to solve the feeling until we were safely back on our own packland - where I knew she and the baby were safe. She huffed in annoyance.

"She gave you her number. You can call her anytime you want now," I reasoned as we boarded the jet. She just huffed again and turned to stare out the window as we took off. I chuckled at her moodiness, finding it more adorable than I should have. My smile widened as she tried, and failed, to stifle a yawn.

"I'm tired from all the traveling. Why don't we have a nap?" I asked, already standing to head to the sleeping quarters in the back of the jet. Scarlett released a soft sigh before accepting my outstretched hand and following me back. I climbed onto the bed after her and crawled between her parted thighs. Pushing her flowy cotton sundress up to rest just below her breasts, I nuzzled my face into the skin of her belly, imagining the life that was growing right there. A life Scarlett and I had made together. I pressed gentle kisses against her soft skin before allowing them to trail farther down to the juncture between her legs.

"I thought you said nap," Scarlett sassed, leaning up on her elbows to watch me as I painfully slowly slid her panties down her legs.

"I did. But you always sleep better after having an orgasm," I stated knowingly. Scarlett pursed her lips, fighting a smile, before allowing her legs to open further to accommodate my wide shoulders. She fell back against the pillows with a happy sigh the moment my tongue swiped up her folds before pulling her engorged clit into my mouth, lavishing it with my tongue.

True to what I knew, Scarlett was out like a light mere moments after she came all over my mouth and face. I spooned her from behind, cradling her non-existent belly with my hand. I mulled over the signs I might have missed, but there weren't any. She hadn't been sick - except for the one time on the plane yesterday morning. Her boobs weren't sore. She wasn't more tired than normal. I made a mental note to send Donovan to the pharmacy for pregnancy tests when we got back just to confirm. Every single cell in my body wanted Jacinda to be correct.

I hadn't been giving any mind to actively trying to get Scarlett pregnant, but we weren't doing anything to stop the process either. We have sex more than what is probably healthy, and I never wear a condom. It's amazing she wasn't pregnant sooner.

On the car ride home from the airport, I finally spoke the thought that has been bouncing around my mind since Jacinda insisted Scarlett was pregnant.

"When we get home, I want to tell my parents right away," I stated, feeling giddy about telling my mom and dad they were going to be grandparents.

"Xander, it's almost midnight. And I haven't even taken a test yet to be sure!" she exclaimed. I could see the stress in her eyes, but I wasn't sure why it was there. Before I could ask, we pulled up to the pack house. Immediately, my anxiety faded. Being back in a place where I had total control and felt comfortable was what I needed. Leading Scarlett inside, I smirked seeing the plastic drug store bag on the counter with a note from Donovan attached that read you better call me as soon as this results.

I ripped the box from the bag and tore it apart to get one of the tests out. Scarlett's face held amusement at my actions, but her eyes were telling a different story. I stretched out the test to her and she accepted it before stepping forward to cradle my cheek with the hand that wasn't holding the plastic stick. I sighed, my wolf rumbling in my head with content at the feel of her soft skin pressed against my own.

"Don't call your parents just yet, okay?" she murmured softly. I furrowed my brows but nodded anyway. I followed barely even a step behind her as she went to the bathroom off of our living room. I bounced back and forth between my feet as I watched her take the test.

"No privacy, huh?" Scarlett giggled, cleaning up and setting the test on the plastic wrap.

"My dick has been in every hole of your body. I think we're past privacy," I joked, but there was no humor in my voice. I was too consumed watching the three digital dots blink across the tiny screen. I could feel her stare against the side of my face, but I didn't look away.

"Xander...if-" her concerned voice began but I immediately cut her off.

"PREGNANT!" I whooped turning towards her and hoisting her tiny body into my arms. I squeezed her tight while breathing in her unique scent I could never get enough of. Releasing her, I came face-to-face with her tearful expression. My stomach dropped.

"What's wrong? Do you not want this?" I asked, forcing the tight ball of emotion that'd wedged its way in my throat at the thought that Scarlett might not want kids yet.

"Just the opposite. I was so worried it would be negative and you would be crushed. You were so excited ever since Jacinda said something," she explained before stretching up on her tip-toes to kiss my lips softly.

"Can we call my parents now?" I asked, a shit-eating grin breaking out on my face as I ran my hand through the hair at the nape of her neck. She shivered from my touch, something that made my dick twitch in my pants. Later I thought to myself as she nodded with a wide smile.

Fifteen minutes later, Scarlett had the test wrapped in a small box with a big red bow as we waited for my very tired and cranky parents to make their way to our place. I knew Scarlett could hear my dad's numerous curses he'd growled at me from across the room as I insisted they come over immediately without telling them why.

"What the hell is so important you woke us up at 12:15 to come over for?" my dad grumbled as he sauntered into our living room where Scarlett and I were cuddled together on the couch. I motioned to the loveseat next to us, waiting for them to sit. When they did, Scarlett handed my mom the small box.

"Consider this our early Christmas gift," Scarlett spoke softly, yet I could still hear the emotion in her voice. My mom looked utterly confused - I attributed it to her still being half asleep. My mom slowly unwrapped the gift, flipping the box open and staring at the plastic test - sanitized per Scarlett's insistence. My mom gasped softly as she picked the test up and held it out to my father. Tears gathered in her eyes as she stared at what I knew was the bolded word pregnant on the little screen.

"You're...?" my father asked, his voice cracking as he started to ask the question.

"I'm pregnant. You're going to be grandparents," Scarlett murmured with a nod.

"Oh my God!" my mom yelled before shooting up off the couch and mauling Scarlett in a tight hug. My mom and Scarlett blubbered together as my dad slowly rose from the sofa. He held a hand out to me and hauled me off the couch into the biggest bear hug he's given me since I turned 18. Tears pricked my eyes as he patted my back roughly before ruffling my hair, all the while not releasing me from the hug.

"I couldn't be happier for you, son," he choked out.

"We have to go shopping tomorrow! I've been waiting for this moment ever since Xander was old enough to find a mate!" she squealed. Scarlett giggled in response.

"We have to get an appointment with the pack doctor first. Sorry for waking you guys up so late. We just couldn't wait to tell you."

"Xander couldn't wait to tell you," Scarlett added, giving me a sweet and knowing look. I just shrugged sheepishly.

"This was the best wake-up call ever!" my mom insisted with a happy clap of her hands. "I'm not going to be able to sleep now! I have to start online shopping!" she rushed out before turning and jetting out the door they came in. My dad chuckled softly before turning back to us.

"It was an incredible surprise - one I would happily be awoken in the middle of the night for, over and over again. I better get going so I can monitor what all she buys," my dad said before pulling Scarlett into a gentle hug. He whispered something into her ear that caused her eyes to water instantly. She sniffled and nodded. My dad placed a soft kiss on her cheek before turning and leaving.

"What did he say to you?" I asked her after we'd gotten changed and were slipping under the sheets in our bed. She rolled towards me and snuggled against my chest, her hand resting right where my heart would be.

"That he's been praying for this for you and it was finally answered."

Scarlett's POV

"Scarlett? Sweetheart, where are you?" Xander's voice floated through the house to where I was folding his laundry and putting it away. He'd been training with the pack warriors non-stop since we got back from our trip two weeks ago and therefore had mounds of dirty workout clothes.

"Up here, baby!" I called out. I could smell him before I saw him - his wolf flooding our entire house with stress hormones. I set the shirt I'd had in my hands down and turned to face him.

"What is it?" I asked, frantically searching his face. His lack of a response paired with how disheveled he looked immediately had my wolf rising to the surface. The response was so fast it made me dizzy and slightly nauseous.

"Xander?" I pressed, my concern leaking into my tone.

"The Council has announced they're going to be hosting the Gathering of the States a year early. They said it's due to numerous leadership changes across all the US packs this year. It wasn't supposed to be for another two years," he said, the worry lines on his face only increasing.

"What does that mean?" I asked, already fearing I knew the answer.

"Every Alpha and their respective Luna are required by pack law to attend. It allows The Council to take inventory of each pack's leaders and presents the opportunity for packs to rub elbows in a strictly controlled environment." My heart pounded away in my chest.

"So I'll see the Alpha of...of Eric's pack." I stuttered out.

"It's not just that, sweetheart. There's a very high chance you will see Eric, too. Alpha Sanford almost always brings his beta with him to every single formal meeting and event. I think it's for a show of power. He's one of the only Alphas that does it," he explained.

"Oh," I husked out, my voice catching.

"All of your female security team and the men I selected to watch you will be coming at my request. He will not get anywhere near you. You won't leave my side."

"When?" I asked, staring blankly at the wall ahead of me as my heartbeat thundered in my ears.

"Two months. I asked for a special circumstance due to you being pregnant, but I was denied - much to Elder Adelia's annoyance," he stated with a frustrated growl. I would be three and a half months pregnant by then - my showing would be more than obvious by that point. I gulped, unsure how to process the news.

"Talk to me, baby." Xander pleaded, gently stroking his hands down my arms.

"We have to go. There's no getting out of it. I'll just stick to you like glue. It'll...it'll be okay," I finally answered. I believed in the words I spoke whole-heartedly; Xander would never let anything happen to me, especially not now that I was pregnant. His daddy instincts were borderline annoying at times.

I was only 6 weeks pregnant and just barely had a belly to show for it, but he acted like I was made of glass. He'd stocked our house with remedies for all kinds of pregnancy-related symptoms. Chocolate and ice cream for if I had a craving in the middle of the night, pregnancy-safe bath salts to soak in if my body ached, a special pillow to sleep with - which hadn't been touched because we couldn't cuddle when it was in the bed, and anti-emetic medication in case I experienced morning sickness.

Despite his efforts that made me love him even more, this pregnancy had been nothing but perfect so far. I wasn't sick or tired and nothing ached - except occasionally my boobs. Xander's mom insisted I was truly glowing. She said it was a product of my wolf; when our wolves are truly content it pours out through our skin side as a reflection of their peace and happiness.

"What can I do?" Xander asked, looking like every muscle in his body was twitching and at attention - ready to burst into movement.

"Get Jackie for me?" I asked. He nodded before kissing my forehead and taking off. I slid onto one of the chairs in the sitting area in our room. Staring out the window I released a shaky breath of air. I never thought this day would come.

"What day?" Jackie asked. I must've spoken my thoughts out loud without realizing.

"When I'd finally have to face Eric after escaping. When I was free. I never thought I'd have to look into his eyes ever again," I elaborated. Her shocked face said it all as she sank onto the cushion next to me. She never expected this day to come either.

"I...Scarlett, how are you feeling?" she asked, reaching out to intertwine our fingers.

"I don't know. It's like I feel nothing," I responded, confused. "For two years I thought every single day about what I would say to him if this moment ever came. What exactly I would do to him. But now, it's like...all those thoughts have just evaporated."

"Because you've healed. Xander has successfully repaired all the cracks. The ultimate revenge is moving on and healing. You've done that, Scarlett," she said, rubbing her thumb back and forth across the knuckles of my hand she'd been holding.

"I have?" I asked, turning my gaze from the forest line just beyond our window to stare into Jackie's eyes. She nodded with a solemn smile.

"For a while, the plots of revenge were what kept you going. It was the fire that sparked your fuel for survival. And now, that need is gone. You have Xander. You have me. You have his family. Hell, you have your own family. And you have this baby, too. You have so much to live for that revenge isn't even a blip on your radar," she reasoned. I swallowed thickly as I realized what she said was true.

"I can't believe how much my life has changed in the span of just two months," I choked out through suppressed tears. The unopened boxes of baby items Xander's mom sent non-stop littering our bedroom was evidence enough to that fact. Jackie pulled me in for a tight hug. I melted in her arms, appreciating the embrace.

"But," she started as soon as she pulled away and wiped the lone tear that rolled down my cheek, "just because we've moved on doesn't mean we shouldn't look good enough to eat. Just as one last fuck you," she insisted with a wink.

# CHAPTER 31



I released an unsteady sigh as the woman doing my hair for the evening added her final finishing touches. My makeup was flawless, including the bright blood-red lipstick they'd applied. My hair cascaded down to my lower back in soft curls. A small section of my hair was pulled back and pinned on one side, accentuating my bone structure. The lipstick shade expertly matched my dress for the evening - the one I'd picked all on my own. It had only been seen by my eyes and mine alone. The girls hurried to finish packing their things before rushing out of our suite. I knew they could sense my wolf's presence and it made them uneasy.

She had been at the surface, bordering on taking over, ever since we'd pulled away from our pack house. Knowing the circumstances, she refused to take a back seat. I removed my bra and pulled the silk material of my gown up my body. It was held up with thin straps over my shoulders and zipped at the side of my hip. Being the middle of June, Colorado was plenty warm for my ensemble. The first time I'd ever shown my scars had been to my pack. I had been forced to show them, but I was ashamed of them; I hid them from the eyes of anyone that wasn't myself or my closest confidants.

But now? Now I would show them to the entirety of the most powerful in our world. No Alpha or Luna would leave here with any preconceived notions about the "sheltered" Luna of the Windcrest pack; a rumor that had been floating around as the approach of this night came closer and closer. I would wear my scars like a badge of honor. I had gone through something no wolf could ever imagine. And I lived.

Not only did I live, I thrived.

I examined myself in the mirror. Stroking my baby bump with my hand, it was clear I was carrying an alpha's firstborn. My bump was larger than the average female wolf's. By human standards, I looked to be about five months, not the three and a half I actually was. The silk fabric billowed around my breasts before tightening across my belly. There was a high slit in the fabric going over my left leg. I gathered all my hair over one shoulder and turned to gaze at my backside. The dress had an almost identical design to the one I'd worn to the the pack dinner previously. Not a stitch of cloth covered my back from the bottom of my spine all the way to my neck. I moved my hair back in its place and quickly put on my jewelry for the night. Grabbing my clutch, I reached for the door of the bathroom I'd been getting ready in. Xander wasn't expecting me for another ten minutes, but I couldn't stand the nerves in my stomach. He was waiting just outside and down the hall. The only reason he was more than a few inches away from me was because all my female guards were in the bedroom while the male guards stood just outside the door.

"Tabby, would you mind buckling my heel straps for me?" I asked. My voice immediately snapped all three of the girls' gazes in my direction. Their jaws dropped. Minnie was the first to release a wordless squeal.

"Scarlett, you look amazing!" Tabby exclaimed before rushing over to buckle my heels. I would've done it myself, but my belly would surely get in the way.

"Alpha Harrington is going to lose it when he sees you!" Minnie added in with a huge smile. I returned it before smoothing my hands down my dress.

"Any last touch ups needed?" I asked. They all vigorously shook their head no before Minnie opened the bedroom door for me.

"Luna Harrington is ready," she stated in a serious voice before walking out in front of me. I was flaked on all sides by both my male and female guards. It felt ridiculous, but I was also incredibly thankful for it at the moment.

"Xander," I called when we were within distance for him to hear me. He immediately dropped the conversation he'd been holding with Alpha Huxley and turned towards me. He raked his eyes over my body. His pupils dilated as his tongue swept out over his bottom lip, his chest rising and falling just a touch faster. When his gaze centered on my belly, the corners of his mouth edged upwards in a soft smile.

As soon as I was within arms reach, he yanked me into his embrace. He leaned down to growl against the shell of my ear, "I would take us back to our room and devour you if our attendance wasn't required." I snickered softly, patting his chest dismissively to try and quell the heat his words had caused between my legs.

"Alpha Huxley, where's Veronica tonight?" I asked. I was still unable to get myself to call her Luna Huxley; it was just too...stiff and formal.

"She went off with her escort to find where they were hiding the good champagne," he retorted, and though there was humor in his tone his expression remained completely unphased. I giggled at his words.

"That sounds just like her. Please tell her she'll have to drink for the both of us tonight," I replied, my hand resting atop my belly as I said so. This caused a true smile to pull at his lips.

"I will be sure to do so. Congratulations by the way. You look fantastic," he complimented politely before inclining his head to Xander in a silent goodbye. I swallowed thickly as I realized now was the time for us to head to the main ballroom - one I'd run around like a maniac with Jackie just six months ago. This entire night felt completely surreal.

"There's going to be a lot of eyes in the room. Our guards can't come in. They will stay in the perimeter, but I'm going to be right next to you. And..."

"And?" I asked.

"Despite my numerous threats, our table is right next to the Obsidien pack. They seat by state and region for this event" he finally revealed. I released a shaky breath before plastering a fake smile on my face.

"Well, let's get this over with then shall we?" I asked redundantly. He nodded before looping his arm around my back. He jerked when his hand glided over my naked back. His shocked eyes searched my own silently before he cleared his throat and leaned down to kiss me deeply.

"Let's do this," he murmured against my lips before guiding us towards the entrance. The extravagant doors were opened for us and all I could see was a sea of people. I never thought I would call the ballroom small but it felt that way with how many people were in here. The pheromones were suffocating. I could feel a sense of panic rising in my chest. The hand that I had wrapped aroudn Xander's bicep clenched around the muscle. Xander tightened his hold on me and pressed even closer. I focused on just his scent, thankful when it relaxed my wolf a fraction.

"Everyone, please take your seats!" Elder Thomas's voice floated over an MC system a few moments later. Murmured whispers followed behind us. They were apparently surprised I'd showed up rather than locking myself in a tower back home. I felt Xander's fingers flex and tighten against the skin of my back. I turned my gaze to where his was directed.

My breath caught in my chest and my heart thundered to what felt like a complete stop. I wasn't sure what I was expecting to feel when seeing Eric for the first time in person since I'd run. Since the final beating he gave me.

Hurt? Maybe. Vengeful? Sure. Tearful? A good possibility. But the all-consuming murderous rage that engulfed my body? Wasn't on the list. The air around us changed as the blood-lust shot through my veins with lightning speed. It was charged with my pheromones. I sensed the other alphas' reactions to my hormones as their skin likely prickled with the threat of a predator nearby. Eric and Alpha Sanford's eyes snapped toward us. I watched as the moment Eric registered what he was seeing. His eyes blew wide with disbelief, as if he was seeing a corpse walking.

To his knowledge, that's what I was. What I should've been. My predatory stare didn't deviate from his face. I couldn't even find it in me to care that I was breaking so many social norms. So many laws. And to do so at The Gathering of the Packs? I was asking for it.

The whispers around us grew in volume as the other alpha and lunas tried to make sense of my stare down with Eric. My skin felt like it was bubbling under the surface with the white-hot anger that seeped through my bones. It threatened to break out as we approached our table - conveniently placed directly in front of his own. Grabbing my hair, I swept it over my shoulder as we came just feet from the man responsible for the mangled flesh on display. My body seemed to have a mind of its own as my mouth moved into a sinister smile.

I couldn't focus on the reactions to my body by those closest to us, I was too caught up in this moment. Eric's gaze darkened as his eyes scanned his masterpiece, silent anger sweeping across his features. No one would know that's what he was feeling if they didn't know him. To unsuspecting eyes, he looked shocked and upset.

But I did. I knew him. Knew what made him tick. What sent him over the edge. This blatant display enraged him. And I loved it. Game on.

I could feel his eyes burning holes into the back of my head the entire night - burning especially hot whenever Xander would caress my skin or press a kiss to the mark on my neck. As each Counsel Elder spoke the flames only burned hotter. Apparently, the formality of tonight included each alpha approaching the podium on the set-up stage one-by-one to state who they were, their pack affiliation, and their rank. It all seemed so stupid to me, but I already had a plan forming in my head.

"I'm introducing myself," I suddenly found myself whispering to Xander. His concerned gaze met mine while his hand stroked my belly from where I was cradled against his body in our seats.

He released a sigh before nodding. Replying with a simple, "okay, baby." I love this man I thought as I stroked his cheek intimately. His unwavering support of me was something he had no idea I needed so badly in that moment.

Our number was called, and Xander stood tall. He extended a hand to help me stand, which I took gratefully. The room was dead silent as we confidently approached the designated spot on the stage.

"My name is Xander Harrington, affiliated with the Windcrest pack of Montana. I am the Alpha of the Windrest pack," Xander stated with a commanding voice. There was no doubt he was an alpha. He took a tiny step back, indicating it was my turn. I swallowed the thick lump in my throat and stepped up to the microphone, steeling my nerves for what I was about to do.

"My name is Scarlett Harrington. Formerly Scarlett Rockwell. Affiliated with the Windcrest pack of Montana. I am the Luna of the Windcrest pack and the mate of Xander Harrington," I repeated the words in the same fashion every female had been introduced before me. I could taste Eric's rage on my tongue the moment the words mate left my mouth. But I wasn't done yet. "I once shared an unconsummated bond with Beta Eric Strickland of the Sablefur pack. I now have a Contract of Retribution signed by all Council members with Eric's name on it."

The roar of gasps and outraged cries forced me to stop talking. Eric's face went so white I would've thought he was a ghost. "That's right Eric," I started back up, focusing my gaze solely on the man in question. "The scars you left have consequences. I hope that scares the fuck out of you. Because it should. I've had two years to think about what you did to me. How you tortured me. Today is your official notice that your life has an expiration date - courtesy of me. It could be today. It could be tomorrow. It could be next month. It could be in five years. I hope you spend the rest of your short, pathetic life looking over your shoulder, terrified that it will be the day I come to end your miserable existence. Maybe then you'll have an inkling of an idea of how you used to affect me," I finished. Backing away from the microphone, I looped my arm through Xander's before placing another comforting hand over my belly. An overwhelming feeling of pride encompassed my chest - no doubt Xander's emotion rather than my own. I held onto his arm tighter as he escorted us off the stage. I looked straight ahead as we left the ballroom - completely ignoring the fact that we would likely get into a ton of trouble for doing so.

It just didn't seem polite to stay and party after threatening someone's life in front of all the guests.

Xander's body shook lightly against my arm as we exited the room. I immediately snapped my gaze to him, confused. I quickly realized he was laughing. "Did I say something funny?" I teased, squeezing his forearm gently.

"Just you, Scarlett. You amaze me," he said before a small chuckle broke out from his lips. My mood did a 180 from tense anger to light-hearted and giggling.

"So, what happens now?" I asked as we both peered over our shoulders at the closed ballroom doors as an uproar of noise - what sounded like numerous people all yelling over each other - suddenly exploded. He sighed softly with a quick shrug of his shoulders.

"We still have to attend the brunch tomorrow morning. We can find out what became of your little speech then," he reasoned.

And find out we did.

The next morning we entered the same ballroom, except now it was set up with multiple tables of various breakfast foods lining nearly every wall. Hungry alphas demanded large quantities of food. I locked eyes with Elder Adelia - who happened to be trying to hide a smirk as we locked gazes. I didn't bother concealing my smile before tipping my head in acknowledgment of her. Xander and I were the center of attention once again - this time I understood why. We put on jovial expressions before approaching the vast buffet tables. Loading our plates up, Xander continued to heap numerous additional items onto my plate murmuring 'for the baby' each time. I just rolled my eyes jokingly while letting him continue his antics.

Finding a table where Veronica and her mate were sitting alongside some men I'd never seen before, I motioned towards the two empty seats with my eyes, silently asking Xander. He brought our intertwined hands up to his mouth before taking off in the direction of the table. Conversation ceased as we got closer. Xander didn't pay it any mind as he set his plate down and pulled out my chair for me.

"Alpha Jameson, Alpha Prescott," Xander acknowledged the other men at the table respectfully. I slightly bowed my head in acknowledgment before beginning to dig into my food.

"Okay, I'm just going to say it. How can you eat like nothing has happened?" Veronica demanded, looking completely shocked. I put my fork and knife down. Wiping my mouth with my napkin, I shifted my body in her direction.

"Am I supposed to lose my appetite because I finally confronted the man who tortured and mutilated me for a year?" I asked, mostly redundantly. She floundered for something to say in response, so I saved her. "I had two years to come to terms with what he did to me. I don't sit and wallow about it any longer. I chose to try and move on. And when Xander came into the picture, I truly did. As crazy as it sounds, I hardly think about Eric anymore - if ever. Seeing him irritated old wounds, sure, but that doesn't undo all the hard work I've put in to get to where I am today." She searched my eyes while processing my words. Xander stayed silent, rather rubbing his hand resting on my shoulder back and forth in a soothing motion.

"So when you disappeared without keeping in contact with any of us...?" Veronica asked. I knew she'd already put the pieces together, but she was the type who needed to hear her suspicions spoken out in the open.

"I was either tied up in his bedroom closet or chained to the floor in his basement," I responded, popping a piece of watermelon in my mouth. "What ended up happening after we left?" I asked, needing a break from the looks of abject horror and pity on the faces of our breakfast companions.

"Shortly after you walked out, a huge argument broke out between Alpha Stanford and all the Alphas he has active alliances with. Many of them were calling for a complete dissolution of their agreements. None of them want to be associated with the pack of a horrific monster that would commit such crimes to warrant a Contract of Retribution - and one against their ex-mate at that. Some people didn't believe what you'd said because of how...preposterous the whole idea seemed. More than 70 percent of alphas are mated to their fated mate. They couldn't fathom Beta Strickland doing such a thing to you. The alpha of Alpha Stanford's closest pack alliance demanded proof. All the Elders had to come in and dispel the chaos. When they confirmed what you said to be true, Luna Harrington, everything really spiraled from there. Alpha Stanford and Beta Strickland quickly left after that. I don't even think they stopped to grab their belongings. It was quite a hostile environment against them."

I chewed slowly while taking in all the information. "I wonder what would happen if people knew that Alpha Sanford was aware of what was going on. Complicit, even," I mumbled absent-mindedly.

"What?" Alpha Prescott scoffed, a baffled look on his face. I just shrugged my shoulders.

"It's neither here nor there. The Elders are aware of his role in the entire situation. I'm sure they'll both be taken care of soon, likely without me needing to lift a finger," I finished, popping a bite of syrupy pancake into my mouth.

"Okay. New topic for table discussion," I insisted. "Who here has been waterboarded? It's not very fun." A cheeky smile pulled at my lips, but no one else joined me. Tough crowd.

# CHAPTER 32

Scarlett's POV

We stuck around at the Gathering of the Packs for a couple of days after the main event held by The Council. Xander had some business to finish with a few ally packs and it was easier for them to work it out now rather than by back and forth conference calls once we all went home. We'd been home for a week now, and I couldn't shake the odd feeling that had loomed over me ever since we arrived back. I never wanted to have to confront Eric after escaping him, but now that I had it felt like my business was left unfinished.

The last I'd heard about the situation was from Veronica at our shared breakfast the night after the confrontation. I wasn't sure if Xander had information regarding Eric and his Alpha; if he did, he chose not to share it with me. I knew there was likely something that transpired beyond Alpha's wanting to sever their alliances with their pack.

I huffed in frustration at myself, unable to concentrate on picking a nursery color when my mind was flooded with other concerns.

"It's just a paint color, sweetheart. No need to get so frustrated," Xander's voice floated over to where I was standing in the middle of the baby room.

"It's not that. I think I already picked the one I like best out," I responded, crossing my arms over my chest and rubbing my hand over the fabric of Xander's t-shirt that was covering my arm. He came up behind me and pulled me against his frame by my hips.

"Then what has you so tense?" he asked before pressing a sweet kiss to the mark on my neck. I shivered at the contact, every cell in my body lighting up with recognition at his touch.

"Have you heard any news regarding the Obsidian pack?" I asked, not bothering to elaborate on why I was asking.

"A few things, yes..." he trailed off, not elaborating either. I sighed before turning in his hold so I could press my nose into his chest and breathe him in.

"Like what?" I pressed further. He hesitated before answering. He cleared his throat before grasping the side of my face in his hand and lifting my gaze to meet his.

"There have been reports from allies of ours that the news traveled back to their pack members. They quickly organized a grass roots uprising and usurped their entire leadership board - Alpha, Beta, Gamma, and head warrior. They figured if there was something so sinister going on with one member of their leadership, there wasn't any way the rest didn't know or at least have a good idea what was going on. They were all banned - including their mates - and officially regarded as rogue. Since being chased off their lands, their whereabouts haven't been able to be located," he revealed. My breath caught in my throat at his revelation.

"So they're just wandering around without anyone knowing where they're at or what they're doing?" I asked apprehensively.

He pursed his lips before nodding. I pressed my face back into his chest and squeezed my eyes shut. Was I somewhat thankful that I didn't have to keep hiding behind my secret now that the world knew exactly the kind of man Eric was? Yes. Was I incredibly nervous about the fact that I had no idea where he was or how to track him now that he'd been labeled a rogue? Yes.

"Nothing will ever happen to you," he assured me. I didn't even need him to say it, because it was a fact I already knew. I nodded in affirmation.

"What about my...my family?" I asked, still feeling the residual awkwardness of the title. "I'm worried Eric could find out about them, or even already knows, and he'll go after them as a way to get back at me for what's happened," I said.

"I was going to speak with you about this, but wasn't sure how to approach the subject. I spoke with their pack's alpha. We discussed transferring their membership to my pack and having them relocate. This way, you could build a true relationship with them and they wouldn't be so far away. Only if you want, though," he quickly added at the end.

"You did that for me?" I asked, tearing up immediately at the fact that he'd taken steps to bring me and my family closer without me even asking or expressing the desire outloud.

"Of course, baby. You deserve to get to know your family," he insisted. I grabbed him by the back of the neck and jerked him down to my height so I could properly kiss him.

The rest of the day was spent making phone calls to various individuals. First my family to see if they were even open to the idea of relocating packs. To my surprise, they said they'd already considered the idea before they knew I wanted them closer. Next was the call to the Alpha to get the transfer paperwork started. Then Xander called the individual in charge of housing for his pack and allocated a couple homes near each other for my family to move into.

Watching Xavier bounce from phone call to phone call arranging for my family to come within 15 minutes of our place got me so hot and bothered. I'd decided that watching him do his job would be a form of foreplay for me. It was so attractive watching him boss people around. Xavier assured me that they would be here within the next few days.

Half an hour later, I was in the middle of straddling Xavier on his office couch when Justin came bursting through the door without knocking. My hands immediately stopped unzipping his pants as I jerked back in surprise.

"Knocking was invented for a reason," Xander growled in annoyance. I shushed him when I saw the terrified look on Justin's face.

"What happened?" I asked, climbing off of Xander - with some difficulty thanks to my belly - and walked to Justin to try and get an answer.

"It's Jackie," he rushed out, voice cracking halfway through his words. It felt like there was suddenly a lump of lead in my stomach as a feeling of dread washed over me.

"What about Jackie? What happened?" I demanded, my heart beginning to pound in my chest.

"She was out shopping for baby clothes - for you," he clarified when he saw my shocked expression, "we were on the phone one minute because she wanted my opinion, then next thing I know she's screaming and the line goes dead," he explained, tears welling up in his eyes.

"Xander-"

"I'm already on it," he interrupted Justin. He was immediately back in business mode, picking up his phone and calling someone he had on speed dial. If the situation weren't so dire, I would laugh at the fact that Xander's pants were still hanging open, his belt clinking freely.

"I know who it was," I whispered, my heart aching at the realization.

"What do you mean?" Justin and Xander demanded at the same time.

"It was Melvin. Her stalker. I was praying he had finally moved on. We haven't heard a peep from him in over a year. There wasn't any indication he was still after her. The Elders swore he would give up when she was finally mated..." I trailed off.

"Where do we find him?" Justin demanded, a fire in his eyes that reassured me my friend would be okay. Justin wouldn't allow any other outcome. I shook my head in response.

"No one knows," I mumbled barely loud enough for them to hear. "That's why Jackie had to be in protective custody for so long. He's incredibly difficult to track down. He blows into town and is gone before anyone even realizes. He doesn't leave a trace," I explained.

"Well he's chosen the wrong woman to fuck with. When I find him, and I will, he's not going to have an issue hiding anywhere because he'll be in convenient, small pieces," Justin growled.

"I need to borrow your phone," I said to Xander, holding my hand out for the device in question. I dialed the number I knew by heart and waited anxiously as the dial tone rang.

"This is Elder Adelia May, head of protective affairs, may I ask who's calling?" Adelia's soft voice sounded in my ears.

"Adelia. It's Jackie. He finally got her," I choked out, doing everything I could to hold the sob that was lodged in the base of my throat down.

"Oh, goodness. Scarlett-"

"We need The Council's help. I need you to fax everything you've ever gathered about Melvin. I don't know how much time we have before..." I said, stopping myself before I said something I didn't want Justin to hear.

"Absolutely. I'll do it right away. I'm going to send a representative down to aid in the investigation as well. Please, let me know what else I can do to help."

The information from The Council was helpful, but there was so much of it we were using a large amount of time to sort through it. Time we didn't have. Every single part of me wanted to break down over the unknown condition of my best friend. I hadn't been more than a day without speaking to her in some capacity for over a year now. I wouldn't even let myself imagine a scenario where I couldn't text, call, or hang out with her whenever I wanted because of Melvin.

Xander entered his office - the place everyone had gathered to try and find somewhere to start looking for Melvin - with a stack of papers in his hands. "Alistair was able to hack into his bank statements and tax filings. He owns two different abandoned warehouses that he tried to disguise. He purchased them both utilizing a shell corporation in the Cayman Islands. One is in the middle of nowhere Wyoming and one just an hour away from The Council's grounds in Colorado," he mumbled, reading the information on one of the papers intently. He handed some of them off to Justin as his eyes continued scanning the documents.

"When was the one in Wyoming purchased?" I asked, setting down the laptop with hundreds of pages of information on Melvin and his life story.

"Looks like...three months ago," Xander stated, looking up to meet my eyes. My brows furrowed as I thought.

"That's right around the time Jackie left Counsel grounds and mated with Justin. When was the Colorado one purchased?" I asked.

"Two years ago. Why?" Justin asked, eyes narrowing at me.

"The timeline of his purchases make sense. He stalked Jackie for a year. Then she was taken in by The Council when she was 19. It probably took Melvin longer to track her down after they took her in. He likely purchased the space in Colorado after locating her as a space to take her to if he were ever able to get his hands on her while she was under The Council's protection. It also probably served as a safe hideout for him to be close enough to continue stalking her without being so close that he would be discovered. The Wyoming purchase likely serves the same purpose. However, it's a point between here and Colorado. If I had to guess, he's going to take her back to the Colorado location as his final stopping point until he figures something more concrete out, and the one in Wyoming he'll likely use to rest and prepare for the final trek back to Colorado," I reasoned.

"If that's the case, we need to send someone from The Council to scout the Colorado space. Break in and see exactly what he has going on there," Xander stated before picking up his office phone to make a call.

"I can't believe I let this happen," Justin whispered, his head falling into his hands as he hunched over with his elbows on his knees.

"You can't blame yourself," I whispered, lowering myself onto the couch cushion next to him. I placed my hand on the shoulder closest to me and gave it a gentle squeeze.

"I've told her so many times to never leave without her security, but she's so stubborn. And headstrong. I know she's capable of protecting herself, but there are a lot of people in this world that don't fight fair. I should've known she was going to give her guard the slip. She already told me it would be horrible strolling through the baby isles with a big mean looking guard following her. I should've just gone with her. Then this would've never happened," he growled, clearly angry with himself.

"Justin, if it wasn't today, it would've been another day. Melvin is crazy. He's shown he will stop at nothing until he's caught. And I know for a fact Jackie is putting up one hell of a fight against him right now. She's so strong. We have to stay strong too so we can finally put Melvin away," I insisted. Justin sighed heavily before nodding in agreement.

"He's not nearly as smart as we thought he was. He's just never been this ballsy before. Alistair hacked the street light footage on the major roads trailing away from the mall she was taken from. These are the images he just sent me," Xavier said, handing Justin his ipad so we could scroll through the photos.

"The cameras stop ten miles from the mall, but we know what direction they're heading and we know what he was driving. I've sent enforcers out in that direction already. We'll get her back," Xander stated with so much conviction in his voice.

"Alistair has sent his drone out in the direction they went as well so we can have aerial coverage. Donovan and Griffin are going to stay here and continue combing through clues in case this is a diversion or dead end. Our car is ready and running, we can be on the road in five minutes," Xander spoke while rooting around in his desk drawer. Justin was off the couch in seconds, clearly ready to go. Xander finally found what he was looking for before pulling out a hulking handgun. He pulled the magazine out, checking how many bullets were loaded before shoving it back into the butt of the gun and tucking it into a carrier in his waistline.

"Xander-"

"No," Xander growled, swiftly cutting me off before I could even ask my question.

"What do you mean no? You didn't even let me speak!" I yelled.

"No, Scarlett. You will not come with us. You will stay here, in this house, under your security's watch," he stated with no room for negotiation.

"But she's my best friend!" I hissed.

"I understand, but you're my mate and the mother of my child. I will keep you updated, but you will stay here. I am not arguing with you about this." I balked at his tone. Xander had never spoken to me in such a way ever before. The onlookers of our argument shifted uneasily. Xander barked for them to get in the car and wait for him. I crossed my arms over my chest as his gaze zeroed back in on me once we were mostly alone.

"You can hate me for this all you want," Xander began, his tone softening considerably as he took step after step closer to me. "Quite frankly, I don't care right now. My cousin's mate is missing, and I refuse to experience what he's feeling right now. I've never asked anything of you, Scarlett. But right now, I'm asking you to allow me to protect my family in the only way I can at this moment," he murmured. By the time he was done speaking, we were so close he was able to bend forward and press his forehead against my own. I released a soft sigh as I uncrossed my arms and slid them up his body to rest on his chest.

"Fine," I conceded. I didn't like it, but he was right. I was in no shape to be putting myself in any line of danger right now. The relief he felt by that simple one word was palpable.

"Thank you," he spoke against my lips before kissing me softly. "Promise me you'll go back to our wing and relax in our bedroom until I'm back," he pleaded.

"I can't wander the house? Now I have to just stick to our bedroom?" I huffed.

"It's the only room in the house that has reinforced walls and bulletproof glass - extra protection since it's the room we sleep in. Just please promise me," he said again.

I pursed my lips before giving in. "I promise," I assured him. He gave me a short, passionate kiss, mumbled an I love you, and took off for the vehicle that was waiting for him.

# CHaPTer 33



I paced around Xander and I's bedroom. The second I watched his SUV drive off, my stomach became a heavy pit of anxiety. I did everything I could to try and distract myself. I took a lukewarm bubble bath, curled my hair, made our bed, even tried to focus enough to read a book. When none of it worked - not even a little bit - I lay in our bed and allowed Xander's potent lingering smell to comfort me. My hands fidgeted continuously with the blankets.

Peering at the clock, I counted how long it'd been since they left. Surely, something had happened by now? Three painstaking hours had passed already. I picked up my phone for the hundredth time only to see no notifications; no phone calls, no text messages, no nothing. I blew a raspberry from my lips before throwing my phone onto the bed again. My female and male guards were taking their jobs very seriously - something Xander would be elated about. However, it meant that not a single one of them would speak to me.

It wasn't until another hour had passed that one of the guards finally opened the door. When they did, I shot out of bed. The ball of nerves in my stomach welled up into my chest The guard's expression remained blank, not giving anything away or relieving my anxiety at all. Until, finally, a battered and bruised Jackie came partially limping into the room.

"Oh, thank God!" I yelped, relief flooding my body as I dashed over to her. I enveloped her in a tight hug, my tears coming fast and heavy as I clutched my best friend tightly. Truth be told, I had no idea if Melvin was a violent man or not. We'd never known much about who he truly was over the years. Only the fact he was a creepy stalker, which was obvious. Despite my words of encouragement for Justin, I couldn't help the niggling of fear that crept into my mind. Seeing Jackie here and safe finally allowed me to breathe.

"I'm a little offended to tell you the truth," Jackie finally spoke when I released her. I backed away just enough to get a good look at her.

"What?" I balked.

"After all these damn years of pining over me, the loser couldn't even get it up. I mean, in hindsight, he's lucky. I would've broken the damn thing if he even came close to me with it, but it was just...a limp noodle the whole time. Maybe that's why he's truly angry," she stated with a roll of her eyes. Despite the humor behind her tone, I knew the joke was her own way twisted way of coping with the situation. I couldn't help the laughter that bubbled quietly from my chest at her words. I knew she just desperately wanted to forget the situation.

"Thank God for that," I said through another soft rumble of giggles before pulling her back in for another hug. She held me just as tight. I could smell the fear finally begin to dissipate from her skin.

"Please tell me he's never going to bother you ever again," I practically begged.

"Unless he comes back as a zombie and can reassemble his body from the numerous pieces that Xander and Justin tore him into, I'm going to guess no," she snorted. My head jerked back at the incredibly violent act she seemed to brush off as no big deal.

"Wow. Justin wasn't kidding," I murmured off-handedly.

"If you'll excuse me. I'm going to go take a scathing hot shower and then sleep for 48 hours," she said before giving me one last hug and a chaste kiss on my cheek. Xander passed by Jackie on the way into our bedroom, stopping her to give her a serious look and ask if she was sure she was alright. Jackie gave him a small smile and nodded, patting him on the shoulder before finally disappearing.

"She's a strong one, that girl," Xander mumbled, his face one of relief when he finally laid his eyes on me. A genuine smile pulled at my lips as I nodded, opening my arms to wrap them around his torso as he stepped in front of me. I soaked in his warmth as I leaned fully into his embrace.

I would stay just like this forever if I could.

It had been two weeks since the incident with Melvin and things were finally starting to feel normal again. Jackie and I holed up in my place for the first few days. She didn't feel safe being alone at home when Justin was gone for pack business during the day. I didn't blame her. I would've felt the same way.

Slowly but surely, she came out of the anxious shell that had been surrounding her and was back to her normal, chatty self.

The July heat had started to pick up, so Jackie and I were working on getting a better AC system installed for the orphanage. We were in the middle of speaking with one of the pack maintenance men when Xander entered my office and interrupted us.

"Is this something that can be picked back up in about an hour?" he asked, glancing between me and the pack member. I nodded and rescheduled for him to come back.

"I've been speaking with a few packs in Europe-"

"Europe? There are wolves in Europe?" Jackie cut him off, just as surprised as I was.

"Yes. About half as many as here in the States," he answered seamlessly before continuing. "I've been in negotiations with them for a few days now. We're working out a temporary treaty to help us hunt Eric down and get his official location. There's a possibility he fled the country to try and hide."

"There must be a catch if you're coming to tell me?" I asked, already apprehensive. Last time this happened, I had to see Eric again.

"In order to even enter Europe and meet with these alphas, we have to meet with the monarch family that rules over the European packs."

"Are all the packs in one country or are we going to have to rub elbows with multiple families?" I asked, completely unsure of how any of it worked.

"No, just one king and queen. The Were Monarchy is different from the human's. There's just one royal family that resides over all the packs in Europe rather than just one country. Once we get their permission, we can go wherever we need," he explained.

"When were you planning for this trip to take place? I'm not getting any less pregnant," I deadpanned, my ever-growing swollen belly making my statement even clearer.

"Within the next week or so. We won't stay long because I don't like the idea of you being an entire continent away from our pack. Just a couple days at the most. I will fly back out on my own for the treaty meetings."

And that's exactly what we did. Just a short three days later, we were touching down on the royal family's personal tarmac in rural England. I was thankful we had the pack's jet because I grew uncomfortable rather quickly when sitting for extended periods of time.

We were ushered into a luxurious SUV. Obnoxious little flags bobbed from the light breeze on either side of the vehicle. Thankfully, the ride to the castle was short. It felt like Xander's child was using my bladder to play their own private soccer game. Or I guess football considering my location.

The whole show they put on once we arrived was a bit overdone in my opinion. From what Xander said, the monarchy was Europe's version of our Counsil. I know if they ever tried to pull something like this, Elder Adelia would've scoffed and put a stop to it.

There was a line of guards in fancy uniforms lining the stairs as we were escorted inside. I suddenly felt very underdressed in my cotton sundress. I held tightly onto Xander's arm as we ascended and entered the castle, my bladder full to the point of pain.

"Bathroom," I quickly rushed out to Xander, rocking back and forth between my feet. He asked the closest guard to him if they could show us the way. The man looked disgruntled by the request, but nodded. Once back, we waited around a few more minutes until a booming voice came from the second level.

"Alpha and Luna Harrington, it's a pleasure to have you!" My eyes tracked the couple as they began descending the grand staircase.

"King Grimaldi, we appreciate your generosity in accepting us on such short notice," Xander stated genuinely, extending his hand for the king to shake. He accepted Xander's hand before his gaze swiveled to me for the first time.

The look he gave me had me subconsciously reaching up to my face, wondering if I had food on it. Or maybe he was thinking I should've put more effort into my appearance. I never wore any makeup these days. Xander's never complained, so I never cared. I cleared my throat uncomfortably as the King continued to examine my face intently. The Queen noticed my discomfort and gave the bicep she was holding a squeeze. The grip seemed to snap him out of whatever was running through his head because a bright smile quickly took over his face.

"Your room has been arranged already. I assume you'll be needing some rest before dinner? What time is it in Montana now?" the king asked.

"Seven am," Xander answered. The king's eyebrows rose a fraction.

"Ah. Well, dinner will be served at 6:30. You've got a bit of time to sleep off some of the jet lag before then." I wasn't going to argue with him. All I wanted to do was take a long nap after the 12 hours it took to get here.

I couldn't shake the uneasy feeling as the King continued to intentionally glance at me while guiding us to our room. At one point, it felt like his eyes wouldn't leave me. It was more than just unsettling. Xander must have eventually noticed too. He slowly started to shield me from his eyes with his body.

After what felt like a million hallways and stairs, we finally arrived at our room. We said our quick goodbyes and I darted to the massive four-poster bed that sat proudly in the middle of the room. The second my head hit the silk-covered pillow, I was out.

Three and a half hours later, Xander woke me with just enough time to find our way back to the entrance and be escorted to the dining room. I did my best to stifle my yawn that I couldn't stop completely as we were seated. The king and queen joined us a few moments after we were seated. The weird feeling both me and my wolf had from the earlier encounter with King Grimaldi came right back. Despite my best efforts at shaking it, it wouldn't subside. It felt like the clothes I was wearing were itchy and two sizes too tight. I gave the king, who was yet again staring intently at me, a terse smile. Thankfully, his attention was pulled from me as a man and woman joined us at the table moments later.

"Ah! Alpha and Luna Harrington these are our children. Luke is my oldest. He's almost twenty-four, so he'll take over for me in just a bit over a year. This is my only daughter, Angelina. She's just turned eighteen," the king stated as his daughter took the seat across from me. She was beautiful and the spitting image of her mother.

As we ate, Angelina and I exchanged small talk here and there. It was difficult due to the scrutinizing gaze of her father. I couldn't get the way he introduced her out of my head either. It was just so odd. 'My only daughter'. The words just kept circling around and around in my brain on repeat. His statement had seemed pointed when he'd said it; different to how he introduced his son - who happened to be his only son.

"So, Luna Harrington, your mother and father must be very proud to have a daughter mated to such a strong leader as Alpha Harrington," King Grimaldi stated as they set our dessert down in front of us. It was the first time he'd addressed me directly since we'd arrived. His voice grated unpleasantly against my skin as he spoke. The hair on the back of my neck bristled.

My hand clenched around my spoon, suspended in the air above the apple crumble I was about to take a bite from. I let a strained smile grace my face. "I wouldn't know. I've been an orphan my whole life," I stated simply. My revelation seemed to knock his world off kilter. He looked utterly distraught. His mouth opened and shut multiple times making him resemble that of a fish out of water.

"That's...well," he began before stopping to clear his throat, "all great Lunas I've met have faced hardship and adversity at some point in their life," he finally finished.

"Well there's been plenty of that," I snorted before taking a large swig of the sparkling water I'd been given in lieu of the wine everyone else was drinking. He looked curious about my statement, but I refused to elaborate.

"That's actually why we're here. We're seeking an alliance to help track down a wolf whose sole intentions could be to further harm my mate," Xander explained, getting right down to business. The King's demeanor hardened immediately as Xander's words registered.

"Harm how?" The King demanded, his gaze focusing on my face.

"Contract of Retribution kind of harm," Xander grunted. The King's jaw clenched multiple times, so hard I thought it might break.

"Whatever you need, we will accommodate. Every pack," the King insisted. This must have been an unexpected response because Xander wasn't able to stop his face from showing his shock.

"We appreciate that, King Grimaldi. If you don't mind, I'd prefer to finalize the details of what we need over the phone or email. With my mate being pregnant, I'd like to get her back home," Xander insisted. The King looked like he wanted to put up a fight, but held his tongue as his eyes flickered from his mate, to his kids, and finally back to me.

I wasn't going to question the king's motives behind agreeing to help us so quickly. I was just thankful that we were possibly one step closer to chasing Eric down. I wanted this to be over and handled before I gave birth. I dug into the warm apple dessert in front of me, sighing happily. My eyes flitted up to the king, who'd just taken a bite of his own dessert. And then, seconds later, I felt all the air leave my lungs as my heart constricted in my chest. My eyes caught a very distinct mannerism - the tapping of his spoon against the plate twice after he took a bite. But it wasn't just that bite. It was every bite after.

I was probably certifiably crazy. It wouldn't be a surprise after everything I've been through. But in that moment, it just clicked.

He's my father.

# CHAPTER 34

Scarlett's POV

After the rocking revelation, I became the one who stalked him like he was my prey. I started to notice every single thing. Our eyes were the same color.

No. No. I got those from my grandmother. Not him. I'm crazy. I'm making this up.

But then there was the way he leaned back in his chair after taking a bite. The way he raised his eyebrows whenever someone was talking directly to him so the person knew he was listening. The way the corner of his mouth curved upward instead of a full-fledged smile. They weren't huge things, but it felt like the earth below me had shifted.

I was off-kilter.

I put my fork down and clenched my fists by my sides, suddenly losing my entire appetite despite still being hungry moments earlier. As if sensing the change in me, the king looked up and met my gaze. I'm not even sure what emotions were showing on my face in that moment, but a knowing look overcame his own as he scanned my demeanor.

"I apologize. My stomach's not feeling right. If you'll all excuse me," I murmured before rushing out of the dining hall, my guards just a step behind me. Xander must have followed me out, too. He caught up with me just as I entered the bedroom we'd been assigned.

"Sweetheart, what's wrong?" Xander prodded. I was so focused on breathing so I didn't pass out that I ignored the question.

"Scarlett, talk to me," he insisted again, his tone sounding more desperate than the first time. Again, I couldn't answer. My mind was a mess of whirling thoughts and emotions. My hormones weren't helping the matter as I struggled to contain the simultaneous tears and screams I wanted to release. Everything felt so overwhelming. I just wanted it to stop.

"Scarlett-"

"JUST SHUT UP AND GO AWAY! GET OUT!" I screamed. I couldn't handle it all, instead lashing out. Xander attempted to pull me into his arms, but I pushed at his chest as he got near me. I immediately regretted the action. The sheer anguish that showed on Xander's face at my rejection made my throat tighten with pain. Seconds later, Xander schooled his face into a stone-cold expression that sent a chill through me almost instantly. He cleared his throat and left the room without speaking a single word.

Unable to speak through the lump of ever-growing emotion and frustration, I couldn't call him back and apologize. I couldn't tell him to please stop and I'm so sorry. The dam of tears broke the second the door shut. The sound of it latching seemed the be the loudest sound in the world.

I was crying so hard I could barely breathe. The thoughts racing around in my mind were too loud. Too much. Too everything. I stumbled to the bed, my knees buckling as I clenched the comforter in a death grip. I gasped for breath as I pressed a hand to my belly, needing something to anchor me back in reality.

My hands shook as I tried to clear my mind. Nothing was helping. Not having Xander nearby for comfort while I was wrestling with my emotions made everything ten times harder. My fingers ached to run over Xander's body and just feel his sturdiness. Feel the comfort that the security of his strength brought me. My guards watched on helplessly, unsure what to do. I finally managed to choke out a request for Xander between my sobs. Millie looked relieved to either get away from my inconsolable crying, or be able to actually do something about it. Probably both.

Xander slowly meandered into the room. The second he saw my tears, he rushed the rest of the way to me. He pulled me against his body and cradled the back of my head as I pressed my nose against his chest. It took what felt like hours, but was likely only a few minutes at most, to calm down.

"What's wrong, baby?" he asked, handling me with kid gloves. Emotion tightened my throat once again.

"I think....I think I'm - ugh I'm probably c-crazy! It's such a stretch and I'm just losing it because of the pregnancy hormones ...b-but- " I started, the words choppy from my hiccups, but I was cut off by one of the king's guards knocking twice before sticking his head in the room.

"Alpha, King Grimaldi is requesting to speak with Luna Harrington," he stated with an uncomfortable expression on his face.

"Tell him she's unwell and we will speak with him tomorrow," Xander instructed.

"He said it's urgent," he pressed further, looking incredibly uncomfortable pushing back against his own alpha's order.

"Tell him my Luna is in urgent need at the moment and we can speak tomorrow," he insisted with more finality in his tone. The guard cleared his throat before nodding and leaving.

"What were you saying?" Xander murmured gently.

"He does that thing! He taps his silverware twice on his plate after taking a bite!" I hissed out. Xander gave me the most confused look. I couldn't help the tortured sob that left my mouth. "I think the King is my father!" I whispered harshly, new tears slipping down my cheeks. Xander's face immediately morphed from confused into shocked in a matter of seconds.

"It would give an explanation as to why your father's DNA isn't in The Council's database..." he finally responded after a few pensive minutes.

I sniffled, shrugging my shoulders. I knew it was still a complete long shot, and likely a little deranged to even think. However, my gut wasn't something I could ignore.

"There's only one way to know, and that's to ask. Well, actually, that's a lie. I could steal something with his DNA and send it to Alistair, but this way is much faster," Xander reasoned.

"I don't....I don't know if I even want to know," I sniffled brokenly. Xander's eyes morphed into an expression of concern. "I mean, all this time I grew up moving from place to place. I never stayed anywhere long enough to ever feel like I had a home. And then when the system kicked me to the curb, everything happened with Eric. Meanwhile, he was here being waited on hand and foot!" I hissed, my hands clutching his shirt in my fists.

"Then we don't have to know," he stated, his words soothing my panic for a moment. "If I could go back and take away every single thing that ever caused you pain, I would. In a heartbeat. But Scarlett, if it weren't for the past, I wouldn't have you. And you - and now our child - are the best things to ever happen to me. My heart beats for you. Only ever for you. Day in and day out. The past makes us who we are and I love every single thing about you," he murmured while cupping my face with one of his big hands. My tears were falling for an entirely different reason now.

"You're my reward for everything I endured," I whispered against his lips. Pressing up onto my tippy toes, I captured his lips with mine. His arms wrapped around my body, pressing me against him as close as he could get me with my belly between us.

"I'm sorry to interrupt again, but the king says he will not wait until tomorrow," the same guard butted in, ruining our moment. And the sex we were probably going to have. Now I'm pissed.

"Where is he?" I grunted out angrily. The man's face morphed into one of unease at my clearly angry expression, but didn't say anything besides 'follow me'.

The man escorted us to a large office. Once inside, the king shooed the guard with a flick of his wrist. His eyes flittered to Xander behind me before finally settling on me. I didn't speak a word and opted to just stare at him as I crossed my arms over my chest. He sighed deeply before standing from his chair.

"I presume you know why I've asked you here?" he finally spoke.

"No, actually. Enlighten me," I said, deciding to play dumb for the sake of the conversation. I could see it in his eyes he didn't believe me.

"You look like the spitting image of your mother," he stated. My entire body tensed at the confirmation of what I'd already suspected.

"Like I said earlier, I wouldn't know. I never got to meet her," I hissed back, my gaze hardening.

"I'm assuming your birthday is sometime around the end of December?" he asked.

"Christmas, actually. The abandonment was the gift that kept on giving," I snarked back.

"That..." he paused, clearing his throat, "that's my fault," he said, a sad undertone to his words. This time, I wasn't angry. Rather, I was very confused by his words. I didn't respond, waiting for him to elaborate. "Your mother and I were not mates. When I was younger, I was...misguided. I did many things I'm not proud of. One of my biggest regrets is the way I treated your mother. When I first took over as king, I was traveling the States meeting each American alpha. It's customary when a new monarch takes over. I met your mother when I was visiting her home pack. At the time we met, I was already mated and Luke was a year old-" his words cut off as I scoffed in disgust. I wasn't sure I wanted to hear another word out of his mouth.

"I know what I did is abhorrent. My mate knows about my lapse in judgment that led to my infidelity. Your mother was an enchanting woman. She had a freeness about her that I couldn't resist at the time. I was only in her pack for a day, but it was long enough for me to get carried away-"

"Did you know about me?" I finally interrupted. I couldn't stop the words from tumbling out of my mouth. My heart began to pound in my chest as I waited for his answer. A few seconds passed before a pained look overtook his face. I had to fight to contain the sob that threatened to break out.

"Your mother managed to get into contact with me after she found out she was pregnant with you. Scarlett, you must understand how lost I was back in those days."

"What did you do?" I hissed, my teeth clenching with barely contained anger.

He released a resigned sigh. "I threatened her. I told her if she ever came around again I would expose her to her alpha. I told her

I would inform him that she'd been coming back to her old pack for months at a time and would even send trackers to help them find her." He paused as the sob finally broke free. Xander grabbed both of my shoulders and gave them a meaningful squeeze.

"I was young and so childish. I was scared. I already had a mate and a child at home. I was worried about what my father and my councilmen would do to me if they found out I'd not only been unfaithful to the Queen but had also gotten the woman in question pregnant."

"Did you ever stop to think about my mother? About me? She was probably scared out of her mind! Pregnant and alone at 18 with the baby of a man who had all the power in the world to make good on his threats!" I yelled. He at least had the decency to look ashamed.

"Not a single day has passed that I haven't thought of you. I had no idea if your mother kept you. I wanted desperately to look for you, but I couldn't risk someone in my cabinet finding out."

"Well, let me enlighten you. She dropped me off at The Council's doorstep and fled. I was bounced from orphanage to orphanage until the day I turned 18. That's when the man I was fated for found me. He would beat me within an inch of life as often as he was able. I didn't have anyone to look out for me. No one to ask why I had suddenly disappeared. He got away with it for an entire year. And it's all your fault," I growled, pointing an accusatory finger at his chest.

"Scarlett-" he began to speak, his voice cracking with emotion. I didn't want to hear it.

"You're a coward. A good-for-nothing man who skips out on his responsibilities to avoid the consequences of his own actions! You make me sick. I don't want anything to do with you!" I hissed, turning and exiting before he could even process my words. I waddled back to our room as fast as my feet would take me. I snatched Xander's phone and called the man who flew us here. I was in the middle of arranging our flight home when Xander made it into the room. He grabbed me and pulled me into his body, taking his phone from me.

"Jamison, rest for the night. We'll leave first thing in the morning as planned," he murmured before ending the call.

"What the fuck was that? What do you think you're doing!" I yelled, wiggling about in his arms to try and get away so I could face him. He wasn't having it.

"Scarlett, enough," Xander barked out, authority lacing his tone. I huffed indignantly, crossing my arms over my chest. "It's late. I know you're tired. You're upset and stressed. None of these things are good for you or the baby. What you need right now is a nice shower and a good night's rest. In the morning, if your feelings are unchanged concerning your father, we will leave first thing," he stated nonsensically.

"They won't be," I snipped out, "...but a shower does sound nice," I conceded. I felt a few feather-light kisses pressed against the delicate skin below my ear. My traitorous body immediately melted into his touch. I allowed him to turn me in his arms as he slowly undressed me and then himself. I returned his knowing smirk with a glare.

"Don't give me that look," I rumbled out as he carefully walked me backward into the ensuite bathroom connected to our quarters.

"What look?" he chuckled softly, his hands always touching me in some capacity as he turned the shower on.

"That know-it-all look." My response only made his smile grow.

"You're so cute when you're grumpy," he snickered before ushering me into the shower. I couldn't help the pout that made its way to my face as I lightly smacked his chest with the back of my hand. "For the record, I don't know it all in a general sense. I do, however, know it all about you," he spoke, his hands traveling south as he did so.

# CHapter 35

Scarlett's POV

The next morning, I was still upset about the situation with my...my father. Simply thinking those words in reference to myself was surreal. I hadn't thought about the concept of having actual parents since I was a child; before I was ten years old, at least. Somehow, within the last three months, I had both spoken with my mother's family and met my father.

My anger no longer burned fiery hot - probably from the multiple orgasms Xander so graciously gave me last night. However, there was still a deep sorrow that lingered.

"You've just woken and your mind is already moving a mile a minute," Xander's deep, gravely voice broke the silence. I just sighed and leaned further into his hold. His lips pressed to my temple before remaining there, soft and warm.

"I feel like I need clarity...but part of me knows his answers will only bring more pain," I whispered. He hummed thoughtfully.

"You won't be satisfied until you get your answers, Scarlett," he stated, knowingly.

"I know..." I trailed off. "I need to talk to him before we leave this morning," I reasoned. I felt him nod against me. "No time like the present I suppose." I heaved a sigh while hoisting myself out of bed. We'd just finished getting dressed when one of the King's men arrived to let us know he was waiting for us in the same place we'd had dinner last night.

I wasn't sure what was going to greet me as Xander and I entered the formal dining hall once again. The King surrounded by his entire family as they ate breakfast and talked like nothing was wrong was not it, though. I stood dumbly by the door as my anxiety shot through the roof.

"Scarlett! I'm so glad you chose to join us this morning!" The King proclaimed, standing from his seat. I swallowed the knot that had formed in my throat before clearing it.

"Unfortunately, we won't be joining you. We need to get back home. I figured we could talk before our plane took off," I stated, avoiding the curious looks from the others sitting around the table.

"Very well," he said, clearly seeing the no-nonsense look in my eyes and knowing not to push me. Good.

We were silent as all of us exited the room and made our way to the office I'd found myself in last night. The King's demeanor was noticeably less jovial than his initial greeting this morning as we all took a seat.

"I'm assuming you have questions?" The King took the lead.

"Do you know where my mother is?" I asked, cutting to the chase. I was more apt to forgive her than I was him. I think I might have done the same thing if I were in her situation. For all she knew, she was putting me in the safest place possible at the time. She...she kept me. She carried me for nine months despite the danger it brought her. That had to mean something...right?

He looked hesitant to answer my question at first.

"My councilmen have kept tabs on her over the years. They wanted to know where she was in case she tried popping back up to blackmail me later in my political career," he revealed. His answer made my heart begin to race in my chest.

"Where...?" I asked breathlessly. I didn't need to finish the sentence. He knew what I was asking.

"There's a...free-spirited pack in South Carolina-"

"The Gold Sun pack," Xander interrupted with a knowing smirk. I'd heard of the pack in passing - they had the best orphanage accommodations according to my friends in the system back in the day.

"Yes, you're correct. She's been there since we were able to first track her down. That was about eighteen years ago," the King explained.

"It makes sense why she's not in the American database. She started running before her original pack could log her, and the Gold Sun pack doesn't believe in the database. They think it's an overstep of The Council's boundaries into our lives," Xander said with a quick roll of his eyes. "They stopped regular DNA reporting when the kidnappings stopped decades ago. If she's been there this whole time, she would've never been put in the system." I nodded slowly, taking all the information in.

"Scarlett..." King Grimaldi murmured, catching my attention and pulling me from my thoughts. I met his gaze, and we just stared at each other for a few moments. I searched hard for any resemblance of myself in his face but came up short. Our eye color was the only thing we shared. I wasn't sure if I found that comforting or disheartening. All of it was hard to process. "I truly am sorry. I wasn't there to protect you and I should have been," he finally finished through a whisper. I swallowed the thick lump that formed in my throat and nodded once, acknowledging his words. "Even though I wasn't there before, I'm here now," he stated fiercely.

My heart mourned for the little girl who cried herself to sleep on scratchy bed sheets, wishing more than anything someone had said those words to her. Praying someone had been looking out for her, all the while knowing she was all she really had in this world.

"I don't need a father now. I have a mate who loves me very much and takes my protection quite seriously," I answered, a hint of sadness in my tone. Part of me wondered if I was being unfair. But then I remembered what he said to my mother and how we ended up in this situation in the first place. I deserved time to grieve and process my emotions in my own time.

"We'll be in touch, King Grimaldi," Xander stated before standing from his chair. I followed his lead, not having anything else to say to my father.

Xander and I didn't exchange any words as we packed and boarded our jet. He knew me well enough to know I was lost in my thoughts.

"I'm gonna take a nap," I murmured as we finally settled into our seats and buckled in.

"I'll have a snack waiting for you when you wake up," he responded. I just gave him a soft kiss on the lips in response. He really was the best. True to his word, there was a large bowl of watermelon - my current pregnancy craving - sitting in front of me as soon as I opened my eyes.

I didn't pay much attention to what was happening around me as I dove into a book I'd been meaning to read for a while. It wasn't until the scenery outside my window caught my attention hours later that I realized something wasn't right.

"Xander?"

"Yeah, baby?" he murmured distractedly as he typed away on his laptop beside to me.

"Where are we?" That definitely got his attention. He gave me a sheepish look before turning so his body was facing me. His hand found my upper thigh, resting on it before giving it a quick squeeze. I pursed my lips before quirking one of my eyebrows upward.

"Xander?" I pressed further.

"We're almost to South Carolina," he murmured.

"What?!" I shrieked.

"Listen to me, Scarlett. Like you said before we left for England, you're not getting any less pregnant. No way are you going to last the rest of your pregnancy without meeting your mother now that you know where she's located. I called the Gold Sun's alpha while you were sleeping. He said we'd be welcome with open arms whenever we chose to visit. I figured we were already in the air so we might as well just do it now," he reasoned. There were a few moments of silence that passed between us.

"You're right," I conceded, grabbing the hand that was resting on my thigh and lacing our fingers together. "How long until we get there?" I asked, already antsy with nerves now knowing our final destination.

"Six hours," he said, a sympathetic look in his eyes. I groaned and dropped my head back against the seat. I did my best to distract myself the rest of the flight, but it hardly stopped me from checking the map every few minutes.

As soon as the pilot announced our descent my heart started to race in my chest, my mouth grew dry, and my palms started to sweat. I couldn't focus on anything as we unloaded from the plane painfully slow. Or that's how it felt, at least.

"Breathe, baby," Xander whispered against the shell of my ear once we were finally seated in an SUV that was driving us to the Gold Sun pack. I drew in a shaky breath.

"I'm trying," I husked out. Resting my forehead against the window, I watched as the terrain flew by. Our baby had been incredibly active the last week, and I'd finally been able to feel all the movements. I closed my eyes and focused on the small flutters I felt. Wanting to cherish this moment with Xander as we often had at night as of recent, I grabbed his hand without saying a word and pressed his palm to my belly where I felt the movement. I laid my hands overtop his own, a smile pulling at my lips as our child gave a particularly harsh kick against Xander's hand. They could always sense when their daddy was near.

"Always showing off for daddy," I murmured only loud enough for him to hear. I peaked my eyes open just in time to see the breathtaking smile on his face as his gaze focused on where our hands were pressed against my rounded bump.

"Only two weeks until we get to find out what this little one is," Xander reminded me, sparing a quick glance up at me. "What do you think we're having?" he asked, gently stroking my belly back and forth. The action soothed me and calmed my nerves.

"A little boy. Strong and smart, just like his daddy," I insisted con-fidently. Truthfully, I had no idea what we were having. However, the idea of watching Xander chase around a chubby little boy that looked just like him made my eyes sting with unshed tears. Damn these hormones. "What do you think we're having?" I asked.

"Don't care. They're gonna be perfect no matter what they are," he said softly.

"Alpha, Luna. We're here," the driver called from the front, bursting the bubble of our intimate moment. Exciting the vehicle, our driver grabbed our attention once again. "Wednesday's are pack dinner nights. Everyone is gathered outdoors just down that way," he explained, pointing towards a cobblestone path that lead alongside the packhouse.

My anxiety reared it's big, fat head with each step we took down the uneven path.

"I think I'm gonna throw up," I hissed as I heard the loud chatter of talking and laughter grow louder and louder.

"I'm right here," Xander reassured me, squeezing my hand a few times. I released a steady breath through pursed lips as we broke through a clearing and were met with the sight of a huge group of people. I wasn't sure where to look first. I shied away from all the prying eyes, partially hiding behind Xander's huge frame like a scared child.

"Alpha and Luna Harrington! I'm so glad you guys could make it on a family Wednesday!" came a booming voice from across the clearing.

"We appreciate the warm welcome," Xander spoke, reaching out to shaking the hand of the man who quickly approached us. I decided to pull on my big girl panties and step out from hiding behind him. I smiled politely at the older couple. They definitely fit the bill for a typical hippy couple, that's for sure. It made sense considering what I'd learned about them. I locked eyes with the Luna as we shook hands. Instead of smiling, her expression looked confused.

"I've seen that face before..." she muttered contemplatively.

"What's that, pumpkin?" The alpha asked curiously.

"It's probably nothing. Feel free to mingle! Food should be done in an hour!" she exclaimed. Xander and I nodded, but I still wasn't sure where to start first. We took a few uncertain steps towards the mass of people. I scanned the crowd of people sitting and chatting. I suddenly locked eyes with an older woman. She looked like she'd seen a ghost. I smiled politely because I didn't know what else to do.

"Oh...my God. Where's Josie? Someone get Josie!" She yelled out. I could just barely hear her over the commotion. The ruckus of the crowd seemed to die down a bit as Xander and I's presence slowly garnered more and more attention.

I had just awkwardly laid my arms over my belly and nodded a few hellos when I heard it.

"What is it, Pamela? Seriously? Gosh, you're crazy after one margarita!" came the soft, feminine voice followed by melodious laughter. My breath caught in my throat. My lungs seized up. My face grew warm. My wolf recognized the voice immediately. Like second nature.

"Josie," the woman who'd spotted me, Pamela, sternly spoke. Her body was blocking the woman she was speaking to. But then she stepped out of the way. And our eyes locked. The wide, bright smile that encompassed her whole face slowly dropped. Her eyes scanned my face frantically. I couldn't tell if the clearing had gone silent, or if the white noise in my ears had grown deafening. I couldn't keep my hands from shaking.

It was like...like looking in a mirror.

I locked my knees, afraid I was going to tumble over if I didn't. My nails dug into Xander's forearm as she took the first step towards me. Slowly but surely, she made her way across the space until we were only an arm's length away. Her eyes glistened in the sun with unshed tears. Her hand shook with a fine tremor as she lifted it to cradle my cheek. Her thumb softly swiped away my tears - the ones I wasn't aware had even fallen. I couldn't help the soft sob that fell from my lips.

"My baby," she whispered.

# CHAPTER 36



Her voice trembled with emotion as she spoke. I could only nod in response, unable to find my voice. A sob escaped her lips before she pulled me into her embrace. With my face pressed against her chest and my hands clutching her body, I cried into the fabric of her shirt. Her hand gently stroked the back of my head. Her repeated murmurs of "thank you, God" soothed me as my tears turned into hiccups. When I finally calmed down, Xander spoke up.

"Why don't we go somewhere with a bit more privacy?" he suggested. I pulled away, suddenly aware of the spectacle we'd made, my cheeks flushing with embarrassment.

"Follow me," my mother murmured, leading us toward their pack house. She guided us into a small sitting room. My mother settled next to me on a loveseat while Xander took a seat across from us.

"What's...what's your name?" she asked, breaking the silence.

"Scarlett," I whispered, still processing the reality of meeting both my biological parents in the last 24 hours and the shock of discovering I was technically royalty. The latter wasn't something I intended to share with people.

"Such a beautiful name. It suits you. I always knew you'd be pretty, but for the first time in my life something has surpassed my imagination." She grasped my hands gently, and for the first time in a long time, I found myself liking the name I'd once resented. The part of me that Eric had beaten down, which had come to hate the name because of its association with him, began to heal.

"Who named you?" she asked.

"Elder Adelia. It was because of the blanket you had me wrapped up in when you...uhm, dropped me off," I mumbled. Her cheek pinched inward, as if she was biting it.

"That was my baby blanket from when I was a child. I snuck back into my parents' place a couple of weeks before I gave birth. I wanted you to have something from me, even if I couldn't be with you for long," she explained. It made me sick to my stomach that I had no memory of the blanket.

"It...it must have been lost with all my moves. I don't remember it; I've only heard about it from Elder Adelia," I said, sadness in my voice.

"I've missed so much since then," she said, glancing between Xander and my round belly. A sad smile tugged at my lips. She had no idea.

"I'm sorry it took us almost twenty-one and a half years to find each other. I started searching a few years after you were born. I thought it was safe by then. There were circumstances that forced me to give you away—" she began, but I couldn't bear the look of helplessness in her eyes.

"I know what my father did to you. I know how he threatened you," I interrupted. Her shocked expression might have been comical if the situation weren't so serious.

"H-how do you..?"

"How do you think I found you? Xander had to meet with him. It's a long story, but he came clean to me. He's known your location since shortly after I was born," I revealed. Her face went pale, as if she might faint any second.

"Oh God," she rasped, pressing a worried hand to her forehead. "I'm glad my search efforts were fruitless, then. But I did try, Scarlett. I've thought about you every single day of your life!" she insisted. "I didn't have many resources and had to be discreet. Every time I thought I found a lead, it ended in nothing. But I always had a piece of you with me." She undid the clasp of the gold locket hanging around her neck and placed it in my hand. I stared at it, unsure of what I was seeing.

"I gave birth to you alone in a motel bathtub not far from The Council's grounds. I spent a few hours with you. At that moment, life felt perfect. I couldn't bear to let you go. When it got dark, I knew my time with you was ending, so I took a stamp pad from the front desk and made handprints of your tiny hands and feet. This one is from your little pointer finger that you kept reaching up to poke me in the eye," she said, her voice choked with emotion as tears slid down her cheeks. I couldn't hold back my own if I even wanted to.

"I've spent most of my life feeling forgotten and unloved. But there's never been a moment when that was true," I whispered, barely audible.

Grasping my chin, she made me meet her eyes. "Not for a single second," she said firmly. "Follow me. I want to show you something." Overwhelmed with emotions, I silently followed her through the pack house to an eccentrically decorated door. She opened it and invited Xander and me inside.

"This is my mate and I's living quarters. Feel free to sit any-where," she instructed. I eased myself onto the edge of the mat-tress while Xander took a small chair in the corner.

She emerged from the closet with a shoe box. It looked like someone hastily covered it in colorful construction paper. The words 'My Little Girl' were written in cursive glitter on the top. She placed it on my lap and sat beside me.

"What's this?" I asked.

She lifted the lid, revealing a stack of envelopes and a few trinkets. "I wrote you a letter every birthday. I refused to give up on finding you. I knew this day would come eventually, and I wanted you to know how much I've always loved you." I slid the box from my lap, turned, and hugged her tightly. She quickly embraced me back.

"Why don't we stay for a few days?" Xander suggested, breaking my thoughts. I turned to him, astonished.

"Is that possible? We've already been gone for a few days," I asked.

"I'll make some calls. I can work remotely from here. My dad can cover for me if needed," he said resolutely. My love for him grew even more.

"Okay, we'll stay," I said with a smile. My mother whooped happily and clapped her hands.

Later that evening, I felt Xander's gaze on me during dinner. His smile and happiness were almost overwhelming. Being so loved by both him and my mother was more than I could handle at once.

Xander, being the intuitive man he is, knew what I needed. Even if I wouldn't ask for it. Over the past month, I'd become fascinated with Disney movies. It was thanks to a movie night with his sister Jade and my aunt. Since then, Xander and I had watched them all. The emotional scenes, particularly those with princesses and their mothers, often brought me to tears. It wasn't just hormones; these feelings had been with me for a long time, growing stronger as I carried our child. I knew Xander noticed.

"Why don't you spend the night with her? Since we aren't staying long, you two should enjoy the time together," Xander suggested, pulling me from my thoughts. My astonishment must have been evident.

"That would be wonderful! If you're comfortable with it?" my mom asked, her voice thick with emotion.

"Yeah, okay," I managed, breathless. This was a big step for me. We were on unfamiliar grounds, and this would be the first night since our mating that I would spend without Xander. I felt his pride through our bond.

A couple of hours later, Xander dropped me off at my mother's room. I was freshly showered and in a pair of my favorite pajamas.

"Your guards will be right outside the door, but I'm only seconds away if you need me," Xander said as we stood in front of the door. I could see the apprehension in his eyes, but I knew he wouldn't say anything. I loved that he was so cautious with me - even though this had technically been his idea. I grasped his chin and pulled him down for a kiss.

"I love you," I murmured against his lips. "You're better than anything I could have ever dreamed of." He swooped back in for another sweet kiss followed by whispered words of love in return. He pecked my lips one last time and knocked on the bedroom door. My mom answered with a big smile, quickly ushering me inside. I immediately noticed the changed bed linens on her mattress. It was likely for my comfort; sleeping on sheets that smelled strongly of her mate wouldn't sit well with my wolf.

I could feel Xander's displeasure at our separation through our bond. Seconds later, he closed himself off, no longer allowing me to hear or feel what he was thinking or feeling. While I disliked the lack of connection, I understood why he did it. It wouldn't make being apart any easier on me if I felt his disdain about it.

"Do you need to brush your hair before we lay down?" my mom asked, eyeing my damp tangly hair pointedly. I snickered softly.

"I probably should or it'll be a rats nest in the morning." She silently pulled out a chair resting in front of a small vanity.

She picked up the brush that was sitting out. "Can I...?" she asked meekly, her gaze looking unsure as she silently asked to brush my hair. I bit the inside of my cheek to contain my emotion. I nodded without saying a word. She smiled brightly. She gathered all of my hair into her hands before laying it down against my back. Every swipe of the brush against my ends was so gentle. I'd never had anyone be so careful before. My eyes fluttered closed as she worked out all the tangles. Resting my hands on my belly, I enjoyed the soothing sensation of the comb working through my hair.

"Your hair is so soft. Like silk," she spoke softly as she gathered it all back into her hands. "So pretty," she whispered as she carefully began braiding the strands.

"Do I have any siblings?" I suddenly blurted, unsure where the question had come from. Her hands faltered for a single second. She sighed deeply, finishing the braid before answering my question.

"Shortly after my mate and I met, we learned he was sterile. It was a complication of a childhood injury. Truthfully...I'm glad for it. After everything I'd been through with you, and never getting closure in the situation, I just didn't want another. It wouldn't have been fair to any other children I might've had. I was so hung up on you," she husked out, her voice thick with emotion. I turned to look at her. She brushed a few strands of hair that slipped from the intricate braid out of my face. "I fear they might have felt emotionally abandoned." I nodded, understanding.

"How come you never tried to contact your family?" I asked, unable to contain the question that was burning on the tip of my tongue. She might see it as rude, but I was too curious to hold it back. "They miss you terribly," I added.

A look of sadness encompassed her face. "I was ashamed and afraid. All the stupid things I'd done as a child had put them in danger. I didn't want to cause any more problems than I already had," she explained. "Have you met them?"

"Yes. They live with us now," I answered. "Well, they transferred to our pack, actually," I clarified. "Grandma says being near me is like a salve over the wound your disappearance left behind," I told her. I could see the sorrow in her eyes. She looked like she wanted to say something.

"Come visit. Come stay. Xander will say yes. I know he will. You'll be safe there," I insisted, my eyes pleading with her. She pursed her lips before a smile pulled at the corners.

"How could I say no to that?" she asked, cupping my cheek softly. She pulled me into an embrace, stroking the back of my head gently. "There's a pack gathering tomorrow to welcome a few new members. We can speak with my alpha during and make the arrangements then," she insisted. "Now, time for bed. I can see your eyes fighting to stay open," she laughed.

Seeing the pack dynamics among the Gold Sun pack was...interesting. Their alpha hung out with his members like he was just another pack member. I knew our pack was comfortable around Xander and trusted him completely, but there was still a separation of sorts. They didn't treat him like they would a fellow friend; they recognized his authority. It was the typical dynamic you saw in every pack. Well, almost every pack I should say.

We had just finished discussing my mother's relocation to our pack and had moved on to conversations I found more than a little boring. Xander was picking Alpha Anderson's brain about his pack security - something Xander was always looking to improve. I tuned into their conversation here and there while talking with my mom. From the bits and pieces I'd picked up on, Alpha Anderson and Xander had very different approaches to pack security.

"Keep my mate company for a few minutes, will you? I need to run to the lady's room," my mom said before walking off. I hadn't yet had a chance to speak with her mate. I was much too focused on making up for lost time with my mom. The atmosphere was a touch awkward as we looked at each other.

"You probably already realized this, but your mother loves you very much," he said, breaking the ice. William was his name - something I had to contain my laughter after hearing. From the numerous stories my mom had already told me, she was the definition of a carefree hippy. She did whatever she wanted and had plenty of crazy stories from her youth to prove it. It didn't seem like a man named William would match her level of crunchiness. However, they appeared to get along perfectly.

"She's keen to never let me forget it. I feel like I won the lottery with her," I answered honestly. Elder Adelia told me that things always get worse before they get better. My life now has proven that to be true; Eric was the 'worse', my life now was absolutely the 'better'. William started to tell me about all the garden plans my mother had conjured up since hearing they would be relocating. According to William, she'd already done some research last night into the different fruits and vegetables that grow best in Montana and in what season.

As William finished talking and the silence settled around us once again, I realized it had been a decent chunk of time and my mother still hadn't returned.

"What's the face for?" Xander whispered against the shell of my ear. I must've had a look of confusion.

"I'm gonna go find my mom, she's taking a while in the bathroom," I murmured, kissing his cheek in parting as I went off in search of my mother.

"Did you fall in?" I jokingly called out as I meandered towards the communal bathrooms. Pushing the door open, a scream left my lips.

"See? I told you she'd come looking for you. Such a bleeding heart your daughter has," Eric sneered. I was going to be sick. My stomach up-ended itself as I took in the scene before me. Eric had my mother in a chokehold, the blade of a knife pressed against the delicate skin of her neck.

"Eric-"

"Shut up!" he screamed, interrupting me. I had no power in this situation - not with him wielding a knife and me being quite pregnant. The look in Eric's eyes scared me the most. It was the same look he had the night I escaped. Deranged. Delusional. Dangerous. I knew one thing for sure - Eric had completely lost it. He didn't have a single care about his own life, and that made him deadly. If he did, he wouldn't be here - and alone at that. He wasn't a member of this pack and my mate was seconds away. He knew he wasn't going to make it out of this alive. I had to be extremely careful.

"You are insufferable. Ever since you came into my life you've caused nothing but problems!"

"Then why me, Eric? If I was such an issue, why didn't you just let me go? After all these years, that's the only thing I want to know.

Why did you do it to me? I was your mate," I husked out, voice thick with emotion. The question served two purposes. For one, it got him talking and if he was talking then he wasn't thinking about hurting me or my mom, but also...the question had always plagued my mind. I never understood why he did what he did.

"Because I could! Because I can! Because breaking someone with an unbreakable spirit is a high that nothing else compares to!" he spat back. That dangerous, crazed glimmer in his eyes twinkled. Something had well and truly snapped. "You were just always so fucking...happy," he sneered the word; as if my happiness had personally insulted him. "You shouldn't have been! You weren't very pretty. You weren't very smart. You had a shitty childhood. You didn't have any parents. You didn't have many friends. There was no reason you should've been happy!" he screamed. "I deserved to be happy! I had it all!" his roar was deafening. The knife as my mother's throat dug just a little deeper. The action forced a pained whimper from my mom's mouth. My hands trembled with the fear I couldn't conceal.

"Eric, please," I pleaded. I always promised myself I would never beg this man for anything ever again. But the words flew from my mouth on instinct at seeing the compromising position my mother was in.

"There was once a time where your begging did something for me. Made me feel...something. Not anymore. Not since you let that mutt mark you. Impregnate you. If you didn't have any value before, you're worth less than nothing now-"

"How dare you speak to my mate that way." My heart leapt in my chest, a sense of calm coming over me instantly. Safe. Safe. Safe. We're safe. Mate is here, my wolf seemed to chant over and over. The look in Xander's eyes was more than just murderous. I could see his wolf was sanguinary; he wanted to tear Eric limb from limb and then drink his blood. I could see the pinch of fear that flashed in Eric's eyes as he eyed Xander up and down. My mate was huge; sizeably bigger in both height and weight than Eric was. It wouldn't be a fair fight.

"I'm going to give you exactly three seconds to put my mate's mother down," Xander stated so calmly it sent a shiver up my spine. "One," Xander squared his shoulders. Eric didn't move a muscle. "Two." Xander clenched his fists as his sides. "Three." It all happened so fast I wasn't able to process exactly what took place. Once the movement stopped, all I saw was red.

Xander was bleeding profusely from a wound that I couldn't identify. He had Eric in a tight headlock, unable to move his upper body at all. Turning Eric to face me, Xander tightened his hold on Eric causing him to grimace.

"Apologize. Right now," Xander demanded. Eric shook his head even as his face contorted in pain. "I said now," Xander growled into his ear. Xander applied so much pressure when Eric continued to refuse that I heard the distinctive snap of a bone breaking. Eric cried out in agony.

"I-I'm sorry," he finally hissed through gritted teeth. I didn't believe the apology one bit, but I loved Xander even more for forcing it out of him.

"Look at her," Xander growled, grabbing his jaw and powerfully jerking it up so he was forced to make eye contact with me. "I want the last thing you ever see to be my incredible mate. Swollen with my child. And I want you to remember this knowing you never get to experience anything even remotely as amazing," Xander taunted. Eric opened his mouth to speak, a hateful look on his face, but he never got the chance. In a split second, Xander snapped his neck.

Eric landed at my mother and my feet in an ungraceful heap. I gasped and quickly stepped back to avoid him touching me. Xander's groan of pain immediately caught my attention. I shrieked when I realized exactly where the blood was coming from. Eric's knife was lodged squarely in his chest, a river of blood flowing out around the blade.

"Xander!" I screamed. My mother and I lunged for him at the exact moment he started falling to his knees. We lowered him as gently as we could with how heavy he was. I had started to sob, dread sinking in my gut like lead.

"It's...it's just a flesh wound, baby," Xander rasped out. He was trying to make light of the situation to make me feel better, but I was having none of it. My mother had already run off to get help, but I was frozen.

"You can't leave me," I cried, trembling hands reaching out to cradle his face.

"I'm not going anywhere, Scarlett," he promised, though the paling color of his face said otherwise.

"You can't!" I hissed, hysterical. My tears were coming faster now. "You can't! Because I need you! I love you!"

"I love you more than life itself, sweetheart. My heart beats for you. Only you, Scarlett. Don't you ever forget that," he murmured, his eyes growing heavy as they began to flutter slowly.

"Xander!"

# EPILOGUE

S carlett's POV

"Alexander?" I hollered at my son. My tone conveyed everything I wanted to say without even needing words. At eleven months old, he was already showing what a mischievous little boy he was going to be.

"Just like his father at that age," Vanessa chuckled. I huffed.

"Well he's his clone. I'm not shocked he acts just like him too," I grumbled.

"Those two are thick as thieves," Andrew commented as he approached where his wife and I were resting by the fireplace in their living room.

"Alexander loves his daddy," I conceded, sighing as I kicked off my sandals to give my swollen feet a break. I watched Xander wrestle with our son on the carpet. The high-pitched boisterous laughter from our infant echoed off the walls, bringing a soft smile to my face. My breath caught as I thought about how this moment could've been so different. It had been almost a year and a half since Xander lay bleeding to death and fighting for his life on the bathroom floor of a foreign pack.

"Dad, take my place for a minute?" Xander called out. I opened my eyes when I felt him relax into the couch cushion next to me. I rested my head back and let it roll toward him, appreciating his handsome face.

"You're thinking about it again," Xander stated, his tone slightly chastising. I released a slow sigh. He always knew when I was reminiscing on the past - even if I blocked him from my mind.

"How could I not? You weren't supposed to survive that," I hissed, getting more upset by the second. The 'that' in reference being Xander getting stabbed mere centimeters away from his heart.

"No. I wasn't. But I did because I love you far too much, sweetheart," he insisted before nuzzling my neck. The Gold Sun's pack doctor said Xander should've already died before he even started tending his wound. It was only because of Xander's wolf's persistence that he held on as hard as he did. The thought choked me up as Xander pressed a few soft kisses against my delicate skin. His hand smoothed over my massive belly a few moments later.

"You look ready to pop, baby," Xander commented. Our children - yes, plural - kicked frantically in my stomach at their father's touch. They always went crazy whenever he was near.

"Baby is exactly what I'm about to pop. And it's all your fault," I mumbled grumpily. Xander laughed softly in return.

"If I do recall, you were just as eager as I was as soon as we got the medical clearance from the pack doctor," he stated. I rolled my eyes.

"Yeah but you were supposed to remember the condoms. Having three kids all under two was not the plan," I chastised. He just smirked and sought out my lips for a sweet kiss. We were soon interrupted by our uncoordinated son slamming into our legs. He had learned to walk quickly. There was no crawling for him. One day, he just got up and took off.

His toothy grin gleamed up at me as he bounced on his feet, thrusting his little butt up and down as he did so.

"Are you dancin' for momma and dada?" I asked. He gave a non-committal screech of happiness that had Xander and I both laughing. He leaned over to press his face against the side of my belly before wrapping one arm around the opposite side. I smoothed my hand over his head of soft, black hair, treasuring the moment.

The skin on my back burned with the pain of having to stretch to accommodate two children this pregnancy. Every move pulled at the scars that would never go away. However, the reminder wasn't unwelcome. Not anymore. It reminded me of everything I had endured to get the things I had today. As my son pulled back, calling out 'mama' in his sweet voice, I knew I would bear it all over again 1000 times just to be right here.

9 781944 260378